THE BEST SHORT STORIES OF 1922

THE
BEST SHORT STORIES
OF 1922

AND THE

YEARBOOK OF THE AMERICAN
SHORT STORY

EDITED BY

EDWARD J. O'BRIEN

EDITOR OF "THE BEST SHORT STORIES OF 1915"
"THE BEST SHORT STORIES OF 1916"
"THE BEST SHORT STORIES OF 1917"
"THE BEST SHORT STORIES OF 1918"
"THE BEST SHORT STORIES OF 1919"
"THE BEST SHORT STORIES OF 1920"
"THE BEST SHORT STORIES OF 1921"
"THE GREAT MODERN ENGLISH STORIES," ETC.

BOSTON
SMALL, MAYNARD & COMPANY
PUBLISHERS

Forest Hill, Oxon, England,
October 10, 1922.

My dear Mr. Herford:

I had just finished star-stamping for the year, and I felt
a bit exhausted when one of those kind friends every one
has, sent me a copy of "Say It with Asterisks," beautifully
bound. Picture my delight when I discovered that a baf-
fling problem which had haunted me for weeks was solved.
To whom should I dedicate "The Best Short Stories of
1922"? I could not inscribe it to our Mr. Anderson always,
and yet he insisted upon writing the best stories year after
year. At last I knew. *Palmam qui meruit ferat.* No
curate's egg this time! The dedication should read:

```
* * * * * * * * * * * * * * * *
*                              *
*                              *
*                              *
*              TO              *
*                              *
*         OLIVER  HERFORD      *
*                              *
*          "SUCH  IS  LIFE"    *
*                              *
*                              *
*                              *
* * * * * * * * * * * * * * * *
```

For we both deserve it.

Cordially yours,

EDWARD J. O'BRIEN.

BY WAY OF ACKNOWLEDGMENT

Grateful acknowledgment for permission to include the stories and other material in this volume is made to the following authors, editors and publishers:

To the Editor of *Broom*, the Curtis Publishing Company, the Editor of *Brief Stories*, the Editor of *The Pagan*, the Editor of *The Dial*, the Editor of *The Pictorial Review*, the Editor of *The Bookman* (New York), the Editor of *The Century*, the Editor of *The Metropolitan*, the Editors of *The Smart Set*, Miss Margaret C. Anderson, the Editor of *The Cosmopolitan*, Mr. Conrad Aiken, Mr. Sherwood Anderson, Mr. Konrad Bercovici, Miss Susan M. Boogher, Mr. Frederick Booth, Miss Edna Bryner, Miss Rose Gollup Cohen, Mr. Charles J. Finger, Mr. F. Scott Fitzgerald, Mr. David Freedman, Mrs. Katharine Fullerton Gerould, Mr. Ben Hecht, Mr. Joseph Hergesheimer, Mr. William C. G. Jitro, Mr. Ring W. Lardner, Mr. James Oppenheim, Mr. Benjamin Rosenblatt, Mr. Wilbur Daniel Steele, and Mr. Clement Wood.

Acknowledgments are specially due to *The Boston Evening Transcript* for permission to reprint the large body of material previously published in its pages.

I shall be grateful to my readers for corrections, and particularly for suggestions leading to the wider usefulness of this annual volume. In particular, I shall welcome the receipt, from authors, editors, publishers, of stories printed during the period between October, 1922 and September, 1923 inclusive, which have qualities of distinction and yet are not printed in periodicals falling under my regular notice. Such communications may be addressed to me at *Forest Hill, Oxfordshire, England*.

E. J. O.

CONTENTS[1]

---

[1] The order in which the stories in this volume are printed is not intended to indicate their comparative excellence; the arrangement is alphabetical by authors.

CONTENTS

INTRODUCTION

INTRODUCTION

During the past year I have had occasion to think often and seriously of disintegration in American literature as a force which can no longer be ignored. There are times in the history of a people when disintegration is a form of creation, and when the cry goes up on all sides: "Écrasez l'Infame," it is not generally recognized that this cry is a passionate prayer. Such a cry is heard in all countries of Europe today, though it is not yet general, and the question arises whether it is historically the moment for that cry or prayer to be uttered by American writers. Well, I do not think so at all, and yet the cry is usually synchronous with disintegration.

I do not think so because the disintegration which I see in American life and literature is the effect of weakness rather than of strong relentless force. It takes two forms in the work of our story writers. First of all, we have the disintegration of laziness and spiritual compromise which is manifest in the commercial short story's surrender to the machine and to business. That is a present fact which can never be sufficiently taken into account. It follows the line of least resistance, and utters no cry of passionate conviction.

The second form of disintegration is often thought to be more subtle, but it is really equally obvious and weak. Those who manifest it are sitting home quietly observing the spiritual disintegration of Europe as a fascinating spectacle, and finding in it only æsthetic values which they long to imitate. They do not see, or perhaps they do not choose to see, that the pattern which they admire is the result of a conflict which they have shirked, and that any attempt to copy it without undergoing the experience which justifies it as expression will result only in pastiche, and in bad pastiche at that. Joyce and Lawrence and other Europeans are not accidents, but their American imitators may prove to be serious accidents. Joyce, who will serve very well to illustrate my point, is subduing the show of things to the desires of the mind, because he is a possessive European male who has suffered. Any one of many American writers whom I refrain from naming perceives the patterned result of this suffering, but is unable or unwilling to pay the price.

We are told in the Old Testament that Dada followed Babel as a penalty, and the European Dadaists have only sought, as critics of a civilization which has become a spiritual failure, to make this clear by symbols. The American Dadaists, who seem likely to spring up like mushrooms from now on, say "Dada" for its own sake, and so revert to infancy at the moment when men are most needed to interpret our obscure desires. I find their assumed superiority to other mortals snobbish, and their æsthetic attitude is only one present manifestation of the intellectualist sterility and anæmia from which we have begun to escape at last. They are taking "Art" entirely too seriously, and forgetting that every great artist is only great in so far as he can laugh at his own pretensions a little sadly.

We are also in some danger of seeking romantic escape from the machine by creating a mysticism of the machine, and by regarding the machine as something transcendental. This is sincere enough, because it is the result of action on the part of those who have suffered from the machine. We know how deeply rooted is the instinct to lay propitiatory offerings before something powerful of which we are afraid. But the artist should not imitate Caliban, even if he does so beautifully, and so while I recognize the truth underlying the work of Stieglitz, for example, I cannot accept this new transcendentalism in American art and literature as a liberating force. It is clear to me that it is really an ostrichlike way of accepting slavery.

These remarks are perhaps less irrelevant to the general reader than he is likely to believe. If our more promising artists are driven into a cul-de-sac, it is because they perceive the banality of Main Street, and are seeking a way out into the country. It is perhaps necessary to continue trying cul-de-sacs until the right road has been found, and it may even be probable that when that road is found, many artists will not be disinterested enough to bring back the news. The romantic escape of many is perhaps necessary for the realistic return of one, and all I am seeking to do is to point out if I can what ways appear to me to be cul-de-sacs, and what artists seem to have stumbled on the way out. If these artists run away, something is lost, but more is lost if they are all driven into narrow cul-de-sacs. Meanwhile, Sherwood Anderson seems to me the man who is nearest to finding freedom, and I believe he is also the man who is most anxious to return to Main Street and report what he has found.

To repeat what I have said in these pages in previous years, for the benefit of the reader as yet unacquainted with my standards and principles of selection, I shall point out that I have set myself the task of disengaging the essential human qualities in our contemporary fiction which, when chronicled conscientiously by our literary artists, may fairly be called a criticism of life. I am not at all interested in formulæ, and organized criticism at its best would be nothing more than dead criticism, as all dogmatic interpretation of life is always dead. What has interested me, to the exclusion of other things, is the fresh, living current which flows through the best American work, and the psychological and imaginative reality which American writers have conferred upon it.

No substance is of importance in fiction, unless it is organic substance, that is to say, substance in which the pulse of life is beating. Inorganic fiction has been our curse in the past, and bids fair to remain so, unless we exercise much greater artistic discrimination than we display at present.

The present record covers the period from October, 1921, to September, 1922, inclusive. During this period I have sought to select from the stories published in American magazines those which have rendered life imaginatively in organic substance and artistic form. Substance is something achieved by the artist in every act of creation, rather than something already present, and accordingly a fact or group of facts in a story only attain substantial embodiment when the artist's power of compelling imaginative persuasion transforms them into a living truth. The first test of a short story, therefore, in any qualitative analysis is to report upon how vitally compelling the writer makes his selected facts or incidents. This test may be conveniently called the test of substance.

But a second test is necessary if the story is to take rank above other stories. The true artist will seek to shape this living substance into the most beautiful and satisfying form, by skillful selection and arrangement of his materials, and by the most direct and appealing presentation of it in portrayal and characterization.

The short stories which I have examined in this study, as in previous years, have fallen naturally into four groups. The first consists of those stories which fail, in my opinion, to survive either the test of substance or the test of form. These stories are listed in the yearbook without comment or qualifying asterisk. The second group consists of those stories which may fairly claim that they survive either the test of substance or the test of form. Each of these stories may claim to possess either distinction of technique alone, or more frequently, I am glad to say, a persuasive sense of life in them to which a reader responds with some part of his own experience. Stories included in this group are indicated in the yearbook index by a single asterisk prefixed to the title.

The third group, which is composed of stories of still greater distinction, includes such narratives as may lay convincing claim to a second reading, because each of them has survived both tests, the test of substance and the test of form. Stories included in this group are indicated in the yearbook index by two asterisks prefixed to the title.

Finally, I have recorded the names of a small group of stories which possess, I believe, the even finer distinction of uniting genuine substance and artistic form in a closely woven pattern with such sincerity that these stories may fairly claim a position in American literature. If all of these stories by American authors were republished, they would not occupy more space than six or seven novels of average length. My selection of them does not imply the critical belief that they are great stories. A year which produced one great story would be an exceptional one. It is simply to be taken as meaning that I have found the equivalent of six or seven volumes worthy of republication among all the stories published during the period under consideration. These stories are indicated in the yearbook index by three asterisks prefixed to the title, and are listed in the special "Roll of Honor." In compiling these lists I have permitted no personal preference or prejudice consciously to influence my judgment. It has been a point of honor with me not to republish a story by an English author or by any foreign author. I have also made it a rule not to include more than one story by an individual author in the volume. The general and particular results of my study will be found explained and carefully detailed in the supplementary part of the volume.

EDWARD J. O'BRIEN.

Forest Hill, Oxon, England,
    November 23, 1922.

THE BEST SHORT STORIES OF 1922

Note.— The order in which the stories in this volume are printed is not intended as an indication of their comparative excellence; the arrangement is alphabetical by authors.

THE DARK CITY[1]

By CONRAD AIKEN

(From *The Dial*)

HIS greatest pleasure in life came always at dusk. Its prelude was the reading of the evening paper in the train that took him out of the city. By long association the very unfolding of the grimy ink-smelling sheets was part of the ritual: his dark eyes dilated, he felt himself begin to "grin," the staggering load of business detail, under which he had struggled all day in the office, was instantly forgotten. He read rapidly, devoured with rapacious eyes column after column—New York, London, Paris, Lisbon—wars, revolutions, bargains in umbrellas, exhibitions of water colors. This consumed three-quarters of the journey. After that he watched the procession of houses, walls, trees, reeling past in the mellow slant light, and began already to feel his garden about him. He observed the flight of the train unconsciously, and it was almost automatically, at the unrealized sight of a certain group of trees, oddly leaning away from each other, like a group of ballet dancers expressing an extravagance of horror, that he rose and approached the door.

The sense of escape was instant. Sky and earth generously took him, the train fled shrieking into the vague bright infinity of afternoon. The last faint wail of it, as it plunged into a tunnel, always seemed to him to curl about his head like a white tentacle, too weak to be taken seriously. Then, in the abrupt silence, he began climbing the long hill that led to his house. He walked swiftly, blowing tattered blue clouds of smoke over his shoulders,

3

revolving in his mind the items of news amusing enough to be reported to Hilda; such as that Miss Green, the stenographer, who had for some time been manifesting a disposition to flirt with him, today, just after closing, when everybody else had gone out, had come to him, blushing, and asked him to fasten the sleeve of her dress. A delicious scene! He smiled about the stem of his pipe, but exchanged his smile for a laugh when, looking in through a gap in his neighbor's hedge, he found himself staring into the depraved eyes of a goat. This would add itself to the episode of Miss Green, for these eyes were precisely hers. He turned the corner and saw his house before him, riding on the hill like a small ship on a long green wave. The three children were playing a wild game of croquet, shrieking. Louder sounds arose at his appearance, and as he strode across the lawn they danced about him chattering and quarreling.

"Daddy, Martha won't play in her turn, and I say—"

"Marjorie takes the heavy mallet—"

The chorus rose shrill about him, but he laughed and went into the house, shouting only, "Out of the way! I'm in a hurry! The beans are dying, the tomatoes are clamoring for me, the peas are holding out their hands!"

"Daddy says the beans are dying. Isn't he silly?"

"Let's get to the garden before daddy does."

As he closed the door he heard the shrieks trailing off round the corner of the house, diminuendo. He hung up coat and hat with a rapid gesture and hurried to the kitchen. Hilda, stirring the cocoa with a long spoon, looked round at him laconically.

"Chocolate!" he shouted, and pulled a cake of chocolate out of his pocket. He was astonished, he rolled his eyes, for it appeared to have been sat upon—"in the train." Hilda shrieked with laughter. He thrust it into her apron pocket and fled up the stairs to change.

He could not find his old flannel trousers. Not in the cupboard—not in the bureau. He surrendered to an impulse to comic rage. "Not under the bed!" he cried. He thrust his head out of the window that overlooked the garden and addressed his children.

"Martha! Bring my trousers here this instant!"

He drew in his head again from the shower of replies that flew up at him like missiles and going to the door roared down to his wife.

"I've lost my trousers!"

Then he found them in the closet behind the door and, laughing, put them on.

II

He ran out of the side door, under the wistaria-covered trellis, and down the slippery stone steps to the vegetable garden.

"Here comes daddy, now," shrilled to him from Martha.

He lighted his pipe, shutting his left eye, and stood in profound meditation before the orderly, dignified, and extraordinarily vigorous rows of beans. They were in blossom—bees were tumbling the delicate lilac-pink little hoods. Clouds of fragrance came up from them. The crickets were beginning to tune up for the evening. The sun was poised above the black water tower on the far hill.

Martha and Marjorie began giggling mysteriously behind the lilacs.

"My hoe!" he wailed.

The hoe was thrust out from behind the lilacs.

"If anybody should drive up in a scarlet taxi," he said to Martha, accepting the hoe, "and inform you that your soul is free, don't believe him. Tell him he's a liar. Point me out to him as a symbol of the abject slavery that all life is. Say that I'm a miserable thrall to wife, children, and beans—particularly beans. I spend my days on my knees before my beans."

"I'll do nothing of the sort," said Martha.

He held his hoe under his arm and walked solemnly among the beans. The two girls followed him.

"Here's a caterpillar, daddy!"

"Kill him!"

"Here's another—a funny green one with red sparkles on his back. Oh, look at him!"

"Don't look at him! Kill him!"

"He squirts out like green tooth-paste."

"Don't, Martha!" he cried, pained. "Don't say such things! Spare your neurotic father."

He shrank visibly and strode off to the corner where his peas were planted and started methodically hoeing the rows, turning the rich loam up about the pale stalks. Now and again a pebble clinked, he stooped and threw it off into the meadow. Mary, the youngest, came to the top of the steps and cried. Martha and Marjorie went to her, and he forgot them. The rising and falling of the hoe-blade, shiny with much polishing in the brown soil, hypnotized him, and his thoughts fell into a sort of rhythm, came and went without his interference. "Ridiculous!" he thought, "that this solemn singular biped, whom other bipeds for convenience call Andrew, should stand here with a stick and scratch the skin of this aged planet. What does he expect to get for it? It pleases the aged planet. She stretches herself in the twilight, purrs like an old cat, and expresses her pleasure in the odd and useful effluvium we call peas. And this biped wears clothes. Think of it! He wears clothes; things made out of plant-fibre and sheep's wool cunningly and hideously made to fit his arms and legs. He has in his pocket—a small pouch made in these singular garments—a watch, a small shiny round object in which he has reduced to feeble but regular iambics the majestic motions of the sun, earth and stars. He takes it out and looks at it with an air of comprehension and puts it back again. Why doesn't he laugh at himself?" . . . He chuckled. . . . "This object tells him that he has time for two more rows before dinner. Clink, clink. Damn these pebbles. My antediluvian anthropoid ape of an ancestor had to walk round them, they were so huge. He sat on them, cracked nuts against them, chattered with his family. He had no watch, and his trousers grew like grass. . . . Thank the Lord they've become pebbles."

He sighed, and for a moment rested his chin on the hoe-handle, peering out towards the tree-encircled swamp. The hylas were beginning to jingle their elfin bells. A red-winged blackbird sailed in the last sunlight from one apple-tree to another.

"All a vicious circle—and all fascinating. Utterly preposterous and futile, but fascinating."

He dropped the hoe and trundled the wheelbarrow to the edge of the strawberry-bed.

"Why can't you stay where you're put?" he said. "Why do you grow all over the place like this?"

With a trowel he began digging up the runners and placing them on the wheelbarrow. It delighted him to part the soft cool soil with his fingers, to thrust them sensitively among the finely filamented roots. The delicate snap, subterranean, of rootlets gave him a delicious pang. "Blood flows—but it's all for the best; in the best of all possible worlds. Yield to me, strawberries, and you shall bear. I am the resurrection and the life." When he had a sufficient pile of plants, he trundled the wheelbarrow to the new bed, exquisitely prepared, rich, warm, inviting. With the hoe he made a series of holes, and then, stooping, thrust the hairy roots back into the earth, pressing the soil tenderly about them. Then he rose, stretched his back, and lighted his pipe, shutting his left eye, and enshrining the flame, which danced, in the hollow of his stained hands. The cloud of smoke went up like incense.

"Water!" he cried. "Water! Water!"

Martha appeared, after a moment, bringing the watering-pot. She held it in front of her with both hands.

"Quick, Martha, before they die. Their tongues are turning black."

"Silly!" Martha replied.

The earth about each plant was darkened with the tilted water, and the soiled leaves and stems were brightened.

"Listen, daddy! They're smacking their lips."

"They are pale, they have their eyes shut, they are reaching desperately down into the darkness for something to hold on to. They grope and tickle at atoms of soil, they shrink away from pebbles, they sigh and relax."

"When the dew falls, they'll sing."

"Ha! ha! what fools we are."

He flung the hoe across the wheelbarrow and started wheeling it towards the toolhouse.

"Bring the watering-pot."

Martha ran after him and put it in the wheelbarrow.

"That's right—add to my burden—never do anything that you can make somebody else do."

Martha giggled in response and skipped towards the house. When she reached the stone steps she put her feet close together and with dark seriousness hopped up step after step in that manner. He watched her and smiled.

"O Lord, Lord," he said, "what a circus we are."

He trundled the bumping wheelbarrow and whistled. The red sun, enormous in the slight haze, was gashing itself cruelly on a black pine tree. The hylas, by now, had burst into full shrill-sweet chorus in the swamp, and of the birds all but a few scraping grackles were still. "Peace—peace —peace," sang the hylas, a thousand at once. Silver bells, frailer than thimbles, ringing under a still and infinite sea of ether. . . . "Peace—peace," he murmured. Then he dropped the wheelbarrow in horror, and put his hands to his ears. "The enemy!" he cried. "Martha! hurry! Martha!" This time Martha seemed to be out of earshot, so he was obliged to circumvent the enemy with great caution. The enemy was a toad who sat by preference near the tool-house door: obese, sage, and wrinkled like a Chinese god. "Toad that under cold stone." Marvelous compulsion of rhythm. . . . He thrust the wheelbarrow into the cool pleasant-smelling darkness of the toolhouse, and walked towards the kitchen door, which just at that moment Hilda opened.

"Hurry up," she said. Her voice had a delicious mildness in the still air and added curiously to his already over-whelming sense of luxury. He had, for a moment, an extraordinarily satisfying sense of space.

III

He lifted his eyes from the pudding to the Hokusai print over the mantel.

"Think of it with shame! We sit here again grossly feeding our insatiable bellies, while Fujiyama, there, thrusts his copper-colored cone into a cobalt sky among whipped-cream clouds! Pilgrims, in the dusk, toil up his sides with

staves. Pilgrims like ants. They struggle upwards in the
darkness for pure love of beauty."

"I don't like bread-pudding," ejaculated Mary solemnly,
"it's beany."

Martha and Marjorie joined in a silvery cascade of
giggles.

"Where *did* she get that awful word!" said Hilda.

"Tom says it, mother."

"Well, for goodness' sake forget it."

Mary stared gravely about the table, spoon in mouth,
and then, removing the spoon, repeated, "It's beany."

He groaned, folding his napkin.

"What an awful affliction a family is. Why did we
marry, Hilda? Life is a trap."

"Mrs. Ferguson called this afternoon and presented me
with a basket of green strawberries. I'm afraid she thought
I wasn't very appreciative. I hate to be interrupted when
I'm sewing. Why under the sun does she pick them before
they're ripe?"

"That's a nice way to treat a neighbor who gives you a
present! . . . You *are* an ungrateful creature."

Hilda was languid.

"Well, I didn't ask her for them."

Her eyes gleamed with a slow provocative amusement.

"They're beany," said Mary.

He rolled his eyes at Mary.

"Our kids are too much with us. Bib and spoon,
    Feeding and spanking, we lay waste our powers!"

They all pushed back their chairs, laughing, and a moment later, as he lighted his cigar, he heard, from the
music-room, Hilda's violin begin with tremulous thin notes,
oddly analogous to the sound of her voice when she sang,
playing Bach to a methodical loud piano accompaniment
by Martha. Melancholy came like a blue wave out of the
dusk, lifted him, and broke slowly and deliciously over
him. He stood for a moment, made motionless by the
exquisite, intricate melody, stared, as if seeking with his
eyes for the meaning of the silvery algebra of sound, and
then went out.

The sun had set, darkness was at hand. He walked to

the top of the stone steps and looked across the shallow
valley towards the fading hill and the black water-tower.
The trees on the crest, sharply silhouetted against a last
band of pale light, looked like marching men. Lights
winked at the base of the hill. And now, as hill and water-
tower and trees became obscure, he began to see once more
the dim phantasmal outlines of the dark city, the city submerged under the infinite sea, the city not inhabited by
mortals. Immense, sinister and black, old and cold as the
moon, were the walls that surrounded it. No gate gave
entrance to it. Of a paler stone were the houses upon
houses, tiers upon tiers of shadowy towers, which sur-
mounted the walls. Not a light was to be seen in it, not
a motion: it was still. He stared and stared at it, following
with strained eyes the faint lines which might indicate
its unlighted streets, seeking in vain, as always, to discover
in the walls of it any sign of any window. It grew darker,
it faded, a profound and vast secret, an inscrutable mystery.

"She is older than the rocks," he murmured.

He turned away and walked over the lawn in the darkness, listening to the hylas, who seemed now to be saturat-
ing the hushed night with sound. "Peace—peace—peace—"
they sang. *Pax vobiscum*. He gathered the croquet mallets
and leaned them against the elm tree, swearing when he
tripped over an unseen wicket. This done, he walked down
the pale road, blowing clouds of smoke above him with
uplifted face, and luxuriated in the sight of the dark tops
of trees motionless against the stars. A soft skipping sound
in the leaves at the road's edge made him jump. He
laughed to himself. . . . "He had no watch, and his
trousers grew like grass. . . ." He took out his watch and
peered closely at it. The children were in bed, and Hilda
was waiting for a game of chess. He walked back with
his hands deep in his pockets. Pawn to king-four.

"Hilda! Wake up!"

Hilda opened her candid eyes without astonishment and
sat up over the chess-board, on which the tiny men were
already arranged.

"Goodness! How you scared me. What took you so
long? I've been dreaming about Bluebeard."

"Bluebeard! Good Heavens! I hope he didn't look like me."

"He did—remarkably!"

"A *nice* thing to say to your husband. . . . Move! Hurry up! . . . I'm going to capture your king. Queens die young and fair."

He smoked his pipe. Hilda played morosely. Delicious, she was when she was half asleep like this! She leaned her head on one hand, her elbow on the table. . . . When she had been checkmated at the end of half an hour she sank back wearily in her chair. She looked at him intently for a moment and began to smile.

"And how about the dark city tonight?" she asked. He took slow puffs at his pipe and stared meditatively at the ceiling.

"Ah—the dark city, Hilda! The city submerged under an infinite sea, the city not inhabited by mortals! . . . It was there again—would you believe it? . . . It was there. . . . I went out to the stone steps, smoking my cigar, while you played Bach. I hardly dared to look—I watched the hill out of the corner of my eyes and pretended to be listening to the music. . . . And suddenly, at the right moment of dusk, just after the street lamps had winked along the base of the hill, I saw it. The hill that we see there in the daylight, with its water-tower and marching trees, its green sloping fields and brook that flashes in the sun, is unreal, an illusion, the thinnest of disguises—a cloak of green velvet which the dark city throws over itself at the coming of the first ray of light. . . . I saw it distinctly. Immense, smooth and black, old and cold as the moon, are the walls that surround it. No gate gives entrance to it. Of a paler stone are the houses upon houses, tiers upon tiers of shadowy towers that surmount those sepulchral walls. No motion was perceptible there—no light gleamed there—no sound, no whisper rose from it. I thought: perhaps it is a city of the dead. The walls of it have no windows, and its inhabitants must be blind. . . . And then I seemed to see it more closely, in a twilight which appeared to be its own, and this closer perception gave way in turn to a vision. For fiirst I saw that all the walls of it are moist, dripping, slippery, as if it were bathed in a deathlike dew; and then I saw its people. Its people are maggots—maggots of perhaps the size of human children; their heads are small and wedge-shaped, and glow with a faint bluish light. Masses of them swarm within those walls. Masses of them pour through the streets, glisten on the buttresses and parapets. They are intelligent. What horrible feast is it that nightly they celebrate there in silence? On what carrion do they feed? It is the universe that they devour; and they build above it, as they devour it, their dark city like a hollow tomb. . . . Extraordinary that this city, which seen from here at dusk has so supernatural a beauty, should hide at the core so vile a secret. . . ."

Hilda stared at him.

"Really, Andrew, I think you're going mad."

"Going? I'm gone! My brain is maggoty."

They laughed and rattled the chessmen into their wooden box. Then they began locking the doors and windows for the night.

I'M A FOOL[1]

By SHERWOOD ANDERSON

(From *The Dial* and *The London Mercury*)

IT was a hard jolt for me, one of the most bitterest I ever had to face. And it all came about through my own foolishness too. Even yet, sometimes, when I think of it, I want to cry or swear or kick myself. Perhaps, even now, after all this time, there will be a kind of satisfaction in making myself look cheap by telling of it.

It began at three o'clock one October afternoon as I sat in the grand stand at the fall trotting and pacing meet at Sandusky, Ohio.

To tell the truth, I felt a little foolish that I should be sitting in the grand stand at all. During the summer before I had left my home town with Harry Whitehead and, with a nigger named Burt, had taken a job as swipe with one of the two horses Harry was campaigning through the fall race meets that year. Mother cried and my sister Mildred, who wanted to get a job as a school teacher in out town that fall, stormed and scolded about the house all during the week before I left. They both thought it something disgraceful that one of our family should take a place as a swipe with race horses. I've an idea Mildred thought my taking the place would stand in the way of her getting the job she'd been working so long for.

But after all I had to work and there was no other work to be got. A big lumbering fellow of nineteen couldn't just hang around the house and I had got too big to mow people's lawns and sell newspapers. Little chaps who could get next to people's sympathies by their sizes were always getting jobs away from me. There was one fellow who

kept saying to everyone who wanted a lawn mowed or a
cistern cleaned, that he was saving money to work his way
through college, and I used to lay awake nights thinking up
ways to injure him without being found out. I kept thinking of wagons running over him and bricks falling on his
head as he walked along the street. But never mind him.

I got the place with Harry and I liked Burt fine. We
got along splendid together. He was a big nigger with a
lazy sprawling body and soft kind eyes, and when it came
to a fight he could hit like Jack Johnson. He had Bucephalus, a big black pacing stallion that could do 2.09 or
2.10 if he had to, and I had a little gelding named Doctor
Fritz that never lost a race all fall when Harry wanted
him to win.

We set out from home late in July in a box car with the
two horses and after that, until late November, we kept
moving along to the race meets and the fairs. It was a
peachy time for me, I'll say that. Sometimes, now, I think
that boys who are raised regular in houses, and never have
a fine nigger like Burt for best friend, and go to high
schools and college, and never steal anything or get drunk
a little, or learn to swear from fellows who know how, or
come walking up in front of a grand stand in their shirt
sleeves and with dirty horsey pants on when the races are
going on and the grand stand is full of people all dressed
up— What's the use talking about it? Such fellows don't
know nothing at all. They've never had no opportunity.

But I did. Burt taught me how to rub down a horse
and put the bandages on after a race and steam a horse
out and a lot of valuable things for any man to know. He
could wrap a bandage on a horse's leg so smooth that if it
had been the same color you would think it was his skin,
and I guess he'd have been a big driver too and got to
the top like Murphy and Walter Cox and the others if he
hadn't been black.

Gee whizz, it was fun. You got to a county seat town
maybe, say, on a Saturday or Sunday, and the fair began
the next Tuesday and lasted until Friday afternoon. Doctor Fritz would be, say, in the 2.25 trot on Tuesday afternoon and on Thursday afternoon Bucephalus would knock

'em cold in the "free-for-all" pace. It left you a lot of
time to hang around and listen to horse talk, and see
Burt knock some yap cold that got too gay, and you'd
find out about horses and men and pick up a lot of stuff
you could use all the rest of your life if you had some
sense and salted down what you heard and felt and saw.

And then at the end of the week when the race meet
was over, and Harry had run home to tend up to his livery
stable business, you and Burt hitched the two horses to
carts and drove slow and steady across country to the place
for the next meeting so as to not over-heat the horses, etc.,
etc., you know.

Gee whizz, gosh amighty, the nice hickorynut and beech-
nut and oaks and other kinds of trees along the roads, all
brown and red, and the good smells, and Burt singing a
song that was called Deep River, and the country girls at
the windows of houses and everything. You can stick
your colleges up your nose for all me. I guess I know
where I got my education.

Why, one of those little burgs of towns you come to on
the way, say now, on a Saturday afternoon, and Burt says,
"let's lay up here." And you did.

And you took the horses to a livery stable and fed them
and you got your good clothes out of a box and put them
on.

And the town was full of farmers gaping, because they
could see you were race horse people, and the kids maybe
never see a nigger before and was afraid and run away
when the two of us walked down their main street.

And that was before prohibition and all that foolishness,
and so you went into a saloon, the two of you, and all the
yaps come and stood around, and there was always someone
pretended he was horsey and knew things and spoke up
and began asking questions, and all you did was to lie and
lie all you could about what horses you had, and I said I
owned them, and then some fellow said, "Will you have a
drink of whiskey?" and Burt knocked his eye out the way
he could say, offhand like, "Oh, well, all right, I'm agree-
able to a little nip. I'll split a quart with you." Gee
whizz.

But that isn't what I want to tell my story about. We got home late in November and I promised mother I'd quit the race horses for good. There's a lot of things you've got to promise a mother because she don't know any better.

And so, there not being any work in our town any more than when I left there to go to the races, I went off to Sandusky and got a pretty good place taking care of the horses for a man who owned a teaming and delivery and storage business there. It was a pretty good place with good eats and a day off each week and sleeping on a cot in the big barn, and mostly just shoveling in hay and oats to a lot of big good-enough skates of horses that couldn't have trotted a race with a toad. I wasn't dissatisfied and I could send money home.

And then, as I started to tell you, the fall races come to Sandusky and I got the day off and I went. I left the job at noon and had on my good clothes and my new brown derby hat I'd just bought the Saturday before, and a stand-up collar.

First of all I went downtown and walked about with the dudes. I've always thought to myself, "put up a good front," and so I did it. I had forty dollars in my pocket and so I went into the West House, a big hotel, and walked up to the cigar stand. "Give me three twenty-five cent cigars," I said. There was a lot of horse men and strangers and dressed-up people from other towns standing around in the lobby and in the bar, and I mingled amongst them. In the bar there was a fellow with a cane and a Windsor tie on, that it made me sick to look at him. I like a man to be a man and dress up, but not to go put on that kind of airs. So I pushed him aside, kind of rough, and had me a drink of whiskey. And then he looked at me as though he thought maybe he'd get gay, but he changed his mind and didn't say anything. And then I had another drink of whiskey, just to show him something, and went out and had a hack out to the races all to myself, and when I got there I bought myself the best seat I could get up in the grand stand, but didn't go in for any of these boxes. That's putting on too many airs.

And so there I was, sitting up in the grand stand as gay

as you please and looking down on the swipes coming out
with their horses and with their dirty horsey pants on and
the horse blankets swung over their shoulders same as I
had been doing all the year before. I liked one thing
about the same as the other, sitting up there and feeling
grand and being down there and looking up at the yaps
and feeling grander and more important too. One thing's
about as good as another if you take it just right. I've
often said that.

Well, right in front of me, in the grand stand that day,
there was a fellow with a couple of girls and they was
about my age. The young fellow was a nice guy all right.
He was the kind maybe that goes to college and then comes
to be a lawyer or maybe a newspaper editor or something
like that, but he wasn't stuck on himself. There are some
of that kind are all right and he was one of the ones.

He had his sister with him and another girl and the
sister looked around over his shoulder, accidental at first,
not intending to start anything—she wasn't that kind—
and her eyes and mine happened to meet.

You know how it is. Gee, she was a peach. She had
on a soft dress, kind of a blue stuff and it looked carelessly
made, but was well sewed and made and everything. I
knew that much. I blushed when she looked right at me
and so did she. She was the nicest girl I've ever seen in
my life. She wasn't stuck on herself and she could talk
proper grammar without being like a school teacher or
something like that. What I mean is, she was O.K. I
think maybe her father was well-to-do, but not rich to
make her chesty because she was his daughter, as some
are. Maybe he owned a drug store or a dry goods store
in their home town, or something like that. She never told
me and I never asked.

My own people are all O.K. too, when you come to that.
My grandfather was Welsh and over in the old country, in
Wales he was—but never mind that.

The first heat of the first race come off and the young
fellow setting there with the two girls left them and went
down to make a bet. I knew what he was up to, but

he didn't talk big and noisy and let everyone around know
he was a sport, as some do. He wasn't that kind. Well,
he come back and I heard him tell the two girls what
horse he'd bet on, and when the heat was trotted they all
half got to their feet and acted in the excited, sweaty way
people do when they've got money down on a race, and
the horse they bet on is up there pretty close at the end,
and they think maybe he'll come on with a rush, but he
never does because he hasn't got the old juice in him, come
right down to it.

And then, pretty soon, the horses came out for the
2.18 pace and there was a horse in it I knew. He was a
horse Bob French had in his string, but Bob didn't own
him. He was a horse owned by a Mr. Mathers down at
Marietta, Ohio.

This Mr. Mathers had a lot of money and owned some
coal mines or something, and he had a swell place out in
the country, and he was stuck on race horses, but was a
Presbyterian or something, and I think more than likely
his wife was one, too, maybe a stiffer one than himself.
So he never raced his horses hisself, and the story round
the Ohio race tracks was that when one of his horses got
ready to go to the races he turned him over to Bob French
and pretended to his wife he was sold.

So Bob had the horses and he did pretty much as he
pleased and you can't blame Bob, at least, I never did.
Sometimes he was out to win and sometimes he wasn't. I
never cared much about that when I was swiping a horse.
What I did want to know was that my horse had the speed
and could go out in front if you wanted him to.

And, as I'm telling you, there was Bob in this race
with one of Mr. Mathers' horses, was named "About Ben
Ahem" or something like that, and was fast as a streak.
He was a gelding and had a mark of 2.21, but could step
in .08 or .09.

Because when Burt and I were out, as I've told you,
the year before, there was a nigger Burt knew, worked for
Mr. Mathers, and we went out there one day when we
didn't have no race on at the Marietta Fair and our boss
Harry was gone home.

And so everyone was gone to the fair but just this one nigger, and he took us all through Mr. Mathers' swell house and he and Burt tapped a bottle of wine Mr. Mathers had hid in his bedroom, back in a closet, without his wife knowing, and he showed us this Ahem horse. Burt was always stuck on being a driver, but didn't have much chance to get to the top, being a nigger, and he and the other nigger gulped that whole bottle of wine and Burt got a little lit up.

So the nigger let Burt take this About Ben Ahem and step him a mile in a track Mr. Mathers had all to himself, right there on the farm. And Mr. Mathers had one child, a daughter, kinda sick and not very good looking, and she came home and we had to hustle and get About Ben Ahem stuck back in the barn.

I'm only telling you to get everything straight. At Sandusky, that afternoon I was at the fair, this young fellow with the two girls was fussed, being with the girls and losing his bet. You know how a fellow is that way. One of them was his girl and the other his sister. I had figured that out.

"Gee whizz," I says to myself, "I'm going to give him the dope."

He was mighty nice when I touched him on the shoulder. He and the girls were nice to me right from the start and clear to the end. I'm not blaming them.

And so he leaned back and I gave him the dope on About Ben Ahem. "Don't bet a cent on this first heat because he'll go like an oxen hitched to a plough, but when the first heat is over go right down and lay on your pile." That's what I told him.

Well, I never saw a fellow treat any one sweller. There was a fat man sitting beside the little girl that had looked at me twice by this time, and I at her, and both blushing, and what did he do but have the nerve to turn and ask the fat man to get up and change places with me so I could set with his crowd.

Gee whizz, amighty. There I was. What a chump I was to go and get gay up there in the West House bar, and just because that dude was standing there with a

cane and that kind of a necktie on, to go and get all balled
up and drink that whiskey, just to show off.

Of course she would know, me setting right beside her
and letting her smell of my breath. I could have kicked
myself right down out of that grand stand and all around
that race track and made a faster record than most of the
skates of horses they had there that year.

Because that girl wasn't any mutt of a girl. What
wouldn't I have give right then for a stick of chewing
gum to chew, or a lozenger, or some licorice, or most
anything. I was glad I had those twenty-five cent cigars
in my pocket, and right away I give that fellow one
and lit one myself. Then that fat man got up and we
changed places and there I was plunked right down beside
her.

They introduced themselves, and the fellow's best girl
he had with him, was named Miss Elinor Woodbury, and
her father was a manufacturer of barrels from a place
called Tiffin, Ohio. And the fellow himself was named
Wilbur Wessen and his sister was Miss Lucy Wessen.

I suppose it was their having such swell names got me
off my trolley. A fellow, just because he has been a swipe
with a race horse, and works taking care of horses for a
man in the teaming, delivery and storage business, isn't
any better or worse than any one else. I've often thought
that, and said it, too.

But you know how a fellow is. There's something in
that kind of nice clothes, and the kind of nice eyes she
had, and the way she had looked at me, awhile before,
over her brother's shoulder, and me looking back at her,
and both of us blushing.

I couldn't show her up for a boob, could I?

I made a fool of myself, that's what I did. I said my
name was Walter Mathers from Marietta, Ohio, and then
I told all three of them the smashingest lie you ever heard.
What I said was that my father owned the horse About
Ben Ahem, and that he had let him out to this Bob French
for racing purposes, because our family was proud and
had never gone into racing that way, in our own name, I
mean. Then I had got started and they were all leaning

over and listening, and Miss Lucy Wessen's eyes were shining, and I went the whole hog.

I told about our place down at Marietta, and about the big stables and the grand brick house we had on a hill, up above the Ohio River, but I knew enough not to do it in no bragging way. What I did was to start things and then let them drag the rest out of me. I acted just as reluctant to tell as I could. Our family hasn't got any barrel factory, and, since I've known us, we've always been pretty poor, but not asking anything of anyone at that, and my grandfather, over in Wales—but never mind that.

We set there talking like we had known each other for years and years, and I went and told them that my father had been expecting maybe this Bob French wasn't on the square, and had sent me up to Sandusky on the sly to find out what I could.

And I bluffed it through I had found out all about the 2.18 pace in which About Ben Ahem was to start.

I said he would lose the first heat by pacing like a lame cow and then he would come back and skin 'em alive after that. And to back up what I said I took thirty dollars out of my pocket and handed it to Mr. Wilbur Wessen and asked him would he mind, after the first heat, to go down and place it on About Ben Ahem for whatever odds he could get. What I said was that I didn't want Bob French to see me and none of the swipes.

Sure enough the first heat come off and About Ben Ahem went off his stride, up the back stretch, and looked like a wooden horse or a sick one, and come in to be last. Then this Wilbur Wessen went down to the betting place under the grand stand and there I was with the two girls, and when that Miss Woodbury was looking the other way once, Lucy Wessen kinda, with her shoulder you know, kinda touched me. Not just tucking down, I don't mean. You know how a woman can do. They get close, but not getting gay either. You know what they do. Gee whizz.

And then they give me a jolt. What they had done when I didn't know, was to get together, and they had decided Wilbur Wessen would bet fifty dollars, and the two girls had gone and put in ten dollars each of their own money, too. I was sick then, but I was sicker later.

About the gelding, About Ben Ahem, and their winning their money, I wasn't worried a lot about that. It come out O.K. Ahem stepped the next three heats like a bushel of spoiled eggs going to market before they could be found out, and Wilbur Wessen had got nine to two for the money. There was something else eating at me.

Because Wilbur come back after he had bet the money, and after that he spent most of his time talking to that Miss Woodbury, and Lucy Wessen and I was left alone together like on a desert island. Gee, if I'd only been on the square or if there had been any way of getting myself on the square. There ain't any Walter Mathers, like I said to her and them, and there hasn't ever been one, but if there was, I bet I'd go to Marietta, Ohio, and shoot him tomorrow.

There I was, big boob that I am. Pretty soon the race was over, and Wilbur had gone down and collected our money, and we had a hack downtown, and he stood us a swell dinner at the West House, and a bottle of champagne beside.

And I was with that girl and she wasn't saying much, and I wasn't saying much either. One thing I know. She wasn't stuck on me because of the lie about my father being rich and all that. There's a way you know. . . . Craps amighty. There's a kind of girl you see just once in your life, and if you don't get busy and make hay then you're gone for good and all and might as well go jump off a bridge. They give you a look from inside of them somewhere, and it ain't no vamping, and what it means is—you want that girl to be your wife, and you want nice things around her like flowers and swell clothes, and you want her to have the kids you're going to have, and you want good music played and no ragtime. Gee whizz.

There's a place over near Sandusky, across a kind of bay, and it's called Cedar Point. And when we had had that dinner we went over to it in a launch, all by ourselves. Wilbur and Miss Lucy and that Miss Woodbury had to catch a ten o'clock train back to Tiffin, Ohio, because when you're out with girls like that you can't get careless and miss any trains and stay out all night like you can with some kinds of Janes.

And Wilbur blowed himself to the launch and it cost him fifteen cold plunks, but I wouldn't ever have knew if I hadn't listened. He wasn't no tin horn kind of a sport.

Over at the Cedar Point place we didn't stay around where there was a gang of common kind of cattle at all.

There was big dance halls and dining places for yaps, and there was a beach you could walk along and get where it was dark, and we went there.

She didn't talk hardly at all and neither did I, and I was thinking how glad I was my mother was all right, and always made us kids learn to eat with a fork at table and not swill soup and not be noisy and rough like a gang you see around a race track that way.

Then Wilbur and his girl went away up the beach and Lucy and I set down in a dark place where there was some roots of old trees the water had washed up, and after that, the time, till we had to go back in the launch and they had to catch their trains, wasn't nothing at all. It went like winking your eye.

Here's how it was. The place we were setting in was dark, like I said, and there was the roots from that old stump sticking up like arms, and there was a watery smell, and the night was like—as if you could put your hand out and feel it—so warm and soft and dark and sweet like a orange.

I most cried and I most swore and I most jumped up and danced, I was so mad and happy and sad.

When Wilbur come back from being alone with his girl, and she saw him coming, Lucy she says, "we got to go to the train now," and she was most crying, too, but she never knew nothing I knew, and she couldn't be so all busted up. And then, before Wilbur and Miss Woodbury got up to where she was, she put her face up and kissed me quick and put her head up against me and she was all quivering and—Gee whizz.

Sometimes I hope I have cancer and die. I guess you know what I mean. We went in the launch across the bay to the train like that, and it was dark too. She whispered

and said it was like she and I could get out of the boat
and walk on the water, and it sounded foolish, but I knew
what she meant.

And then quick, we were right at the depot, and there
was a big gang of yaps, the kind that goes to the fairs,
and crowded and milling around like cattle, and how could
I tell her? "It won't be long because you'll write and I'll
write to you." That's all she said.

I got a chance like a hay barn afire. A swell chance I
got.

And maybe she would write me, down at Marietta that
way, and the letter would come back, and stamped on the
front of it by the U.S.A. "there ain't any such guy," or
something like that, whatever they stamp on a letter that
way.

And me trying to pass myself off for a bigbug and a
swell—to her, as decent a little body as God ever made.
Craps amighty. A swell chance I got.

And then the train come in and she got on, and Wilbur
Wessen come and shook hands with me and that Miss
Woodbury was nice and bowed to me and I at her and the
train went and I busted out and cried like a kid.

Gee, I could have run after that train and made Dan
Patch look like a freight train after a wreck, but socks
amighty, what was the use? Did you ever see such a fool?

I'll bet you what—if I had an arm broke right now or a
train had run over my foot—I wouldn't go to no doctor
at all. I'd go set down and let her hurt and hurt—that's
what I'd do.

I'll bet you what—if I hadn't a drunk that booze I'd
a never been such a boob as to go tell such a lie—that
couldn't never be made straight to a lady like her.

I wish I had that fellow right here that had on a Windsor tie and carried a cane. I'd smash him for fair. Gosh
darn his eyes. He's a big fool—that's what he is.

And if I'm not another you just go find me one and I'll
quit working and be a bum and give him my job. I don't
care nothing for working and earning money and saving it
for no such boob as myself.

THE DEATH OF MURDO[1]

By KONRAD BERCOVICI

(From *The Pictorial Review*)

"OH, Murdo, grandson of the mighty chief Lupu, but
father of none worthy of thy blood. I shall tell of
thy death to the 'other ones' so that they might know
how to die themselves. I have already told them of thy
great wisdom; that wisdom which was far greater than
that of the snake, yet had none of its poison; and thy
great wing-strength, more powerful than that of the eagle,
on which thou hast lifted thine own soul above the dirt
and the dust of the valley, but never soiled with the blood
of prey.

"Murdo, grandson of Lupu, the Wolf. Eagle and Snake.
Man. Of all who have seen thee die I am the only one to
know the truth. The tribe is scattered to the four winds.
'Lilith' has done her dreadful work. Murdo, my teacher,
my chief, thou who hast been more than father or brother
to me, forgive me if I do not tell the story as thou, incomparable one, wouldst have had me tell it."

I had been away from the camp for over a year. Civilization and father and mother had claimed me; but hardly
had the green shown itself from underneath the snow and
I rejoined Murdo's tribe again. An old Tzigany had told
me that Murdo was mortally ill and that the whole tribe
was stranded near the Black Sea. The morning after I
reached Konstanz, through marshes and mire, found me
by Murdo's cot. The great chief had grown considerably
older. The knife-wound he had received from Yorga, the
fiddler, the previous fall, had not healed, and the concoc-
tions and incantations of Miora had not successfully replaced a needed physician.

[1] Copyright, 1922, by The Pictorial Review Company.
Copyright, 1923, by Konrad Bercovici.

"It is well thou art here," Murdo greeted me. "I have called thee with my soul. It is too soon for me to die. Though I am advanced in years, my tribe still needs me. Nicolai, son of my own blood, is no man to be chief of a tribe. He dreams away on his violin. Oh! that a pigeon should be born in an eagle's nest! The starost of the village has told me many a time to go to one of your doctors. But I have believed and still do believe that illness and recovery from it is Fate; with which neither doctor nor witch can interfere. Yet your people, who have made wagons go without horses, a bridge span the Danube, who can talk with one another across distances without the aid of witches—by stretching wires that the sparrows stand upon—perhaps you do know something about diseases which we neither believe nor understand. So do take me to one of your doctors and talk to him and tell him I must yet live a short while. It is not health I want, but life. Life until I choose a chief in whom my people shall believe. Their trust in me is so great—too great—they will never be satisfied with another man unless it be proved he is as good or better than I."

I looked at Murdo's wound and marveled that he was still alive. Only his great powers of resistance had enabled him to live that long. I wondered that he had not died long before of blood-poisoning! He was emaciated beyond belief. His long arms were so thin that it looked as though his bones had been shaved down to spindles. The veins of his neck and around his temples showed like blue cords from which the hemp had been worn and loosened. The cheek-bones of his dark-grained face edged against the parched skin and gave him a haunted aspect. Even his voice, that great and haughty drum-voice, though still big and commanding, had lost the firmness of its tissue. It rasped like drumsticks upon the loosened skin of a bass drum.

The tribe, nervous and restless, wandered hither and thither in narrow circles, like lost children, uncertain and afraid, forming little groups behind the trees in the forest, or under distant tents, discussing in subdued voices every detail, bickering, quarreling, doing their best to keep disagreeable things away from the ears and eyes of their chief. The horses and the dogs looked worn and forlorn, sick and sorely in need of a master. For the horse of the Gipsy and the dog of the Gipsy are happy when their master is happy, and sad when their master is sad, and grow restless and nervous when sojourning too long in the same place.

"But why are you all so sad?" I asked Lica, the son of Miora, the witch, who had somehow assumed some sort of command during the chief's illness.

"How can we be happy," he replied, "when we no longer hear the song of the hammer upon the anvil, when the smith dares not blow his bellows lest he disturb Murdo from his sleep? When we have looked upon the same hill so long the pegs of our tents are rotting in the ground? Look! Our horses have lost half their hoof-bones. It is an age since they have been shod. Look! We have muzzled our dogs, and when our goats bleat in the morning, our women rush out with knife in hand to cut out their tongues. Because our chief battles with death we have become like old women; fussy and afraid of noise."

That very afternoon, having bedded Murdo as comfortably as possible in the wagon, I started on my journey with him to the town of Braila on the Danube. The trip lasted several days.

"Now tell me what thou hast learned while away from my camp," Murdo turned upon me suddenly the night of our first stopover at an inn kept by a Greek.

I was certain the doctor would have to operate and cleanse the wound where Yorga's knife had struck. Fearing Murdo might oppose such operation, I began to explain the cause of infections and the means employed for staying them, and the existence of microbes in the human body. Murdo listened very attentively as though I were telling him some interesting story, but I could see that he did not believe what I was telling him. After a long pause he said to me:

"It is a well-knit tale thou hast put forward. But thou, who hast argued against the existence of spirits and goblins in the air, how is it thou wantest me to believe in your tale of the existence of worms which I do not see. Surely our fairy-tales are nicer than yours!"

He called me over to his cot the following night and asked me to continue my "fairy-tale."

"But since you do not believe, Murdo—" I objected.

"And hast thou ever believed our fairy-tales? Yet thou hast insisted we tell them to you!"

I recalled to him a telescope we had once seen together and explained how by increasing the number and the power of these glasses one could see things placed at enormous distances. He believed that. Then I told him how with the aid of such powerful glasses very small things could be magnified and how upon increasing the power of these glasses things too small to be seen with the naked eye could be made visible.

"I should love to see with my own eyes through those glasses those invisible little goblins of which you speak so convincingly," he answered sarcastically.

"Thou shalt see," I assured him.

"Truly," Murdo rejoined, "thou art a good story-teller. Thou even believest what thou tellest. Go off to sleep now. Perhaps I shall dream of what thou hast told me— of those powerful glasses through which thou hast magnified thy story!"

I knew I had won my point. I knew I had won because the doctor to whom I was taking Murdo, an old friend of the family, possessed a microscope.

No sooner had the doctor seen the old man's wound than he called in another physician. Without asking any questions, they put Murdo under ether, and before long they had opened and cleansed the wound. When Murdo awoke he found himself solidly strapped to the bed. I had urged that method upon the doctor, for I feared what Murdo might do upon his awakening from ether. But he was very mild and submissive. He asked me to sit near him. A few days later Murdo, who for the first time in many moons had slept peacefully, was completely restored. The doctor had allowed him the use of a room in his own household. Another few days and Murdo was ready to return to his camp.

"I hate to make thee feel guilty," Murdo said when we were ready to leave. "If what thou hast told me on the road hither was but a fairy-tale, well and good. If, however, it is a true tale, I shall willingly give a year of my life to see it proved."

Within five minutes the microscope was brought to light, and the doctor himself put underneath the lens a few pieces of glass upon which he had made different smears. He allowed Murdo to look at the whirling mass of squirming matter. Murdo looked for a full hour. Having fully satisfied his curiosity, he walked out of the room and asked me to leave him by himself.

The following day we were upon our homeward journey. Murdo was driving. I was sitting near him. The whole day long he remained silent.

"Well?" I inquired that evening. "Art thou satisfied about the existence of *these* goblins?" He turned two very sad eyes upon me; then replied:

"I never knew there were things alive and yet too small to kill. Living things that could destroy a man, but whose smallness saved them from our wrath! I have been thinking of them the whole day long. In size those little worms are about in the same relation to the ant as the ant to us. A drop of water, which they in their infinitesimality cannot see, is enough to drown millions of them. A little child passes over an ant-hill and under its little sole destroys the work of a whole season of millions of them. The ants do not understand what has crushed them. They only feel its power. They are too small to see the child from sole to head as a whole being. They only feel its strength. You blow your softest breath, and it is like a devastating hurricane.

"If we stand in the same relation to some other bigger being as those little worms stand to the ant and the ant to ourselves, when one of those huge beings moves its hand, a great storm arises, a tempest. A drop of sweat falls from his brow, and our fields are inundated; it forms a lake, a river upon which sail large ships. He looks at us, at all of us, because we too are too small to be seen singly and —we have light! We are warm! Perhaps the sun is one

of his eyes. Who knows upon what other little thing his
other eye may rest? A speck of dust—our hills, our mountains. Think of what all our wisdom means, what our time
and space are to him, the earth and the oceans and the
waters all perhaps so small that he, too, needs some powerful glass to see us! And there may yet be still other beings
standing in the same relation to him as he to us——"

When Murdo was in one of his reflective moods he was
better left undisturbed. But the following day he continued the conversation.

"And if this be so—and I am almost certain it is so—
then we are so small that one's life is not worthy of the
slightest consideration. It is the good of the whole tribe
one must think of; and if I, Murdo, will soon be too old
to rule—for man should rule only when he is able to enforce
his commands—should I not beforehand choose a man fit
to follow me? What matters it which ant is alive just so
that the ant-hill lives? So I shall choose a chief in my
own manner. One in whom they shall have absolute con-
fidence; for the wisdom and the power of a ruler are in the
belief of his people. And I shall choose the best one in my
own manner. And I shall choose him while I am yet able
to do so, before old age has dimmed my mind and while I
am yet ruler. But one thing I want of thee. Never a word
to the others of what thou hast told me! Never a word of
what we have seen through those glasses! Never speak of
our stay at your doctor's! A witch has cured me! And
never question when I ask thee to do something! Just
do it!"

Another day and we were in camp. Seeing him restored,
the happiness of the Gypsies broke all bounds. Wine began to flow freely. The musicians brought out their fiddles
again, and song and dance continued through days and
nights. The smith set up his anvil and was singing loudly
to the accompaniment of the hammer while fashioning
shoes out of red-hot iron. Of all music, the clang of the
hammer, alternating from the hard steel of the anvil to
the soft hot iron, pleased the Gypsies most. When the
smith and his helper hammered together, they composed and
improvised melodies and accompaniments for the hammer.

The lustrous, black hair of the maidens was plaited with early violets and evergreens, in thankfulness to the Great Spirit who had restored Murdo to life. Fresh holes were bored in the lobes of the men's ears and new rings of white gold were inserted. In their frenzy, even the little boys came and offered their lobes to be pierced. Little cries of pain were mixed with great cries of joy. At last they could again be noisy. They could allow the horses to neigh, the dogs to bark, and the goats to bleat at will. They could shout, they could quarrel, they could fight. There was no need of hushing one another. No need of soul-torturing restraint. If one were hurt, he could cry aloud. They could be Gypsies again!

Postponed weddings were celebrated. Oh, since the wine was flowing so freely and the musicians were playing, since the women were at their best and the men at their happiest, let it be; for the good of future generations. Let Tanase marry Nitza and Andrea marry Tina; so they could remember and say later on they married the spring Murdo was restored to life. Great joys should be remembered through great joys.

At the camp-fire one night, Lica, the son of Miora, who was believed to have great witch-power, asked Murdo, "What has restored thee to health? Some great 'gagiu' in high silk hat and long black frock? Or who else?"

"No!" answered Murdo. "A witch who knew more incantations than I have ever heard. Who brought down goblins from the air so near to me I could see them. Who brought them down in millions and had them dance before me. And by payment of much gold I have not only been restored to health, but obtained from her immunity. No harm can befall me—except from a knife. And immunity of danger even from that source could have been assured, had I been willing to pay what she asked, and stay there a longer time. But for what I paid she has given me immunity against many things. Look!"

And as he said that, Murdo rose and handed me his pistol. "Here I stand." Then turning to me, he added, "Stand six feet away. Now. Raise your arm and aim. Here!" he commanded, exposing his chest.

Murdo's words, followed by his immediate action, took all the men by surprise. "What did he say? What did he ask that boy to do?"

I, standing there, facing Murdo, trembling, held under the spell of Murdo's eyes, which were immeasurably dilated with his own excitement, only remembered his words, "Don't question. Do what I tell thee."

"Pull the trigger!" he ordered. And I did as he told me. There was a loud report. I fell exhausted with my own emotions. Yet Murdo remained standing and laughing.

"That is what the witch I met did for me! Until some man meets a more powerful one, I shall be immune. That's what makes a great chief. Immunity from disease and murderous weapons."

When I recovered I saw that the Gypsies no longer crowded their chief. Awe kept them open-mouthed at a distance. Only Miora, the old witch, allowed a little cynical smile to play around her lips as she looked at Murdo and her son. I was fully aware that Murdo had noticed that, and was also aware that Miora's disbelief in the power of that great witch about whom Murdo had spoken was not displeasing to the chief.

The following day Murdo, who recuperated more rapidly than I thought possible, was up and about his work. I had never before seen him as quarrelsome. He found fault with everything. The horses had been neglected too much. The dogs were too lean. The canvas of the wagons had not been kept in order. The goats were dry. Murdo, who had never paid any attention to the work of the women in the camp, now found fault with it and censored the women for their lack of order. When Sunday came he quarreled with the younger women for having too many jewels; too many dresses, he said, had been wheedled out of their men, who had become as soft as old women. Some of the children whom he inspected closely had sores and boils which had broken out among them while Murdo was ill. And then he accused Miora of knowing as little of incantations and witchery as the cat in the tree.

While Murdo was talking to Miora, Lica came nearer the chief. Murdo sailed savagely right into him, telling him that he was the worthy son of his mother, that he was sloppy, that his whip was not strong enough to hurt a chicken, that his boots were as dirty as those of a beggar, and that while he had carefully waxed his mustache he had not washed his face.

"Has all the water dried up?" Murdo asked sarcastically, "or are you waiting for your mother to wash your face clean with her tongue, as a mother cat her kitten?"

The big, taut frame of Lica shook upon hearing his chief's words. He loved his mother passionately and believed implicitly in her supernatural powers. That Murdo should have singled him out, him and his mother, for such unjust reproaches, when he had done his best to keep some order when Murdo had been ill, pained the big Gypsy.

"If thou hast lost entire belief in the power of my mother's witchcraft," Lica answered, "why not bring here the one thou hast newly met to replace her? At any rate, I thought she had only coarsened thy hide, but I see I was mistaken——"

I could hardly believe my ears. What man dared use such language to Murdo and hope still to live?

By that time a number of men and women of the camp surrounded the two.

"Lost my belief!" Murdo exclaimed, laughing. "I never had any!"

"Never had any!" Lica echoed, and looked around at the other men. His mother's face twitched, her body became contorted. She gave one long hiss, like a snake, and hobbled away on her stick.

"Never had any! What about the time she had darkened the sun? When she had sailed away on a broomstick in open daylight?" many of the other Gypsies repeated. They put as much space between themselves and their chief as they could. It was blasphemy. Murdo was calling down the wrath of the evil one upon himself and the camp. And if Miora were no witch at all, why had he not told them before? Was it possible they had lived so many years without protection from evil spirits? From "Ciuma," the mother of the forest!

When they had all gone Murdo said to me, "Keep

as near my tent as possible, for, though thou hast not
insulted them, their anger may turn upon thee." I sat in
front of the tent watching the men busying themselves
feverishly each at his work. I could hear them muttering
as they worked. I could see them grouping themselves and
talking in subdued voices as they shot out glances from
underneath their lashes toward where Murdo was sitting.
Only Lica and Miora were not to be seen. Curiously
enough, Murdo's face, which had been so choleric only
a while ago, had suddenly turned a glossy white. A certain beatitude seemed to be enveloping him. His eyes
were very wide open and an unearthly smile played about
his lips. It was the same smile that played when he confused an adversary in a discussion, when he was tremendously satisfied with himself.

"One can never rule too well," he said to me after a
while. "If a ruler is kind, men think him a weakling. So
he is a bad ruler. If a ruler is severe, his men think him
a tyrant. So he is a bad ruler. One should rule well
according to his own lights. A kind ruler should be kind
and a severe one severe."

That night Murdo remained awake. He came over several times to my tent. He said he could not sleep; but I
knew he was watching over me, fearing something might
happen.

I had attempted several times to make conversation with
the men and the women of the tribe, but they avoided me
and sent me unceremoniously about my work. Only Miora
had come nearer, and, passing her bony hands through my
hair, she asked, "Were you with Murdo when he visited
that witch?"

"No," I replied. "He was alone. I never saw the
witch."

Miora looked into my eyes to see if I had told the truth.
Satisfied, she hobbled away to the tent she occupied with
her son.

In two days Murdo had worked up the men and women
of his tribe to such an extent that they were in almost open
revolt. He had used the whip mercilessly. He had insulted and beaten them. He had taken away the jewels

from the women, broken the cask of wine, smashed the jugs of whiskey, and fed to the dogs the quarters of dried lamb which hung inside the tents. At the smithy he had elbowed away the smith to show him how shoes ought to be made and put on. He accused the wheelwright of putting the iron rims upon his wheels when too cold. It made the spokes become loose too soon and ruined the carriages. He tore the big needle from the hands of the harness-maker and showed him how stitches should be made in thick leather. He even kicked the boys currying the horses; told them that their hands were made of cotton and their feet of putty and that they were not worthy of attending to horses.

I could not understand the reason back of Murdo's action. I was certain that there was a motive and a good one, because he was not at all as grouchy when alone in his tent or talking to me. On the contrary, he seemed satisfied with his own attitude toward his men, and talked glibly and banteringly of what he might yet do to them.

Miora had evidently spread the news that I had had nothing to do with the chief's finding of a new witch. For the men and women in the tribe renewed old friendships with me. Murdo found me talking to one of the young women. He called me aside.

"She is married now," he told me. "So you had better keep at a distance from her."

"But I have talked to her before, Murdo, and neither thou nor her husband ever objected!"

"No, he has not objected; only he is no longer your friend. It is the way with women. They want every man who comes near them to forswear all his men friends. A woman hates less and fears less the mistress of her husband than she hates and fears his men friends. It is the reason she separates her man from his friends. All means are fair—jealousy as well as others. And another thing I will tell thee. Women do not want you to tell them the truth. They want men to lie to them. They urge them on, and the more they know that he lies the more satisfied they are, the more they like him. For she knows that it is because of her that he lies, that he has done what is most contrary to his own nature. For man needs never lie to a woman if she did not compel him to do so. It is the lies a man tells a woman that chains him to her more than his love. Each lie is a link forged to the chain. And another thing I will tell thee. It is well it is so. Two things a woman has to hold a man near her when he no longer wants her—her tears and her children. It is well she has a third one—his lies.

"And still another thing I will tell thee—this time about high mountains. The higher the peak the deeper the root. And about large wheels moving slowly but covering great distances. But all this thou wilt in time know, coming to the knowledge in a different way. Oh, you who have discovered how to see things too small to kill, yet not learned how to live! Oh, you with your books and solidly walled houses, with your customs and your manners, with your kings and your doctors! You neither understand how to live nor know how to die. And though you have knowledge, you have no wisdom. You are like overfull barrels. You cannot flow. You ooze. Your brains are clogged; stuffed, leaving you no room for thought."

Sunday. The inn at the market-place. The peasants of the neighborhood are there to buy horses. The plowing done, they are soon to begin to harrow. They use horses for that work. Murdo's men are out with their brown little ponies, proving their speed, endurance, and pulling strength. Two fiddlers on chairs upon a table are scraping furiously away with their bows. A few of the youngsters are already dancing, though it is far from midday. The village tippler, chronically drunk, stands with his full, white-trousered legs wide apart, holding an enormous earthen pitcher in his outstretched hand, and offers drink to all passers-by. "Drink, for spring is here!"

The girls stand in little groups, like field-flowers, and talk among themselves, nod approval or bend in laughter, looking from between long and lowered eyelashes in the direction from which the young men arrive on their way to the inn. They know one another so intimately that they remark the slightest change of detail in apparel.

"Oh, look, Stan has put a new ribbon on his hat!"

"Oh, did you ever know Dan had a shirt with red-embroidered sleeves?"

"No, I know of one embroidered with yellow and another with black. This one with red is a new one."

"Had his mother bought any red wool?"

"No, but Fanutza did."

"Then it must be Fanutza! And I had always thought he was to marry Viora!"

And among the young men they talked of the girls.

"Angelica has added a new silver piece to her necklace. It looks a bit too long; dangles too low."

"Her father resoled his boots the other day and quarreled with the cobbler."

"The innkeeper broke a new pitcher last week. Fell on the stairs coming from the cellar and broke the pitcher."

"Which one?"

"The one with blue flowers on a yellow background."

"Innkeepers are so clumsy!"

"Clumsy and rich."

"Nae, the musician, snapped three strings in one month. It is a good omen. Never let the Gypsy use the same strings at two weddings. Either you or your wife will be unfaithful within the year."

Every little thing is noticed. Every little thing is discussed, is food for thought and talk. And if one bought a horse the whole village is ready to give him advice. And even after the man and horse are buried, the story of how he began the bargain, the first price asked, the price offered, every word, every gesture and word of the Gypsy and the buyer are repeated for years and years; standing near the fences in the summer nights or sitting at the fireside in the winter.

"Do you remember when George bought his horse? It was the year Stan married and Maren's bitch gave him a litter of six black little puppies."

The chief topic of that Sunday, however, was Murdo's marvelous recovery and the tale he had told of being immunized from bullets and disease by a great witch he had met somewhere along the shores of the Danube.

When Murdo appeared at the inn he was surrounded by

older peasants who plied him with questions. The younger ones kept respectfully aside.

"But really," said one who had great faith in Miora's great powers, "you will not tell me, Murdo, that the one you recently met can do what Miora is able to do? That she can ride upon a broomstick through the air as well as Miora, or stay the pest as Miora has done? Don't we know how many times Miora has saved this whole world from destruction with her incantations! And what the other one can do, Miora can and better. I am sure of that."

Murdo listened smilingly, allowing his interlocutor to wax warmer and warmer on the subject of Miora and attracting more and more people around him.

When the crowd was big enough Murdo turned around and said, "There is Miora and there is her son, Lica. He is the truest shot of all my men. He is a good man. And were he not to believe as much in his mother's power as he does, he would be still a better man. Here is a test. I shall go away for two days to my witch. While I am away let Miora immunize her son against pistol-shots. Then we will stand six feet apart with raised arms and cocked pistols. Who remains standing is chief."

Murdo's proposition was received with astonishment and awe by his listeners. Something worth while remembering had already happened. A legend was in the making. A great chief, Murdo!

I shall never forget the face of Miora after Murdo had spoken. The locks of her lower jaw seemed to have slipped out of their hinges. She was incapable of articulating a word. The gurgling, moaning cry she let out was so unearthly; it sounded more like the faint howl of packs of distant wolves than that of a human being. In her anxiety to protect with her own body the stature of her son, she stretched herself so high, it seemed her humped back was flattening out. Big as he was, Lica seemed a small baby near that knotted, bony, hardened frame of his old mother.

Murdo vanished from the place as though the earth had swallowed him. As everybody was looking for him and he was not to be found, the tale quickly spread that he had

ridden away on the proverbial broomstick of the witches.
Children playing in front of the inn pointed to a lone, wild
duck high up in the air. They assured their elders that it
was Murdo; that they had seen him rise. Before nightfall the miracle was believed. Even Miora believed it.

No horse-trading was done that day. When night came
everybody felt that the thing had resolved itself into a
fight of witches. That the contest was to be fought between Miora and that other witch who had cured Murdo.
And that the price was to be the chieftainship of the tribe.

How could it be otherwise? If Murdo's witch knew
more powerful incantations, more effective ones than Miora's, then Miora was a useless member of the tribe; then
both she and her son Lica should have to go elsewhere.
But if Murdo, who had courted and obtained the disap-
proval and hatred of Miora, if Murdo's witch was not all
he pretended her to be, then he could not remain the chief
of the tribe. For a man had to be protected against evil
and had to be able to recur to witchery if he were to rule
effectively a tribe of Gypsies. What if a disease befell the
cattle? What if a disease befell the people? And how
frequently those two afflictions came together! How could
a man be without the protection of a witch? And when
that man was a ruler he had to be immune from many
evils and had to be able to consult with the supernatural.

It was strange to see how the absence of Murdo affected
his tribe. During the following two days life became an
unbearable burden to me. Miora and her son kept to their
tent. The rest of the tribe, men, women and children,
huddled pell-mell, cried, yelled, scratching, pushing, at
times moving like a flabby, will-less mass of soft flesh,
hither and thither, without aim, without reason.

The soul-shattering experience made them remember old
words and old curses. Customs and habits which had long
ago fallen into disuse, fallen by the wayside at the Ganges
River, on the Turkestan roads, rose to the surface again.
The women formed a circle holding each other's braids and
pulling hard, yelling and turning round and round. The
men stripped and flogged one another. At one time during
the night, when I had seen an altar built, I feared a return

to human sacrifice. But the fire was not lighted. An old Gypsy spoke and stayed whatever was about to take place. He urged them to keep their minds away. Not to commit themselves. For if Moira were stronger and they had committed themselves mentally to the other one, they were sure to be punished. So they danced rhythmless dances and sang tuneless songs, buried their nails in the flesh of their faces and their breasts, and howled with delight. In the end some one started to repeat incessantly two words, "Cirtra, vatra; cirtra, vatra; cirtra, vatra." Soon they were all repeating the same words, holding one another under the spell of their feverish, dilated eyes and the jerking, nervous movements of their limbs and shoulders.

The loud moaning of Miora rose above the din of the monotone, which soon became like an accompaniment to the wailing song. From time to time this unearthly cacophony was punctured with a dry and piercing report from Lica's pistol.

In their distraction the Gypsies had not noticed the appearance of Murdo in their midst. When they had noticed him they remained silent and surrounded him. Oh, they believed in him and his witch! He could see that in their eyes. Why had he thought it necessary to test them?

Murdo was in his bare feet and dressed only in a white shirt, held closely to the hips with a wide red sash.

"Call Lica," he ordered, "but let two men keep Miora in her tent."

Lica came out. He was not too sure on his feet. I could see Murdo remarked that. The old chief walked to where the young Gypsy was standing, measured six feet away from him, opened the shirt at his chest until the gray-haired surface was exposed, and said:

"Aim well, Lica, for I want no excuse afterward. It is known thou art the best shot of the tribe."

Miora howled her loudest. The others were awe-struck and silent.

"Now," and the old chief leveled his pistol. "When I say 'three.' "

Lica was pale, but he had regained his composure. It was evident both men were anxious to end the affair.

"One."

"Two."

"Three." Both men emptied their pistols; and Murdo fell flat on his back. The blood trickled.

"Murdo!" I cried, leaning over the dying man.

Lica was untouched, wondering, amazed at what had happened.

"In—my—left—hand—take it—" Murdo murmured softly.

"He—is—a good shot. They will believe in him. It's what—they need. A chief—in whom they believe—a great witch, Miora—greater than mine——"

From his left hand I took the lead of the bullet Murdo had fired at Lica!

He died to give them a chief they could believe greater than he was.

So they danced and made merry. And there was song and wine, and the women were again at their best and the men at their happiest.

"Oh, Murdo, grandson of the mighty chief Lupu, but father of none worthy of thy blood. I shall tell of thy death to the 'other ones' so that they might know how to die themselves. I have already told them of thy great wisdom; that wisdom which was far greater than that of the snake, yet had none of its poison; and thy great wing-strength, more powerful than that of the eagle, on which thou hast lifted thine own soul above the dirt and the dust of the valley, but never soiled with the blood of prey.

"Murdo, grandson of Lupu, the Wolf. Eagle and Snake. Man. Of all who have seen thee die I am the only one to know the truth. The tribe is scattered to the four winds. 'Lilith' has done her dreadful work. Murdo, my teacher, my chief, thou who hast been more than father or brother to me, forgive me if I have not told the story as thou, incomparable one, wouldst have had me tell it."

AN UNKNOWN WARRIOR[1]

By SUSAN M. BOOGHER

(From *The Junior League Bulletin*)

SNOW was falling over London; a great blur of zig-zagging flakes; the embankment was deserted; the streets half-filled; in the houses of Parliament long windows etched themselves in light; Westminster Abbey was almost obliterated by the downfall, its time-stained crevices had filled, like cups, with drifts of snow.

Out of the obscurity and the snow a soldier approached Westminster.

He paused a moment on the opposite side of the street to peer at the great pile before him, and in his eyes was the half-incredulous amazement of one who finds himself at home again after strange, unhappy wanderings.

For an instant the Abbey seemed subtly changed; vague, intangible, unearthly. It was the drifting snow, of course, that obliterated the stains of time in its multitudinous delicate crevices; the drifting snow that was like a veil about his vision.

The zig-zagging flakes momentarily blinded the soldier, confused him . . . for an instant in the falling snow, he saw the Abbey white and stainless like a transcendent chalice lifted to the sky.

Then the soldier passed through the high-pointed portal. The padded doors fell to behind him. Dim and quiet, the great nave stretched away into the gloom.

After a moment the soldier raised his bared head; his eyes, grown accustomed to the twilight, lifted to the rose window above the altar.

He had taken off the heavy coat he wore; shorn of its bulk, he seemed extremely young, boyish, child-like even.

There was something of childhood in the hidden, secret happiness of his eyes; something of childhood in the furtive way he fingered the column at whose base he stood, then quickly withdrew his hand.

As one touches a flower, his gaze fondled the dim Abbey. Presently he moved slowly down the splendid nave, pausing now and then to drink in with thirsty eyes the beauty about him. . . .

In a distant chapel, candles like captive fireflies were flickering amid the gloom of drooping banners, and the furled flags of forgotten wars. . . .

The vastness of Westminster, the stateliness, lifted him as wings lift.

It had always been so; throughout his childhood the Abbey had held for him the beauty and romance that other boys find in sport, in girls, in love.

He was remembering how often and often as a child he had brought lunch with him and spent whole days exploring the Abbey—its great naves and chapels, its crypts and tombs.

And it was still the same. War had not changed the Abbey.

The soldier now was standing before the chancel at the high altar, his face lifted to the rose window that glowed above it. And suddenly, like light, transcendent happiness was about him.

War had not changed him either!

The thought that was like light about him bore him in an ecstasy of thanksgiving to his knees. His prayer was incoherent; a feeling of infinite, lifted happiness: to have gone from college, physically untrained for war, psychologically unprepared, to have spent three years in the mud and blood,—and to have remained unchanged!

War had not changed him. War was an interruption, a suspension, a holding of one's breath . . . the things for which he had lived—poetry and beauty still were first.

Irrelevantly, and with an overwhelming longing, he remembered the casual eyes of men who dwell in peace; he remembered English lanes that call out to be trod; violets like music in the grass; the cloistral quality of libraries; that first faint tremble in the trees of spring; moonlight like snow upon the night. . . .

And then, a tremendous symphony, the poems he had loved broke over him. For an interval he was breathless, remembering the unbearable beauty of Shakespeare's sonnets; Chaucer, like a dayesie in the grass; the music of Milton; Shelley's "luminous wings"; Wordsworth, "whose dwelling is the light of setting suns."

Poetry! English poetry! He felt abased and purified and lifted. In a sudden flash he re-beheld his England as the land of poets. Not of shopkeepers, sailors, empire-builders. But of poets—the winged voices of the race!

There were Ireland, of course, and India, and Egypt, and opium; dreadful ills! He shuddered imperceptibly. But these things, in the final analysis, were not England. England was the poets whose voices sing always of freedom; England was the barons at Runnymede; Magna Carta; England was America, too; the pilgrims who planted a dream upon the wilderness; and that still prophetic voice speaking today above the roar and belch of war to the heart of the world. England was Westminster: Shakespeare and Wordsworth and Wilson.

"Cloud-capped towers" . . . "and visions splendid" . . . "men too proud to fight."

Then the young soldier thought of his king; instinctively his eyes lifted, his hand rose to the salute. Not as a kindly, middle-aged man, slightly shrunken with mediocrity, did the young soldier think of his king. To him, he was a knightly, shining figure, splendid with romance. Medieval mysticism; crusaders faring forth to holy lands; the glamour of Elizabeth's bright reign; all the lesses poets like fugitive and falling stars upon the night; these things were England to the young soldier, were his king. King and Country! The phrase lifted him again in exaltation. King and Country! It was for that he was a warrior; it was for poetry and peace—tranquility like the silence here in Westminster, where dreams unfold.

War was a cloud that would pass from before the shining beauty of life. Others would know it again. *Others.* . . .

Bitterness and grief for a moment assailed him. He had

felt life poignantly. A poet does; most poignantly, perhaps, the man not quite a poet. Beauty had been so vividly acute; the laughter of forsythia in the spring; summer's perfumed, star-sown nights, the flaunting flags of autumn, the thrill like military music on the wind. These things to him were happiness as sharp as pain. And winter, too, with its largo of snow.

It was winter now . . . and snowing.

As the exaltation of his mood subsided, the soldier found his down-cast gaze caught by an insignia on the overcoat that hung across his arm; the number of a regiment, a division. The symbols seemed to him suddenly utterly divorced from himself, alien. War was not possible, *the war was not*. It could not be that yesterday he had been in France; tomorrow he would be there again.

Incredulity swept him.

In the silence and the solitude and the twilight of Westminster, the thing that he had left, the thing to which he must return, seemed impossible, an unreality, delirium.

He thought suddenly of death . . . it was the first time he had thought of death since he had entered the Abbey. It seemed incredible that men were dying at that instant, killing each other with terrible guns, when the quiet here was so profound.

For an instant one of those moments of distorted sensation assailed him, of familiarity with what occurs; the silence was acute with soundless sounds; in the shadow about him crowded unseen presences; the pounding of his heart was louder than a drum . . . and suddenly he knew that he had never been surprised, always the things that had come to him he had foreseen. Suddenly he knew that he had always known that this would happen to him; war and death. For an instant he closed his eyes against memory, against war, presentiment.

Like terrible and bitter waters, despair engulfed him; he was conscious of a fumbling, still-born gesture after the youth that he had lost, the beauty forgotten, the poems he would not write.

He had meant to be a poet.

Always, as a child, a youth, he had meant to be a poet,

and write phrases like the "vision splendid," and sleep in Westminster with the mighty dead.

A strangling agony was in his throat. . . . He felt betrayed. War had betrayed him. Fate had. Now he would never be a poet and sleep in Westminster. He was only a soldier, a warrior . . . an unknown warrior.

The terrible and bitter waters, the strangling agony at length subsided. He felt spent, exhausted, devoid of emotion.

And after a moment he rose from his knees; he was remembering why he had come back to England on this strange leave; he was remembering he must hurry if he were to stand again among the mighty dead.

The look of childhood, the look of hidden, secret happiness returned to his face as he turned away from the high altar and traversed the transept.

When at last he had come to the Poets' Corner, he paused, he relaxed, he drew a deep breath, as one who has indeed come home.

Above him in the stained glass windows myriad colors gleamed. It was lighter there than any place in the Abbey, than any place in England, the young soldier thought . . . any place in the world.

England's poets! He found himself again among them.

It was a tryst he kept!

As he stood there, the twilight, and the storm, and war, all the weary weight he carried, vanished from about him. Like a rush of purifying waters, poetry and beauty swept his soul.

It was for this he had come home!

Hot, unexpected tears in his eyes startled the young soldier. Poetry! He had not until today really thought of poetry for three hideous years of war. Poetry! The very word was the loveliest in the language. Unexpectedly, he remembered his bookshelves, his volumes of poems, certain pages—words themselves were before his eyes.

"Whither is fled the visionary gleam?"

"Where is it now, the glory and the dream?"

Like a deep-toned organ, the music of Wordsworth's Ode was about him. "Our birth is but a sleep and a forgetting." . . . The words suggested phraseless things; they lifted him, he soared upon their beauty.

Suddenly illusion swept him. . . .

Visions swirled upon the dark; about him the dim distances leaped into light; the great Abbey was ablaze with candles; through its windows gleamed the sun; a thronging multitude was gathered beneath the drooping banners and the furled flags of forgotten wars; upon the silence pulsed the slow beat of funeral music, as a vast procession passed in insubstantial pageantry behind a flag-draped bier to where the mighty dead of England sleep.

Illusion crowded upon the young soldier; blinded him; dazzled him. . . . Life had been too stabbing to last, poetry too poignant. And now it did not matter; *his* life, *his* death, *his* poetry.

"Another race hath been, and other palms are won."

A flag-draped bier! Like great protecting wings about his soul presentiment enfolded him. . . . Peace comes after war; death after life; and always to the poet, come poetry and beauty. A shining something, like light, was about him, was in his eyes and soul. Unsung songs . . . a voiceless poet . . . a soldier, an unknown warrior . . . *sleeping in Westminster with the mighty dead!*

The swirling visions vanished. Illusion fell away.

The young soldier sank to his knees; for an instant his head was bowed in prayer . . . "thoughts too deep for tears."

The vision he had seen had blinded him, and humbled him and healed. Gradually his eyes re-focused to the dark, but the shining something, like light, remained in his soul.

In the stained glass window the colors had blurred together, but still a lantern, in the hand of a figure grown shadowy and dull, retained its fire; the soldier watched it fade.

And then he rose and moved away. Beyond a transparent dimming window, he glimpsed a gargoyle vague with snow. The great nave as he traversed it was a well of darkness. Out of the silence came the muffled sound of a padded door.

In the vestibule, a ragged newsboy flitted past him like a bat; his face and the papers under his arm made white blots in the gloom. " 'Ello! A soldier hin the Habbey!" The boy drew up at his side. "Paper, sir? News from the front?"

The soldier looked about him tentatively, as one waking from a dream. In the shadows the newsboy's face was strangely white, and he had eerie eyes. The man wondered what he was doing in the Abbey.

"Hit's the quiet 'ere hafter the streets," the boy volunteered, as if in answer to the unspoken thought. His strangely white face and his eyes fascinated the soldier, hypnotized him.

"Hit's quiet 'ere too hafter the guns!" The boy was pirouetting from one foot to another.

"Yes," the soldier said. He wanted to tell the boy to come here often. He wanted to tell the boy about poetry and beauty—the Intimations of Immortality.

"Hi come to the big shows they pulls off 'ere, too," the child said unexpectedly.

For an instant his illusion recurred to the soldier; a vast crowd, lights and banners — funeral music, a *flag-draped bier!*

"But Hi likes hit better when hit's dark and quiet— like now!"

The newsboy's eerie eyes re-focused to the soldier's vision. It had come to him that this boy, other boys, loved the Abbey as he had. For an instant he realized the linked chain of life. He saw a passing torch.

Then he got into his overcoat. Shrinking a little as one does who leaves home for the darkness and the cold, the young soldier passed out from Westminster.

Snow was falling over London; a great blur of zig-zagging flakes. . . .

THE HELPLESS ONES[1]

By FREDERICK BOOTH

(From *Broom*)

EDDIE GORDON sprawled face upward on the living-room couch, asleep. His head was at the foot of the couch, hanging partly over the edge, and his shod feet lay nearly buried where the pillows and his overcoat were jumbled together. One arm hung over the side of the couch, and his hand, crumpled against the floor, lying limp in the shadow, resembled a cast-off gray glove. He lay so still with his clothes all tumbled and his head turned and hanging back against one shoulder, one might have thought him dead. But he only slept.

At six o'clock a lively step sounded in the hall. A key snapped in the lock. The door opened and Sally Gordon came in.

She turned her head deliberately toward the couch as she closed the door. A sigh, rather tremulous but brief, whispered in the gloom. She went quickly to the table in the middle of the room, felt about for a match, and lighted the gas chandelier. Without looking again toward the couch she removed her overcoat and hat, went into the bathroom, turned high the gas and washed her face and hands, vigorously brushing the ink-stains from her finger-tips. She turned from the bathroom into the bedroom, turned up the light there, and brushed her hair with soft, slow strokes. She touched her face rather indifferently with a powder-puff, and stood then stroking her eyebrows with the tips of her fingers, looking long into the mirror. She gazed at her reflection and her face wore a look of pleasure. Once with her palm she smoothed back the hair from her forehead with a slow, caressing stroke, as one

[1] Copyright, 1921, by *Broom*.
Copyright, 1923, by Frederick Booth.

would stroke back the hair from the forehead of a child. She regarded herself steadily with the unaffected and unconcealed tenderness with which she would have regarded a child.

At last, reluctantly, she turned down the light and walked back into the living room.

She stood by the couch and stared down at her husband. Her eyes had the peculiar intent look of a mother who watches her sleeping baby. Her eyes roamed the whole length of his body, looking at his untidy clothing, his uncombed hair, at his muddy boots that had muddied his overcoat and the pillows. At last she slipped one arm under his shoulders and with a great effort pulled him up on the couch so that his head had a better resting place. She reached for a pillow and tucked it under his head. She picked up his limp, hanging arm and laid it across his body, pulled his gaping coat together and buttoned the bottom button. She made quick, sure movements, the movements of one who performs an accustomed human task.

Having made him easier, less ungraceful in his inertness, she sat down on the edge of the couch and gazed intently into his face. Her eyes dwelt in turn on every one of his features and to every one she gave some sort of touch, his tousled hair a pat, his forehead a slow stroke, his closed eyes a touch of her finger-tips, and still in her face was that peculiar intent and anxious look, the look of a mother who dotes on her fragile treasure.

Eddie Gordon slept, hardly breathing, not moving. His sleep was profound, sodden, the sleep of a hard and habitual drinker who gets drunk every night and sleeps until morning, drunk every morning and sleeps until night. His face had a greenish yellow color about the forehead and eyes, was flushed at the cheeks and swollen at the mouth.

Sally knew what ailed him. It was a daily event in her life, and she found herself reacting to it this time exactly as she had many times before, as she did every time she saw her husband lying so still and helpless, his heart barely beating, his breath barely stirring. Always when she saw him thus, so profoundly helpless, so utterly and mystically

babelike, the feelings of a mother for awhile possessed her
completely. It possessed her as one is possessed by a mood.
It possessed her against her will, this common emotion that
had not yet found expression in her life. She dreaded this
slow welling up of morbid desire to fondle and nurse that
helpless, still baby, her husband. But it was not to be
resisted while it ran its course. In that desire, during its
beginning and even during the moments of her surrender
to it, was something that filled her with self-horror. She
felt herself tricked and made worse than silly. She felt
herself infected with moral decay. Always she had fought
against it, as she had this time, with little devices, delays,
as one in sleep fights the approach of a bad dream which
comes on regardless. And always she surrendered, for
awhile. Always, for awhile, something in her was glad to
have this man even thus dependent, thus her own.

So she sat, prinking her husband's hair, straightening
his disordered clothing, lost in this strange little orgy of
motherliness.

But after awhile a look of distaste ruffled a little her
face. Little dimples puckered the middle of her forehead.
The wide pupils of her eyes narrowed a little. She turned
her face a little away, still looking, cocked her head a little
sideways, bit her lip and drew her hands back, hesitating.
The man's mouth was sagging open, and impulsively, with
a studious, earnest air, like a child modeling clay, she took
his face in both her hands and firmly pressed his mouth
shut, and for a moment held it so. But when she took her
hands away his mouth again sagged open. He slept.

She frowned and again put out her hands, but drew them
back. She recoiled a little and turning her head swept his
body from head to foot with one swift glance. She took
his limp hand in hers, held it up to the light and looked
at it narrowly. His hand was unclean all over and the
nails were black. She flung it down hurriedly, and without
getting up she turned her back to him, and bending over,
her elbow on her knee, her mouth resting against her fist,
stared at the floor a long while. The silence was absolute.

Minutes passed. She arose and walked aimlessly about
for awhile, tucking at her hair, rearranging the furniture.

Once she glanced at her watch. She came and leaned back against the table, looking at her husband. Her hands arranged and rearranged a bunch of violets pinned between the buttoned lapels of her jacket.

After awhile she called sharply, "Eddie! Eddie!" Silence.

She bit her lip and shook her head slowly a long time, gripping the edge of the table and holding her body rigid. She lifted up her head and gazed at the ceiling.

"Oh, God!" she whispered, as though she believed God might be in the room above. Her body sagged while she gazed at the ceiling. She sobbed without making a sound. Tears glinted in her eyes but did not roll down her cheeks.

The man lay regardless.

At last the woman smiled, a wry smile; looked at her watch; and turned toward her coat and hat.

A step sounded in the hall, heavy and rather slow, coming toward her door. It stopped at her door, there was a wait, a firm rap. She opened the door at once.

"You, Allen?" she exclaimed in an undertone.

A tall man was looking in at her. He was rather angular and awkward. His eyes were deepset and gray, and his large, rather bony face had a sober look.

"May I come in?" he said.

She led the way into the room. He followed slowly, closing the door behind him. She looked at him with a question in her face.

"I could not stay away any longer," he said.

"I never told you not to come," she replied.

He had not appeared to notice the man on the couch. Now, as if he had known all the time, he turned slowly and looked down at Eddie. After some moments he again faced her.

"The same as ever," he said.

She shrugged her shoulders and a poor smile flickered on her lips. He looked at her steadily but not offensively, and she could not take her eyes from his face. The steady, full breathing of this man could be heard in the room. He put out his great hand and stroked back the hair from her forehead as she herself had done when she stood before the mirror in the bedroom. Her head was thrust a little back by the weight of his hand, but she continued to look up into his eyes. Her hands trembled on the edge of the table.

"You've had enough," he said at last. "You're going away with me this evening. You are going now."

The pupils of her eyes widened. Her face grew pale and her lips seemed brilliant by contrast. She put both of her hands against his shoulders. The quick gesture seemed to warn him not to come any nearer, yet the touch of her hands against his coat was almost like a caress.

A sort of eagerness animated the face of the man, tempered by hesitancy and grave concern. The look of his face plainly said, "I want you, but I wouldn't hurt you."

He held his head in an awkward fashion and moved his lips, searching for words. They gazed at each other without speaking.

The man on the couch flung his head fretfully about, opened his eyes and blinked up at the light, turned his body a little more and raised himself on his elbow. His swollen lips made a grotesque attempt to draw themselves down, and failed; but the stare of his eyes was fixed, unwinking and terrible. He saw how her bare arm, the sleeve slipped back, gleamed like a bar of silver against the tall man's shoulder. He stared and then his face became dull. Quietly he laid himself down again.

The tall man said at last, "Pack your suitcase and come away. I'm not asking you to . . . You know. You understand me, don't you, Sally? I love you. But that's not it, not entirely. I wouldn't try to break up your home, not if you had a home. I see you wearing yourself out here. This is breaking you, this business. You've said so yourself. Now it's time to cut it out, anyway, for awhile. I saw that look in your eyes when I came in. Leave him a note. I'll take you anywhere you say. You can go to my mother's, or you can go to a hotel. But you've got to have a rest for awhile anyway. I saw that look in your eyes when I came in. Now you've got to give this business a let-up. Don't worry about him. Leave him a note and some money. Anyway, I have always managed to look him up every day or so, I'll see to it that he gets along.

You know that Eddie and I understand each other, Sally, I mean, when he's sober. And I don't have to tell you, do I Sally, that I am honest about it with both of you, no matter how much I want you? You and Eddie and I, we've always been friends, and we always will be, no matter what happens. I'll see him and I'll talk to him straight out. It will be for the best all the way round, for him too. He'll see the thing straight. He's not so unreasonable, not when he's sober. I know he will consent. I know it can be settled in the right way. Pack a suitcase and come away with me tonight."

His heavy manner, his blunt speech, his awkwardness, revealed the heaviness of his desire and his anxious earnestness.

The woman had slowly drawn away from him. Now she leaned back against the table, one hand braced against the edge, the other hand smoothing down the lapel of her jacket. She held her head sideways and cast at the floor a troubled and pensive look, its pathos heightened by the whiteness of her face and supple neck.

She thinned her lips and a frown puckered her forehead. "No," she said slowly, in a small voice. "No, I couldn't do that. You know I couldn't, Allen. No. No."

The tall man looked at her with an expression of benign indecision and puzzlement. He turned his head toward the sprawled shape on the couch. He bit his lip. A deep flush mounted to his forehead and made the arteries in his temples swell. He stroked his chin, meditating.

"Sally," he said at last. The constraint in his voice made the woman look quickly up. "I'll tell you, Sally, I haven't talked to you about this thing the way I feel like talking. Now I'm going to talk the way I feel like talking. Maybe it's brutal of me to do it, but I can't help that. I have to say what I think. I'm that way and you know me well enough not to mind too much."

But he paused and studied her face, hesitating, half afraid. Then he said:

"You loved me before you met Eddie, didn't you, Sally?"

"Yes."

"I knew it." His voice trembled a little, and he stopped

for a moment because he did not want to show how pleased he was at her confession while he was still under the disadvantage of her resistance.

His slow voice went on, "Yes, I used to feel almost sure of it. Even though it was presumptuous of me, I did think so. You were always straightforward. You were never ashamed of your feelings. But I couldn't ask you to marry me, not then. You remember how things were with me—my kid sisters and all to be looked after. I had to wait."

"I understood," said Sally in a low voice. "I knew you cared, and why you—didn't say anything."

"But you married Eddie just the same! And it wasn't because you didn't care for me. I know why you married him. I'm going to tell you why you married him."

"Don't! You needn't tell me. I know. I didn't know then. I just felt something that was too strong for me. I didn't know why I had to give in to it. I just had to. Now I know what it was. I know why I had to give in to it."

She paused, pressed the back of one hand against her mouth. She bent her head. Her hand trembled against her mouth and her shoulders trembled a little too. She took her hand away from her mouth and began to tug at one of the buttons of her coat. Her lips were white. She pressed her upper lip against her teeth to keep it from quivering.

"I could have waited for you. I knew you would ask me some day. But there was one thing I couldn't wait for. I was twenty-four, and natural. My whole feeling for life and people was full of a woman's desires. I didn't know it then, but I know it now. I was strong, I could have waited if I had known it then. I know now that my whole feeling for Eddie was that I wanted to mother him. I had to mother somebody. But I didn't know it was that, not then. I didn't understand it at all. I used to be afraid and ashamed because I still loved you and here all the time Eddie and I were coming closer and closer together. I didn't understand myself at all. Yes, I still loved you, but . . . I couldn't have children then, it takes money to have children. Those days you were having your own struggles and I could barely make my living. I couldn't even allow myself to think of having children."

She stopped, turned her head and looked at the sleeper on the couch. She knitted her brows and compressed her lips. The tall man moved his lips as if to speak, but she went on:

"One night he came to see me. That was when he was on *The Sun*, and he had made such a hit, you remember? He was drunk that night. He came to the house drunk. I used to wonder how he could get drunk—how he could— such a sweet boy. Now I know why. He got himself drunk so he could run away from responsibilities—so he would be helpless—so he could be a child, just as he is now. He was beautiful that night—drunk. He was beautiful partly because he was drunk. Can you understand that? Some men are that way. He was that way then. His cheeks were flushed, his eyes sparkled, and his yellow hair stood up all over his head, glittering in the lamplight. He sat on the couch and drew up his knees so that his feet were on the couch too. He sat there and talked to me. He lisped when he talked. His head was unsteady on his shoulders, like a baby's. He talked to me about his mother. You know she died when he was five. He had to grow up unfinished. He had become a man but he was still a child. He told me how beautiful his mother was and how he would have been different if she had lived. I was like her, he said. He sat there and talked to me just about as he would have talked to his mother, I suppose, if she had been there in my place. The room was warm and after awhile he couldn't talk at all. But he was beautiful, as a child is beautiful. His yellow head fell over against me. I put my arms around him and pulled his head down and held him close to me. I didn't know what I was doing. Maybe I didn't want to know.

"After that I couldn't resist him. I didn't try. I wouldn't let myself think about you. Eddie needed me. The whole thing with me was pity. A woman must pity something! I told myself that Eddie needed me. I loved him for his weaknesses."

The tall man slowly nodded his head. "I knew that was why you married him," he said. "I can see how a woman would do that."

The woman went on: "After we were married I used to go out and hunt for him when he didn't come home. I still do sometimes. I hunt for him in the back rooms of saloons, at the bar, down at the Press Club. I go along the streets where I know he is likely to be. I lead him home by the hand. Yes, and he leans on me, and he babbles to me like a baby as we go along the streets, he says the same things over and over again the way a baby does. He comes with me through the streets like a child that was lost and is glad to be found again. And when I get him home I wash his face and feed him. I put my arm around him and make him eat. I undress him and put him to bed. And he is glad of it. He is glad to be like a baby; then he can live that part of his life that was never finished. And I used to be glad too."

"You used to be glad?" the tall man said. "That is hard to believe."

"Yes, I think I must have been glad of his helplessness. Do you understand? His helplessness gave me an excuse to mother him. I had to mother somebody! The worst thing is, no good at all has come of our being married— no good to either of us. No, it has hurt us both."

She turned her head, holding it a little sideways as she had when she sat on the couch by her husband, and looked at him again. There was something childlike in the expression of her face and in her pose. Her whole body expressed ingenuous bewilderment and trouble. She put her finger to her lips.

The tall man, his hands at his side, studied her face. He said nothing. He waited for her to go on.

She made a little gesture with her hand as if she were brushing something away.

"See, now he has got to where he no longer wants even to be helped. Now he doesn't even want to be cared for."

Her voice was tired and plaintive, the voice of a tired child.

"To be a coddled baby doesn't satisfy him any more.

He wants to be a sleeping baby. Sleep! Sleep! Only let him sleep! He gets drunk at night and sleeps till morning. He gets drunk in the morning and sleeps till night. That is what drinking is with him. That is what drinking is for. That is the way he escapes—he has always drunk to escape —he is backing out of life entirely. Do you see? Now he doesn't want me to take care of him any more, for that reminds him that he is alive and in the world. I know. He is trying to find again the deep sleep that a baby has before it is born."

The tall man would have spoken but she went on.

"Can't you see how it is with me now? There is no longer any satisfaction, not even the kind of satisfaction I got from it at first. Maybe I should have known better at first. But we always say that afterward, when it is too late."

"It isn't too late," the tall man said. "You know it was a mistake. It's a simple thing to correct that mistake, and you know it's perfectly straight. As far as Eddie is concerned we will take care of him."

"But I couldn't do it. I just couldn't, somehow. You don't know how it is. But I know. The whole thing is like a habit, only it's worse than a habit. I know. I have tried to break it. But I didn't use much will power. Maybe I didn't want to break it.

"You think I am strong. Maybe I am strong. But I am like most women. My strength does just about as it pleases with me."

She bowed her head and looked hopelessly at the floor.

The tall man had already taken her by the shoulders. She lifted her head quickly. Her face wore a look of surprise and fear because of his sudden and strong grip on her shoulders.

"You may call it a habit or whatever you like, you've had enough of it," he said. His face had turned pale and his mouth was stern. But his eyes regarded her kindly. She made no attempt to pull away from him. The frightened look left her face.

"You'll put an end to this business. I'll make you. Then you'll be glad."

They looked at each other in silence. The sleeper on the couch seemed to be holding his breath.

"I don't know," said the woman at last. "Maybe I would be glad. Yes, maybe I would be glad. But I don't know — I just don't know how I could make myself do it."

"How about me?" said the tall man in a voice that had changed since last he spoke. "Why do you always leave me out of it? Maybe if you let yourself think about me once in a while . . ."

He had turned pale and his lips were trembling. He stopped speaking, but not because he was ashamed of his emotion. He stopped speaking because he was ashamed of what his emotion had impelled him to say.

She was looking at him in surprise and wonder. She put out one hand and touched his coat with her finger-tips, unconsciously, lightly. Her chin quivered.

"Allen," she said softly, "Allen, I didn't mean—please—"

"Never mind," he said slowly, in a constrained voice. "You know I didn't mean to talk to you that way. I don't want to appeal to your sympathy. And I don't want to make you do anything. You know that. I meant all along to appeal to your understanding. You know that. I still mean to. And as far as understanding goes, you understand everything as well as I do. It's all a matter of making up your mind. I don't want to force you to do anything. I know how hard it is for you. You take your time about it. Don't think about me. Try to think about what is the best thing to do. And just take your time about it."

She still kept her head lowered and still her fingers touched his coat. He knew that if he had taken her in his arms then and there the decision would have been entirely of his own making, and to his own liking. But his pride rebelled at the thought of reaching a decision, above all a decision in his own favor, by such a primitive method, by a method so contrary to his idea of how an issue between a man and a woman should be met. He would have her make her decision through her own understanding and by her own will! His hands left her shoulders and he stepped a little away from her. They no longer touched each other.

She nodded her head a little, looking at the floor.

He studied her, a little puzzled. "Then, may I come back next week, say, next Monday evening?"

Again she nodded her head, without looking up.

"Will you try to make up your mind between now and then? Will you be ready to tell me what you have decided to do?" He spoke almost as he would have spoken to a child.

For a moment she still looked at the floor. Then she lifted her head. She met his kind gaze timidly.

"Yes, Allen, I will," she replied in a low voice.

He drew a deep breath. "Good night," he said, awkwardly holding out his hand.

"Good night, Allen."

He was gone and she closed the door quickly behind him.

She stood by the door while the sound of his footsteps rang in the hall. She looked wistfully about the room, sunk again in silence. She puckered her brows, thinking.

She understood Allen. She knew why he had not followed up his advantage. She respected him for it. But she almost hated him for it as well.

She walked slowly back into the middle of the room. Again she leaned back against the table. The uneasy breathing of the man on the couch could be heard.

"Eddie," she called.

Slowly he turned his face away from the wall. He opened his eyes and for a moment stared without winking down the length of his body. Then he crooked one arm, raised himself to a sitting posture, turned and pulled his feet off the couch. He sat with his body toward her. But he looked down at her feet. He put his hands down on either side of him against the couch, as if to brace himself. He moved his dry lips two or three times.

"So you let Allen go away without you," he said.

"You were awake?"

"Most of the time." He looked up at her. He had slept a long time and he was quite sober. The pupils of his blue eyes were like black pin-heads. He tried to control the uneasy movements of his swollen upper lip.

"I heard what you told him," he declared in a high, assertive voice. "You're right about me. I know it. But it's worse than you think. I'm done. I'll be glad when I'm dead. Not on your account either. On my own account. I'll be glad when I'm dead, I tell you. You ought to have gone away with him. What makes you so silly?"

"Please, Eddie."

"I mean it. I wish you'd go away and leave me. I wish to God you would."

He stared defiantly at her, blinking his eyes.

She tried to speak. She moved her lips, searching for words. Exasperation struggled with the pity in her face.

She looked at him without trying to hide her pity. Her forehead was puckered with little dimples. She tilted her head a little to one side and half extended one hand.

"Eddie!" she cried. "Eddie, my poor boy! If you'd only let me—"

"Ah-k!" He waved his hand in front of his face, brushing away her words.

"Don't I know what you're about to say!" he sneered, twisting his face and making his light-colored eyes glare at her.

"Save me—eh? Want to try that again, eh? What do you want to do that for? You've tried that before. Now you want to try it again, eh? I know. I know. What makes you so silly? I'm done. You know I'm done. Allen's right. Better chuck the whole thing and forget it. You'll be glad afterward."

He wagged his head, smirked at her and added: "And maybe you don't know it but I'll be damned glad of it too."

"You mustn't talk that way, Eddie. You mustn't."

"Yes I will," he declared, pulling down his puffed upper lip. He looked around at the floor, at the furniture, at her, with an unchanging, hard stare. A silence followed. Nothing could be heard but his quick, uneasy breathing and the uneasy motions of his body on the couch. His hands moved all of the time. His yellowish face moved. His eyes rested nowhere.

She came and sat by him. She put her hand on his shoulder. She regarded him with a look of pity, watching his face. Her feeling for him trembled on her lips. Her eyes watched every movement he made, dwelt on every one of his features. Her fingers trembled.

But he would not look at her. He looked sideways at the floor.

"When he comes Monday you'll go with him. You'd better." His voice was high and harsh.

"No I won't go!" She put her arms around him and began to cry. "I just couldn't, somehow. What would become of you? How could I when I know you would be alone and nobody to take care of you! Eddie, I feel so sorry for you. I feel so sorry for you. As long as you need me I shall stay. I shall stay. I don't know what will become of us but I shall stay. I can't help myself."

He stiffly put up his hands and pulled her arms away from his shoulders. She turned away from him. He, bending over, propping his elbows on his knees and his chin against his fists, stared at the floor. He blinked his eyes and puckered his forehead as if he were trying to think.

She stood half turned from him, with her head bent, staring at the floor. She was half ashamed, half pensive. The silence lasted a long time. In the silence the man made a despairing gesture and ejaculated:

"Oh, Jesus, what's the use!"

Minutes passed. The woman stood without moving. The man's lips writhed, his forehead scowled, his eyes stared.

"There's no use in talking about it, is there Eddie?" The woman turned and looked at him with patient weariness. He let his hands fall and dangle between his knees. He shook his head.

"Christ, no! What's the use in talking!"

She slowly crossed the room and began putting on her hat.

"I'm going to dinner; will you come with me?" She

looked at him with a flash of wistfulness in her eyes.

He shook his head without saying anything. She put on her overcoat and came over to him, stood by his side and stroked his hair. He stared at the floor.

"I'll be back in about an hour," she said at last. "Good-by, Eddie."

"Good-by."

He listened to her footsteps in the hall until they died away. He sat thrusting his head forward. The fixed stare of his light-colored eyes defied the lines of his mouth which changed all of the time.

At last he stood erect in a crumpled sort of way and walked into the middle of the room. His wrinkled trousers clung to his calves and bagged at the knees. His coat had come unbuttoned and he held it together with one hand like a woman wearing a shawl. He frowned, sticking out his upper lip; and his forehead was broken by many little wrinkles. His forehead was greenish-yellow in the gaslight. He shivered and a whisper rang through the room:

"Jesus, it's cold!"

He let go of his coat, felt in his pockets and brought out a sack of tobacco and some papers, rolled a cigarette, lighted it and began to smoke greedily, inhaling the smoke. He looked at the table, at the chairs, at the floor. And all the time he made grimaces, scowled and shivered. His movements were uncertain and halting, but he stared intently this way and that. He was trying to reflect. But he was dizzy and cold. His blood felt yellow.

Once he looked at the door where they had gone out. He listened a long time while the cigarette smoked in his fingers.

At last he turned away from the door, back toward the middle of the room. He happened to see her handkerchief lying at the foot of the table. He threw away the cigarette and picked up the handkerchief and stared at it. He shivered more than ever and pulled his coat together at the bottom, but forgot to button it.

With a gesture of finality he threw the handkerchief from him, on the table. With the manner of an idle or a sick man he walked to the window, drew aside the curtain and looked down at the glittering street. His mind became clearer and his thoughts began to arrange themselves in more orderly fashion.

After a long time he turned away from the window.

"Yes," he drawled in a fretful voice, "yes it would serve me right. Christ, yes, she'd be doing the right thing."

His forehead became smooth. His face ceased to pout and wrinkle. It became calm. The pupils of his staring eyes became a little larger. He lifted his head a little. His face had almost an eager look. One would have said that he had reached some sort of a decision.

He found some paper and envelopes in the table-drawer and took a pencil from his pocket. Craning over the table, his intent face pallid in the gaslight, his hair gleaming like disordered gilt plush, he began to write in a shaky large scrawl.

He wrote one sheet almost full; signed it; folded it crookedly; put it in an envelope and scrawled a single line across the face of the envelope. On another sheet he wrote six or seven short lines, underlining each one; signed it boldly at the bottom and put it in another envelope, which he addressed.

He stood the two envelopes against some books and looked at them as he put the pencil back in his pocket. On the first envelope was written: *For My Wife*. On the other: *For the Police*.

He rolled and smoked another cigarette slowly, looking at one spot on the carpet.

At last he tossed the remnant of the cigarette on the floor as if something in him craved disorder. He walked slowly into the bedroom, thrusting his head forward and his elbows out.

In the bedroom he turned up the light and without hesitation opened a little drawer in the old-fashioned bureau, taking out a revolver. He held it in both hands and cocked it. He stared into the mirror, and with something of the manner of a man who prepares to take a new kind of medicine he lifted the revolver and pointed it at his temple.

Then something in his whole mechanism seemed to stop

and something else seemed to start. His body sagged and quivered at the same time. His eyes bulged. His mouth opened in such a way that his teeth glittered. A loud groan rang through the room. Quickly he laid the revolver down and walked back into the living room. He took unsteady steps and held his hands against his forehead.

"Oh, Jesus!" he cried.

He stood still a long time, pondering. It seemed to him that the silence of the room was lost in another silence.

His eye fell on a quart whiskey-bottle standing on a corner of the table. The unusual character of his awakening had made him, thus far, forget all about it.

It was nearly a third full of liquor. A little gleam came into his eye, the faintest color into his cheeks. He looked at the bottle with a sort of eagerness and went hopefully toward it.

He was thinking of the revolver on the bureau and it seemed to him that some of the whiskey would make that business easier.

He picked up the glass and the bottle and poured out a large drink, shuddered and swallowed it, making a face. He had eaten nothing all day and at once the whiskey was racing in his blood. Color flashed into his cheeks. He felt his blood becoming red again.

He took another drink and waited for the effect. After a little while he took still another. There was only a little left in the bottle.

Now his eyes were brighter and they had a misty look. The pupils were larger. He blinked his eyes and looked about. His face looked almost cheerful. He appeared to be reflecting. Indeed his thoughts raced rapidly but they began to tumble over each other. He hardly understood his thoughts. Vague emotions stirred him.

A sort of courage was mounting in his body, warming him like a new-kindled fire. But he felt mournful too.

He waited. He was about to have great thoughts. He was about to discover some magnificent solution of everything.

He stood still a long time, pondering. A little smile began to tremble on his mouth.

He poured out the last of the whiskey and shook the bottle to get the last drop. But now his head was rolling a little and his eyes were vague.

He lifted the glass. Just then his uncertain glance fell on his wife's handkerchief. He looked long at the handkerchief, blinking. His head wobbled a little. He was trying to seize some idea that eluded him. Thoughts rose up in his mind but they fell over one another. His face wore a crippled look.

A long while he stood in thought, staring feebly at the handkerchief. But at last a faint, self-satisfied smile appeared on his trembling mouth.

Visibly swaying he turned around, his gaze wandering a little; steadied himself a little bit, and began to look uncertainly in the direction of the door. The smile flickered over his face like a blue flame. His mouth moved. His lips picked at words.

But he remembered the whiskey. He lifted the tumbler and emptied it, spilling some on his chin, half turned and with a single motion flung the glass ringing on the table.

He turned toward the door again, peering uncertainly as a man peers in the dusk. His head wagged. His voice blurred the silence:

"Di' think I was 'sleep?"

Pleased, he laughed, rolling his head. But he stopped laughing to look toward the door, listening. His mouth got ready to talk.

"Di'—di' y' think I was 'sleep? Di' y' think I was 'sleep?" he called. No reply. Silence beyond the door. He smiled a satisfied smile. He laughed at the silence beyond the door; wagged his head; turned away; made two or three sidelong steps and brought up against the table. He flattened one hand out on the table-top and leaned against that hand. He stood there. His body swayed back and forth to a certain rhythm, like a weed in a creek. A smile flickered back and forth across his face like shadow on a shaking leaf. Sunk in drunken revery he blinked his drunken eyes, smirked and blinked. Now and again, when he leaned harder than usual, the legs of

the table creaked under his weight. The hiss of the hot
gas-lamp mingled with the noise of his breathing.

The little handkerchief lay on the table just under his
nose. He had to see it if he looked. And when at last,
tired of leaning against the table, he roused himself a
little from his revery, he did see it at once. Pulling himself up as straight as he could he confronted the handkerchief with all his unsteady dignity, and with a righteous
smirk, as one confronts an offender. He took the handkerchief in both his hands and turned it over and over.
He stared at it as a baby stares at a new plaything. He
moved his mouth all the time, breathing noisily. He
blinked hard and often, looking and pondering. He seemed
to be trying to recall something the handkerchief almost
reminded him of, something he had forgotten.

At last he made the sort of motion a baby makes when
it throws down a plaything, and threw the handkerchief
on the floor. He looked pleased with himself and smirked
down at the handkerchief. Satisfied, he pondered no
longer. He turned with studied care, aimed himself at
the bedroom door, made crooked long steps and went un-
steadily in.

He looked at the revolver a long time. Sometimes he
scowled. Sometimes he smiled. After awhile he picked
up the revolver in both hands; turned and swayed back into
the living room. He stood in the middle of the room, his
body bending to and fro, and peered at the revolver with
idiotic eyes. He stuck out his lips; blinked his eyes with
great deliberation, pondered over the thing he held in his
hands.

Now he began to look at the door again, listening and
watching more and more attentively. At last he fixed his
gaze wholly upon the door. The pupils of his eyes were
distended. Bending in the middle, his legs trembling, his
body swayed this way and that. His lips no longer smiled,
but writhed.

"Think I was 'sleep?" he called. "Di' y' think—steal
m' wife when I was 'sleep?"

His voice shrilled in the room. He began to hurl at the
door inept anathemas against the treachery of wives and

the cowardice of men. He made uncouth accusations. He delivered himself of bizarre philosophies; sometimes mumbling, sometimes shrilling his words. He twisted his shoulders, stepping about in a small space. His voice quavered, rising and falling. His head tossed as if he rode in a boat.

But the silence at last reduced him to silence.

The labor of thought again showed in his face. Something was eluding him. Yes, he had forgotten something he was going to do. He tried hard in his own way, opening and shutting his mouth, blinking and searching the floor with his aimless eyes. Sometimes mutterings fell out of his mouth.

He smiled again. Something stirred him. Now he remembered what he had forgotten. He lifted the hand that held the revolver and aimed his wavering gaze down toward it. He raised his eyebrows and blinked. He turned the gun over this way and that, staring and blinking as if he had never seen one before in all his life. His face was pulled out of shape with the labor of cogitation. He began to smirk. He looked toward the door again, opening and shutting his mouth; and at last he delivered himself:

"Di' y' think I was go' shoo' m'self? Di' y' think I was go' shoo' m'self?"

His head sank on his breast and his eyes half closed. But he heaved his head up again and opened his eyes.

"Ah, sure, sure," he called. "Steal m' wife an' I shoo' m'self. Sure! sure!"

He laughed. But the laugh crumpled up in the silence.

His eyes were witless. It looked as though his pale head had talked without his knowing it. He wagged his head and announced solemnly:

"I'll shoo' you." He waited a moment, trying to keep his gaze on the door ,and repeated more loudly:

"I'll shoo' you. I'll shoo' you."

He smiled down at the revolver and patted the barrel with an aimless motion.

"We know where fin' 'im, don't we?" he said to the revolver.

His eyes brightened and he became a little steadier

smirking at the door, he called loudly, "We know where fin' 'im. We know where fin' 'im."

He turned, and like a man walking in the dark he made his way to the couch. Here he laid the revolver down. With much labor and fumbling he gathered up his overcoat. With much labor he began to put it on. Half way through the job he paused, turned, and sent a wavering look toward the door.

"Di' y' think I do' know where fin' im?" he jibed.

He got his overcoat on and put on his hat. He stood a long time with a solemn expression on his face. He blinked studiously. He had become steadier. A fixed purpose seemed to have got him under its control. With great care he buttoned the overcoat and settled his hat as straight on his head as he could. Now his eyes were no longer blurred and wavering. They glowed as with fever and a flame was mounting in his cheeks. But his mouth was a woeful thing, a wound that opened and shut, writhing.

He picked up the revolver and looked at it, smirking. With the smirk on his face he turned toward the door and began to shove the revolver down into the inside pocket of his overcoat.

"We know," he said, wagging at the door. "We know where—"

The trigger of the revolver must have caught in some part of his clothing. The crash of the discharge tore the wavering smirk from his face. Piteously intent, he stared for a second at the door. Then he lay quickly down, as if he accepted everything.

He lay first on his face, and muzzled his face snugly between his hands. Presently he turned over quietly on his back. One hand knocked once or twice against the floor.

The look fixed on his countenance was the look of one who has at last discovered something real.

FOREST COVER[1]

By EDNA BRYNER

(From *The Bookman, N. Y.*)

THE ribbon of road wound down through the forest. A woman followed it. The road seemed to come from the town of a thousand souls but it only came through there, just as it came through forest on the other side of the town, and through another town on the other side of the forest, and through forest again on the other side of that town. The woman followed the road just that way. At some time or other she had stepped out upon it from some place through which it came and ever since she had been following it. Somewhere she would stop following it, she would make an end of it. The road itself would go on, ceaselessly, in and out of forest, through towns and again through forest.

As the woman walked, a sharp, long needle of words, "No one must ever know," drove itself in and out of her brain. The words made a thin pattern that spread out sprawlingly to form a lid, like the pan of some cunning trap, which shut down automatically over every projection of thought that tried to make of her an articulate being, conscious of her own exigency. At the same time, something of her beyond the reach of words, finely hidden away from all snares, escaped like a thin cloud and entered the forest, crept along the dark leaf-mold earth, over the mossed rocks, up the dark, strong trunks of trees, out to the tips of the branches, to the edges of the leaves, swaying there until by its own motion it was dissipated—and again she was a woman walking along a piece of road.

The woman was in a daze with her following of the road.

When she bent her head down and stared upon its yellow dirt surface, she was one with it, a piece of itself walking upon it. When she lifted up her head, she was separate from it, a living thing walking upon a piece of dead earth. Then she looked upon the wall of forest to right and left and became aware that the trees were intimate with the earth. She felt heavily their greater intimacy with the earth.

This intimacy bothered her. The forest came up out of the earth in trunks swelling into branches that burst into leaves. The earth was proud of this, proud of the roots that bored into it and sucked at it, at the trunks that went up, swelling into branches, a network between it and the sky, mesh to sift sunshine through. The trees were proud, too, proud of the earth that lay quiet and heavy with nourishment under them, receiving their roots, feeding them. The deep, unfathomable intimacy made them proud. They were joined in understanding, one. Their oneness bothered the woman. At the same time she felt strangely protected by it. She walked quietly and firmly, not fast, as she did in the towns. In the towns she hurried through, looking at no one, eager to get into the safety of the woods, eager almost to be in the bother of the oneness of earth and trees.

There were times when she wanted to stop, to leave the road, go up the side of the forest-clothed mountain and lie down; but she did not dare. Something within her urged her on. The Something was her Sin. Her Sin made her put one unwilling foot before the other and follow the winding strip of dirt road.

It was her Sin that set her out upon the road. Through long months she had kept it secret, hidden quite from knowing eyes. She kept it secret, shutting out admission that the hour of its triumph would come. She had hoped to kill it, had encased it in prison bars, ruthless, holding herself impervious to the pain of the hurt that wrenched her with the hurting of the thing secret within her. She had tried to starve it, suffering in silence from the lack that she caused herself in withholding food from it. But her Sin lived. It was alive and strong. The day came

when its strength moved terribly within her and that set
her feet upon the road. While she walked, it was quiet,
sleeping like a child carried in its mother's arms. When
she sat down to rest, it moved and urged her on, on down
the narrow road winding through the forest around the
side of the low mountain.

Many turnings and windings the road had. By and by
it would come to a swift creek, with a bridge set across,
and a mill beside it, and there would be human habita-
tions, imitations of houses, rough hemlock shells, with
people carrying on an imitation of living, going through
motions that made time slip by. The woman knew all
this well. The road had taught her as she came. At some
such place her Sin would have its hour of triumph.

There must be an end soon. She stopped to drink at
a little spring under a jutting bank. Her Sin grew angry,
threatened her. She straightened up and went on round-
ing the turn. A heavy team dragging its load of deftly
packed shingles came up the flank of the mountain, its
driver walking slowly beside. The brawny blue-shirted
lumberman did not speak but drew the horses aside to let
good footing be for the woman and his eyes looked with
friendly respect upon the neat young figure in the gray
print dress.

The woman felt the look penetrating deep, into a place
thin and clear, a place that existed long before her Sin
came upon her. She bent her head and moved quickly
past, down the long slope of the road toward the swift
creek.

A rough shack set high on the bank above the big mill
dam came into view. Would this be the place? Her Sin
gave no sign. Now that she was in motion it lay quiescent,
pacified. She stood still in the road. Her wide, gray
eyes rested in appraisement on the house. A dirty old
woman smoking a corn-cob pipe slouched around the corner from the back. On her wrinkled face greedy curiosity
showed itself. She took her pipe out of her mouth and
started to speak.

The woman of the road began walking again very fast.
She went down across the bridge and past the mill from

which came forth the rhythmical high hungry whine of the saw cutting virgin timber, the slap-thwack of boards thrown from one receiver to another.

The road was going up again past a house set high to the left, a large house with an air of well-being. Perhaps here? She went up the steps from the road, walked the single board path to the porch, knocked against the casing of the open door. From an inner room a woman came, in a blue wrapper, young and blowsy, with red eyes, holding a sleeping baby to her breast.

"Will you give me a drink?"

"Yes. It's hot today, ain't it? Come right in. You must be tuckered out walking in the sun." Voluble, she led the way to the back porch. "There it is in the big tin pail. Wait a minute. I'll git you a glass." She fetched a heavy tumbler from the kitchen shelf. "It's prob'ly warm. I can't git water many times with this baby to look after. He cries every time I put him down. It's all I kin do to git the men's meals. They's two from the mill besides my husband."

There was no place here for her. The woman drank the water hastily. "I'm much obliged." She turned back through the house. "I'll be going on." She was on the porch.

"Better set a minute. Needn't be hurryin' off so quick." There was slight resentment in the tone.

The woman was on the walk. "I have to be going. I'm much obliged." She went down the steep steps into the road.

She followed the road doggedly. A little house to the left, door and windows shut. She went up and peered in. It was empty. Here? She looked around fearful. Her Sin gave a great lurch within her. She shuddered. She could not be alone with it here.

She went out into the road again and toiled on up the curve, crossed the slide where the logs came shooting down, moved slowly up the straight, nearly level piece. More buildings came into view, to the right a large rough barn, to the left a watering trough and a long picket fence front-ing a cleared space with a big hemlock house set in the middle and a spring-house a stone's throw away. Farther ahead to the right a little shack squatted on the flat side of the road and near it a woman's figure in bright blue was tying a bony horse to a stake.

The woman walked past the watering trough and approached the figure. She saw a stringy woman in a tight blue sateen dress, face the color of old leather, a great bang of hair falling down into faded blue, piglike eyes, a little knot of hair in the back twisting tightly away from the cordy neck. A frowsy child came out of the shack. "Ma, ma," it cried like a little animal. A wailing arose from within the house, a sound of violent rocking. "Not here," said the woman in a cold fear to herself.

"Will you give me a drink?" Automatically the words came.

"I sure will. We got the best drinkin' water anywheres around. Liz!" she shouted into the house. An ungainly elder girl appeared in the dark hole of the doorway. "Git some fresh water from the spring!"

The girl stood sullen a moment, then disappeared. She came out with a small tin pail dangling against her dirty legs.

"Git a move on you. Seems like I can't make her do a thing."

Sullen, the girl moved across the road, swung open a gate, and took the path to the spring-house.

"Who lives there?" asked the woman. Hope burned low in her.

"That's Bennet's. He's the lumber boss. He don't take no boarders neither. They got too many children for that, five boys an' two girls, an' Mrs. Bennet's pertickiler. I allays scrub the floors for her. See this dress? I saved the money she give me an' got it last week come Sataday."

A great despair came over the woman. She made a couple of steps forward.

"Where air you goin'? Air you all alone?"

Anything to put an end to questioning. She spoke at random, strangely in accord with the custom of the forest dwellers. "My husband's coming along behind with our goods. We're moving."

"Oh, movin'? What's your husband do? Gonno work in the mill or in the woods?"

"He's going into the mill."

"You ain't gonno walk all the way to Goff's, air you?" The woman felt fright. "How far is it?" Her Sin was threatening her again.

"Must be a matter of five miles."

"Is that the nearest mill?" She could never walk that far.

"By the road 'tis. If you cut through the woods you kin git to Fox's mill down the path back of Bennet's barn, but that mill's shet down. You kin cut up back of their house an' git to Sumner's. That's a mile or so an' a good path. Mrs. Sumner, now, she comes over to see Mrs. Bennet an' brings Gertrude. She ain't tied down like the rest of us. She ain't but the one, an' a good little girl, too. Not like my good-fer-nothin' Liz."

Hope suddenly leaped high, a sense of surety crowned its leaping. "And the path to her place is back of the house over there?"

"Yes. Walk right past the spring an' cut up over the hill, an' there's a path." The woman started to go. "But I thought you was goin' to Goff's? An' your husband?" Suspicion came into the lines of the leathery face.

"I must have misspoken myself." The woman kept her head turned toward Bennet's. Her voice was calm. She had a slight wonder at her calmness while her mind searched out through the forest back of Bennet's. "I came the wrong way, I guess. It was Sumner's I wanted."

"But you said your husband—"

"He isn't coming for a few days." She spoke with decision. It was easy to say anything, anything that any one wanted her to say. "I came on first to kind of look around and it was Sumner's I wanted but I forgot the name."

"Well, it's a good thing you found me. You'd been to Goff's not knowin' no better." She laughed a hoarse chuckle.

The woman said, "Yes, I'm glad I found you. Now I know how to go."

"But you ain't had your drink. Liz!" the raucous voice

screamed. "Fetch that water or I'll tan your hide good!"

"Never mind, I'll get a drink as I go past. I'm much obliged to you." The woman crossed quickly over the road, took the path past the spring, not stopping to drink, cut up back of Bennet's, and was swallowed up in the forest before the figure in blue had recovered from surprise.

She was surrounded by forest, by trees growing out of earth. She was full of pain. Her head was a ball of fire and her body a world of pain. Roots were twining in her trying to get a foothold, roots were sucking away at her vitals trying to extract nourishment. She was earth and she could not lie down, for she had a Sin that kept urging her on.

Blindly she followed the pathway. The pathway led to Sumner's where there was a woman who had time to visit and a little girl who was good. If Sumner's was not the place, there was only the forest. She was in forest now but she was on a path that divided forest. Forest on both sides of her, trees and earth in a great swelling together and the sky smiling through the network of branches and leaves. She went on. She went quickly. Roots caught at her feet. The smart of branches fell on her face. Her Sin clamored for its hour.

She ran, she could not see, her feet kept the path like a miracle. Suddenly the path gave out on a road. Across the road was a house. She felt that there was a house, she did not see it. She made her last effort against the Sin that was tearing her to pieces, taking at last its deep revenge. She fell toward the blur that she felt was the house. She gave way at last to the strength of her Sin. . . .

The woman awoke. She was lying in bed in a ceiled room whose windows looked out on low branches of hemlock. There was a patchwork quilt on the bed. She felt light, light and drowsy. She slept. Again she awoke. She felt light, light and her head was clear. Her Sin? It had triumphed. She felt like laughing. Her Sin had triumphed, yet she felt light, light and quite clear. She stirred. A large, motherly form appeared, an anxious face bent over her. "I'll lift it up and you can see it."

The woman looked upon it. It was her Sin. She had
lost her Sin. But here it was beside her still. Would it
never leave her? She stared hard at it. Yes, it was her
Sin. She closed her eyes to shut out its sight.

"I'll put it right beside you where it'll keep warm. It's
so tiny, we must take good care of it."

The little bundle lay beside her. She could put her
hand upon it, pick it up. Her Sin was outside of her now.
Everyone could see it. A Sin should be hidden, kept secret,
covered over. . . .

She dozed. She was walking along a road. The road
went on and on, hard, smooth, implacable, hard and hurting under her soft feet. The wall of the forest rose up on
both sides and mocked her. The wall to the right bowed in
derision. The trees leaned over and swept their branches
on the road in front of her. The wall to the left bowed in
derision and swept its branches before her. "Come this
way," one said. "Come this way," said the other. They
swept their branches in front of her making it difficult for
her to walk.

She tried to placate them. She bowed first to the one
wall and then to the other. As she bowed, the one wall
said in a great voice as though all its trees were many-
forked tongues demanding together, "Speak!" and as she
bowed again, the other wall said in a great voice of many
tongues, "Speak!" They settled their trunks stiffly across
her way like dark crossed swords and waited for her to
begin.

She saw now that they were full of eyes, terrible accusing
eyes, an eye on every leaf, thousands of eyes. "If I
could change their eyes to ears," she thought, "then I
could tell them." She became clever. She shut her own
eyes so that they could not see her. No sooner had she
done so than she remembered that this was a game she
had played with Him when she was a little girl. She stood
in the corner with closed eyes and said, "Now you can't
see me." He hunted from corner to corner until he stumbled upon her. Then she opened her eyes and he shouted,
"Now I see you!" She knew all the time really that he
saw her. So she knew now that the thousands of eyes saw

her and there was no use trying to play a silly game with them.

"Perhaps he will be here now if I open my eyes," she thought, "and he will tell them." Dismay swept over her. "But how can he? I never told him. How could he know if I did not tell him?"

She opened her eyes and looked upon the walls of forest. They were waiting for her to speak, unsettling themselves uneasily. The eyes began to move back and forth and as they moved they read words out of her through her own voice: "His mother never would have forgiven me. She wouldn't have believed he did it. She'd have thought I made him do it."

The words seemed weak, thin, a flimsy covering for something that lay underneath. The trunks of the trees rubbed against one another, complaining at her words. The eyes glowered upon her, piercing into her. "They want to know everything," she thought desperately, "everything, from the beginning." She addressed them as though they had commanded her. "But that would take too long, all of it, the whole thing."

The forest ruffled itself still more uneasily and murmured against her. The eyes became sinister. In fear, she spoke: "His mother took me in when I was little, from the city, nobody's. She brought me up to be his sister. She called me daughter, gave me things."

The forest began sweeping its branches in front of her. "It doesn't believe me," she thought in terror. "It won't let me pass, ever." She began to cry. "He might have hated me if I told him. He might have hated me." The branches swept in front of her. She could not see the road. It was covered with sweeping branches. . . .

She awoke. Her face was wet, quite wet, as though she had been in the water. Her hand lay on the bundle that held her Sin. She became wide awake, alert. She felt cunning arise within her. She stirred in bed. No one came. Sin should be covered. Her hand was on the patchwork quilt, grasped it, drew it up over the bundle of Sin, held it close. Her hand unclosed after a while, dragged the quilt back a little. She lay still. Her eyes slept. . . .

Some one came in, over to the bed, leaned over, jerked the quilt away. The bundle was taken up. At last they were taking her Sin away. They had left it too long beside her. She felt herself looked steadily upon. She opened her eyes. "Did you—have you been awake since I left the room?" The motherly voice was stern, suspicious, reluctant, too.

"I was asleep."

"I fixed the quilt carefully before I left. It was over the baby's face when I came back."

Why did they trouble her about a baby? It was her Sin she had covered up so that no one could see it. "The quilt," she whispered painfully. "I pulled the quilt up. I was cold." She settled down in bed.

A breeze, soft and full of the resinous breath of hemlock came through the slightly opened window and blew her eyelids down. Leaves began piling upon her in layers, soft and pressing, trying to smother her.

The dream began again. She was walking on a road through the forest. The road was narrow, oh, so narrow, she could hardly keep on it, narrow, and hard and smooth like glass. The wall of forest to the right kept bowing, the trees swept down, their branches lashed her. The wall of forest to the left kept bowing, its branches lashed her. The branches were full of eyes, eyes that burned when the branches lashed.

The eyes *knew*. "I must tell them the whole truth," she said to herself, but she knew that she said it aloud and that the forest heard it. "Huah! Huah!" The wind swept through the branches. "The truth! The truth!" The wind blew the words through the branches. A tall strong tree with great bulging eyes swept down upon her. "I wanted him!" she screamed.

The trees stopped lashing. The eyes became ears. She knelt before them feeling their compassion. "I tried not to, at first—but when he touched me, I wanted him. He spoke words of poetry, words that he knew out of a book he brought back with him from his travel. 'Your gray eyes are like pools. I lose myself in them.' He took the pins from my hair. 'Your hair is a mesh. I am caught in it. I cannot escape.' He held me to him. 'Your body is softer than this milkweed down. Shall I float away with it?' He had never spoken that way before. His mother wouldn't have believed that he talked that way."

Now that the forest was compassionate, her mind unloosed itself all at once in a great rush of hurrying thoughts that went out like waves into the leafage, communicating her secret without the tedious use of words. "I had no right to him. His mother meant us always to be brother and sister—to keep us apart. She didn't really think I was as good as he. She only took me because his father wanted me. She didn't know what his father said, once, when he teased me: 'I chose you because you were the prettiest of all the children. Your gray eyes asked me to take you, and so I had to. You were a little fairy without any father or mother.' She would have given him up some day to some one else. But I wanted him. I needed him. She would never forgive me if she knew. I never told anyone, not even him. He would have married me. His father would have made him marry me. But I kept away from him, after I knew. And he—"

"And he, and he," whistled the trees. The sky became dark, the wind came in a gale, the branches crashed together and began lashing her. Despair overwhelmed her. "Now I shall be destroyed. They were only trapping me." She submitted herself to annihilation. The branches lashed her, lashed her clothes away, lashed into her flesh. . . .

"Poor thing! She didn't know what she was doing. I thought at first she had done it on purpose. She doesn't seem to know she's had a baby." She lay and listened with closed eyes. She felt she was lying in a pool of water that softened her flesh, took life away from her. "It looks real pretty in that little dress of Gertrude's. I always felt I'd have use for those baby clothes some day, but I didn't think it would be like this."

They brought it for her to see. She looked upon it dry-eyed. She knew that they wanted her to cry. Foolish people! Why should one cry for a Sin once it is dead?

She was sitting up. . . . She could walk a little. . . . She dressed herself and came out on the porch. They were kind. They never asked her anything. She knew they hoped she would tell them. The husband spoke clumsily to her. They were sorry—could they help her? She shook her head.

Early in the morning she awoke. She felt quite clear. She must be on the road. She dressed hastily, quietly, was out of the house. The road led her. She walked fast, following it through the forest. She did not know where she went. She simply went on. By and by she would come out of the forest and there would be a town and there she would step off the road.

She walked quickly, she felt so light. She was light for her Sin was gone. She walked quickly for a long time. She became tired. She sat down to rest. Nothing within her urged her on. There was a great emptiness within her, a consuming emptiness. She felt how heavy her breasts were and how great her emptiness was. She wanted to go up in the forest and lie down. She did not dare. The forest and earth seemed allied against her, trees and earth together, their oneness held her out.

She had a desire that the roots of the trees should take hold on her, disintegrate her, find a place for their support and nourishment. A great and horrible yearning took hold on her. She yearned that her emptiness should be filled, she yearned for her Sin, for the bundle that held her Sin, she yearned to nourish her Sin. . . .

She threw herself in the dust of the road and sobbed. The forest repudiated her. The wall of the forest pushed her into the road. She was one with the road. Nothing grew out of her; she nourished nothing. She was a way, to be passed over, trampled upon. . . .

She felt the throbbing ache of her breasts in the dust. She arose and stood quiet, looking sombrely at the dark, unrelenting wall of forest. Then she walked slowly along. Sadly, drearily, the life that lay behind her, the life that she had shut out from her when her feet first set out upon the road, began to filter back into her bruised mind. It came as something she had known long ago, so long that it seemed as though it must have been quite another life, and she another person, a young dreaming girl, moving

about in the big white house set on the great planted space
up against the forest, learning from a shadowy placid
woman who called her daughter the ways of the little
world of which she was a part, teased by a shadowy kindly
man when the woman was not there to hear, captured by
the shadowy grown-up figure of the little boy who had
played games with her, come back from school and travel
a mysterious young man. . . .

How far away it was, how far and how long, long ago!
Slowly, slowly, she walked along the road through the
forest, carrying in her the dream fragments of her shattered
world. Soon she would come out of the forest and there
would be a town and there she would step off the road.
She would leave the road that went on ceaselessly, in and
out of forest, through towns, and again through forest.

NATALKA'S PORTION[1]

By ROSE GOLLUP COHEN

(From *The Pictorial Review*)

SABINKA lay buried in snow. The hills, the forest, the lake, all lay hard, white, glittering, and the air also glittered and stung and cut.

Looking toward the village, the two rows of huts looked small, insignificant, mere specks of time-grayed timber weighed down with snow. Over each speck a thread of smoke rose, going straight up into the still, glittering air. Within, doors and windows sealed, the peasants huddled for warmth, here and there, together with their animals, to keep them alive, or for the life that they could give. In the chimneyless huts even the smoke was kept in for the warmth it gave. It poured from the oven into the room and hung there from the ceiling. Beneath it the peasants went about, their bodies bent to the ground. When at last the smoke settled on ceiling and walls they still went about bent, from habit now, and peering with weakened eyes.

Then winter ended! Suddenly, as if it spent itself in its own cruelty, it ended. The sun came out warm. From the ragged straw roofs of the huts the snow slipped and melted and fell in a thick shower. Birds appeared. The peasants came out to look at their fields. Their faces were sallow and pinched, and the smoke soaked into the skin showed plainer in the strong light.

The snow blackened with every moment, and suddenly the earth lay bare. The men began to scatter over the fields. The women tended nearer home.

One afternoon, when the air was sweet with the warmth and the moisture of the earth, and in the pastures about the village Sabinka a tint of green showed faintly, Katherina came to her husband, Gavrelo, where he was mending the fence around the field to be planted with wheat.

"Gavrelo," she said, "I have come to plead with you again about the marriage portion of our daughter Natalka." She stood meekly, a clumsy little body in a red plaid shawl. Her face was steaming with heat and perspiration, and her worn birch-bark sandals were clogged with earth from the soggy fields.

Gavrelo had not looked up when she had been coming to him through the fields, and now it was as if she were not there. Near him lay a pile of poles, a heap of freshly cut twigs and a hatchet. He selected a long, pliant twig and began twisting it in and out between two poles as a bar-rest. His face was sullen. He was short and wide and brown; his thick hair and beard, and worn homespun clothes, and his weather-beaten skin, all were brown. He was like the powerful trees about him, and, like these deep-rooted trees, he looked as capable of being moved.

Katherina turned her eyes away from him. It crushed her to see him so. It had always crushed her—even so long ago when he used to come to court her at her father's house—the way he would sit there of a Sunday, sullen, silent, never a kind word, never a smile, contrary, scowling at the whole world.

"Gavrelo," she repeated her sentences in a way peculiar to the people of Sabinka, "I have come to plead with you about Natalka's marriage portion." Her voice was full of restrained passion.

"Look, Gavrelo, at your home." She pointed to a hut across the great field. In one of the two dingy windows a young girl could be seen, though vaguely, at a spinning-board.

"There is your home. Moldy and rotten, it is sinking to the ground. You were supposed to have built twenty years ago, soon after we were married. All you have built are barns. There they stand, shaming your house. And there is your daughter, as pretty as the prettiest in Sabinka, in that rotting home. Yet, Gavrelo, have I ever pestered you about it? But now it is about Natalka that I beg you."

Her clumsy little body leaned toward him. But her voice became more patient, more restrained.

"Gavrelko!" She used the diminutive, and then stood dumbly looking down a moment. Yes, she could have cared for him if he had let her. "Gavrelko, you are not going to send Natalka away without a portion to her husband's home, a strange home in a strange village! You are not going to do it!"

Dumb and silent, Gavrelo's scowl never relaxed. It was always so, always—except—except when he stood looking at his fields — at his wheat. Then his furrowed face smoothed and the light in his eyes reflected the light in the fields.

Gavrelo now selected a long pole, sharpened it, and began driving it into the ground. "Hagh!" his breath echoed, and the pole sank deep into the earth.

"And you have so much, Gavrelo." She glanced about. Their hut stood a good distance away from the village, and all surrounding it was Gavrelo's.

"All that, all about us is yours, and your barns are stacked with wheat. You will not send Natalka away with empty hands." Her own clasped in agony. "You won't do it. I know, Gavrelo, how bitter it is to come with empty hands." Her head drooped, her voice sank low.

"I know how it is. I came to your home, Gavrelo, without a portion. My people were very poor. You have never thrown it up to me, Gavrelo, but your mother cast it in my face every day as long as she lived. And I was never able to lift my head."

Gavrelo's face was turned from her, and he worked on steadily.

"And Natalka, too, is marrying into a large family. It is perhaps a disadvantage to marry into a large family. There are so many to find fault with your ways, a mother-in-law and sisters-in-law and brothers-in-law. All watching and criticizing you. And when you have come without a portion—Ach! Gavrelko! They will throw it up to her, the mother-in-law and the sisters-in-law—and—and even Simyonka—Simyonka is a fine fellow. And yet—in a

quarrel— would he not remember?" She began to weep
passionately. "You won't do it, Gavrelo. And Natalka
has really earned it. You know how she can spin and
weave. Her cloth is straight and fine. And during the
harvest she has been among the quickest hands. You won't
bring this shame upon her, Gavrelo!"

Gavrelo turned to her. At last she had touched him.
His face was distorted with anger, and he stopped his work
for a moment. "Why does she want to marry, the fool!"
The words burst from him through his teeth, and he bent
down to pick up his tools. He had finished the fence.
Katherina stared at him.

"What—what else do you expect? Oh! It is a harvest
hand you are thinking of!" Then realizing that he was
going, she ran to him.

"Gavrelo!" she cried, "what do you say? What will
you say when at the wedding Simyonka's father will ask,
'And what do you give Natalka as her portion?' What
will you say, Gavrelo?"

Gavrelo lifted a few poles to his shoulder and slipped the
hatchet into his girdle. "I told you," he said doggedly.
"Simyonka has enough!" And he walked away with his
long, even stride, his sandals making deep prints in the
soft earth.

Katherina staggered to the newly mended fence and
buried her face in her arms. *"Ach, Boshi Moi!"* she cried.
With the habit of the lonely she talked to herself. Gavrelo
did not tolerate neighbors. Indeed. he was hated because
of his hardness and meanness.

"Life is bitter," she wept. Her own had been a cruel
fate.

"You have come like a beggar." Her mother-in-law had
cast it in her face. And now her own fate was to be
Natalka's fate! And why? Because Gavrelo was an unnatural father, because he was stingy and cared for nothing
—but—his fields, his wheat, more and more wheat. His
barns were stacked with wheat. He kept them under lock
and key, and he sowed still more wheat. She raised her
head and looked about. This field was to be all wheat, acres
and acres. And Natalka was to go to her husband like a

beggar. "They will throw it up to her, the mother-in-law
and the sisters-in-law. And Natalka is young; she will
never be able to lift her head!" Her own head sank into
her arms again.

It was late when she started for the hut. The red sun
hung on the very edge of the forest. She picked her way
to a back road not far off which would be less soggy than
the fields, though roundabout and longer. Trudging along,
her eyes on the path, her sandals heavy with the mud, she
at once upbraided and defended Gavrelo, and analyzed and
schemed.

It would take so little to give Natalka a fine portion.
There, for instance, was the little pig, only a year old, but
so aggressive that he had to be fed with the old hogs.
Parshuchuck would be an excellent gift. He could take
care of himself anywhere. Even in a litter of strange pigs
he could hold his own. Also there was Chulka, a heifer, for
whom no fence was too high. She used her knobby little
horns with such skill that often won a long stare of surprise
from the old cows. Chulka, too, could take care of herself
in a strange herd. These two would be an excellent gift.
It would be pleasant for little Natalka to have something
of her own that was alive, in a strange home, in a strange
village. Parshuchuck and Chulka might even be an example to her, not to bend her head too low.

But what was the use in thinking about it? "Ach! The
mean peasant! The unnatural father!" She stumbled,
unable to see the path through her tears.

"Bah! They are fools, those wise men," she shook her
head disgustedly. "They are fools who say that it is better
to have a relative rich, though a miser, than one who is
poor and generous. Both are like death. Can you take
from the miser? Nor can you take from the one who has
nothing to give."

Presently, on reaching a sudden turn in the road, she
heard a merry voice babbling incoherent fits of song. That
was Addom on his way home from the *kabock*. Addom
was a drunkard. He drank like a fish. Addom, too, was
often idle, she mused. Gavrelo never drank, though he
liked a glass of vodka. But what would Gavrelo do in a

kabock where men talked as they drank? Gavrelo never talked to any one. He only worked. That was why her parents had made her marry him instead of Addom, who drank and who never kept his word, just as Gavrelo never broke his word. But Addom's daughter Anulia, who was also to marry this spring, was to receive one of her father's two cows as her wedding-gift. Anulia Addom also wore machine-made stockings which she bought from the Jewess Deborah—stockings and boots every Sunday! Natalka bound her ankles in cloths and wore birch-bark sandals to church. Katherina shook her head. A man who drank was perhaps better-natured, more generous.

Reaching the yard, she saw Natalka still in the window spinning.

Natalka was eighteen. She was small like her mother, but she was rosy and healthy. Her hair lay in two thick, brown braids on her back. Her faded red kerchief was tied with a coquettish knot, and her little round nose had a mischievous tilt. But just now she was neither coquettish nor mischievous. She was very earnest. Her wedding was to be the first in the village this spring, and she was hurrying to finish all her mother's spinning before it came. Her hands twirled the spindle rapidly; her head scarcely moved except to moisten the thread with her lips, or to extricate a knot in the flax with her small white teeth.

Katherina watched her a moment. Should she tell her —that her father would send her away with empty hands? No! There was time enough. But as she stood watching she saw Natalka stop her work suddenly; her hands became still, her head drooped for a moment. In agony, Katherina wondered. Could she know, then? Perhaps she guessed! Katherina turned away from the window.

About the yard all the buildings stood facing in a semi-circle, the hut, the barns, the pig-pen, the chicken-coop. Katherina went toward the coop. In the barn she heard Gavrelo. He rarely forgot the keys. "He rarely forgets them," she muttered to herself. The corners of her mouth lifted firmly. "Well, Natalka shall have a fine trousseau, anyway. Her *kubial*, at any rate, shall not go off empty!"

Late that night the full moon rose, and Sabinka, with its

two rows of huts, its hills and dales and lakes, lay transformed in silver light.

In the shadow of the fences a woman went stealing along. Climbing, here forcing a way through the bars, running a step where the shadow broke, and again lingering where it resumed, she reached a small hut standing in the full light. She rapped on the door and shook the latch impatiently.

"Open, Deborah!" she whispered. "It is I, Katherina." A tall, thin woman with a white kerchief about her head came out on the threshold.

"So late, Katherina!"

"Yes, and I must hurry back. Here." Katherina took a large ball of thread from her *swita* pocket. "You are to knit a pair of stockings for my daughter Natalka's wedding," she whispered. "But mind, Jewess," her voice rose suspiciously, "you are to return to me what is left of the thread."

"We are not thieves!" came from Deborah in a tone hurt, yet patient.

"Well, perhaps not," Katherina said, softening slightly. "Perhaps not. But all Jews are swindlers."

"We are what we are forced to be." Restraint and infinite patience were in Deborah's voice. Hesitating an instant, she turned suddenly. "Look, Katherina, would you not much rather come along the road, in the light of day, to order stockings for Natalka, instead——"

"Do you mean to insinuate, Jewess?" Katherina flamed.

"No, no," Deborah hastened to assure her. "I am not insulting you. I am not blaming you. I just want you to see, Katherina, how one may be forced to become what one does not want to be."

"Well," said Katherina, somewhat mollified, "I suppose so. I suppose Jews, like people, have their troubles."

Carefully she put her hand into her bosom and counted slowly six eggs into the apron Deborah held out. "There," she said, brushing her hands with an air as if the transaction was quite satisfactorily completed.

"My dear Katherina!" Deborah exclaimed, "you expect me to knit a pair of stockings for six eggs?"

"How much then?" Katherina's voice was suspicious again and cross.

"Twelve, Katherina; at least twelve. This is not winter, you know."

"In the next village——"

"I know," Deborah broke in. "In the next village lives a Jewess who knits a pair of stockings for six eggs. Don't believe it, Katherina. It's a fairy-tale. Anyway, I cannot do it. We have to live, too. And little Miriam is growing up. There is no chance for a penniless girl here, a girl without a dowry." Deborah's voice came brooding.

Katherina put her hand into her *swita* again. The trouble of a dowry she could easily understand.

"Here, Deborah," she said sympathetically, "here are twelve eggs. But remember every inch of the thread you are to return. And don't let your blind mother-in-law knit the stockings. She might drop a stitch!"

A whispered good night followed, and Katherina stole forth into the shadows again.

The village peeped through a mist of tender green buds. Warm sunshine, dazzling blue skies were continuous. Scattered over the fields far and near the peasants were. Mere specks between earth and sky, their bodies moved slowly, heavily, all day long. Nearer the homes the women labored, digging in the gardens, bleaching at the lake. At dawn and after dark they took the time to prepare for the weddings in the village.

When the mud in the road had dried a peddler came driving through the village with summer finery and pots to sell.

"Pots to sell! Earthen pots to sell!" the peddler cried in a ringing voice. And the dogs barked, and the children stared, and the women left their work and hurried to the wagon with their bundles of rags.

Katherina was digging a draining-canal between two long beds in the garden. When the peddler stopped at her gate she left her spade and looked around. Natalka was at the lake bleaching. And Gavrelo—she could see him in a far field, his arm swinging rhythmically back and forth. Hastening to the outhouse, she came out with two bundles, one of rags, and one small sackful of wheat. She carried it with difficulty and threw it over the fence into the road, where it lay hidden among some weeds.

"Did you see, little Jew?" she called to the peddler. "It is wheat!"

"I saw," the peddler answered significantly. He was as accustomed to this kind of transaction among the peasants as they themselves were.

Katherina hurried out to the wagon and climbed onto the axle.

"Quick, little Jew, let me see what you have. And don't think you can rob me. Wheat is dear now! Have you ribbons? And I want two red bandannas, but of different patterns. And show me beads. Have you got rings? Yes, show me that one with the red stone."

And the peddler measured, using the length of his arm, and watched Katherina. And she picked and fussed and worried in indecision, her eyes never quite leaving the distant field where Gavrelo was working.

Her selections made finally, she gathered them into her apron jealously, and a haggling ensued between the two, not unlike the transaction some weeks earlier at Deborah's hut.

"Now, peddler, how much? That sack of wheat is almost a bushel."

"Almost!" he cried. "That should have been a full bushel for all you have taken."

"Don't shriek!" she paled. "There are those rags. What do you give for the rags?"

"The rags go to make up the full bushel of wheat." His dark eyes snapped.

"Oh, very well," she said. "Take it! Take it! You are a robber." She climbed down and hurried away. The peddler threw his bundles into the wagon and touched his pony with the end of his whip, his dark eyes measuring the distance to the next hut.

Katherina breathed a sigh of relief as his wagon creaked away, and she slowly entered the deep interior of the out-house which adjoined the living room. It was late afternoon, and the road was hot and dusty. But here it was

cool and dark; the only light came from the door opening
on the garden path.

In the dimmest corner Natalka's *kubial* stood, filled with
her trousseau. Katherina reached it by a small step-ladder
and dipped down into its tank-like body. She touched
and patted the cool, smooth linens, heavily embroidered
and plain pieces. She added the newly-purchased treasures.
Yes, Natalka's *kubial* was filling—but of the portion there
was no prospect. She sighed hopelessly. There was no
prospect, and the day of the wedding was drawing nearer.
Gavrelo had ordered vodka from the *kabock*, and told her
she might have all the pork she wanted for the wedding-
feast. But that was all. Natalka must enter into a strange
family owning nothing, come with nothing belonging to
her, nothing familiar. Everything she will look at will
be strange, his! Nothing that she had brought, that she
could feel pride in. *"Ach, Boshi Moi!"*

She finally climbed down the ladder. It had grown late.
Outside the mellow sunset lay full on the path and the bit
of road she could see before the gate. But in the outhouse
the dimness was quite deep. And the living room, through
its door, looked out at her, a dark hole with its sooty
walls; the two tiny windows in it admitted but little light.
Only one bright spot—the icon in vivid red and blue of the
"Gracious Mother" looked out at her from the dimness.

"Boshi Moi!" Katherina's eyes went out to it in a
dumb appeal, *"Boshi Moi!"* Wearily she sat down after
a moment on the lower step of the ladder. Voices came
from the road. Presently she saw, from her seclusion, Natalka and Simyonka enter through the gate. Their young
forms stood out clean, clear, in the soft light. This was
Simyonka's market day, she remembered. He had evidently met Natalka at the lake on his way from market.
They were talking heatedly. The little chit Natalka was
arguing, smiling, coquetting. The youth seemed to be
entreating her, begging earnestly. Simyonka was not much
older than Natalka. He was tall and lean and brown,
clean-featured, clean-looking in his coarse, home-spun linen.
Katherina watched, and her soul filled with gratitude that
he was so beautiful, for Natalka.

They came a few steps nearer on the garden path and she caught their words.

"Just one! Just one, Natalka!" His face was lifted. His eyes were beseeching her. And Natalka, laughing, radiant, mischievous, turned and was backing away from him toward the house, her hand raised between them.

"*Lublue ya tibya.*" (I love thee.)

With the palm of her hand against his mouth, she pressed him away. He was murmuring, "You are like a little flower, Natalka. You are like a little birch-tree, a little white birch growing in the field."

Katherina's own face was radiant. "*Ya tibya lublue.*" He loves her! Yes, he loves her. She herself had never known such love. "Simyonka loves Natalka!" The words filled her with dizzy joy.

Then her face twisted with agony. But soon, very soon, he would look upon her with shame! At once! At her wedding! His father will ask Gavrelo, "What is your daughter's portion?" And Gavrelo will say, "Nothing!" And the whole vliiage will laugh and jeer. And little Natalka will bend her head with shame. And later, again, when he brings her home and the villagers and relatives gather about him, and he has nothing of hers that he could tell them she brought, that he could show—

She rose. Carried away by this thought, she no longer saw nor heard them outside, and she went staggering into the living room of the hut and fell upon her knees before the icon.

"Gracious Mother Maria!" Her clumsy little body crumpled to the hard-trodden earth.

"Blessed Mother Maria, can you hear me?" she pleaded in the crude way of Sabinka people. "Can you hear me? I have come to beg of you for Natalka. You know, Mother, I have never come to you for myself. But now I come for her. Mother," her voice rose brokenly, "you know how hard my life has been. At home when I was young we were so poor. Often I was hungry for just bread. In marriage—Gavrelo is a strange person." She fell silent a moment, her tears choking her.

"The children were all I had. And when little Zacharka

died I felt as if my heart would break, Mother. He was so
sweet to look at with his golden hair and blue eyes. He
would have been fifteen years old now. Oh, Mother! It
is hard; it has been hard to see other little lads in the
village and not see Zacharka. In the spring, when the
sky is blue, and the fields are covered with grass, I miss
little Zacharka. I miss him when from each home in the
village a little lad goes forth with his father's herd. The
mothers wait for them all day, and in the evening they
meet them at the gate. I, too, wait all day, but it is a
strange little lad that brings our cattle home." She lay still,
sobbing brokenly.

"It has been hard, Mother Maria. Yet, have I complained? But now I beg pity for Natalka." Her hands
clasped, her forehead pressed to the earth. "Pity, Mother,
pity for Natalka!"

The trees were in full leaf. The meadows were dotted
with the first flowers. The wheat in the great field stood a
foot high. It was Saturday at dusk. The cattle had long
passed, and the dust they had stirred was laid. Swarms
of tiny insects danced in the open spaces of the road. Far
out frogs croaked at regular intervals. The air was warm
and sweet with the breath of the flowers and the dew.
The village seemed quietly at rest. Yet there was a silent
stir—preparation for the morrow, the first wedding in
Sabinka this spring.

The fence enclosing Gavrelo's hut was strung with
branches of green foliage. High over the gate a wreath of
orange-colored flowers hung to mark the bride's dwelling.
Inside the yard was swept clean and sprinkled with yellow
sand, and long benches stood along the walls. On the door-
step of the outhouse Natalka sat with her two bridesmaids
trimming her veil. Natalka herself was making the little
rosettes of red or green ribbon, and the maids stitched
them on all over the long strip of white muslin. The maids
were talking and giggling, their heads bent over their work.
Natalka was quiet and solemn.

In the deep interior of the outhouse Katherina was giving the last touches to the *kubial*. She lifted and replaced
and folded and finally fitted the cover and slipped in the

bar. It was done! Her hands fell at her sides. Katherina
had grown thinner, paler, more pinched. Since she prayed
before the icon she had spent the time from day to day,
from hour to hour, waiting. But nothing—nothing had
happened to save Natalka. Since that hour at dusk, she,
Katherina, had spent morning and night kneeling before
the icon. She had been to the cemetery many times, where
her dead were laid, and hung their moldy wooden crosses
with new little aprons of many colors. She had watched
Gavrelo from day to day, hoping for a sign of relenting,
of softening. But none had come. Sullen, stolid, he went
about as usual, working early and late in the fields and at
the barns, only coming in to eat his three meals of black
bread and cabbage soup, and to sleep the few hours between the extreme dark and early dawn. Standing there,
she could hear him now at the barns, still working—still
working—while others were long at rest.

"Ach, Gavrelo!" she cried to him silently, "what is it
all for? What are you doing it for, Gavrelo?" She lifted
her coarse apron and wiped away stinging tears.

The shadow before the door had just fallen on the
threshold. By clock time it would have been perhaps ten
in the morning. A wagon lined with green leaves and
buttercups, harnessed to four pair, stood at the gate in the
road. The horses were snorting and beating the ground
impatiently, and a sturdy youth sat holding the reins
mightily. Within, the yard flashed with color—red, short,
wide skirts, blue and green streamers, red bandannas, white
shirts, patent-leather boots, sparkling black or green beads,
shining brass buttons.

The guests sat primly on the benches along the walls,
chanting solemnly. Katherina and Gavrelo sat among the
elders of the village. Gavrelo looked browner in a well-
bleached shirt, and he was the only man who wore birch
sandals instead of boots. Katherina sat beside him, her
head swathed in a white linen scarf decorated with little
red crosses. Her head was bowed, her hands were folded
in her lap, her face as white as her scarf. Simyonka, in
patent leather boots and white shirt , looked solemn.
Natalka was tearful. Natalka looked like some strange

wild-flower, a poppy perhaps, with all the red and green,
and her loose brown hair. Her scarf flashed with every
possible color. Her skirt was red; her breast was covered
with many strings of beads.

Suddenly the chanting stopped. A hush fell. Solemnly,
between her two maids, the bride rose to ask a blessing
of her parents before starting for church. She walked
with studied and becoming dignity, her head bowed, her
hands clasped in front of her. She reached her parents.
And here she forgot her rôle. Overcome by emotion, she
fell upon her knees rather clumsily, humanly, and a low
cry, half song, half wail of the braid song, pierced the air.

"Boshi Moi———"

"My braids—my beautiful brown braids."

Blindly and convulsed, Katherina rose and made the
sign of the cross over her. Gavrelo did the same. Katherina watched, still watched and hoped for a sign of relenting. But his face looked more stubborn than ever. And
Katherina now suddenly knew that she must not expect
him to relent. When had Gavrelo ever relented that she
should have expected it? Fool that she was! It had
always been just the contrary even when it was to his own
disadvantage. His word given became law. Fool that she
was to have expected Gavrelo to change his word!

Meanwhile, Natalka, kneeling before each guest for a
blessing, reached the gate. There was a burst of song. All
pressed forward. The horses pranced, a whip cracked and
a cloud of dust rose before the gate, and the bride was
gone. Katherina and Gavrelo followed in a vehicle. Dazed
and crushed, she was sped along. What could now happen? The beginning of Natalka's shame a mere few hours
off.

Noise and confusion filled the yard. There was a
babble of voices, thick voices, incoherent, affectionate,
querulous, crying of children, snatches of song, the strains
of a fiddle rising a moment over the clamor, a rhythmic
thomp, thomp of dancing feet.

It was late in the afternoon. The bridal pair had long
returned from church. The yard was now divided in two
parts. One-half was occupied by the dancers, and in the

other half two long tables stood spread with food—roast pork, dishes heaped with sour pickles glistening in juice, salt herring, thick slices of black bread, tall green bottles of vodka, white and stinging.

The guests sat about the tables, while the children clamored at their elders' elbows. The feast was at its height. Among the men several of the guests already lay under the table. Of the women most were intoxicated. Some sat wagging their heads. Others were awakened now and then to shrill merriment. Still others drank little and sat chanting solemnly, keeping up dutifully the burden of the rites.

In the dancers' corner several couples whirled in a quadrille. In one of these Natalka flashed in and out. Natalka's face was still solemn and dignified. But a twinkle of mischief and coquettishness was in her eyes. Her husband was dancing in the same quadrille. Whenever they had to dance opposite each other her eyes teased him; her little red hand extended and withdrew half-way, and Simyonka was tantalized and radiant.

Further a circle of young folk surrounded the great-grandfather of the village, dancing a jig.

His hands on his hips, his white beard flowing, his head high, a smile on his lips, his aged limbs performed with wonderful agility. He toed to the right, he toed to the left, here he crossed, there he kneeled. And the fiddlers fiddled with all their might, and the women clapped, and the men cheered and stamped.

"Trala-lala-lala."

At one table Katherina sat among her guests. Leaning to this one and that one, she urged:

"Another piece of pork? Some more *kvass?*" She herself neither ate nor drank. Her face was ashen white. Her eyes were fastened on Gavrelo, who sat at the side of Simyonka's father. At the other table Gavrelo, urged by Simyonka's father, had drunk deeply. This was the second time in his life he had drunk. His face was purple, he talked incoherently, and he sat gazing about him helplessly, as if he could not make out what had happened to him. Simyonka's father was leaning on the table to keep

his balance; but being accustomed to vodka he had not
quite lost his wits.

"You— you half a fine stock of cattle," he told Gavrelo,
dealing him a complimentary blow on the back. "You half
fine cowsh!"

Gavrelo threw his head back to drain a glassful, and drew
it back with difficulty, then sat swaying.

"Fine cowsh," mumbled Simyonka's father. Gavrelo
turned his head and eyed his new relative with a vacant
stare. Then came the dreaded question. Katherina,
watching from her table, sat as still as if cut from stone.

"What—what ish Natalka's portion, Gavrelo?" Many
bleared eyes were turned on Gavrelo. This would be the
first time Gavrelo had given anything in his life. Some of
the villagers actually sobered for a moment and stared.

"Natalka's portion?" Simyonka's father insisted with
drunken stubbornness.

Suddenly Katherina's face turned from its ashen pallor
to a live red. Oh, yes! Yes! She would! Why not?
She would do it, yes, she would! Or why would it have
come into her head? Could it be that the Sacred Mother
had not forgotten her? She sat a moment staring stupidly,
then rose quickly, elbowed her way to her husband and
stood at his side.

"Natalka's portion?" Simyonka's father clamored with
piggish persistence. His voice rose to a squeal. Katherina
bent over Gavrelo and whispered.

"Say Parshuchuck."

"Parshuchuck," Gavrelo repeated, and looked up at her
as though he were trying to recognize her.

"Natalka's portion a pig!" the father-in-law called out
to the guests.

"And Chulka," Katherina again whispered to her husband. Gavrelo stared at her doubtfully, but repeated
"Chulka."

"And the large field of wheat," Katherina urged hoarsely.

"Wheat!" repeated Gavrelo. His head fell forward and
his mouth dripped water.

"Three pishes!" Simyonka's father bawled out.

"Three pieces!" It was repeated around the yard.

"Simyonka! You lucky hound!" a young man shrieked. All were now staring, eyes bleared, at the three. Natalka came over to her mother. Her face looked white and scared.

"*Matushka!*" she exclaimed, "what have you done?" And Katherina suddenly realized that Natalka had known all along that her father would give her nothing.

"It is all right," Katherina said. "Go dance. Go. But tell Simyonka to come and fetch his father-in-law to a cool place. And Natalka—you better tell Simyonka to take the pig and the heifer tonight. The wheat you will get in the fall."

"But, *Matushka*——"

"It is all right, Natalka. You know your father is a man of his word. Go dance."

A few minutes later Gavrelo lay stretched on a bench in the cool, dim outhouse. Natalka and Simyonka were congratulated on their generous portion. New quadrilles were formed, a new jig was being danced. Katherina went back and sat among her guests. And as she clapped her hands for the dancers she wondered, "And what about the morrow? Will he think he did it of his own accord, or will he remember?" But what mattered the morrow? Just now Anulia Addom was screaming into her grandmother's deaf ear:

"Natalka received three things, *Babushka;* you hear me, three things!" And Katherina clapped.

"Trala-lala-lala-lala."

"Ach, they were wise after all, those men," she thought; "they were wise who said that it is better to have a relative rich though a miser than one who is poor and generous. The miser, sooner or later, in one way or another, you may overcome. It is poverty that is like unto death."

THE SHAME OF GOLD[1]

By CHARLES J. FINGER

(From *The Century*)

"L'INTRANSIGEANT" recently printed a short account of the failure of the Franco-Brazilian ornithological expedition. Reading, you may have caught a hint of tragedy in it; but it may have escaped you, because our papers barely noticed the matter. I was specially interested because of a conversation I had had with a stranger who knew Brazil in a peculiar way.

Knowing Columbus, Ohio, you cannot fail to remember the place where the C. D. & M. Traction crosses the main business street. It is crowded at the corner, for a newspaper office is there, and bulletins of the world happenings are posted every hour or so. On the day that I have in mind, Hall and I paused there for a moment. A new bulletin was being put up, which read:

Franco-Brazilian expedition formed to explore upper Amazon territory.

Hall made a remark laughingly as to new markets to exploit, and hurried on his way to meet his investment broker; but I, gazing upward, unaware of his disappearance, said:

"Yes, there are still spots on this little world untrodden by the foot of man."

Turning, I discovered his absence, while from another man who stood where he had been came the words, very decidedly:

"I doubt it."

"But why?" I asked, mildly interested.

"Good reason," he replied, with a little shrug of his shoulders. There was a moment of hesitation, then, simultaneously, we both started off in the same direction, and

[1] Copyright, 1922, by The Century Company.
Copyright, 1923, by Charles J. Finger.

for half a block walked almost side by side. At a word it transpired that we were both bound for the depot, for the Cincinnati train.

Later, on the train, he resumed the subject. "I know Brazil a little," he said, "and far out of the beaten track, but I know it superficially. Others have been there—many others, and their lines are crossed and crisscrossed."

"White men?" I asked.

"Certainly, white men. That's how I was surprised into the remark I made there at the bulletin-board. Men poke everywhere about the world." The man sketched out roughly on the palm of his hand, and with his pipe-stem, an imaginary map. "You recall the outline of South America," he went on, "nearly pear-shaped, an elongated pear. Now, here is Peru, a little above the base of my thumb. Over here, under the little finger, is Cape St. Roque. I have been here. Cut across like this." He drew a bold stroke entirely across his hand. "That means Callao, into the Andes, and so north. North to strike the head-waters of the Amazon, and then trouble, fever and hunger. Wealth, too, in a way."

"Love of adventure?" I hazarded.

He regarded me intently for a moment. I noticed his iron-gray hair and queerly wrinkled face. He was not yet middle-aged.

"No. I never tried to analyze. I don't know. I'm not really adventurous. I like to be alone. Also, I drift, perhaps. When in a crowd, nothing seems to be worth while, and one is an ant in a hurrying mass. Alone, thoughts come with force. They strike one as bluntly as seen things impress themselves. I can't explain."

I was unwilling to press him with questions. He was not the kind of man that could be drawn out. When he spoke again there was a note of quiet, pleasant excitement.

"By the way, in Prescott's 'Peru' there is a passage somewhere telling of one party of Spaniards crossing the Andes and discovering silver. Then, being unable to get back, they built a boat and floated down the Amazon, and presently turned up in Cuba again. It's there somewhere. Or in Irving. In Prescott, I think."

I told him that I had a faint recollection of something like that.

"Well," he continued, paying little heed, "that was, roughly, four hundred years ago. No modern things to use, no chart, no map, no compass, no tools, or camp paraphernalia; just plain, dogged go-at-it and keep on. Keep in one direction, and you get somewhere. That's how Magellan felt his way, and Columbus his. Then the old Norsemen in open boats. It excites me thinking of that. It was always that way, one man pushing on."

Again he lapsed into one of his ruminating moods.

"But about Prescott— Once I was nearly all in. Over the Andes I'd gone, and if I didn't hit the trail of the Pizarro men, I'm crazy. I never saw a helmet in my life until then, and I came across one under an overhanging rock. A mighty thing it was—the rock I mean—a kind of excavation under it that formed a cave.

"The helmet was there, and a few pieces of steel—short pieces; a broken sword, perhaps. I took the helmet and carried it for days, then threw it away. A man can't be burdened with plunder like that.

"You see, I'd been on the trail for more than three months that time. Now and then I caught sight of an Indian, and once I got an arrow through my left shoulder. There were days and weeks in which I saw no sign of human life, but, by George! there was plenty of good company. Insects, you know, great glorious things. Butterflies, too—butterflies that run and make a little noise like a rattle when they fly away. It's laughable. Living things are great fun to watch. And then the concerts at evening at sunset, crickets and things. I don't know their names. Magnify insects, and I reckon you'd have a fantastic world.

"When I did see a human face again, it gave me a start. I'd found a good spot in the jungle to rest in. The stream ran clear there, this stream I'd been following, and the bottom of it was sandy. One does not often find a place like that. Thinking of an ideal spot, you imagine a stream in the shade of a tree, with grass all about. But when you get your stream, there is often mud, and where there is shade there is no grass. Here there was everything; a pleasant kind of spot, and I didn't move all day. I just rested and smoked and bathed my feet and watched the insects. It was quiet, too, still as midnight, and the sun never pierced the leafy roof. It was just a great, green arch like a cathedral, with smooth, lofty tree-trunks, chamber after chamber of green, and, what was specially fine, the place was clear of lianas. So I rested there and read an old newspaper I had picked up in Callao and brought along. I'd read it before dozens of times. Then my eyes would tire of the print, and I'd doze off. I did that dozens of times. The peace of the place was too much for me—too much both ways. The perfectness of it overcame me, and drove me to the little thing, the silly newspaper.

"Once I woke with the notion that some one was watching me. What I saw gave me a shiver. There was a big flowering-bush not ten yards away. They were great red flowers, meat color, like raw beef, and right between two of the flowers, as if it was stuck in a cleft, was a man's face, snag-toothed, red-bearded, shock-haired. It might have been a great ape. The eyes stared straight at me. Remember, I'd seen no natives for a long while, nor was there a settlement near, and it was a region as big as the State of Illinois, and no white man, I thought, had ever set foot there. Yet here was a face, and it was not the face of a native. I knew enough to keep still, and only peered through the narrowest slits I could make with my eyelids, so I judged that the face in the flower would think I slept. Believe me, I watched closely.

"It moved my way, but cautiously as a snake, and I saw a hairy chest, a hairy human being, and stark. He came on hands and toes, and I knew that he was a fellow used to the jungle and no native. Noiselessly he came, not stirring leaf or blade, hardly. The smell of his body assailed me unpleasantly, for there were sweetly smelling spice-trees, and the human smell was rank as poison.

"I sat up suddenly when the fellow was not more than five yards away. He stopped, rigid, expectant. Fear was in his eyes. Perhaps he saw it in mine. In such cases men hate each other. Each resents the presence of the other where white men should not be. Then he rose to his feet, turned without a word, his feet making no sound, and made for the flowering-bush again. I knew in a moment, somehow, that he was ashamed of his nakedness in the presence of another of his race. So I hailed him. At that he stood, regarding me with doubt.

"Well, he was one of those queer fish found everywhere. He told me his tale that night. Of months and of years he had long lost count, and he wanted to know of things strange to me. Queer things he had been interested in, it seemed—a Londoner I guess, with the peculiar sharpness of interest in political things that they have. It must have been meat and drink to him, his interest in public affairs. He talked of Gladstone and wanted to know whether some fellow named O'Donnell who had killed some informer was hanged or not. From such things we located the date when he left as about 1883. So he had been there nearly thirty-five years. Think of it!

"But as to the unbelief of people who are credulous on some things—tell people that for that length of time a white man, an Englishman, had lived with savages, and every single one would jump to the conclusion that he was chief among them. Naturally. On the general principle, I suppose, that it is better to reign in hell than to serve in heaven. But was he king? Boss? Chief? Not by a long chalk. And naturally. The man from civilization was the servitor. The savages were the superiors. Such things as he once knew were useless in the wilds. Mind you, in civilization machinery is master, and man the servant of the machine. Take him away from the mechanical things and cast him on his own resources, and ninety-nine cases out of a hundred he starves. He can't make a fire, catch his food, build his shelter. He is afraid to test things as to their edibility. He cannot run, fight or climb. Among animals he is a weakling. Face to face with nature he despairs. His education he finds to be ignorance. His overpowering fear is that he may be hurt. You see, in civilization man is protected, he does not have to struggle. All that he needs to do is to sell himself, his time, his life, for the best price he can command. So he becomes soft. He is unfit for liberty. Turn him loose, and he is as useless as a

canary-bird or a common hen turned adrift. So was it
with this fellow, Elfner. The savages were his superiors,
and he was the servitor. He had ceased to concern himself about anything more than the needs of the body; and
his brain had gone. Once, I gathered, he had told them
tales of the city life, but the things he tried to picture they
could not conceive; so he was lowered still further in their
estimation and set down as a liar.

"From this Elfner I learned of the Chequa tribe. He
warned me against them as a vicious people that had no
dealings with other tribes, and indicated their valley as
farther east. That I was not to be led to his tribe was
made very clear. Obviously, he was ashamed of his degradation. But really it was not degradation in one way of
looking at it. There are almost no men who would not
rapidly find their level in a savage tribe, and that level
would be below its general average, because of the new
valuations that the man from civilization cannot compass.

"There was a stranger tale he began to tell me—a tale
of a swamp-land to the southeast and of monstrous, yellow
earth creatures that heaved themselves out of the mire.
Then I was sure he was crazed. I knew of the giant arma-
dillos and great sloths, but it was none of these. He was
loath to continue, and parried my questions. He wanted
to know of things in the world that he would never again
see. He wanted to tell me of John L. Sullivan and of Jake
Kilrain, or of sordid crimes that had interested him. Above
all he wanted to talk of eating, of ham and eggs, of bread
and cheese and beer. Once, for instance, when he had begun to tell me something of the Chequas, he broke off quite
unexpectedly, and apropos of nothing went into a little
rhapsody. 'Say,' he said, 'this 'ere is a dull place. I often
think of colors, and there's a bird all colors, and I always
think of when you hold a glass of whiskey up to the light.
Lord! Lord!' At that he fell into a reverie and sat
hunched, his chin on clenched fist. Then he grew melancholy. 'These 'ere fellers in my tribe, they got me goin',
they 'ave. It's work, work, work. An' if I don't, it's punishment tied up to a ant's nest.'

"His talk was jumbled, disjointed, and I had much ado

to get something from him relative to the country. Very little I got, after all. We had talked for perhaps a couple of hours when a ululation filled the air. 'It's them blacks callin' me,' he said, leaping to his feet. Now, while I was not anxious for his company, I felt an urge to invite him to go with me; but, to my relief, he refused on the ground that his masters would follow, capture and kill him. When the ululation was again heard, he seemed panic-stricken, stood a moment irresolute, then turned and fled into the bush as a dog would on hearing the insistent call."

The man stopped, and I hazarded the remark that it was strange to meet a white man thus, because the chances against an encounter were slight.

"That's so," he said.

"And the reference to those strange earth creatures. Didn't you learn anything further?"

He looked at me and shook his head doubtfully, and a little puzzled frown appeared and disappeared.

"No. But I may have seen one, too. I don't know."

"May I hear?" I asked.

"There's nothing to tell, because I'm not sure. And yet—" He passed his hand over his brow. "I may have been mistaken. It was after I had left the gentle people, and I was not myself then. I was worried, grieved, half-starved. It is all muddled.

"You see, after Elfner left I decided to find the valley he had told me of, and I did find it without any particular difficulty. It was a bird that attracted me, a quetzal. If I had not gone toward it, I might have missed the place. But I never could resist watching a quetzal, for it is the most wonderful thing that God has made, the most exquisite thing in creation. To see it, a living thing of metallic green—gold-green and scarlet-breasted, with tail-feathers of jet and ivory—is an experience. You watch it and lose yourself in admiration. Nothing else is so gorgeous. I have watched as the light struck them, and have seen them change from violet to steel-blue, but colors that live. Then the bird moves slightly, and the blue is blue-green, then again gold-green, and there are crimson flashes and purple. And there was the valley, and it was the valley of quetzals and butterflies, and in it lived the gentle people. I stayed there many months, peaceful months, only to leave in sorrow. A gentle people, indeed! Never did I hear a harsh word or see an ungentle thing. I do not think that they knew of war or of violence. To live was sweet in that valley of flowers and birds. There were sounds of living things as sweet as the musical ripples of a little brook, and the breeze was soft and laden with perfume. So I came to love the gentle people and their land.

"It may seem odd to tell you this, but I have told you much, and the mood is on me, and the place in which I tell it to you is odd, here where there is the noise of people and of the moving train and where there is glaring light or sooty smoke, and where every one is burdened with the stern anxiety of duty. And yet it all comes to me as the memory of a summer day may come to some poor fellow in prison—the memory of that spot where existence is facile and where trifles give joy and where people live as birds live. While there I knew a fresh vigor of soul. I always seemed to be on the point of grasping and understanding things, and the thought lived in me always that I should never do a thing to bring the sorrow of the outside world among this people. The memory is strong upon me now, and it came to me as a dull blow when I read the bulletin uptown. I felt as the prisoner might when the judge said the death sentence. It seemed to mean that, you know."

The man paused and relit his pipe. He gave a puff or two and laid it aside again. Then he leaned back in his seat, folded his arms and dropped his chin on his chest.

"All this noise about us must make what I tell you seem unreal. I appreciate that fully. Sometimes I think that out there I lost something well worth the losing, and found instead a precious thing. Looking back, I seemed to have touched the supernatural. I wonder if you understand. What I lost enriched me, and I seemed to have lost forever my own people and the sins of avarice and anger and pettiness. It was no illusion. There *was* the valley of peace. There *is* the valley of peace. But I fear the ravening hand now stretched out.

"There was a child there, a thing of beauty, who led me about at times after I had been accepted as a visitor. Endol was her name, and she was a dancing creature, who weaved circlets of flowers and often brought to me, laughingly, water to drink, bearing it in a flattish shell which held only a taste. I see her now, a bright fairy, dancing and chasing the cloud shadows on the green, playing with the birds, clapping her hands as she ran after butterflies, but never trying to catch them. Do you know, at such times the memory of my own land was as a dark and fearful dream. I remembered slum children. The memory of the things that clatter about us in houses and in cities, and the fret and the evil and the filth and the sickness—these things bore upon me and oppressed my spirit. Now, sitting here, remembering that valley of joy, it is as if I were in hell, and it is from that hell that I am trying to escape, for all has been dark and ugly since I left.

"One day Endol brought me a golden-colored flower, a new one to me. I saw that she bore a shell in her left hand. When I made a motion to take it she prevented me. Playfully, I held her, and as I did so, she chanced to tip the shell, and a yellowish sand poured forth and lay lightly on a large leaf. Looking, I saw that it was gold dust. At that Endol laughed, stooped, scattered the gold, and, gathering the grains that lay on the leaf, threw them afar.

"That naturally set me to wondering as well as wandering, for thus far I had confined my walks to the upper end of the valley. As it fell out, the next day I came upon a flat rock at the foot of a vine-hung tree, and there in plain view was a shell, much larger than that which Endol had had. It held gold dust, and a few nuggets, the best of them not larger than a small pea. The shell had apparently been set there and forgotten with the carelessness of a child tired of a plaything. The gold was not free from iron dust, but I saw at a glance that the vein from which it had been taken was extraordinarily rich. So it came to me to think that this people knew nothing of the value of gold and perhaps used it as a plaything. I suppose I should have left it there, but I did not. Few men living as you and I have lived in a workaday world could resist the temptation to bear it away. So I took it to the bower in which I slept.

"Now, Endol and another child met me on the way and, chattering and laughing, reached for the shell. I handed it to them. Their actions astonished me. They drew slightly aside; their merriment fell from them, and they held a rapid, whispered conference. Endol's friend, the older of the two, seemed the most urgent, and her counsel apparently prevailed, for they set off running down the valley with the gold. They seemed possessed of a new fear, one that I could not understand.

"Soon after they returned with others, men and women, and I could see that there was consternation. I was reminded of a crowd I once saw running to the pit-mouth when the news of trouble came.

"Sima, a handsome youth with a splendid head ornament of quetzal feathers, addressed me. He was gentle, almost persuasive. At first I could not understand what he was driving at. There were evidently references to a people and the setting sun, and in the midst of his discourse others came up and now and again tried to aid him in making me understand, as people will do all over the world when a foreigner is dense. Presently Sima ceased, and another, an older man, took up the parable. He grew excited in the telling of the tale and, as I gathered, was eager to impress upon me that there was an evil time when hate and murder and greed, until then unknown, had come into the land. But it was not until he roughly fashioned a cross with a couple of sticks and broke it to pieces that a light dawned on me. Then when he told me of white men from the north, it dawned upon me with clearness that here was a tribal memory of the coming of Pizarro into the land of the Incas. Understanding that, I could piece things together, the ancient wrong done to a gentle people in the name of the cross, the white man's greed for gold, which had been a specific cause of strife and disorder, the hopeless resistance of an unarmed people, and the cruel acts of retaliation. From another point of view I saw what the lust of empire meant, and I saw how those who preached civilization, philanthropy and religion came burning, shooting, destroying and subjugating the weak, the simple, the harmless. The forefathers of this people had escaped. What wonder, then, that to them gold stood as an evil, something to hide and thrust away as unclean lest its glitter again attract these who bear death in their hands.

"I saw all that in a flash, and I understood the vague sense of imminent chaos that must have possessed the simple, happy folk when they pondered on what might happen if gold-mad white men again came ravening. The wonder was that they did not slay me when first I came.

"The gold-bearing sand was exceptionally rich in the little river. Grubbing about, I found pockets in the bed-rock full of gold. I even amused myself for a time extracting some of it and piling it in little heaps here and there on stones, and once I dammed up a section of the stream, turning the current so as to expose the river-bed, thus laying bare a new and unexpected vein. But it meant nothing to me then, for I still enjoyed the sighing of the wind through the silky grass, the sweetness of the day, and the fullness of the earth. The water that dripped sparkling from my finger-tips was finer to me than the sifting gold.

"One day I found the cave. I had not found it before simply because I had not sought it. There was no attempt on the part of the folk to conceal its location, nor was there displayed any desire to keep me from it.

"It was an opening in a hillside almost six feet long and four high, a square, natural gap, and the chamber within was at least thirty by thirty. The rays of the western sun flooded the place. For over three hundred years, perhaps, the people had hidden their gold there. From that you may have some idea how things were. The stuff lay scattered over the floor of the cave. I worked my fingers through the gold near the opening, and it was knuckle-deep before I touched the rock. In the farther corner was a sloping heap of the stuff, and it had been there so long that the iron dust had blown away. It shone dully as the sun touched it. Here and there were small nuggets, some as large as a cherry. Leaving the cave, I found a pile of them, oddly shaped, laid along a large, flat rock. They

were evidently the playthings of children. I remember
noticing one, flattish and almost heart-shaped. It had a
hole through it, and I strung it and hung it round my
neck. Look at this."

As he spoke he fumbled at his soft shirt-collar and
pulled up a little nugget, which he handed to me.

"It's all I have to show," he said as he returned it to
its place. "That night I did not sleep. Strangely enough,
my mind took a twist. The life I was living fell behind
me, as it were, and I was filled with a new desire. It
was not really a desire for wealth, but rather a desire for
power. That was it, a desire for power. That old newspaper I told you of came to my mind, with all that it
stood for. I began to dream of walking into my native
town, into Hillsboro, and showing off. Crazy, isn't it?
But it was so. They were day-dreams that might have
pleased a boy, and it is almost too banal to tell, the rapid
succumbing to temptation. I had a vision of becoming the
local 'big man,' of buying out the banker, of building a
fine house, of owning a splendid automobile, of servants,
and all that kind of thing. Things! things! things! The
pageantry of wealth! So dreaming, the quiet of the valley
and the peace of it became a hateful thing, and I longed
for the sound of a thousand footsteps and a thousand
wheels, for the noise of streets, and the haste and the
clatter and the excitement. Gradually the idea took possession of me that the gold was mine and that it was a
weak sentimentality which would prevent a capable white
race from using that which a brown-skinned folk knew not
how to use. I planned and dreamed, planned and dreamed.
The poison was at work.

"Weeks and weeks it took me to carry the gold to the
hidden canoe. I thought at the time that I was unwatched,
but I do not think so now. Some of the stuff I loaded
direct from the river sand, but by far the greater part I
bore from the cave. Of course there were days when I
hesitated, half repenting. But, on the whole, greed had me.

"One day I saw Sima and Capaca, standing side by side,
looking at me, and I was suddenly overcome with shame.
There fell away from me my desire to leave. The glamor

faded. It was as if I had been discovered handling filth by those whose good opinion I valued, and the hot blood rushed tingling to my cheeks. I wanted to make my peace with the people again, but knew that to do so was hopeless now. So I stood irresolutely by my canoe, and I hated myself for my insincerity.

"Sima came down to me. He said no word, but, with a look half pity, half contempt, handed me his spear, and with a gesture dismissed me and turned his back. For a moment I wished that he had thrust the spear through me.

"So it was that I came to leave the valley where I had known peace, and from then time was for me little but physical weariness. There were days when I lay half-dead in the canoe on my bed of gold, tortured by flies and things that bit and stung—days and days of misery when I wished myself dead. Once, it seemed ages, a hovering cloud of insects followed me, sometimes settling on me so thickly that my arms were black. My bodily suffering was great, but greater still the suffering within.

"I think that day after day in that jungle drove me mad, and there were times when I was aware of nothing in the world but the rank smell of decaying vegetation and a black strip of water winding, winding, winding through a canon of dark brown earth through which great roots thrust themselves like snakes. Days of impenetrable gloom there were, and there were days when all about me there seemed to be hushings, then hissing whisperings and pointing fingers and peering eyes. Again there was a sensation that music was about me, and I seemed to hear at a distance the opening chords of a brass band. I knew that I was fever-stricken.

"Once I dared to land at a place where the virgin forest seemed to end. There was a great green, open space, a mighty clearing, and a fringe of trees between that and the river. I was the victim of a strange hallucination, and it was as if the whole world were moving swiftly to the right, swiftly, horribly swiftly, and I alone stood still. I fought against it, fought myself. Do you understand? It changed to a sensation of rushing backward. So dizzy I became that I was constrained to squat at the foot

of a tree, pushing against it hard with my back, and press
my temples until I felt the pain of it. Then I heard a
sound and looked up. I saw, or thought I saw, something.
The earth seemed to tremble and heave. Out from it came
swiftly a hideous thing, clay-colored and huge, a mighty
mass of living flesh. The mud fell from it to right and left.
I was breathless and unable to stir. The thing pushed
upward and forward with clumsy, lumbering movements,
side to side, extricating itself, growing huger each moment.
Then I realized that what I saw was only the head and
shoulders. The head turned slightly, so that I saw the
upper part of it, blunt and triangular beyond the shoulder.
The heavy-lidded eyes I saw. Then I noticed the mud
dripping heavily, and part of the fore leg coming from the
slime. My God! Send that there are no such things on
earth and that I was really mad!

"I remember rolling down the steep bank and falling into
the river, so shaded and still, and then there was an awe-
inspiring roar, dreadful to hear. I swam. I do not know.
I cannot talk of it."

The man sighed deeply. It was almost a stifled sob.
He was ashen-faced. When he spoke again, his voice was
perceptibly huskier.

"There is no more to tell," he said. "There were weeks
and weeks of misery in that jungle, and wanderings that
I forget—wanderings in the swamp lands, and most wonderfully I came to Mannos and, in time, to Para, where the
consul was good to me."

He ceased suddenly and fell to smoking. It was a long
time before I dared to speak, but said at last:

"And you propose to return?"

"I want to get back to the people, to where the superstition of gold is absent," he said. "Only there is the world
sane. Only there do people enjoy their days and love the
earth and know the beauty of life. Gold blinds all others.
So I must go to the gentle people again. That is, if they
will have me. Then there's this expedition."

His voice was tense now.

"Suppose. You see, once I might have been a traitor to
them. I dreamed of something of the sort, a betrayal to

my own people. If this expedition is a success— Well, where white people go and where there is gold, sorrow and disease and death follow. The consul at Para knew something of my story. Would it not be a good thing to save a race, a gentle people, from destruction?"

The man's story stayed with me. And, as I said, since learning of the failure of the expedition, I have wondered much.

TWO FOR A CENT[1]

By F. SCOTT FITZGERALD

(From *The Metropolitan*)

WHEN the rain was over the sky became yellow in the west and the air was cool. Close to the street, which was of red dirt and lined with cheap bungalows dating from 1910, a little boy was riding a big bicycle along the sidewalk. His plan afforded a monotonous fascination. He rode each time for about a hundred yards, dismounted, turned the bicycle around so that it adjoined a stone step and getting on again, not without toil or heat, retraced his course. At one end this was bounded by a colored girl of fourteen holding an anæmic baby, and at the other, by a scarred, ill-nourished kitten, squatting dismally on the curb. These four were the only souls in sight.

The little boy had accomplished an indefinite number of trips, oblivious alike to the melancholy advances of the kitten at one end and to the admiring vacuousness of the colored girl at the other, when he swerved dangerously to avoid a man who had turned the corner into the street, and recovered his balance only after a moment of exaggerated panic.

But if the incident was a matter of gravity to the boy, it attracted scarcely an instant's notice from the newcomer, who turned suddenly from the sidewalk and stared with obvious and peculiar interest at the house before which he was standing. It was the oldest house in the street, built with clapboards and a shingled roof. It was a *house*—in the barest sense of the word: the sort of house that a child would draw on a blackboard. It was of a period, but of no design, and its exterior had obviously been made only

[1] Copyright, 1922, by The Metropolitan Magazine Company.
Copyright, 1923, by F. Scott Fitzgerald.

as a decent cloak for what was within. It antedated the
stucco bungalows by about thirty years and except for the
bungalows, which were reproducing their species with pro-
digious avidity, as though by some monstrous affiliation
with the guinea-pig, it was the most common type of house
in the country. For thirty years such dwellings had satisfied the canons of the middle class; they had satisfied its
financial canons by being cheap, they had satisfied its
æsthetic canons by being hideous. It was a house built
by a race whose more energetic complement hoped either
to move up or move on, and it was the more remarkable
that its instability had survived so many summers and retained its pristine hideousness and discomfort so obviously
unimpaired.

The man was about as old as the house, that is to say,
about forty-five. But unlike the house, he was neither
hideous nor cheap. His clothes were too good to have been
made outside of a metropolis—moreover, they were so good
that it was impossible to tell in which metropolis they were
made. His name was Abercrombie and the most important
event of his life had taken place in the house before which
he was standing. He had been born there.

It was one of the last places in the world where he
should have been born. He had thought so within a very
few years after the event and he thought so now—an ugly
home in a third-rate southern town where his father had
owned a partnership in a grocery store. Since then Abercrombie had played golf with the President of the United
States and sat between two duchesses at dinner. He had
been bored with the President, he had been bored and not
a little embarrassed with the duchesses—nevertheless, the
two incidents had pleased him and still sat softly upon his
naïve vanity. It delighted him that he had gone far.

He had looked fixedly at the house for several minutes
before he perceived that no one lived there. Where the
shutters were not closed it was because there were no shutters to be closed, and in these vacancies, blind, vacuous
expanses of gray window looked unseeingly down at him.
The grass had grown wantonly long in the yard and faint
green mustaches were sprouting facetiously in the wide

cracks of the walk. But it was evident that the property had been recently occupied, for upon the porch lay half a dozen newspapers rolled into cylinders for quick delivery and as yet turned only to a faint, resentful yellow.

They were not nearly so yellow as the sky when Abercrombie walked up on the porch and sat down upon an immemorial bench, for the sky was every shade of yellow, the color of tan, the color of gold, the color of peaches. Across the street and beyond a vacant lot rose a rampart of vivid red brick houses and it seemed to Abercrombie that the picture they rounded out was beautiful—the warm, earthy brick and the sky fresh after the rain, changing and gray as a dream. All his life when he had wanted to rest his mind he had called up into it the image those two things had made for him when the air was clear just at this hour. So Abercrombie sat there thinking about his young days.

Ten minutes later another man turned the corner of the street, a different sort of man, both in the texture of his clothes and the texture of his soul. He was forty-six years old and he was a shabby drudge, married to a woman, who, as a girl, had known better days. This latter fact, in the republic, may be set down in the red italics of misery.

His name was Hemmick—Henry W. or George D. or John F.—the stock that produced him had had little imagination left to waste either upon his name or his design. He was a clerk in a factory which made ice for the long southern summer. He was responsible to the man who owned the patent for canning ice, who, in his turn was responsible only to God. Never in his life had Henry W. Hemmick discovered a new way to advertise canned ice nor had it transpired that by taking a diligent correspondence course in ice canning he had secretly been preparing himself for a partnership. Never had he rushed home to his wife, crying: "You can have that servant now, Nell, I have been made general superintendent." You will have to take him as you take Abercrombie, for what he is and will always be. This is a story of the dead years.

When the second man reached the house he turned in

and began to mount the tipsy steps, noticed Abercrombie, the stranger, with a tired surprise, and nodded to him.

"Good evening," he said.

Abercrombie voiced his agreement with the sentiment.

"Cool"—the newcomer covered his forefinger with his handkerchief and sent the swatched digit on a complete circuit of his collar band. "Have you rented this?" he asked.

"No, indeed, I'm just—resting. Sorry if I've intruded —I saw the house was vacant——"

"Oh, you're not intruding!" said Hemmick hastily. "I don't reckon anybody *could* intrude in this old barn. I got out two months ago. They're not ever goin' to rent it any more. I got a little girl about this high," he held his hand parallel to the ground and at an indeterminate distance, "and she's mighty fond of an old doll that got left here when we moved. Began hollerin' for me to come over and look it up."

"You used to live here?" inquired Abercrombie with interest.

"Lived here eighteen years. Came here 'n I was married, raised four children in this house. Yes, *sir*. I know this old fellow." He struck the door-post with the flat of his hand. "I know every leak in her roof and every loose board in her old floor."

Abercrombie had been good to look at for so many years that he knew if he kept a certain attentive expression on his face his companion would continue to talk—indefinitely.

"You from up north?" inquired Hemmick politely, choosing with habituated precision the one spot where the anæmic wooden railing would support his weight. "I thought so," he resumed at Abercrombie's nod. "Don't take long to tell a Yankee."

"I'm from New York."

"So?" The man shook his head with inappropriate gravity. "Never have got up there, myself. Started to go a couple of times, before I was married, but never did get to go."

He made a second excursion with his finger and handkerchief and then, as though having come suddenly to a cordial decision, he replaced the handkerchief in one of his bumpy pockets and extended the hand toward his companion.

"My name's Hemmick."

"Glad to know you." Abercrombie took the hand without rising. "Abercrombie's mine."

"I'm mighty glad to know you, Mr. Abercrombie."

Then for a moment they both hesitated, their two faces assumed oddly similar expressions, their eyebrows drew together, their eyes looked far away. Each was straining to force into activity some minute cell long sealed and forgotten in his brain. Each made a little noise in his throat, looked away, looked back, laughed. Abercrombie spoke first.

"We've met."

"I know," agreed Hemmick, "but whereabouts? That's what's got me. You from New York, you say?"

"Yes, but I was born and raised in this town. Lived in this house till I left here when I was about seventeen. As a matter of fact, I remember you—you were a couple of years older."

Again Hemmick considered.

"Well," he said vaguely, "I sort of remember, too. I *begin* to remember—I got your name all right and I guess maybe it was your daddy had this house before I rented it. But all I can recollect about you is, that there was a boy named Abercrombie and he went away."

In a few moments they were talking easily. It amused them both to have come from the same house—amused Abercrombie especially, for he was a vain man, rather absorbed that evening in his own early poverty. Though he was not given to immature impulses he found it necessary somehow to make it clear in a few sentences that five years after he had gone away from the house and the town he had been able to send for his father and mother to join him in New York.

Hemmick listened with that exaggerated attention which men who have not prospered generally render to men who have. He would have continued to listen had Abercrombie become more expansive, for he was beginning faintly to associate him with an Abercrombie who had figured in the newspapers for several years at the head of shipping boards and financial committees. But Abercrombie, after a moment, made the conversation less personal.

"I didn't realize you had so much heat here, I guess I've forgotten a lot in twenty-five years."

"Why, this is a *cool* day," boasted Hemmick, "this is *cool*. I was just sort of overheated from walking when I came up."

"It's too hot," insisted Abercrombie with a restless movement; then he added abruptly, "I don't like it here. It means nothing to me—nothing—I've wondered if I did, you know, that's why I came down. And I've decided.

"You see," he continued hesitantly, "up to recently the North was still full of professional Southerners, some real, some by sentiment, but all given to flowery monologues on the beauty of their old family plantations and all jumping up and howling when the band played 'Dixie.' You know what I mean," he turned to Hemmick, "it got to be a sort of a national joke. Oh, I was in the game, too, I suppose, I used to stand up and perspire and cheer, and I've given young men positions for no particular reason except that they claimed to come from South Carolina or Virgina—" again he broke off and became suddenly abrupt, "but I'm through, I've been here six hours and I'm through!"

"Too hot for you?" inquired Hemmick, with mild surprise.

"Yes! I've felt the heat and I've seen the men—those two or three dozen loafers standing in front of the stores on Jackson Street—in thatched straw hats." Then he added, with a touch of humor, "They're what my son calls 'slash-pocket, belted-back boys.' Do you know the ones I mean?"

"Jelly-beans," Hemmick nodded gravely, "We call 'em Jelly-beans. No-account lot of boys all right. They got signs up in front of most of the stores asking 'em not to stand there."

"They ought to!" asserted Abercrombie, with a touch of irascibility. "That's my picture of the South, now, you know—a skinny, dark-haired young man with a gun on his hip and a stomach full of corn liquor or Dope Dola, leaning up against a drug store waiting for the next lynching."

Hemmick objected, though with apology in his voice. "You got to remember, Mr. Abercrombie, that we haven't had the money down here since the war——"

Abercrombie waved this impatiently aside.

"Oh, I've heard all that," he said, "and I'm tired of it. And I've heard the South lambasted till I'm tired of that, too. It's not taking France and Germany fifty years to get on their feet, and their war made your war look like a little fracas up an alley. And it's not your fault and it's not anybody's fault. It's just that this is too damn hot to be a white man's country and it always will be. I'd like to see 'em pack two or three of these states full of darkies and drop 'em out of the Union."

Hemmick nodded, thoughtfully, though without thought. He had never thought; for over twenty years he had seldom ever held opinions, save the opinions of the local press or of some majority made articulate through passion. There was a certain luxury in thinking that he had never been able to afford. When cases were set before him he either accepted them outright, if they were comprehensible to him, or rejected them if they required a modicum of concentration. Yet he was not a stupid man. He was poor and busy and tired and there were no ideas at large in his community, even had he been capable of grasping them. The idea that he did not think would have been equally incomprehensible to him. He was a closed book, half full of badly printed, uncorrelated trash.

Just now, his reaction to Abercrombie's assertion was exceedingly simple. Since the remarks proceeded from a man who was a Southerner by birth, who was successful—moreover, who was confident and decisive and persuasive and suave—he was inclined to accept them without suspicion or resentment.

He took one of Abercrombie's cigars and pulling on it, still with a stern imitation of profundity upon his tired face, watched the color glide out of the sky and the gray veils come down. The little boy and his bicycle, the baby, the nursemaid, the forlorn kitten, all had departed. In the stucco bungalows pianos gave out hot, weary notes that inspired the crickets to competitive sound, and squeaky graphophones filled in the intervals with patches of whining ragtime until the impression was created that each living room in the street opened directly out into the darkness.

"What *I* want to find out," Abercrombie was saying with a frown, "is why I didn't have sense enough to *know* that this was a worthless town. It was entirely an accident that I left here, an utterly blind chance, and as it happened, the very train that took me away was full of luck for me. The man I sat beside gave me my start in life." His tone became resentful. "But I thought this was all right. I'd have stayed except that I'd gotten into a scrape down at the high school—I got expelled and my daddy told me he didn't want me at home any more. Why didn't I know the place wasn't any good? Why I didn't *see?*"

"Well, you'd probably never known anything better?" suggested Hemmick mildly.

"That wasn't any excuse," insisted Abercrombie. "If I'd been any good I'd have known. As a matter of fact— as—a—matter—of—fact," he repeated slowly, "I think that at heart I was the sort of boy who'd have lived and died here happily and never known there was anything better." He turned to Hemmick with a look almost of distress. "It worries me to think that my—that what's happened to me can be ascribed to chance. But that's the sort of boy I think I was. I didn't start off with the Dick Whittington idea—I started off by accident."

After this confession he stared out into the twilight with a dejected expression that Hemmick could not understand. It was impossible for the latter to share any sense of the importance of such a distinction—in fact, from a man of Abercrombie's position it struck him as unnecessarily trivial. Still, he felt that some manifestation of acquiescence was only polite.

"Well," he offered, "it's just that some boys get the bee to get up and go North and some boys don't. I happened to have the bee to go North. But I didn't. That's the difference between you and me."

Abercrombie turned to him intently.

"You did?" he asked, with unexpected interest, "you wanted to get out?"

"At one time." At Abercrombie's eagerness Hemmick began to attach a new importance to the subject. "At one time," he repeated, as though the singleness of the occasion was a thing he had often mused upon.

"How old were you?"

"Oh—'bout twenty."

"What put it into your head?"

"Well, let me see—" Hemmick considered. "I don't know whether I remember sure enough, but it seems to me that when I was down to the University—I was there two years—one of the professors told me that a smart boy ought to go North. He said, business wasn't going to amount to much down here for the next fifty years. And I guessed he was right. My father died about then, so I got a job as runner in the bank here, and I didn't have much interest in anything except saving up enough money to go North. I was bound I'd go."

"Why didn't you? Why didn't you?" insisted Abercrombie in an aggrieved tone.

"Well," Hemmick hesitated, "Well, I right near did but —things didn't work out and I didn't get to go. It was a funny sort of business. It all started about the smallest thing you can think of. It all started about a penny."

"A penny?"

"That's what did it—one little penny. That's why I didn't go 'way from here and all, like I intended."

"Tell me about it, man," exclaimed his companion. He looked at his watch impatiently. "I'd like to hear the story."

Hemmick sat for a moment, distorting his mouth around the cigar.

"Well, to begin with," he said at length, "I'm going to ask you if you remember a thing that happened here about twenty-five years ago. A fellow named Hoyt, the cashier of the Cotton National Bank, disappeared one night with about thirty thousand dollars in cash. Say, man, they didn't talk about anything else down here at the time. The whole town was shaken up about it, and I reckin you can imagine the disturbance it caused down at all the banks and especially at the Cotton National."

"I remember."

"Well, they caught him, and they got most of the money back, and by and by the excitement died down, except in the bank where the thing had happened. Down there it seemed as if they'd never get used to it. Mr. Deems, the first vice-president, who'd always been pretty kind and decent, got to be a changed man. He was suspicious of the clerks, the tellers, the janitor, the watchman, most of the officers, and yes, by golly, I guess he got so he kept an eye on the president himself.

"I don't mean he was just watchful—he was downright hipped on the subject. He'd come up and ask you funny questions when you were going about your business. He'd walk into the teller's cage on tip-toe and watch him without saying anything. If there was any mistake of any kind in the bookkeeping, he'd not only fire a clerk or so, but he'd raise such a riot that he made you want to push him into a vault and slam the door on him.

"He was just about running the bank then, and he'd affected the other officers, and—oh, you can imagine the havoc a thing like that could work on any sort of an organization. Everybody was so nervous that they made mistakes whether they were careful or not. Clerks were staying downtown until eleven at night trying to account for a lost nickel. It was a thin year, anyhow, and everything financial was pretty rickety, so one thing worked on another until the crowd of us were as near craziness as anybody can be and carry on the banking business at all.

"I was a runner—and all through the heat of one God-forsaken summer I ran. I ran and I got mighty little money for it, and that was the time I hated that bank and this town, and all I wanted was to get out and go North. I was getting ten dollars a week, and I'd decided that when I'd saved fifty out of it I was going down to the depot and buy me a ticket to Cincinnati. I had an uncle in the banking business there, and he said he'd give me an opportunity with him. But he never offered to pay my way, and I guess he thought if I was worth having I'd manage to get up there by myself. Well, maybe I wasn't worth having because, anyhow, I never did.

"One morning, on the hottest day of the hottest July I ever knew—and you know what that means down here—I left the bank to call on a man named Harlan and collect some money that 'd come due on a note. Harlan had the cash waiting for me all right, and when I counted it I found it amounted to three hundred dollars and eighty-six cents, the change being in brand new coin that Harlan had drawn from another bank that morning. I put the three one-hundred-dollar bills in my wallet and the change in my vest pocket, signed a receipt and left. I was going straight back to the bank.

"Outside the heat was terrible. It was enough to make you dizzy, and I hadn't been feeling right for a couple of days, so, while I waited in the shade for a street-car, I was congratulating myself that in a month or so I'd be out of this and up where it was some cooler. And then, as I stood there, it occurred to me all of a sudden that outside of the money which I'd just collected, which, of course, I couldn't touch, I didn't have a cent in my pocket. I'd have to walk back to the bank, and it was about fifteen blocks away. You see, on the night before, I'd found that my change came to just a dollar, and I'd traded it for a bill at the corner store and added it to the roll in the bottom of my trunk. So there was no help for it—I took off my coat and I stuck my hankerchief into my collar and struck off through the suffocating heat for the bank.

"Fifteen blocks—you can imagine what that was like, and I was sick when I started. From away up by Juniper Street—you remember where that is; the new Mieger Hospital's there now—all the way down to Jackson. After about six blocks I began to stop and rest whenever I found a patch of shade wide enough to hold me, and as I got pretty near I could just keep going by thinking of the big glass of iced tea my mother 'd have waiting beside my plate at lunch. But after that I began getting too sick

to even want the iced tea—I wanted to get rid of that
money and then lie down and die.

"When I was still about two blocks away from the bank
I put my hand into my watch pocket and pulled out that
change; was sort of jingling it in my hand; making myself
believe that I was so close that it was convenient to have it
ready. I happened to glance into my hand, and all of a
sudden I stopped up short and reached down quick into
my watch pocket. The pocket was empty. There was a
little hole in the bottom, and my hand held only a half-
dollar, a quarter and a dime. I had lost one cent.

"Well, sir, I can't tell you, I can't express to you the feeling of discouragement that this gave me. One penny, mind
you—but think; just the week before a runner had lost his
job because he was a little bit shy twice. It was only carelessness; but there you were! They were all in a panic
that they might get fired themselves, and the best thing
to do was to fire some one else—first.

"So you can see that it was up to me to appear with
that penny.

"Where I got the energy to care as much about it as I
did is more than I can understand. I was sick and hot and
weak as a kitten, but it never occurred to me that I could
do anything except find or replace that penny, and immediately I began casting about for a way to do it. I looked
into a couple of stores, hoping I'd see some one I knew,
but while there were a few fellows loafing in front, just as
you saw them today, there wasn't one that I felt like going
up to and saying: 'Here! You got a penny?' I thought
of a couple of offices where I could have gotten it without
much trouble, but they were some distance off, and besides
being pretty dizzy, I hated to go out of my route when I
was carrying bank money, because it looked kind of strange.

"So what should I do but commence walking back along
the street toward the Union Depot where I last remembered
having the penny. It was a brand new penny, and I
thought maybe I'd see it shining where it dropped. So I
kept walking, looking pretty carefully at the sidewalk and
thinking what I'd better do. I laughed a little, because I
felt sort of silly for worrying about a penny, but I didn't

enjoy laughing, and it really didn't seem silly to me at
all.

"Well, by and by I got back to the Union Depot without
having either seen the old penny or having thought what
was the best way to get another. I hated to go all the
way home, 'cause we lived a long distance out; but what
else was I to do? So I found a piece of shade close to the
depot, and stood there considering, thinking first one thing
and then another, and not getting anywhere at all. One
little penny, just *one*—something almost any man in sight
would have given me; something even the nigger baggage-
smashers were jingling around in their pockets. . . . I must
have stood there about five minutes. I remember there
was a line of about a dozen men in front of an army
recruiting station they'd just opened, and a couple of them
began to yell: 'Join the Army!' at me. That woke me up,
and I moved on back toward the bank, getting worried now,
getting mixed up and sicker and sicker and knowing a million ways to find a penny and not one that seemed convenient or right. I was exaggerating the importance of
losing it, and I was exaggerating the difficulty of finding
another, but you just have to believe that it seemed about
as important to me just then as though it were a hundred
dollars.

"Then I saw a couple of men talking in front of Moody's
soda place, and recognized one of them—Mr. Burling—
who'd been a friend of my father's. That was relief, I can
tell you. Before I knew it I was chattering to him so quick
that he couldn't follow what I was getting at.

" 'Now,' he said, 'you know I'm a little deaf and can't
understand when you talk that fast! What is it you want,
Henry? Tell me from the beginning.'

" 'Have you got any change with you?' I asked him just
as loud as I dared. 'I just want—' Then I stopped short;
a man a few feet away had turned around and was looking
at us. It was Mr. Deems, the first vice-president of the
Cotton National Bank."

Hemmick paused, and it was still light enough for Abercrombie to see that he was shaking his head to and fro in a
puzzled way. When he spoke his voice held a quality of

pained surprise, a quality that it might have carried over
twenty years.

"I never *could* understand what it was that came over
me then. I must have been sort of crazy with the heat—
that's all I can decide. Instead of just saying 'Howdy' to
Mr. Deems, in a natural way, and telling Mr. Burling I
wanted to borrow a nickel for tobacco, because I'd left
my purse at home, I turned away quick as a flash and
began walking up the street at a great rate, feeling like a
criminal who had come near being caught.

"Before I'd gone a block I was sorry. I could almost
hear the conversation that must 've been taking place between those two men:

" 'What do you reckon 's the matter with that young
man?' Mr. Burling would say, without meaning any harm.
'Came up to me all excited and wanted to know if I had
any money, and then he saw you and rushed away like he
was crazy.'

"And I could almost see Mr. Deems' big eyes get narrow with suspicion and watch him twist up his trousers and
come strolling along after me. I was in a real panic now,
and no mistake. Suddenly I saw a one-horse surrey going
by, and recognized Bill Kennedy, a friend of mine, driving
it. I yelled at him, but he didn't hear me. Then I yelled
again, but he didn't pay any attention, so I started after
him at a run, swaying from side to side, I guess, like I was
drunk, and calling his name every few minutes. He looked
around once, but he didn't see me; he kept right on going
and turned out of sight at the next corner. I stopped then,
because I was too weak to go any farther. I was just
about to sit down on the curb and rest when I looked
around, and the first thing I saw was Mr. Deems walking
after me as fast as he could come. There wasn't any of
my imagination about it this time—the look in his eyes
showed he wanted to know what was the matter with *me!*

"Well, that's about all I can remember clearly until
about twenty minutes later, when I was at home trying to
unlock my trunk with fingers that were trembling like a
tuning fork. Before I could get it open, Mr. Deems and a
policeman came in. I began talking all at once about not

being a thief and trying to tell them what had happened, but I guess I was sort of hysterical, and the more I said the worse matters were. When I managed to get the story out it seemed sort of crazy, even to me—and it was true—it was true, true as I've told you—every word!—that one penny that I lost somewhere down by the station—" Hemmick broke off and began laughing grotesquely—as though the excitement that had come over him as he finished his tale was a weakness of which he was ashamed. When he resumed it was with an affectation of nonchalance.

"I'm not going into the details of what happened, because nothing much did—at least, not on the scale you judge events by up North. It cost me my job, and I changed a good name for a bad one. Somebody tattled and somebody lied, and the impression got around that I'd lost a lot of the bank's money and had been tryin' to cover it up.

"I had an awful time getting a job after that. Finally I got a statement out of the bank that contradicted the wildest of the stories that had started, but the people who were still interested said it was just because the bank didn't want any fuss or scandal—and the rest had forgotten: that is, they 'd forgotten what had happened, but they remembered that somehow I just wasn't a young fellow to be trusted——"

Hemmick paused and laughed again, still without enjoyment, but bitterly, uncomprehendingly, and with a profound helplessness.

"So, you see, that's why I didn't go to Cincinnati," he said slowly; "my mother was alive then, and this was a pretty bad blow to her. She had an idea—one of those old-fashioned Southern ideas that stick in people's heads down here—that somehow I ought to stay here in town and prove myself honest. She had it on her mind, and she wouldn't hear of my going. She said that the day I went 'd be the day she'd die. So I sort of had to stay till I'd got back my—my reputation."

"How long did that take?" asked Abercrombie quietly.

"About—ten years."

"Oh——"

"Ten years," repeated Hemmick, staring out into the gathering darkness. "This is a little town you see: I say ten years because it was about ten years when the last reference to it came to my ears. But I was married long before that; had a kid. Cincinnati was out of my mind by that time."

"Of course," agreed Abercrombie.

They were both silent for a moment—then Hemmick added apologetically:

"That was sort of a long story, and I don't know if it could have interested you much. But you asked me——"

"It *did* interest me," answered Abercrombie politely. "It interested me tremendously. It interested me much more than I thought it would."

It occurred to Hemmick that he himself had never realized what a curious, rounded tale it was. He saw dimly now that what had seemed to him only a fragment, a grotesque interlude was really significant, complete. It was an interesting story; it was the story upon which turned the failure of his life. Abercrombie's voice broke in upon his thoughts.

"You see, it's so different from my story," Abercrombie was saying. "It was an accident that you stayed—and it was an accident that I went away. You deserve more actual—actual credit, if there is such a thing in the world, for your intention of getting out and getting on. You see, I'd more or less gone wrong at seventeen. I was—well, what you call a Jelly-bean. All I wanted was to take it easy through life—and one day I just happened to see a sign up above my head that had on it: 'Special rate to Atlanta, three dollars and forty-two cents.' So I took out my change and counted it——"

Hemmick nodded. Still absorbed in his own story, he had forgotten the importance, the comparative magnificence of Abercrombie. Then suddenly he found himself listening sharply:

"I had just three dollars and forty-one cents in my pocket. But, you see, I was standing in line with a lot of other young fellows down by the Union Depot about to enlist in the army for three years. And I saw that extra penny on the walk not three feet away. I saw it because it was brand new and shining in the sun like gold."

The Georgia night had settled over the street, and as the blue drew down upon the dust the outlines of the two men had become less distinct, so that it was not easy for any one who passed along the walk to tell that one of these men was of the few and the other of no importance. All the detail was gone—Abercrombie's fine gold wrist watch, his collar, that he ordered by the dozen from London, the dignity that sat upon him in his chair—all faded and were engulfed with Hemmick's awkward suit and preposterous humped shoes into that pervasive depth of night that, like death, made nothing matter, nothing differentiate, nothing remain. And a little later on a passerby saw only the two glowing disks about the size of a penny that marked the rise and fall of their cigars.

JOHN THE BAPTIST[1]

By WALDO FRANK

(From *The Dial*)

THE room was bright with the sun. Three stories up.
Three dark halls, three worn stairs, the mustiness of
walls to which grimed hands, worn shoulders had rubbed
their intricate soiled burden, held up this room that was
all bright with the sun.

The door was open: two windows with their mesh Dutch
curtains were thrown high: Clara Jones dusted.

She was a short woman, colored a dark brown in which
were shadows of blue and orange. She was of indeterminate age. She worked slowly, diligently, with a sort of submissive rhythm to the sweep of her arms, the sway of her
head, as if an invisible Master timed her work with gentle
strokes on her bent back. The contours and objects of
the room were a familiar haze against her hands. Her eyes
did not take in the books upon the mantel, the morris
chair which her hands groomed and shifted, the blue cover
of the couch which the room's tenant used for a bed. Her
eyes were focused dimly beyond the room, beyond the
sunlight also that did not make them blink—beyond the
sun. At times a murmur as of words answering in herself,
a shred of tune, came from her. And these were in unison
with the rapt measure of her work. And it with the distant
fixedness of her eyes that moved as if to remain upon some
point either far within or far without herself. Or both. . . .

A tall young man . . . almost a boy . . . stood in the
door. He buttressed both his palms against the threshold's
sides: he watched her.

Her face turned to her shoulder, then fell forwards back
into its somnolent rhythm.

"Lor'! that you already? You-all *quick* this mo'nin'."

[1] Copyright, 1922, by The Dial Publishing Company, Inc.
Copyright, 1922, by Waldo Frank.

"May I come in?"

"Sho'ly, sho'ly. Sit down over th'ah."

She did not stop. She held a broom in her two brown hands. With a steady stroke of shoulder, back and forth it went, rasping . . . swinging; her small, soft body cadenced with its stiff advance.

"Th'ah you are, Mr. Loer!" She waved a musty rag over his desk, over a picture nailed above it. "Th'ah you are."

She turned and smiled at him. He was still standing in the threshold. She had a round, small face, and her big mouth smiling seemed to cover it. Her eyes still focused distantly.

She dropped the broom against a shoulder and flung the rag into the fold of an elbow. She laughed.

"What yo' got, this mo'nin'? I'm done. Come along in."

"I don't feel like being alone this morning, Clara."

Clara's smile was tender. Her face tilted to a side.

"Lonely, Mr. Loer?" she said. He felt caressed.

"Oh, no." He stepped into the room, lifting his knees unnecessarily high. He sank down in the morris chair and primed a pipe.

"Clara," he seemed to hold her, "how'd you sleep last night?"

She folded her hands.

"Oh, fine, Mr. Loer. You know I always sleeps fine."

"Well I slept rotten."

"I wouldn't sleep none at all, Mr. Loer . . . ef I went to sleep same as you does."

He looked up from his pipe. "What do you mean?"

" 'Thout prayin'. Yo' tole me so yo'self. No wonder you sleep rotten. Lor'! I wouldn't sleep none at all . . . ef . . . I went to sleep 'thout prayin'." She paused. "Watch out, Mr. Loer," she said with a sweet tremulousness. "Supposin' the time comes when you cyant sleep at all."

"I don't know whom to pray to."

The old woman looked at the broomstick standing against her shoulder.

"And you so—eddicated," she declared.

She ambled out, still keyed to that impalpable warm measure kindling her feet, her hips, the drone of her soft voice.

The door's gentle click made him alone.

He relaxed forward in his chair. Crumpled hands held his sharp, fine chin. His eyes were disturbed. They wandered. They saw his room: sharply each object in his room caught in his eyes and held there. His eyes were hurt because they saw no farther.

He jumped up, flung his coat. He ran his fingers through the high, blond hair. He faced his books.

Spencer's "First Principles" . . . "Introduction to Anthropology" . . . Dewey's "How We Think" . . . caught like long splinters in his eyes. He shook his head as if to shake them out.

Then he took the psychology book and settled, rigid in his chair, to read.

His mind held back. It seemed stiff and small, dry and remote. It gave no attention to the book. It gave no attention, now, to the movement of his body as the book fell from limp hands and he was stepping to the corner where stood his 'cello.

He placed a stool. His body flexed and grew co-ordinate as it received the instrument. Softly, with eyes arching beyond him and his mind still gone, he began to bow. His mind held away no more. It broke forward. It leaped, it sang: his fingers moved with delicate precision making slow music.

. . . The street. A woman, tall, clouded in dark glow, whom he had seen, whom he had seen in the street. His mind out there beat against her uprightness; it was a sea beating and breaking against her. It went up, it went down—as did his fingers—avail-less.

. . . . Then his mother. There was no doubt, she reminded him of his mother who had died when he was a lad in Holland.

Karl Loer bent his face upon his loved 'cello and played deep, plaintive words. He saw the woman whom he had passed so often in the street. . . . She has arms piteous towards a man who is her husband. She pleads with her arms. She wears a straight black dress. And underneath her dress he saw her breast. It is bleeding! There is an iron bar, clamped hard and close, on the breasts of the woman!

His fingers stopped. He drew his bow dazedly back and forth. He jumped up.

"O you! O you!" he cried, clutching his loved instrument. "I could wring your neck. I could dash you to bits—" He lifted his 'cello in violence with both hands above his face. Softly he laid it on the couch.

He stood now with eyes free and found that he was thinking of his life.

"What nonsense! what nonsense!" he began. He had forgotten how he had begun. . . . "Mother, this woman . . . two women I have never known." He loved his mother. She was French. He recalled her stately and dark in a town of light, plump people. He recalled her lovely in a world of clods.

The whole world knew that she had been unfaithful, and had disappeared . . . disappeared for ever and for ever: that was eternity, her disappearing . . . after his father turned her out. He and his two brothers knew how sensual indulgence grew like the fat upon his father, clogged him, clotted his brain . . . and he had turned her out. His father's soul shrank famished, he was a sucking brute. Then he was mad . . . she was gone . . . and Karl had come away.

America! He brought to it, he thought, his yearning and his music. He dwelt in misery. He dwelt, it seemed to his free eyes, in misery that grew more deep, more blind.

He wondered why.

"I have a good mind," he said aloud. He swung his chair to face the row of books upon his mantel. So he sat looking at his books. Proud of them—I wonder why?

And as he sat, he forgot the books that stood within his eyes. He thought again of his mother. Why had she been unfaithful? What had driven her, and what his father? Was his brutality the way of sorrow? Had she found joy in that eternity where he had lost her? . . . Sudden like a stroke across his brain, the woman with white breasts crushed in a clamping iron: her piteous arms stretched towards a man—not he.

He walked up and down. He forgot the vision.

"There," he said aloud, with an emphasis that was a plea, "there is what comes of music . . . of emotion. Idiotic ideas . . . visions. That woman . . . what do you know about that woman? Rot!"

He bent down and picked up the book that he had failed to read.

"Here's the place for your mind," he said aloud.

"You," he turned to his 'cello, "you'll go on earning my living." He stroked the fragile wine-hued wooden breast. "For a while . . . But you'll not boss me, hear?" He stood the instrument away.

There was a knock. Clara with a letter.

He took it. He seemed strangely perturbed. He laid the letter, unread, aside. As she reached for the door, "Clara," he said.

She turned.

"Clara," he said again, "why are you so happy? What have you, Clara?"

Her round face was all warmth and smile. She found her ease on her feet.

"I had fo' babies, Mr. Loer. An' ev' one of 'em died afo' they was six. An' my husband that I nussed fo' ten years—he was sick ten years a-dyin' on his back—he's gone too. They is all in Heaven, Mr. Loer. They is all waitin' th'ah fo' me. Ev'y onct in a while, they comes to me at night. I sees 'em, sees 'em standin' th'ah as clar—why as clar as you is! An' they speaks to me: wuds as clar—as clar as mine is. They's all gone and safe, awaitin' for me up th'ah. Tha's why I'm happy, Mr. Loer."

Old woman and young man stood very still, looking at each other. Karl stirred first. His hands, then his head. He walked up and down. She was still.

"But Clara—but Clara—"

She beamed on him. He stopped. He smiled also. He grasped his cap. He rushed into the street.

Into the street his smile and her words went with him
. . . shredding his speed, eating into the mood of his release, until his smile went and he stood stock still.

The sun splintered into the block, from the east, through
mouldy cornices of houses. Men and women moved separate upon stone, moved from sun to shadow, brokenly.
The day was yet too young to have welded them into the
substance of the block. Each was a particle thrown out
from a separate home.

Karl stood, looked down through the scatter of men and
women, the scatter of shade and sun. Athwart shoulders
and skirts and hats that bobbed like dark flotsam in a
golden sluggish stream, he saw a man move up.

A weight rose from his bowels, clutched at his throat.
The man he had seen once, with the woman he had seen
often!—Her husband . . .

A sense of omen cloaked his head and made him dizzy.
He felt only his body free, his head was cloaked. The
street was suddenly a force, physical and relentless, fixing
him there within the channel of this man.

He could no longer fight for the fading word in him:
Folly!

The man was almost abreast of him standing to face
him. There, in himself he heard, sharp like a fusillade,
the words that were his own.

*"I'm stopping you! Because your wife's in danger!
Look at her! Who put the iron bar across her breast?"*

A young man leisurely moved up. A smile in his ruddy
face, his red lips mumbling as if he discoursed amiably to
himself. His eyes wandered amenably. He saw Karl.
Something furrowed his brow into a question. Karl
swerved aside. They passed each other. . . .

And now the word that had been fading . . . "folly"
. . . shrieked. It besieged him and shrieked. It was very
brave.

"Fool! Fool!"—what did the words mean? Why am I
in the street? Why did her husband cross me in the street?

His mind reached for the surety of his mantel and of its
row of sober books. These casual things could be explained. He was lonely. Perhaps he was a bit . . .

unreally, of course, since what did he know of her? . . .
in love. Nonsense.

He jerked his cap over his eyes. . . . *Look at her! Take
away the bar! Place your arms there!* . . . he returned
to the house he lived in.

The area-gate was open, so he went in by it.

His mind, he was very sure, was master now. It was a
hard fight of course. He had had so little training! For so
very long, he had weltered in emotion. At home, the emotion of rage and of salvation against the brutal gluttony of
his father: the emotion of faith against the crass certainty
of his world that his mother was bad. And in America,
above all, the emotion of hunger. With one way only to
destroy it . . . his easiest gift . . . the emotion of music
with which he earned his bread.

—But it shall not master!

His mind pictured the book on psychology upon his
mantel. I'll learn about that. And then some day I'll
dash the old 'cello . . . no, absurd! . . . I'll sell it.

His feet led him into Clara's kitchen.

She was alone. An ironing board was laid from table to
low shelf. He saw her back. A bent old back . . . a
small round head . . . a mass of tousled hair dusted with
white. Yet as the bare arm pressed the steaming iron to
and fro, he felt with a new poignance how a wind, tropical
and fresh, wielded this woman.

He tiptoed in, sat down and watched her. The rhythm
fleshed. . . . A naked woman, tall and firm and glowing
like red earth. Her hands are above her head. Her hands
are flowers with the wind in them. There is a tree above
her. And her long, bare feet, with the straight toes, are
intertwined to the tree's roots.

Clara moved to the farther side of the board so as to
iron and see him. Her shoes were huge misshapen shreds
of leather barely holding about her feet, so that but for the
glide of her body, her moving might have seemed a shuffle.
He saw her smile now over her board at him. He thought
of a cloud saturate with sun.

"Clara," he said, "I should be studying. But I'm a good
for nothing."

"Yo' mustn't say that, Mr. Loer!" As her words came, her arms went to and fro, pressing the steamy steel. Her shoulders spoke in concord.

—Nigger woman . . . you are all *one!* . . . What a strange thing to think about a person!

"No, Mr. Loer," she crooned, "yo' mus'n't say that! We is all good fo' som'p'n. We doan know what a heap o' de time. But we all is—"

"How can you be so sure of Heaven?"

She rested her elbow on the board. "I done seen it, Mr. Loer. I sees it . . . *offen.*"

"How do you know you see it?"

"How do I know I'se a-seein' you?"

"You could describe me, Clara. Could you describe Heaven?"

"Why, ob co'se I could! What I sees I can describe . . ." She ironed. "It's a great big place! Mos'ly light . . . glorious, golden light! An' angels in white wings an' harps a-singin', a-singin' . . . When yo' plays sometimes, Mr. Loer . . . dem waily shatterin' tones . . . dey sings like dat. Dey music . . . it starts *away* down an' it leaps *away* up!"

She ironed.

"Clara, what would you say if I told you that was all a dream—what you saw?"

She beamed and ironed.

"The wise people, Clara, the wise men who study deep and who write books . . . they say all that is nonsense."

Clara beamed. "Dey ain't wise ef dey say dat, Mr. Loer."

She was bent over her towels, beaming upon her towels. Towel after towel she ironed, folded, laid upon the pile of towels at her side . . . her brown face beaming.

She stopped. She straightened and looked at Karl. Then she went back to her work. . . .

II

Karl was at work. From twelve to half-past-two, from half-past-six to twelve, six days of the week, Karl played in the Trio at The Bismarck. Played sentimental music . . . grime of German and Italian soil, froth and scum of Broadway. He drew with his bow complacencies and veiled obscenities . . . at work. His mind and his senses in revolt leaped away towards life: swirled, delved, circled; beaten, brought back to his heart which sent them a burden whose eternity he could not understand, would not accept: of Pain.

His eyes saw the café for whose lounging patrons his hand fingered, his hand drew a bow. His eyes saw his associates . . . clever, ugly: Stumm with bald, blond-ruffed head at the piano; Silvis, the leader, dark, agonizingly eager to be artistic, swaying, who was a muddy cloud about his violin.

Karl was at work and his mind and senses beating out of tune.

The flamboyant German Hall: smoked woodwork, paneled and carved in Gothic sayings, beermugs and flags under the sombre rafters like brittle colors falling, unable to rest. And in the sudden alcoves, men and women: idle eyes that took in so little, moist mouths, distended bellies that took in so much. Karl bowing an aria from Bohème; and the crass glint of the hall with its arrogant beer mugs, its mottoes, its elbow-leaning guests currying his mind and his senses as they yearned forth towards purer air. . . . The bald head of Stumm was round, it rested upon his neck like the head of a pin. His wrists bounced up and down. They dragged Karl back from the purer air he sought. Silvis crossed a knee upon the other and swayed with a small finger fluttering from his bow. His eyes were half shut in an absorbent leer . . . absorbing Puccini whom he loved. The weak grace of his body, swaying, leading, sucked Karl from his need to be away. . . .

Last chord. *D A F-sharp D.* . . . Stumm swung about on his stool. Silvis' legs stretched forward, abdomen collapsed—like a bug stiffened no more into organic form by its creamy fluid . . . the music . . . now all oozed out. Their words scraped Karl's head. When their words spoke to him, it was, this day, as if their fingers touched his lips.

"Lehnstein says, next fall we are going to move for a raise—"

"Did you hear about his wife? I guess she's his wife—"

"Why don't Max bring that beer?"

The hard loom of the hall, the coldness of men and women abject before their senses, taking in heat . . . heat of air, heat of sound, heat of food, heat of sex . . . into their coldness: the soil of these two men, his partners, playing this parody of life for an unreal living: himself with truant senses reeling back and bringing to his heart what pitiful crumbled fragments?—a woman stately with white breasts clamped in iron, a woman with brown beaming smile, all One, a woman of whom he knew no good, no ill, save that she had been his Mother—or to bar him from these a row of brittle books upon his mantel? . . . Karl with a burst of pain he could not understand, at work making his living to know that this was life?

He covered his 'cello and stood it away in the corner made by the piano.

"Ain't you going to eat?"

"No, thank you."

He was in the street.

Where was his mind? What was he suffering for? What about?

A lovely day. Here was pure air. Why did he breathe it and not taste it? He wanted more of it than he could breathe. What was air? Why was it pure ironically to him?

Long stiff rows of dirty houses exuding like sweat and excrement his sisters and his brothers. Cold houses sweating in the spring. Sick houses emptying their bowels upon the pure air.

He climbed by stairs into a house.

A swarthy little man in a great white vest with gold chain larding it from arm-pit to stomach, opened the door. Hands brandishing, lying, welcomed him.

"Well, Loer! . . . Come in."

"Just a moment, Dooch. I'm in a hurry." Hurry for what? What am I hurrying towards? "Will you, as a great favor, Dooch, take my place tonight at The Bismarck?"

Brandishing lying hands: "O, my dear fellow. Y' know I'd love to—anything to help you out. But I'm so busy . . . lessons . . . lessons . . . all day. I must have my rest. At night . . . the only time. Why don't you ask, let me see . . . well Facker'd be glad. . . ."

Another visit? "Ten dollars, if you'll do it, Dooch."

Hands dropping from lying. "Well, you know, I'd do anything for you. . . . Half-past-six?"

"Thank you, Dooch."

Hands sincere, palm upward: waiting. A bill in a hand happy, silent. Once more the air. . . .

Sudden Karl heard these words in himself above the beat of his feet: "I have never learned to use my mind. It's hard. That is what hurts. . . . It will come."

His legs walked on. He walked through desolation.

"O God, let me find *something*—" He stiffened, hearing his words. "Of all prayers, if one is absurdest, this is the one."

But he walked still through desolation. He sensed how he walked swiftly. Interminable houses were a heavy, fluttering canopy that passed him: banners they were of some arrogant dominion, dragged through mud, stiffened in frost. They shut him out.

Warm air. It was spring.

Children went under his beating knees like the drip of frozen houses melting in spring.

"Let me think! What do I want? . . . Something more solid than air. . . . Something as pure that is more solid than air."

His right hand clasped his left wrist behind him. His knees and chin thrust forward. From waist to shoulder he tended back. So he walked.

He walked through his life. He ached as he walked through his life. He felt himself trample. He trampled what he felt. Was it not clear? Clarity. He had lived in a pigsty. He had come forth. He was young. He would make a better way for himself in the world than the way of Silvis and Stumm. He would study, he sensed already,

and was it not good that already beyond the bowing of
fiddles he had won the trenchant accent of Reason—
Spencer, Darwin, Huxley? He yearned towards the ecstacy
of their release from mist and frowziness . . . from beer
and Puccini. A crumble of old churches falling in dust,
drenching the air with dust. He had hands to tear down.
He partook of the ecstacy of the release that lay in clear
books, clear eyes, hands tearing down. . . .

His father went to church. He saw again the great
stomach and the little eyes and the twist of the wreathing
mouth . . . the heft of fat red hands he felt . . . they
were sodden in hair . . . beating against him, beating the
children of his father's house. Karl's arm swung at his
side, his chin no longer thrust. He felt now his mother's
voice: it lay like a warm purple scarf against the chill
of his thoughts; his mother had a red, sweet mouth shut
upon her mystery; she moved beyond the shoulder of the
town like a sunset bleeding. Karl's hand clasped a wrist
once more beyond his back. . . . The woman whom he
had seen in the street and who haunted him . . . he struggling against her.

"Think! Think! Conquer yourself!"

He walked now heavy and stiff.

"Very well. What is she?" he fought.

He turned upon this woman with clamped breasts . . .
this myth . . . this nonsense. Why was she like green
fields? Why was his mind like lead? Married . . . a
stranger! Oh, she was suffering, he knew.

—Once I spoke to her; but my lips trembled.

"No, I am married," came her pleading whisper. But
her hand moved toward him. . . .

A complacent clod of a little man. But husband. Married. A stranger. . . .

Why was his mind a forest of hot trees when he needed
a path? A pavement. Hard, clear, cool, like here where
his feet were pounding.

Tedium. He played in a waste of soiled senses. He
walked through a waste of frozen thoughts. He was frozen
in tedium.

He sat down, for he was tired. He opened his eyes.

III

The East Park gasped its scanty green between the loom
of the streets of men and the black tumult of the river.
Here he, sitting upon a bench. . . .

Before his eyes first, two boys playing tether-ball. One
of them strong and with fresh eyes swung his racket well:
it rose from a clear forearm, muscle moulded, mazed with
faint gold sleeping hair. His mouth shut firm as he
stroked. Against him, a boy, shorter, dark, older. He
lunged with mouth slant open, and dull feet. One of his
eyes stared wide, the other was half shut. He lost swiftly.

The victor stood bored, easefully; looking beyond for
a comrade who did not come. Saliva wet the chin of the
other, whose effort had been great. His hand hung, palm
forward, near his knee.

"Let's try again," he said. "You give me your side
where the sun's not in my eyes. That's fair." They exchanged places. The battle went on, the same.

Karl was very tired. He leaned back in his bench.

In three straight strokes came to his passive eyes sky,
river, park. The sky was steadfast and still. The river
was dense and still, boats and waves moving upon the river
were like the shiver of sun-motes upon a steadfast sky.
The park swayed under the stillness of sky and water. Its
swaying was a word that came from moveless lips; its
swaying was a word issued from moveless lips. Three hori-
zontal strokes in the eyes of Karl, of a world that did not
move.

Stillness came within him.

He turned his head from side to side, as within stead-
fastness, not stirring it. He saw no more, no less, by turning his head. He was within a focus where all was steadfast and where stillness was all. He moved his hands, and
felt how he was wrapped in movelessness. He was not
prisoned. He felt free, fluent, felt the accessibility of
flight within stillness, within changelessness as within air.

He sat upright on his bench and was not tired.

He swung his left arm slowly under his face; he felt
how the world swung with him so that naught had moved.

Upon the cuff of his left sleeve a spot caught him and

made him focus his eyes. . . . A cockroach moved on his cuff. It moved. It moved against the world. It lied.

It flowed into the mass of his right hand. It was crushed. It was killed.

He said aloud: "I am sorry, life. But I cannot have you around." He was not surprised at his words.

But his words were another stroke, perpendicular to the three-fold stroke of park and river and sky. A stroke cutting along and lifting a veil before his eyes. The movelessness of life won by this fourth stroke of his words another dimension still. So it was that things seemed to happen. Within his immobile vision, he watched things happen . . . people move, sun slant farther beneath the green fingers of trees . . . as if this fourth stroke of his words saying, "Things happen," were a knife cutting a cord, unfolding a magic parchment.

Men sat upon benches as he sat upon a bench. Men had feet on a pavement as he had feet on a pavement. Men had faces written with thought as he had a written face. All this he saw as if it were happening just now. There was ease in his soul which took each happening and put it away and knew that all was one.

A man with a black, thick, filthy beard, black, bushed eyebrows beneath which glistened black eyes, a man with a nose inordinately long, falling sheer from his sooty brow, moved upon legs that carried him circularly, level, as if they were wheels . . . moved about. He dipped his talonous hand into a refuse can: his shoulders swung like the walking-beam of a boat. He dipped the other hand. There was refuse in his hand. He put it in his mouth. He dove under benches; he ransacked the scanty grass; he sought refuse. He put it in his mouth.

As he ate, his black eyes looked at Karl; they gleamed with a joy so full that Karl breathed against the glisten of his eyes sparking the air.

A little man with a face ghostly white, lips red like a gash of blood soaking through chalk, a little man with up-pointed shoulders and sleeves that were tatters to the elbow, moved, isolate, intent; picking up scraps of paper. Each scrap his fingers feverishly smoothed, his lean eyes

bent and read what was there to read. Then his fingers
tossed the paper from his eyes behind his back . . . eyes
roaming, roaming to another scrap.

As he read each message, his lips moved; as his lips
moved they bled.

A man wide as a hogshead, short as a boy, wider than
long, black as black earth, a negro dwarf with a huge head
sat with legs dangling from a bench and looked at Karl.
Karl saw him. The dwarf raised a hand to his head and
doffed his derby hat. Courteously he smiled, swinging his
hat and his arm. He had white separate teeth and no lips.
Beneath the frowze of his muddy trousers were patent
leather boots. And they dangled.

As he bowed, Karl knew that within the patent leather
boots his toes were twitching.

Karl sat easefully and still, and was not surprised to
find beside him on the bench the bearded tramp whom he
had seen so often, here and elsewhere, on his walks.

The tramp had always interested him; he had always
wondered what could be his story. But a terrible reticence,
savage or divine, fended this shambling blond man who
with great tender eyes, long beard and skin transparent,
blue-veined, now sat beside him. This man, he felt, speaks
to no one. There is an embryon word, yet dumb, sheathed
by his presence. They had sat before in this park on a
single bench; it had been impossible to touch his eyes.

Slight and frail man beside him. Karl did not turn his
head to look at him. By virtue of the four-stroked vision
within which he dwelt, he saw him clear with his eyes
beyond.

He saw between the straight, blond beard and the arching forehead touched with delicate hair, a face young and
worn. Sunken cheeks with blue shadows; blue eyes gleaming in red sick lids; a hidden mouth; a nose straight and
fine and singularly sharp. He saw, lost within the aged
suit of brown, a tenuous body, and at the hip beside him a
huge excrescence . . . a sort of tumor . . . swelling the
trouser leg which elsewhere hung in folds.

Karl sat and let the world play and was aware of himself and was aware sharply that he was at ease as he had

never been before. Yet it was ease, for he knew it so, and somehow he remembered.

A voice very thin, articulate like the faint etch of acid on a copper plate, from his side:

"I shall call you what you like as we sit here. My name is Peter Dawes. What shall I call you?"

Karl answered: "I have no name."

"You call me Dawes, then," said the bearded tramp, "and I shall call you Peter."

Karl-Peter nodded within himself, to himself he nodded.

The tramp went on: "Across the city the sun goes down. It will soon go down to the Palisades. They are high there, that makes the sun low. Do you see?" He was looking eastward.

Karl-Peter nodded within himself, to himself he nodded.

"Look at the little park," said the bearded tramp.

From the park's straight plane, the sun was away. The hands of the westward trees were empty. But beyond his shoulder, above the wall of tenements stood a flame: it leapt into the sky and fell upon the park. The park was thick now with stillness. It was low and leaden-green: it was thickly still under the leaping glow of the sun that was not there.

Within it, moving . . . steadfast in Karl's eyes . . . were busy men. They pressed to and fro, furtive, intent, secret from one another. The two boys at tether-ball kept exchanging places: the game was forever the same.

Under Karl's eyes was the black face of the long-nosed man. All of it that was not under hair was under grime of coal, save the huge nose that was white and the eyes that were clean and hard like a clear, black sky.

He spoke: "My name is Theophilus Larch. Thank you, Theophilus."

His quick hand delved into the cuff of Theophilus-Karl's trouser. It held up the dead cockroach. The long-nosed man had teeth very white; they closed on the cockroach with a joyous crack.

The little man of the red mouth was in Karl's eyes.

"My name is Martin Lounton. Call me Lounton, Martin. . . . And permit me . . ."

He seized Martin-Karl's hand. He smoothed it with feverish fingers. His lean eyes sought the palm of it and read. He tossed it from him, and was gone, feverishly peering under bench, in grass, for scraps of paper.

The black dwarf bowed under Karl's eyes.

"My name is Cæsar Dott. Call me Dott, Cæsar. And allow me to congratulate you upon your wedding. Your bride gave me a favor, from her own hands she gave it. Look, Cæsar . . ." He raised his trouser leg and there against the obscene mass of blackish flesh was an iron bar, toothed and clamped in the flesh.

"It makes my foot go to sleep. I have to wriggle my toes." . . .

Karl sat still.

The strong boy and the idiot who played tether-ball for ever, for ever; the eater of dirt, the dwarf, the picker and reader of scraps . . . joined hands. They were unknown to one another. But they knew Karl. They joined hands. They danced.

A heavy shattering measure. It made the glow of the gone sun tremble, bounce up, join in. It shook the trees until their branches with little leaves like bells reached down into the park and the trees danced also. It broke into the sheerness of the house walls and they rose stiffly and danced. All danced . . . moveless in Karl sitting upon the bench beside the bearded tramp.

He breathed in measure. A row of houses swung into the park and the park swung into the river; and the river suddenly straightened up and thrust like a lance, quivering white, to the sky. The sky came down in a great gust of wind and lifted the beating feet and garlanded the trees among the dancing legs of men, and stuck branches into the windows of the rollicking houses. Karl breathed in measure.

The stillness was very thick like a night without clouds and with neither moon nor stars.

Now, in the dancing stillness like a single star, a voice: "Think!"

The tramp was moveless beside him. His voice: "Think! for the time is not yet."

The star-voice neared, no longer the moveless tramp's. It pierced, it was a shriek. . . . "Think! Think!"

Karl jumped up from the bench. "Think, think!" he echoed.

He thought. He beat with his thought against the dancing world. He lunged and thrust: he hewed with his thought and beat. He beat the sky up. He beat the houses back. He thrust the trees down. The strong boy and the idiot boy, the eater of dirt, the dwarf, the picker and reader of scraps he hewed and beat apart from their thick dance. He trampled with his thought the park into the ground. . . .

Then all was as it should be. . . . And it was as if he had fallen an unfathomable distance.

He sat upon his bench under the darkling sky, alone, beside the bearded man whom he had seen so often.

He turned to him and nodded.

The tramp's reticent blue eyes nodded and turned away.

"It's getting late," said Karl.

He was tingling, as from a mighty fall that had not killed him, that had made him drunk. It was as if an infinitude of space coursed through his veins, as he had coursed through an infinitude of space. He was daring as never before.

"Would you mind," he turned again, very courteous, very quiet, towards the tramp, "would you mind, sir, telling me who you are?"

The look of the frail man was steady and far beyond him. His words came very still, very far away through the straight gold beard.

"You have seen me often," he said, "and asked me nothing. You have thought. What did it seem to you, I was?"

Karl was light with the abandon of his infinite flight, sitting so commonly upon a bench. He was brave and clear, for his mind held one memory—what this strange man, the first time, had seemed to him to be. The words came unhindered.

"It seemed," he stopped . . . he began again, "the first

time that I saw you, I said to myself: 'He looks like a ridiculous Jesus.'"

The bearded man gazed on beyond him. His head moved dreaming. His hands floated underneath his beard.

"You were right in what you said to yourself," he spoke. "For I am John the Baptist."

MENDEL MARANTZ— HOUSEWIFE[1]

By DAVID FREEDMAN

(From *The Pictorial Review*)

WHAT is a landlord? A bore! He asks you one question all the time—Rent! What is rent? A fine you pay for being poor. What is poverty? Dirt—on the surface. What is riches? More dirt—under the surface. Everybody wants money. Money! What is money? A disease we like to catch but not to spread. Just wait, Zelde! The time will come! I'll be a landlord on Riverside Drive! We'll have our own home——"

"In the cemetery!" Zelde said bitterly.

"Not so fast," Mendel replied, sipping his tea. "Cheer up, Zelde! What is pessimism? A match. It burns the fingers. What is hope? A candle. It lights the way. You never can tell yet! What is life? A see-saw. Today you're poor and tomorrow——"

"You starve!" Zelde muttered, as she rubbed a shirt vigorously against the wash-board.

With a sudden impulse she slapped the shirt into the tub, dried her hands on the apron, and, resting her fists on her hips, turned to Mendel.

"Why shouldn't I be mad?" she began, replying to a previous question. "Here I stand like a fool scrubbing my life away, from morning till night-time, working like a horse, cooking, washing, sewing, cleaning and everything. And for what? For this I eloped with you from a rich father? Did you marry me—or hire me?"

"I stole you. Now I got to pay the penalty. What is love? A conquest. What is marriage? An inquest. Don't worry; your father was no fool. He made believe he didn't see us run away. We felt romantic—and he got off cheap! What is romance? Soap-bubbles. They look nice, but taste rotten."

"Never mind! Mister Mendel Marantz, I know you too good. You talk a lot to make me forget what I was saying. But this whole business must come to a finish right here and there!

"You talked into yourself you're a great man, so you don't want to work and you don't want to listen. Sarah sweats in the factory, Hymie peddles papers, Nathan works by the telegrams. And what do you do? You sit like a king and drink tea and make jokes—and nothing! I betcha you're waiting Jakie, Lena and Sammy should grow up so you'll send them to work for you too!"

Mendel shrugged his shoulders.

"What's a woman's tongue? A little dog's tail. It wags too much!"

"I know what I talk. You hate work like poison. You like better to smoke a cigaret and close your eyes and invent schemes how to get rich quick. But you'll get crazy quicker!"

"Zelde, you're a old woman. You don't understand. All I need is one drop of luck and that drop will sweeten our whole ocean of troubles. If only one of my inventions succeeds, none of us will have to work. Then Sarah will have dowry. What is dowry? Every man's price. And we'll move out of the fish-market. What is success? Fifth Avenue. What is failure? Fifth floor.

"Some day, you'll see. I'll be president of the Refillable Can Company and save the world millions in tin. Just wait!"

"And who'll buy bread in the meantime? Mendel, remember what I tell you. Knock out this craziness from your head. Forget about this can business!"

Mendel's dignity was roused.

"Crazy! That's what you all are! You and all your relatives think I got water on the brain!" He pointed with conviction to his brow. "But up here is the refillable can. Zelde, you see it? It's in the brain, the whole scheme. Up here is full with ideas, plans and machinery. Thinking, scheming, planning all the time. It don't let me sleep. It don't let me eat. It don't let me work. And I should forget it—ah?

"You're all jealous because God was good to me. He gave your brother Morris a shoe factory, your cousin Joe He gave a real estate, your sister Dora a rich husband. But God gave me *brains*—and that none of you got!"

Mendel paced the floor excitedly.

Zelde stood silent and bit her lip. For years she had heard the same flow of rhetoric, the same boast of intellect, and the same trust in luck. The net result was always an evasion of work, and the responsibility shifted back to her and the children.

Mendel Marantz had brains, all right. Otherwise, how could he have existed so long without working?

He always confused her with clever phrases and blurred the issue by creating fictitious ones. And he always succeeded in infecting her with his dreams, until she let him dream on while she did the work. It was that way when they had the candy-stand which her brother Gershon bought for them; it was that way when they kept a vegetable-store which sister Dora financed and later reduced to a push-cart; and it was that way now when they had nothing.

By trade a mechanic, by inclination an inventor, and by nature a dreamer, Mendel abhorred the sordid commonplaces of labor and dreaded the yoke of routine. He had been everything from an insurance agent to a night watchman in rapid succession, and had invented at least a hundred different devices for the betterment of civilization while changing jobs. None of these inventions had as yet received proper recognition, least of all from Zelde. But that could not discourage him to such a point as to drive him to work.

He really believed in his powers. That was the tragedy of it. All geniuses have an unalterable faith in their greatness. But so have most cranks. And Zelde was not sure as to which of the two species Mendel belonged.

She was sure of one thing—that the family was hovering perilously near the brink. A single feather added to its burdens and it would topple over. Mendel might take it lightly, but she knew better. She had seen families in that neighborhood crumble to ruin over night. She had known many who—like Mendel—started as harmless dreamers, hopeful idlers, and ended—God forbid—as gamblers, drunkards, and worse.

"How was it with Reznick? Every day he had a scheme to make millions while his wife got sick working in the shop. She died working, and the children went to a orphan asylum and he still wanted to make millions. So he made a corner on the coffee-market and he lost everything what everybody else had, and the only way they could stop him from signing checks with Rockefeller's name was to send him to Bellevue.

"Or Dittenfass? Wasn't he the picture of Mendel? Didn't he hate work like poison, and didn't he pay for it? He thought he was smarter from the rest. Didn't his wife used to told him, 'Dittenfass, look out!'? But he laughed only. He looked out for himself only. And one day she threw in his eyes vitriol! That's what she threw in his eyes, and then he couldn't look any more!

"You can't be too smart. Didn't Karneol try? And it's two years she's waitin' already with swollen eyes he should come back. But he's got to serve three more.

"The best smartness is to do a day's work. If you wait it shall happen miracles—it happens! But the wrong way!"

Zelde knew. She wished she didn't know.

"Maybe you can invent something to make you work," she offered as a possible solution. "Somebody else with your brains could make a fortune. Why don't you make at least a living?"

"Brains make ideas; fools can make money. That's why your relatives are rich. What is business. Blind man's bluff. They shut your eyes and open your pockets!"

"Again you mix me up," she said warily, sensing this new attempt to befuddle the issue. "What's the result from all this? You joke and we starve. It's lucky Sarah works. If not, we would all be thrown out in the street, already."

At this moment Sarah entered. She was pale and tired

from the climb of stairs. She dropped her hat languidly on the couch and sank into a chair.

Zelde was too surprised to speak. It was only one-thirty. She never expected Sarah before six. An ominous thought flitted through her mind. She looked anxiously at her daughter. Sarah's gaze shifted to the floor.

An oppressive silence gathered over them. Then Sarah tried to mumble something. But Zelde understood without hearing. Her heart had told her.

"It's slack! Everybody laid off. Sarah, too!"

What she had dreaded most had happened. The family of Marantz was now over the brink. Zelde stood crushed by the thought of the morrow. Sarah sat staring vacantly, her chin against her clenched hand. Mendel stopped smoking to appear less conspicuous.

Four female eyes detected him, however, and scorched him with their gaze.

The handwriting on the wall was unnecessarily large.

Mendel Marantz knew that his crisis was at hand.

Zelde spoke.

"That settles it. Either tomorrow you go to work or go altogether! Yessir! You, I mean, mister!"

Mendel had faced crises before. Some he had overcome with a jest, others with a promise, still others with a pretence at work until the novelty wore off. But there was a grimness in Zelde's manner this time that looked fatal. Nothing but a permanent job and lifelong drudgery could save him now. But that would also destroy him.

Tying him down to a position was like hitching a lion to a cart. His mind could not travel on tracks. It was too restive and spirited. He could never repeat an act without discovering how much easier it might be done by machinery, and immediately he set himself to invent the necessary machine. That was why he could not be a tailor. After he once threaded a needle, he started to devise a simple instrument for doing it, and in the meantime lost his job. And that happened in every case.

His head was so full of ideas that he often had to stand still to keep his balance. His mind sapped all of his powers and left him powerless for work. In order to work he would have to stop thinking. He might just as well stop living. Idleness was as essential a part of his make-up as industry was of Zelde's.

"I wasn't made for work," he said with finality. "I mean —for just plain work. Some people work with their feet, others with their hands. I work with my head. You don't expect I shall sit like Simon, the shoemaker, every day, and hit nails till I get consumption. One—two—three, I invent a machinery which hits nails, cuts leather, fits heels, makes patches, and I sit down and laugh on the world. I can't work like others, just as others can't work like me!"

"You can make me believe night is day and black is white, but it won't help you. It's a new rule in this house from today on—those who work, eat; those who don't, don't. If you think you can invent food, go ahead. So long I live my children is not going to starve. From today on I'm the father from this family. If you don't want to go to work—I will!"

Mendel was skeptical.

"What is a woman?" he thought. "A lot of thunder, but a little rain."

Still, the shower was more drenching than he supposed.

"Tomorrow morning I go back to be a dressmaker by fancy dresses. Sarah, you come with me. I learn you a real trade."

Then she turned to Mendel with a sneer.

"You thought I play around in the house, didn't you? All right! Now you stay home and play like I did. You want to eat? Cook, yourself. You think in the house it's easy? You'll find out different. Send the children to school, go up on the roof to hang clothes, run down with the garbage five floors, buy groceries, wash underwear, mend stockings, press shirts, scrub floors—go on! Have a good time, and I'll pay the bills!"

Mendel admitted that Zelde had worn for some time the family trousers, but he believed that he still wore the belt. However, her inexorable decision disillusioned him. He admitted having been caught slightly off his guard. He had never suspected that a type of work existed so near

him, into which he might be forced out of sheer necessity.
Not that he intended to do it! But still——

"What is a woman?" he reconsidered. "Lightning. It's
nice and bright till it hits you."

The next morning Mendel discovered perpetual motion.
The children had taken possession of the house. He dodged
flying pillows, tripped over upset furniture, slipped on
greasy garbage from an overturned can, found salt in his
coffee and something sharper on his seat. He kept con-
stantly moving to avoid falling objects and fell into others.
He had planned to have nothing to do with the house,
but the house was having a great deal to do with him.

The youngsters seemed to be under the impression that
with Zelde all law and order had passed away. Mendel
found it hard work to change their minds. It was monotonous to spank Lena, then Jakie, then Sammy. Then over
again. It would be better to send them off to school. But
they had to be dressed and fed and washed for that!

He was tempted to snatch his hat and coat and leave the
house. But what would he do in the streets?

He hesitated, gritted his teeth, and set to work by scrubbing Jakie's face till it resembled a carrot.

"What's a wife?" he muttered, and Lena started at the
question. "A telescope! She makes you see stars!" And
some soap got into his eye.

"Sammy, don't you never marry!" he exclaimed with a
profound look of warning at the frightened little boy.
"What is marriage? First a ring on the finger and later—
on the neck. Lena, stop pulling Jakie's hair. She's like
her mother. Don't do that, Sammy. A table-cloth ain't a
handkerchief! Ai! Little children, little troubles; big children, big troubles. What is children? Life insurance. Some
day they pay you back—when you're dead. But you like
them anyhow. Such is life! You know it's tough, but you
try it once, anyway.

"After all, what is life? A journey. What is death? The
goal. What is man? A passenger. What is woman?
Freight.

"Jakie, you bad boy! Don't cry, Lena. He didn't mean
it. Here's an apple. Go to school. Sammy, get off the

banister! Look out, children! It's a step missing down there! Who's crying? Jakie, give her back the apple! Did you ever hear such excitements? My goodness!"

Mendel, perspired, exhausted, sank into a chair.

"I'm working, after all," he noted with surprise. "If this lasts, I don't."

But the trials of Mendel Marantz had only begun. The sensation of womanhood did not thrill his bosom, and the charms of housekeeping failed to allure him. A home like a warehouse on moving-day tumbled about him. The beds were upset, the table and floor were littered with breakfast leavings, the cupboard was bare, the dishes were piled in the sink, the dust had gathered already as if cleaning were a lost art, and the general atmosphere was one of dejection, confusion, chaos. The magic touch of the housewife revealed itself by its absence.

Zelde had now proved to him conclusively that her presence and service were essential to his comfort. As if he had ever questioned the fact. Why did she go to all this trouble to drive home a point?

"Zelde, a glass tea," he used to say, and the tea stood steaming hot before him. "Zelde, it's a draft. Shut up the window," and presently the draft was gone.

"Zelde—" he would call, leaning back in his chair, but why torture himself with things that were no more?

That night when Zelde arrived, masculine and businesslike, through with work and ready for supper, she beheld a pitiful spectacle.

The house was in hopeless disorder. The children had managed that. The cat was on the table and Jakie was under it, while Lena kept him there with her foot. Sammy's eye had been darkened by a flying saucer which Hymie let go in a moment of abandon. Everything was where it should not be. The kitchen furniture had been moved into the dining room and the feather beds were in the wash-tub.

Mendel was nowhere within the range of Zelde's call.

"Where is papa?" she asked sharply, after calming the youngsters with her two convincing hands. "Everything is upside down. I betcha he didn't do a thing all day. My goodness, that man will make me crazy!"

A crashing sound as of dishes in hasty descent issued from the next room.

Zelde and her retinue rushed to the scene of disaster. With one foot in the sink and the other on the wash-tub Mendel Marantz was poised on high, searching through the closet. Dishes, pans, bottles and rags lay scattered in ruined fragments beneath him.

Zelde blazed.

"Gozlen!" she almost shrieked. "What do you want up there!"

Mendel steadied himself. His heart having missed a beat, he waited a moment, then answered quietly, "Iodin."

"What for iodin, what for?" She was still furious, but also a little anxious.

"A small scratch," he explained without moving. "My finger got caught—under the meat-chopper."

"Oi! You clumsy! And what's all the rags and the water on the floor?"

"To put by my side and my leg. I—slipped and—the gas-range fell on me. My ankle turned around. The soup was good and hot. Maybe you got something for burns?"

Zelde was a little less furious and a little more anxious.

"Then what are you climbing on the walls for? Go in bed. Go—you look broken in pieces!"

She sighed heavily and shook her head.

"After all, he's only a man," she soliloquized. "What can you expect? He don't know if he's alive!"

She continued to scold, but nursed him tenderly.

"How is it? You're a inventor, and you don't know how to light the gas without blowing up the house? A man who can't help nobody else can't help himself!"

After a pause she said, "Maybe I should stay home? Ah?"

"Maybe," he murmured weakly.

Zelde vacillated.

"So what'll be if I stay home?" she prodded.

"It'll be better."

"That I know, but what'll be with you?"

"I'll get well."

"And—?" She expected him not only to recover, but to reform.

"And if I get well I'll feel good. What is health? A garden. What is sickness? A grave. What is a good wife? A gardener. What is a bad wife? A grave-digger."

"He's as bad as ever," she thought.

She finally resolved, "It's not such a terrible! He won't die from it and we can't live from it. He'll learn a lesson and I'll earn a living."

And the experiment continued.

It was very hard on Mendel. It was harder on Sarah and hardest on Zelde. But time subdued Mendel's protests and improved his work.

Zelde was surprised at his altered attitude of gradual submission. It almost alarmed her. She had never really intended this radical change to last. She had expected Mendel to rebel more and more violently as time went on and finally to make a break for his freedom and exclaim, "I'm sick and tired of this slavery. I'm going to work!"

Instead he was getting actually to like it. By degrees Zelde found less to do in the house after her return from the shop. True, his work was crude and slovenly to her practiced eye. She never would have cleaned dishes as he did, with a whisk-broom, or swept dirt under the table, or boiled soup in a coffee-pot, or wiped the floor with a perfectly good skirt.

But withal, Mendel was doing things, and as his domestic craftsmanship improved, Zelde grew more disappointed and depressed. She felt that he was planning to displace her permanently. She pictured him bending over the wash-tub as she used to do; or arranging the dishes in the closet, which was once her favorite diversion; or scouring the pots and pans as only she knew how, and a genuine feeling of envy and longing seized her.

"Thief!" she was tempted to cry. "Go out from my kitchen! Give me back my apron and let alone my housework!"

For she had become nothing more than a boarder in that home, to be tolerated merely because she earned the rent. She saw the children only at supper-time, and they looked curiously at her as if they hardly recognized her.

At table all eyes were turned to pa.

"Papa, Sammy took my spoon!"

"Take his," Mendel decreed.

"Pa, I want some more meat!"

"Take mine."

"Pop, Lena stealed my bread!"

"Take hers."

"Pa-ah! The thoup ith too hot. I tan't eat it!" Jakie complained, and turned a bruised tongue to his father.

"Take some water from the sink," was Mendel's motherly advice.

Zelde felt like a stranger. They did not seem to know that she was present. She tried to interfere.

"Don't put water in soup, Jakie! Better blow on it."

But the little boy slipped down from the chair without noticing her, wriggled out from under the table, and soon returned, gaily carrying a cup of sink-water.

Her maternal instinct rebelled.

"No!" she said warningly, as Jakie tilted the cup over the plate of bean-soup.

But the child, with his eyes fixed on Mendel, poured the contents bravely.

Zelde slapped his hand, and the cup fell with a clatter. It was not a hard blow, but an impulsive one. It created a strained and awkward silence. Jakie burst into tears. He ran to Mendel and buried his little face in daddy's lap. Lena began to whimper in sympathy.

Something snapped in Zelde. Her appetite was gone. She rose and went into the bedroom and shut the door behind her.

She did not want them to hear her sobs.

It had all turned out so different!

Instead of driving Mendel to work she had driven herself into exile. Mendel the housewife was now further from ever getting a man's job than Mendel the idler had ever been. Zelde felt she had made a grave mistake. Rather should she have permitted him to idle and mope—he would have tired of it eventually—than that he should be wrongly occupied and contented.

If only she could undo what she had done, she'd be satisfied.

"After all, a house to manage is for a woman," she began, bent upon re-establishing the old order. "A man should do housework? It can make him crazy yet!"

"I believe you," Mendel conceded.

"It don't look like housework should agree with you," she observed.

"Looks is deceiving."

There was a pause. A good deal of understanding passed between them.

"Mendel, hard work will kill you yet," she insisted.

"So will idleness—in the long run. What is death? An appointment. You got to keep it some time."

"But you don't look good."

"I don't feel bad."

Zelde became a little dizzy. Did he mean to say that he intended to stick to housework? She tried to tempt him.

"Wouldn't you like, like you used to, to have nothing to do, and sit and cross your legs, and, without you should move, somebody should bring you hot tea?"

Mendel blew rings of smoke at the ceiling.

Zelde continued, scarcely breathing.

"And wouldn't you like to lie on the couch with your hands together behind your head and look on the sky from the window and dream what a great inventor you are?"

An impressive silence followed. On Mendel's face were fleeting traces of an inner struggle.

"And—I'll clean the house," she added softly to clear any doubts that he might still have.

Mendel shook his head.

"It'll be too hard for you," he said gallantly.

"It's not such a terrible!"

"I haven't the heart to let you," he complained feebly.

"You'll get over it."

His tone became firmer.

"No! Housework is not for a woman. Like the Masora says, 'Be good to your wife and give your children to eat.' That means a man should clean the house and cook for his children. What is a wife? A soldier. Her place is on the field. What is a husband? A general. His place is at home!"

Zelde was chagrined.

"So this is the future what you aimed for?" she chided. "To be a washerwoman and a porter! Pooh! You ought to be ashamed to look on my face! Think what people say! They don't know which is what! If I am the husband or if you are the wife or how!"

Mendel carefully rolled a new cigarette. There was a plaintive note in her anger. He could afford to be defiant.

"Didn't you make me to stay home and work? So! I'm working! What is work? Pleasure!— If you know how!"

And he struck a match.

Zelde sat down to avoid falling down.

"Work is pleasure," echoed through her mind like an explosion. Maybe solitary confinement at home every day had gone to his head. Or maybe—maybe—! She slowly repeated to herself his sally. "What is work? Pleasure!" and "What is pleasure?" she wondered. The shock of the answer almost made her scream.

So that was it! She had suspected something, but *that* would never have occurred to her in a million years. Those floor-brushes that she found the other day under the bed, and the mop and the tin pail. They did not belong to the house. To whom *did* they belong? She had certainly seen them somewhere before. Now she knew! At the janitor's!

"No wonder he likes to stay home," she muttered to herself. "I should have knew; it's a bad sign if Mendel likes work all of a sudden!"

Her suspicions were still hypothetical, but fragments of evidence were fast falling in to shape an ominous and accusing picture.

One day, upon her return from work, Zelde found Mendel sitting near the window, restfully smoking a cigarette. His legs were crossed under his apron and his arms were folded over his lap. He gazed wistfully out upon the city.

Zelde looked about her in astonishment. The house was

tidy, the kitchen spick and span, the wash dried and ironed, the floor freshly scrubbed. A model housewife would have envied the immaculate perfection of the work.

Zelde gasped. So early in the day and already through with all his work! And what work!

"Sarah, I wonder who did it," she finally said to her daughter when she had somewhat regained her composure.

Her groping suspicions now became a startling conviction. Evidence fairly shrieked at her from every corner.

"Only a woman could do this," she thought, overcome by the shock of the revelation.

"Who do you think?" Sarah asked innocently.

"Did you see the way she looks at me?" Zelde exclaimed with mounting fury. "No wonder she laughs in my face. No wonder she tells all the neighbors, "Such a fool! She works and he plays!' No wonder!"

"What are you talking about?" Sarah inquired, bewildered.

"Never mind! Your father knows what I mean! *She* did it! Rifke! The janitor's wife! I know her, all right. She made eyes to Mister Mendel Marantz lots of times! She's older from me by four years, but she paints up like a sign and makes her hair Buster Brown and thinks the men die for her. Ask your father. He knows!"

Mendel sat dumbfounded. His eyes opened like mouths.

"Don't make believe you're innocent. I know you men too good," Zelde broke out violently. "I slave like a dog and that dirty old—" Tears of rage stifled her. But with a swift change of tone she added, her finger shaking under Mendel's nose, "Mister Marantz, remember, you'll be sorry for this." And she walked out of the room.

Mendel was sorry for her. He turned a puzzled face to Sarah. "When the house was upside down she said I made her crazy. Now when it's fixed up she tries to make me crazy! What's a wife? An epidemic. If it don't break out here, it breaks out there!"

The next day Zelde fidgeted at her work. She was prompted to fling it aside, rush home, and catch them together—Mendel and Rifke—and pull out the old vixen's hair and scratch out her eyes. But she bided her time.

Mendel was, no doubt, expecting a surprise attack and perhaps had warned his paramour to stay away.

Zelde decided to be wily. She would make believe that she had forgotten and forgiven. But how could she?

That night, on the landing of the fourth floor, she met Rifke coming down from the fifth. There were only two tenants on the fifth floor—Mrs. Peril Tzvack, a widow who hated Rifke and would never let her into her house, and Mendel Marantz. From which of the two was Rifke coming?

As Zelde entered her home the same neatness, the same cleanliness and smartness stung her sight. In fact, she herself could not have done better. To be honest—not even as good. The house was a mirror of spotlessness. It was so obviously the accomplishment of the wicked woman she had met on the stairs that Zelde spent a tortured and sleepless night.

She went to work the next morning with a splitting headache, and mists swam before her eyes as she tried to sew. Weird thoughts revolved in her mind. If it were only a question of Mendel, she would not hesitate a moment to leave him forever. But the children! A daughter of marriageable age and the tiny ones! What would people say? And even Mendel. True, there was no excuse—absolutely none—for his abominable treachery. She would never forgive him! Still, Rifke, that superannuated flirt, was the kind of woman that could turn any man's head! With that double chin of hers and the shaved neck and a dimple like a funnel in her cheek! That's what the men liked!

After all, Mendel was a helpless male, all alone in a house. He probably did not know the first thing about housekeeping and would have starved or been buried in dirt if he had not appealed to somebody to help him. And Rifke was just the type to take advantage of a defenceless man in such a predicament. She doubtless opened her eyes at him like two coal-scuttles, and pursed her lips— she had a way of doing it which gave the women of the neighborhood heart failure. And Mendel must have been grateful and kind to her for her assistance, and she must have mistaken his attitude for something else. She always misunderstood kindness from men.

So that's how Mendel managed to clean the house so well! And that's why work was pleasure to him! Judging by the amount and quality of the work Rifke was doing for him, their affection for each other must have developed to an alarming degree.

Zelde visualized the hateful scenes of faithlessness in which Mendel probably danced fawningly about Rifke, the fifty-three-year-old "vamp," who cleaned dishes and washed clothes for him as a reward. She must have nudged him with her elbow while she boiled the wash and said invitingly, "Mendel, dear, why are you blind to beauty?"

And Mendel, edging closer, must have answered, "What is beauty? Wine! The older it gets, the rarer it is!" Then pressing his cheek against hers, he undoubtedly added, with tenderness, "You're so fat! It's a pleasure to hold you around! What is a man? Dynamite. What is a woman? A burning match. What is passion? The explosion!"

"Stop it! Your whiskers tickle me," she probably replied with a coquettish laugh, and slapped him playfully over the hands with a rinsed shirt.

But she was only jesting, and was perhaps ecstatic with joy when Mendel courageously kissed her on the cheek despite her protests, and exclaimed, "What is a kiss? A smack for which you turn the other cheek!" And she probably turned it.

Then Rifke amorously rested her head on his chest and looked up with those devilish eyes of hers, and, linking her plump arms about his neck, she whispered, "Love me, Mendel, love me! I am yours!"

And Mendel, planting his feet more solidly to bear her weight, and carried away by the flames of desire, must have gripped her in his passionate embrace and murmured in a throaty voice, "What is love? A broom. It sweeps you away!"

"What's the matter with you, Zelde?" cried Marcus, the tailor, biting the thread from a seam. "You stitched the skirt to a sleeve and you're sewing up the neck of the waist!

"You look white like a ghost!"

Zelde drew herself up, as out of a lethargy.

"Eh! W—where am I? Oh!"

And her face sank into her palms.

Instantly there was a tumult in the shop.

A startled group of frightened men and women gathered about her.

But Zelde regained her self-control without aid, and pale and faint though she was, she smiled weakly to reassure them all.

"It's nothing. A dizziness. I'm better," she said. But Sarah insisted upon taking her home at once.

"That's right," Marcus advised. "Go home and take a hot tea with lemon. It'll sweat you out."

He added in an undertone to his neighbor, "It's a shame! Such a fine woman! She's got a husband who's a nix!"

Zelde refused to have Sarah accompany her home.

"We can't afford you shall lose a half day," she argued. But the real reason was that she did not wish her daughter to behold her father's infamy.

At eleven o'clock Zelde left. As she neared the house her breath became short and rapid. She stumbled several times going up the stairs. She stopped at the door.

Was it voices or was it her imagination?

No. Yes. It was. A man's voice, then a woman's laughter, then some—oh! She could stand it no longer. She broke wildly into the room and dislodged a bulky person who had been leaning against the door. Zelde stood electrified.

It was Rifke. And she was laughing in her face! And there was Mendel. And the janitor, too—Rifke's husband. And two men! With stovepipe hats and cutaways and spats! Detectives, no doubt! Brought by the janitor to catch his wife and arrest Mendel! Oh, heavens! And there was Morton, Mendel's nephew, a lawyer!

"Oi! A lawyer in the case!" she moaned to herself. "Then everything is lost!"

Zelde was ready to drop, but Mendel took her by the hand, and she heard him say, "This is my wife. It's all her fault. She drove me to it."

"We want you to come with us now," one of the strangers said to Mendel.

"What's the matter here, anyhow?" Zelde exclaimed at last.

"I got to go with these people," Mendel replied. "But you can ask—Rifke," he added significantly. "She knows all about it."

Mendel, his nephew and the two gentlemen departed before Zelde had time to protest. She turned with burning eyes to Rifke—the hussy!

"I wish they could take my husband where they take yours," Rifke began by way of explanation. "You don't know what kind of a husband you got. It's gonna be in all the papers. He did something. Those men what was here watched him, and when they seen it they jumped up like crazy."

"What did he do?" Zelde asked in great alarm. "I betcha you made him to do it."

"I? He says you made him. I only brought up the people. They knock by me in the door. They say, 'Do Mendel Marantz live here? Where is it?' So I bring them up."

"What for did you bring them up—what for? A blind one could see it's detectives!" Zelde muttered angrily.

"How shall I know it who they are? When they came in your husband turned white like milk. 'Are you the man which done it?' they ask him, and he says, shivering, 'Yes.'"

Zelde wrung her hands.

"What for did he say 'Yes'—what for?"

"Because it's true," Rifke explained.

"What's true?"

"That he done it."

"What did he done—what? You'll make me crazy yet. Why don't you tell me?"

"But I told you already!"

"When did you told me—when? You're talkin' and talkin' and it don't come out nothing! What happened here? What did they want here? Why is your husband here? Why are you here? Why were they here? What's the matter here, altogether, anyway?"

"It's a whole lot the matter—with you!" Rifke exclaimed impatiently. "Come over here and look and maybe it'll open your eyes!"

She led the dazed Zelde into the kitchen.

"You see it?" Rifke asked triumphantly, pointing out a mass of wrinkled canvas in the middle of the room.

"What shall I see?" Zelde answered skeptically. "Rags, I see!"

"But under the rags!" Rifke insisted. She lifted the canvas. Zelde stood completely bewildered. Her eyes opened wide, then her face reddened. A feeling of indignation welled up in her.

"You can't make a fool from me!" she began at last with rising momentum. "What do you show me—what? An ash-can on wheels! What's that got to do with you and my husband? Don't think I don't know! You show me this, I should forget *that!*"

Rifke began to perspire. She mopped her face with her apron as she struggled to keep calm.

"You don't know what I'm talkin' about and I don't know what you're talkin' about. It's mixed up, everything! Where do you see a ash-can? This ain't a ash-can! It looks, maybe, like it. But it ain't. All my friends should have such ash-cans! It's a wonder in the world!"

Zelde's head was reeling.

"So what is it, I'm asking you?" she gasped helplessly.

"It's a whole business!" Rifke replied. "We seen it, my husband Shmeril and me and the people which was here. Your husband showed us. He winds up the can like a phonograph and it begins to play. The dishes go in dirty and they come out clean like after a bath. You see it? On these straps the dishes take a ride. They go in from the back and come out on the front. When it's finished the dishes, your husband opens the box—I thought a man will jump out from it—but it's only wheels and straps and wires and pipes inside! Did you ever?

"Then he pulls off the feet and the box sits down on the floor, and he takes out the straps from the back door and puts in such a board with bumps and brushes, and he turns the handle and the box rides around like a automobile and washes up the floor till it shines! I tell you the people was standing and looking—I thought their eyes would fall out!

"Then your husband stands up the box and puts back the feet and takes out the bumpy board and sticks in a whole machinery with pipes and wheels and winds up the machine and pumps in fresh water and throws in all the old clothes, and you hear inside such a noises, and then the clothes come out like frankfurters, clean and washed and ready to hang! Such a business! You don't have to work no more! It works itself! I wouldn't mind to have such a box by me!"

Zelde, dumb with amazement, gazed at the mute, ugly monster before her. She recognized the wheels from the old baby-carriage; the legs were from her kitchen chair; the handle from the stove. And now she remembered the can, the brushes, and the mops that Rifke had probably discarded, and that Mendel had used in the creation of this freak.

So this was the rival she had been jealous of, the usurper of her rights!

"It makes in five minutes what I do a whole day," Rifke rambled along. "They call it such a fancy name—Combination House-Cleaner. It cleans everything. The strangers is from a company which goes to make millions cans like this.

"You're gonna be rich, Mrs. Marantz!

"Who would think from house-cleaning you could get rich! Here I'm cleaning houses for twenty-nine years and I never thought from such a scheme! You gotta have luck, I tell you!"

"And I thought all the time it was Rifke! Oi, Mendel, you must think I'm such a fool!"

"Forget it. If not for you I never would have did what I done. You made me to do it."

"I didn't, Mendel."

She added in a caressing tone:

"Your laziness did it, Mendel. You invented that machine because you were too lazy to work."

"What's a wife? An X-Ray. She knows you through and through!"

BELSHAZZAR'S LETTER[1]

By KATHARINE FULLERTON GEROULD

(From *The Metropolitan*)

"BELSHAZZAR had a letter,
    He never had but one,"
murmured Fenwick.

I should never have suspected Fenwick of having read,
much less having memorized, the works of Emily Dickinson.
Fenwick does not read—much; and how should he have
got hold of Emily, anyhow? It appeared presently—for of
course he was questioned—that he had picked up her
poems in the home of a New England foreign missionary,
where he had once perforce been marooned during a cholera
epidemic. Fenwick himself is, I fancy, outside all creeds;
but he can't help—given his life—running into missionaries,
and he usually speaks well of them. He takes them, at all
events, as all in the day's work, as he reports, from very
strange places, to the "interests" that employ him. They
have an eye out, those "interests," for a good many different
commodities, though I incline to believe that rubber is the
chief. Adventure has never seemed to pry Fenwick loose
from his very American moorings, though he told me on a
certain occasion, with a dropped jaw (in a kind of wry
whisper) that he had lost his religion once—just like that
—in a typhoon.

I mention these facts concerning Fenwick for reasons
that will appear later. He was leaving for San Francisco
and the East the next week, by the way, and this was a
scratch gathering of friends and acquaintances more or less
to do Fenwick honor. Ben Allis and Mrs. Allis were giving
the "party." Nora Pate, Mrs. Allis's niece, was spending
with them an enforced holiday from school. She was at
the dinner-table on sufferance merely. It was Nora, with

her giggling flapperish reference to a ouija-board occurrence at school that had elicited Fenwick's humorous quotation.

Now you must also know that we were a fairly intimate but more than fairly eclectic group at the Allis's table. Most of us were bred to one or another form of the Christian religion, went to church spasmodically (except Nora, who of course had to go every Sunday), and comfortably or uncomfortably, according to temperament, let the whole thing slide—took it for granted, or permitted it euthanasia, as it and our souls chose. But Mrs. Conway was a Catholic—"just the ordinary kind," as she had once said herself, with a sidelong glance at Mrs. Medford, who was waveringly "High"; Allis was a scientific skeptic, and Fenwick a reverent free-thinker. Or so I had gathered. The typhoon had made him a free-thinker, and his inheritance and temperament had apparently kept him reverent. My personal convictions do not matter, but when it comes to ouija-boards, I am all with Allis.

Young Nora had been rather stumped by Fenwick's quotation. She had probably heard of Belshazzar, but she had never heard of Emily, and she certainly did not see what it had to do with the ouija-board revelations at midnight in Betty Dane's room.

After we had found out just where Fenwick had read Emily Dickinson, the talk swung back to the occult. Mrs. Medford's pearl-powdered face and naturally red lips were eager. She even wanted the complete account of what had happened in Betty Dane's room. Nora needed no more encouragement than that.

"Why, Betty was desperate because she couldn't be at home when her cousin had his leave; and she asked ouija if there wasn't any chance of his leave being changed. And ouija said, 'Measles will make you free,' and of course we all laughed. Then we thought probably her cousin would have measles, so he couldn't come, and Betty would be free of disappointment. And the next week Pauline Case came down with them—and Betty *is* at home with her cousin, and she's going to bring back a book that tells all about everything depending on the way the breath circulates in your body."

The flushed Nora, at a glance from her aunt, sank out of sight below the conversational tide. But Mrs. Medford had smiled comfortingly at her.

"Prophesying is one thing they won't usually engage to do, you know," someone threw in. "I believe even Doyle and Lodge say that?"

"Naturally—since they have to get it out of your sub-conscious." This was Mrs. Conway.

Mrs. Medford turned upon her, a little acrid. You may have noticed that the two kinds of "Catholic" don't mix very well. "Has the Church decided that it's all your sub-conscious?"

Mrs. Conway's smile was all that she herself could have wished it to be. "Why, I believe so. Where else could they get it?"

"Whom do you mean by 'they'?" the other woman challenged.

"Why, the evil spirits." Mrs. Conway reached for a mint drop. "You see, the Church has had all this to settle so *many* centuries ago. It's hardly a new phenomenon."

If there was irony in Mrs. Conway's tone, it was not sharp enough to wound Fanny Medford. She looked rather pleadingly at the other woman's clever, gentle face. "Always evil spirits?" she murmured. "Never good ones?"

Mrs. Conway murmured back, and the two seemed for a moment to be isolated together. "Never good ones; and *never* the real dead. That is forbidden, you know."

I had hoped that our moving from the dining room would break the current, but I had reckoned without Fenwick. We had our coffee all together in Allis's big library—so much the nicest room in the house that I didn't much wonder at Maud Allis's refusing, except under great pressure, to drag the women away elsewhere. Nora Pate was sent upstairs to study, and we were freer. As soon as she had gone, Fenwick led us back to the subject. Mrs. Conway sat apart in the shadows, moving a fan slowly. Mrs. Medford fixed her eyes hungrily on Fenwick. The rest of us listened. After all, it was Fenwick's party.

"Of course you see all kinds of trances, and miracles, and levitation, and tricks, out in the East," he began. "I con-

fess I'm not much interested in what Hindus and such do.
They're so different, anyhow. But it does interest me to
come back to America for the first time since the war, and
find everybody going it this way. The Americans and
English out there do it, too. But there's an epidemic
here, as far as I can make out. Look at your niece and
her ouija-board. And all of us ready to argue about it.
Honestly, I'm interested. I'm perfectly open-minded about
it, myself. I'm not psychic, or whatever you call it."

"You don't have to be 'psychic.' There's no such thing."
This came out of the shadows where Mrs. Conway's fan
waved.

Mrs. Medford turned and gazed at her, as if trying to
penetrate even deeper shadows that lay between them.

"Oh, well, I mean—I've sat in on table-tipping once or
twice, but I don't think I added much. I never saw any
ghosts, or had anything queer happen to me. I know a
man out in Singapore who does automatic writing, though
—gets stuff through from his mother. At least, he says he
doesn't believe it's his mother, but he keeps right on, all
the same. He says she has told him things that no one else
could have known about."

"*He* knew about them, didn't he?" asked Allis, with
heavy matter-of-factness.

"Why, yes—he and she."

"Well, it all came out of his subconscious."

"I daresay." Fenwick set down his coffee-cup and took
a cigarette proffered him by Mrs. Allis. "Only I'm sick of
you people all wagging your heads and saying, 'the subconscious' every time you're up against it. Why don't you
get busy and explain how the thing works?"

"Ah, yes, why don't you?" Mrs. Medford seized on Fenwick's challenge as if it were her own.

Allis pulled his moustache and spoke judicially. "I'm not
a psychologist myself, as you very well know—not even a
biologist. I don't know that science has explained the
technique of it yet, though they are working on this sort of
thing all the time. Hysteria, secondary personality, dreams
—all these things are being put under the microscope, and
they're finding out."

"I'd rather believe in spooks than in Freud, any day."
This was Carter, a gay soul.

Allis ignored him. "I daresay you do know, though,
that alienists are using automatic writing in their treatment
of patients now. They find that some traumas, too deep-
laid for hypnotism to probe to, can be brought to the surface by getting the patient to write automatically. That is
one for the subconscious, anyhow."

"But—" this was Fanny Medford, brave on her own
account—"what about the things that never were in your
subconscious; couldn't have been there? They get those
too—indeed they do."

"I agree with Fanny and Mr. Fenwick," said Maud Allis.
"I don't believe it's the spirits of the dead; but neither do
I believe that the psychologists have explained it yet. I'm
open-minded."

"I'm open-minded, too," laughed young Carter. "Ready
to try anything. Except Nora's ouija-board. That's too
darned easy."

A slim form in white came out of the shadows—Mrs.
Conway, gray-eyed, ivory-cheeked, like a warm ghost.
"Can't you see," she said, "that an open mind is the most
dangerous thing there is? Because if your mind is really
open, any evil thing can get in."

She put her arm round Fanny Medford's waist, with a
soft, sidelong gesture, though she faced our host, directly
questioning him. Mrs. Medford stirred a little against the
light encircling arm—barely noticing it, it seemed. Her
face was flushed beneath her pearl powder. She addressed
Allis and Carter, now standing abreast before the fireplace.

"Have you ever tried automatic writing?"

"No."

"Nor I," cut in Mrs. Allis, "but I'm going to try some-
time. Has anyone here tried it?" Maud Allis went on,
looking round at her group.

I shook my head, Fenwick and Carter theirs. Mrs. Conway merely said, "You forget I'm a Catholic."

"How about Mrs. Medford herself?" Young Carter
marked us off on his fingers.

"Oh, I—I've tried it, yes. But I can't do it!" She bit

her lip and turned away, and before we quite realized that she was crying she had made a soft plunge through the wide doorway into the next room. Maud Allis followed her, but returned in a few moments.

"She'll be all right presently. She'll come back. It's just that she is so interested. Ever since her brother, Jack Hilles, was killed, she's been trying to 'get through' to him; and she can't do it herself. She began going to a medium, and the woman had no sooner established communication for her than she died. Now, Fanny's rather up against it. She's not the kind that likes to go to mediums, you know. I'm awfully sorry you started the subject."

"Why didn't you stop us, if you knew all that?" Ben queried.

"I didn't. She just told me about the medium now. Oh, she'll pull herself together all right. It may do her good to have it out with a sensible crowd like this. We didn't put it into her head. It's there all the time—has been, ever since Jack Hilles was killed in the Argonne."

"Well, we'll drop it right here," Allis replied.

But Mrs. Medford was back among us and heard him.

"You won't drop anything on my account, I hope. Maud may have told you it's the one thing I'm interested in. It's just awfully hard luck that I can't do anything by myself. If you people really feel like trying anything, don't let me stop you. I daresay the rest of you are as bad as I am, anyway. Not 'psychic'—though Mrs. Conway says there's nothing in that."

"There isn't," Mrs. Conway averred again.

"Let's try it, anyhow," cried young Carter. "Not table-tipping. Let's sit about and turn the lights out and each take a pencil, and see if we can do automatic writing."

Fanny Medford clapped her hands. "Oh, do! Only, of course, I can't. But perhaps"—she looked us over hungrily —"some of you can, and I might get a tip as to the right way to manage. And, anyway, it's so interesting." Certainly she had recovered.

"I'm not going to sit with the lights out all the evening," grumbled Allis. "This was supposed to be, in its humble way, a dinner-party."

"Well, of course, not all the evening," Maud conceded. "Quarter of an hour. And then we'll stop and play bridge."

"It would be rather fun." This was Genevieve Ford. I have not mentioned Miss Ford before, simply because she had taken no part in the conversation that I have detailed. She happened to you, once in so often, in somebody's house, and you didn't much care, one way or the other. She was just a nice girl, a little more restful than some, perhaps. I think the Allises hoped against hope that some day she and Carter . . . I don't know why."

Somehow, Miss Ford's quiet speech clinched it. Perhaps because she had been an outsider through the talk.

"Good for you. Let's!" Carter dashed to Ben's table and swept some pencils off it. "Paper, Allis? And more pencils. We'll scatter about through the rooms so that everyone can have a table-edge or a chair-arm."

Allis found us pads of paper and pencils—all except Mrs. Conway, who refused to join us and went off to fetch her knitting. We all looked at each other rather helplessly.

"How do you begin?" I asked.

"I suppose you douse the glim." Carter snapped off the light nearest to him.

"That's perfectly unnecessary," Fenwick commented. "The man I know in Singapore does it any time—in broad daylight, between courses at tiffin, if he feels like it. All you do is to let your hand go slack, and think about something quite different."

Mrs. Conway, who had returned with her knitting, intervened. "I wouldn't think too hard about something quite different, if I were you. That is, not if you want results."

"But we want to play fair," Maud Allis protested. "There's no sense in trying this kind of thing unless you do your best."

"I only meant," Mrs. Conway explained, "that if you really want to let them in, you must make your mind as blank as possible. Don't make an effort to think of anything. Just open the door and wait. You make me feel like an accessory before the fact"—she smiled a little—

"except that I really don't believe anything will happen."

She withdrew to a sofa and began to knit.

"You just have to be quiet." Fenwick gave his last explanations. "And let your right arm be comfortably slack, and don't look at the paper if you do begin to write. And if nothing happens in twenty minutes"—he looked interrogatively at Maud Allis—"then we play bridge, do we?"

Mrs. Allis nodded. "And I'm going to put out some of the lights, whether it's necessary or not. We'd be rather ridiculous in a glare, and we'd probably all be looking at each other to see if anyone's else arm was moving." So she reduced the room to a demi-obscurity, very soothing and non-committal.

Fenwick sat at the other end of Mrs. Conway's sofa, resting his pad on his knee. "Won't your knitting spoil it?" he murmured.

"Dear no," she whispered back. "I'll stop, if you like. But knitting-needles won't keep them away."

"No fooling, Ben." Mrs. Allis's admonishing words were the last spoken. After that, silence.

I did my best to play the game, but my hand did not move. I became, somehow, perfectly sure that it never would move, and that conviction edged my voluntary slackness of spirit. The corners of the room were too dark for me to see how each fellow guest was faring; but I noted idly the little stir of Mrs. Conway's needles, the faint fireglow on Mrs. Medford's bent blonde head, Ben Allis's comfortably hunched position, Miss Ford's graceful, pensive attitude. After fifteen minutes, I constituted myself timekeeper, moving my left hand so that the radium dial of my wrist-watch showed. I stared at it until I began to feel prickly all over. If my arm didn't move then, I thought, I was surely no good at the business; for I was half hypnotized by my concentrated stare at the dial, and my left hand certainly had no physical knowledge of what my right hand, off in space, was doing.

When twenty minutes were up, no one stirred. I decided to give them a little more time, for good measure. The minute-hand crawled as it does when you are taking a pulse or a temperature. Before the half hour was quite reached, Ben Allis leaped to his feet.

"I'm tired of this. There's nothing in it. Switch on the lights, you people."

But the others were stretching cramped limbs, rising slowly from their fixed positions, tottering in the half-gloom. I had not risen, myself, and I watched them. They looked drugged, unsure, wan and ungraceful in the dim light—purgatorial poor souls. Only for a second; but just for a second the only normal thing in the scene was the implacable motion of Mrs. Conway's fingers. Then Carter turned on the light at my elbow, and I saw my own pad of paper. The page, ten inches by eight, was covered with the huge scrawl of two words: "Ask Fenwick." And I had not known, staring at the dial of my watch, that my arm had moved.

The other lights went on, then. People held their sheets of paper up before them like shields, and moved to the nearest lamp. All except Fenwick, who still held to his corner of the sofa.

"Nothing—of course." Mrs. Medford spoke first, then flung her pad down on the table.

"Nothing here." Ben Allis grinned over his.

"Mine says something!" Maud Allis cried, as she bent over it under a lamp. "But I can hardly read it, it's so queer."

Miss Ford and Carter pressed towards her.

"Oh, I see now," she said. "It's 'Ask Fenwick.'"

I bit my lip and delayed my contribution to knowledge. But while Carter and Genevieve Ford were examining the unsoiled whiteness of their sheets of paper, I looked at Fenwick. He sat in his corner, open-eyed now but tired, surrounded by white things. Mrs. Conway had stopped knitting and was looking at him with concentrated interest. Her hand fluttered over the sheets of paper that lay between them on the sofa, but never once quite touched them.

The group at the table turned to me. "Did you get anything?" they chorused. Their backs were all more or less turned to Fenwick and Mrs. Conway, you understand.

I came forward. "Just like Maud's. 'Ask Fenwick.' Pick up your manuscript, Fenwick," I called, "and let us see it."

They all turned, then.

"Why, he's written *heaps!*" Mrs. Medford rushed to the sofa, but Mrs. Conway's lifted hand fended her off from the papers. "Give him time," she murmured; "he doesn't realize yet what he's done."

Mrs. Medford stopped, but Carter was not so easily dealt with. He strode over and began picking up the sheets of paper.

Fenwick yawned. "Can I have a cigarette? By gum! I think I must have pulled something off, my arm is so tired." He flexed it as he rose.

"You did, my boy, you did! Well, who says we aren't psychic?" This was Carter, arranging the sheets in the order in which presumably they had fallen from Fenwick's busy hand.

An odd look passed between Mrs. Conway and her host. Both started to speak together. Then she yielded to him, nodding acquiescence as Ben said: "They are Fenwick's property. It's up to him whether or not he gratifies our curiosity."

But, Fenwick, jaunty now, uncramped, waved his cigarette. "It belongs to the company. I'm delighted to have been successful. But isn't it extraordinary that I shouldn't once have realized that I was writing or that I was tearing those sheets off?"

"You did it very quietly. There was no noise," Mrs. Conway volunteered.

"Can't we read the stuff, right off?" Carter inquired anxiously.

Allis leaned over and took the papers from him. There must have been four or five sheets. Neither he nor Carter had examined them.

"Fenwick's property. It's up to Fenwick."

"I don't want the stuff. Let's read it aloud if it makes any sense."

Mrs. Conway rose with determination. "Why not hand it over to me? I won't read it."

But Mrs. Medford cried out. "Mr. Gregory wrote, 'Ask Fenwick.' So did Maud Allis. We *must* ask Fenwick."

"Yes. What's the use of spending all this time in an experiment if we can't see what we've accomplished?" Miss Ford voiced her own and Carter's grievance.

"Well, Fenwick"—Allis's bantering voice threw in—"if you are ready to vouch for the absolute purity of your subconscious, shall we oblige the ladies?"

Fenwick looked sheepish. "Oh, I say! You don't mean to load that stuff, whatever it is, off on me. Why, it may be a résumé of the last French novel I read—or anything."

Mrs. Conway spoke, for the first time, with some sharpness. "You don't, any of you, know what may be there. It may be utter nonsense, or it may be a sermon. But whatever is there comes from no good place."

Some of us laughed. "You're very hard on Fenwick's subconscious," Allis said.

"It's the first time you've ever done it?" Mrs. Conway asked.

"Absolutely the first." Fenwick nodded.

"Well, then" — she sighed — "it's probably all right. They're usually careful how they begin." She shrugged her shoulders.

We moved in a body to the big lamp on Allis's writing-table. "Thank goodness, Nora's upstairs," Maud Allis giggled in my ear.

Fenwick now had let himself go in the spirit of Carter and Genevieve Ford, as they chaffed him. "All right," he said; "I may be done for, but who wrote 'Ask Fenwick'? Seems to me we're all tarred with the same brush anyhow."

He held up the first page, getting the light over his shoulder, and began to read:

" 'Jack Hilles speaking.' " The manuscript opened like a telephone call.

Fenwick broke off. "Oh, I say, you don't want me to read this. There can't be anything in it, and we'd all be sorry to go any further——"

But Mrs. Medford came close to him, her eyes almost glaring with the intensity of her feeling—a queer, soft, mad glare. I saw, like a shot, that she wasn't going to be easy to manage.

"Mr. Fenwick, you've no right to stop," she panted.

Ben Allis had gone completely white under his pink-and-tan. Later, I knew why, but then I was merely surprised. Ben was not the man to be upset by preposterous hints of the supernatural.

Fenwick tried to temporize. "But, Mrs. Medford, we can't play with serious matters. We must respect the dead." Fenwick had not looked ahead; it was obvious that he simply did not wish to be responsible for anything that purported to be a message.

"He's my brother! And if he gets through to you while I'm here, it's for me. That is my property."

Allis came up and looked shamelessly over Fenwick's shoulder at the writing. "No, it isn't, Fanny. It's Fenwick's. He shall do absolutely what he pleases with it in my house. I'm responsible."

There was a curious morbid note of confession in his voice. But no one paid any attention to tones of voice, because a very undignified scene followed immediately on his words.

Mrs. Medford clutched the papers that Fenwick held. She got away with the first page, too, and turned her back on us—heading for the drawing room beyond. "Don't you dare, as you believe in a God, to destroy any of it," she threw back over her shoulder.

She had to fight for even her one page—not very hard, for of course Fenwick couldn't struggle with her physically. The two men, Allis and Fenwick, looked ridiculous as they faced each other in the tacit admission that they couldn't help themselves. Ben pulled himself together quickly. "Get that away from her, Maud—by force, if necessary."

"But, Ben——"

"I said, 'by force, if necessary,' Maud," he repeated sternly.

She flew ahead after Mrs. Medford, obedient, but sowing her path with protesting murmurs.

Genevieve Ford giggled nervously. Carter raised his eyebrows to the ceiling. "What *is* up, you fellows?" he asked weakly.

I heard Allis whisper to Fenwick: "Did you ever know him—Hilles?"

"No. Never heard his name till tonight?"

"Then what the devil——"

"I thought you'd come to the devil in time." This was Mrs. Conway on the outskirts.

An indignant cry came back from Maud Allis. "Really, Ben, I can't. You'd better come yourself. She won't give it to me. Fanny, be sensible!" Then the sound trailed off further.

We followed—Allis, Fenwick, Miss Ford, and I. We passed through the drawing-room where they had been a few seconds before, and out into the hall. Maud Allis stood there furious, a little dishevelled, sucking a hurt finger. "She's locked herself into the telephone closet. I don't know what you expect me to do."

"Not anything more. We can't help it now. We'll go away and leave her. She'll come out."

But Maud was shaking with anger and nervousness. "How do you know she will? If it's anything so bad that she oughtn't to see it, she may never come out. She may just die there."

Allis smiled in spite of himself. "People don't just die in telephone closets. And she'll come out, if for nothing else, because she wants to see the rest of it."

"But if it should be so dreadful——"

"It doesn't make any difference how dreadful it may be. She'll feel she's got to see it. Oh, damn!"

Then he moved over to the door of the closet. "Fanny," he shouted, "we're going back to the library. If you don't come out inside of five minutes, we'll break down the door. Now what a fool thing that was to say," he murmured, precisely as if we were to blame for his words.

A slender figure in white Spanish lace became suddenly manifest among us. "Mrs. Allis, can I telephone?" Mrs. Conway asked softly.

"No, I'm afraid you can't." Maud's answer was grim. "Fanny Medford has locked herself into the telephone closet with the first sheet of that wretched stuff."

"Then will someone go out and telephone for me"—she

gave the number—"and ask them to send my car at once?"

"Ben can telephone from the extension upstairs," Maud suggested sullenly.

"Oh, thank you. I wish he would."

Allis turned suddenly upon Mrs. Conway. "I can't pretend that, as a host, I'm proud of my hospitality. But don't you think it would be kinder all round if we didn't break up? We might be able to get that poor thing out of her hysteria if we all stuck about and did our best?"

"I have no intention of going before Mrs. Medford does, Mr. Allis," was the very quiet reply. "I thought it might be a good thing to have the car waiting. Mayn't I go up and telephone, myself? I think Mr. Allis ought to stay here."

Maud nodded. "It's in my room." And Mrs. Conway moved upstairs. She leaned over the stair-rail on the first landing and spoke to Fenwick. "Don't destroy those other pages. If she still wants to see them, she'd better—much better."

"You don't know what's in them," Fenwick answered. Nor did he, but he evidently considered they were not to be lightly treated.

"It doesn't make any difference what's in them. Not even if it were the Black Mass." She went on, up.

We went back into the library then, and Allis stood, watch in hand, waiting. He was beginning to mean it, about breaking down the door, I could see. Allis had had a good glimpse of the first page. Fenwick had seen a little. None of the rest of us knew anything but those three first words like a telephone call: "Jack Hilles speaking."

Before Allis moved, Mrs. Medford came slowly through the drawing room, holding the sheet of paper very carefully in her hand. A little behind, Mrs. Conway's white form gently stalked her.

Fanny Medford's poor little head was held very high. "I suppose you people have read the rest—and doubtless Mr. Fenwick has told you what is in this." She tapped the paper.

"Not one of us knows anything or has read a word," Maud Allis declared.

Allis frowned. "That's not quite true, Maud. I saw a little—a few sentences—of what Mrs. Medford took with her. I daresay Fenwick saw as much. But no one has seen all of it except Mrs. Melford, and no one has seen any of the other sheets. That is the exact state of the case."

"You will kindly give me the rest of the writing," Mrs. Medford went on, to Fenwick.

But Mrs. Conway stepped forward and slipped the sheets from Fenwick's grasp. He let her take them, though he looked at Allis anxiously. The situation was becoming Mrs. Conway's.

"I have them, you see," She turned to Mrs. Medford. "And if you insist, *you* shall have them. Of course I wish you would let me destroy them all, here and now. It isn't true, you know, that the dead communicate. They don't."

Mrs. Medford was shaking, but her voice was still her own. "They do. I know they do. Jack talked to me through Mrs. Weale, who's dead now. But not this kind of thing. It's wicked, it's beastly, what you've done!" she cried to Fenwick.

"But, Mrs. Medford, I don't even know what's there—except the first sentences. I never knew your brother. I don't believe this stuff, of course."

"Nobody believes anything, Fanny." Allis corroborated him. "This sort of thing has been shown up, time and again, for the most arrant trash. It's just our bad luck that something got written that was upsetting for you."

"You believe it—you know you do." Her voice was half a choke in her throat.

To my consternation, Allis did not deny it, at once and with passion. "Fanny, don't be absurd. You know perfectly well what my attitude to these matters is—purely scientific skepticism."

"I say that you believe those things of Jack. As for Mr. Fenwick"—she disposed of him then and there with a look of loathing—"I leave him to the rest of you."

Maud Allis followed her out of the room.

Allis took out his handkerchief and wiped his forehead. "Any one of you men feel like seeing her home?" he asked. "Fenwick and I would seem to be out of the running."

Mrs. Conway put out her hand. "Good-night, Mr. Allis. Of course I'm going to take her home. What did you suppose I ordered my car for?" She did not bid the rest of us good-night, but she seemed to address us all in parting. "Naturally, I don't know what's in these papers. But I take it, it is something pretty bad—about her brother. Mrs. Medford may have to see them, since I promised her; but I guarantee you they shall be destroyed without my, or anyone's else, reading them. It's all nonsense, of course, but you see she half believes. Truly, I'm the best person to see her through, because I can explain it."

"It's just some foolish trick of muscles—and re-arranging all the words in the dictionary," burst in Fenwick, hotly.

"Yes." She smiled. "But *what* foolish trick? That's what you can't explain to her. And I can. You may not think my explanation is correct, but at least it begins at the beginning and sees you through to the end. That is why I shall try to convince her. You open-minded people can't."

"Even so," Allis said, "I don't see how you're going to manage it."

She had turned to go, but she stopped and answered him. "I've this advantage, you see. You can't tell her *why* it happened. I can. Malice accounts for everything."

"There's not an ounce of malice in this crowd," Carter remarked.

"No, not among us. But the things you let in to your foolish minds are all malice. Believe me, they've had a ripping time to-night. They have to take what they can find—yes. It's the way they use it that counts."

"But suppose whatever it is were true," Miss Ford murmured. "Suppose it was her brother, after all, getting through."

"I've told you the dead can't get through—not the real dead. It's only spirits pretending."

"You'll never get her to believe that," Allis said ruefully. "None of us could believe that."

"Pardon me, I could," Mrs. Conway threw back. "And if I can make Mrs. Medford believe it, too, it will be the best way out of the mess you've made."

"Good luck go with you," he called after her. But he
seemed dazed.

When Maud Allis came back, Miss Ford made her adieux,
and Carter left with her. They had been, from first to last,
outsiders, and perhaps it was the most tactful thing they
could have done. I prepared to follow them, and Maud
Allis, saying good-night to them, bade me good-night, too.

"I've got to see Nora," she said. "I promised her I
would before she went to bed. I meant to cut out from
bridge. Probably I shall see you again, Mr. Fenwick.
Sorry you have to go, Mr. Gregory." There was certainly
no urge to stay, in her voice. She was more done up than
she owned. Yet she had not seen those sheets that Fenwick had written—any more than I had, or Mrs. Conway,
or Genevieve Ford, or Carter.

I let Carter and Miss Ford get away a little in front of
me, thinking that they were best by themselves, in the fel-
lowship of their detachment from it all. Whatever had
happened to the rest of us had left them unscathed. They
had not been touched, apparently, by the episode, except to
see that Mrs. Medford's exit was a cue for them to break
up the party. I lighted a cigarette in the vestibule, and
craned my neck to see them turn the corner. It was jerked
back by a clutch on my collar, and I dropped the cigarette.

"Come back in here, you idiot!" said Allis in my ear.
"Did you really think you were going?"

Yes, I really had thought so; but I went in again.

I found, when I reached the library (Allis locked the door
behind us) that he had furnished Fenwick with a precious
drink. He offered me none, and was taking nothing himself. Whiskey is medicine, in these days.

"Fenwick and I need some one else to sit in with us,"
Allis declared. "I may have to tell Maud later. That's
neither here nor there. I'm glad those two young people
had the sense to go. If they hadn't, I'd have kicked them
out."

"Well, of course, I'm eaten alive with curiosity," I admitted. "Only it all sounded like the sort of thing that
wouldn't be mentioned again unless necessary. I never saw
a word of the stuff, remember."

"I saw precious little of it, and Fenwick here saw no more than I did." Allis began to walk about with his hands in his pockets. "You can see the effect it has had on Fenwick."

Fenwick's head was buried in his hands. "I wrote the damned stuff. That's what gets me." I saw why Allis had fetched whiskey for him.

"We aren't going to quote it for your benefit—even if we could," went on Allis. "But you can take it from us that it was unmitigated filth. We judge by sample."

"Then why did you give the rest of it to those women?" I shouted. "Why didn't you burn up what you had your hands on, at least?"

"Easy, now, easy." But Allis was troubled. He made an eloquent gesture over Fenwick's bowed head. "We practically had to do what Mrs. Conway said. I believe she *is* the person to deal with Fanny Medford. Evil spirits are the best way out—if she can take it. And Mrs. Conway is a clever woman. But we three have got to sift the matter. It seemed to be autobiographical, by the way—statement of things done in the past. Buck up, Fenwick. It's more my fault than yours."

"Your fault? You didn't even write 'Ask Fenwick,'" our friend retorted. The whiskey was strengthening him a little.

Allis paid no attention. "I take it for granted that none of us now present subscribes to Mrs. Conway's theory. Very well. That's that. Fenwick wrote automatically a lot of stuff of which he and I have seen a little. It all purported to be Jack Hilles speaking, and on that basis it was Jack Hilles very much giving himself away. Of course, it wasn't Jack Hilles any more than it was the Secretary of State. Mrs. Conway is right, at least, when she says the dead don't communicate."

"Then this kind of thing just flowers naturally out of the rich soil of my mind, I suppose?" Fenwick asked sarcastically.

Allis smiled faintly. "I wouldn't say that. But you've knocked about the world more than most of us, and you've seen more than your share of exotic rottenness. Gregory and I would have had to go out and hunt for it. You've had it thrust upon your notice. If your subconscious stores it up, it isn't your fault."

"But what on earth should make me drag out horrors and attribute them to a man I never laid eyes on, who died fighting for his country in the Argonne?"

"That," said Allis deliberately, "is where I come in."

"You?" We both exclaimed.

Allis leaned against the chimney-piece, his hands still in his pockets. "Well, yes. Of course Jack Hilles' name was bound to appear if any name appeared — after the way Fanny had gone on. But if that sort of thing was dragged out of you, about Hilles, instead of nice, sweet, comforting things, it was probably because my mind was stronger than Fanny Medford's."

"Do you mean that you were thinking that kind of thing about Hilles all the time?" Fenwick queried.

"No, I wasn't *thinking* those things about him," Allis answered slowly. "I merely *knew* those things about him. That is—I never knew he did anything so bad as what was written there, but I knew he was a bad lot."

"Then why didn't you write the stuff?"

"Like Mrs. Conway, I'm not open-minded. I disbelieve it too utterly. I'm prejudiced. But I don't doubt my knowledge acted telepathically on your more sensitive — what shall I say?—mental mechanism. It's all suggestion. Mrs. Medford involuntarily suggests Jack Hilles to you, and I involuntarily suggest the kind of person I knew him to be."

We were silent for a moment.

"It's hideous, all the same," I said finally. "He's dead, after all—in the Argonne."

"But not fighting for his country," Allis remarked quietly. "He was shot—for other reasons. I've no particular business to know that for a fact, but I do. Fanny Medford never knew the worst of Jack Hilles, but she had no illusions about him until he went into the war. Then he became a hero. When he was 'killed in the Argonne'— which is all *she* knows about it—he was *a fortiori* a hero; a super-hero, if you like. You may have noticed that Fanny isn't exactly impersonal in her attitude to life."

He went on, after a pause. "I hope no one saw anything in my expression. . . . I was rather shaken by the
glimpse I got. I never thought even Jack Hilles went so
far as that. I wonder if Fanny saw. She accused me of
believing it all. She must have meant she thought I believed it on the score of Fenwick's automatic writing. I
believed it on the score of knowing that Hilles was capable of anything. And that, I perhaps didn't conceal
sufficiently—and all of it—I'm banking heavily on Mrs.
Conway to explain."

"I still don't see why I had to write the miserable stuff,"
argued Fenwick—though he seemed a little more at ease
than he had been.

"Well, I can't tell you that," Allis replied. "I'm inclined
to believe that Mrs. Conway is wrong about people's not
being, more or less, 'psychic.' Certainly, even she would
have to admit that some are more sensitive, readier vehicles
than others. It looks to me as though you were a corker,
Fenwick!"

Fenwick brooded for a time in silence, while Allis and
I smoked. At last he spoke. "No, it's too queer. Evil
spirits would explain everything, but I haven't gone back
to the Middle Ages yet. You try to explain it, Allis, by
arranging an intricate system of mental telephone wires—
installed in an instant, ready for the emergency. That may
be accurate, but it's extremely complicated. Too complicated, I'd say. I'm not contradicting you, you understand.
But for myself, I usually take the line of least resistance."
He rose and faced us. His fingers twitched a little as he,
in turn, lighted a cigarette.

"Meaning—?" Allis queried.

"Meaning that if Jack Hilles was the kind of person you
say he was, the easiest place for that sort of screed to have
come from is—Jack Hilles."

Allis's lips folded themselves firmly. "If you choose to
admit the supernatural hypothesis, I suppose it *is* easy. I
was ruling out impossibilities."

"The fact that you haven't proved a thing possible
doesn't mean that you've proved it impossible, does it?
How about you, Gregory?" Fenwick turned to me.

I threw up my hands. "Oh, I'm with Allis. It sounds queer and far-fetched and all, but anything is more reasonable than believing the dead communicate in that way. Even Mrs. Conway is more reasonable."

"Well, I wish to God they had rigged up their wireless on Allis's roof instead of mine!" Fenwick exploded. He turned his back on us and walked over to a dark window.

I tried to be judicial. "If Allis was thinking about the sort of creature Jack Hilles really was, that in itself accounts for the telepathy business."

Allis glared at me. "I wasn't thinking of Jack Hilles. I knew he was a very bad lot, but I wasn't thinking about it—not at all. I was wondering if Carter and Genevieve Ford would pull it off. And, anyhow, I couldn't have thought that kind of thing about Hilles. It just wouldn't naturally have occurred to me. Whereas, it might have, to Fenwick, with his background."

Ben Allis stopped, suddenly, and I felt the blood in my body, for an instant, back up in its channels. For just as Allis finished speaking, Fenwick drew back from his window and crumpled up against the sofa. No, he did not faint. He was, rather, at bay there, against the world; against Allis and me, who rushed to him at once. I did not try to read that face, though it shouted at me silently. I turned my head away. "Damn you all, damn you all!" Fenwick's white lips were saying. "And I thought I'd got rid of it forever. Oh, damn you both!" Yet he did not seem to be standing outside his own curse.

Fenwick roused himself at the sound of a knock on the library door, and we faced about. The knock saved us three from something pretty awful.

It was Maud Allis, and in her hand she carried a ouija-board. "I found Nora playing with this thing," she said; "and after to-night it was more than I could bear. Will you please burn it up now—so I can see it burn?"

"You bet I will!" Allis broke it over his knee, and went to the fire which had almost died out.

With one eye on Fenwick, slowly, very slowly, composing himself to a normal posture and a normal expression, with a sense that I must keep Maud off him, I drew her away in the direction of the door. "I hope"—and I laid my hand on her wrist—"the thing hasn't been worrying Nora. She didn't get any echoes, did she?"

"Oh dear, no. It had just been writing foolishness— probably the kind of foolishness you would expect to come out of Nora's subconscious."

"Nothing about Jack Hilles?" I tried to laugh.

"I should hope not! Betty Dane's cousin, they're all in love with; and their matinée heroes; and their school commencement. But I've put her to bed and taken it away. I will not have my niece ouija-ing."

Ouija was now burning brightly above the Cape Cod lighter. Ben Allis called to his wife. "Maud, do get a taxi round at once for Fenwick. He's tired and doesn't want to walk."

"Certainly, I will. Did you people come to any conclusion?"

"Ben has the right of it, I'm sure. Telepathy." I spoke quite loud. "He'll tell you all about it. We're going."

Maud went off to the telephone.

Fenwick's voice cut in. "Thanks for thinking of the taxi, Allis. I believe I do want one. Good-night."

"Shall I come along with you?" I asked, thinking of Mrs. Conway's brave support of Fanny Medford.

Allis frowned, and Fenwick, though he had got himself in hand, seemed to cringe a little before the frown. "No, thanks. I'm going straight to bed. It's needless to say, I suppose, that this thing shall go no further, as far as I am concerned. I can't say it has been a pleasant evening, but it has been interesting. It's funny, isn't it"—he spoke rapidly, but carefully—"that a party of friends can react so differently? Mrs. Conway thinks it's evil spirits; I think Hilles did get through; and you and Allis think it was all communicated from Allis's subconscious to mine. But we all hope that Mrs. Conway will convince Mrs. Medford."

No; he could evidently take care of himself now. And he obviously wanted to be alone. Mrs. Allis, returning, rallied him as she said good-night.

"Your taxi is there already, I think, Mr. Fenwick. What do you think of Belshazzar's letter *now?* I'm sorry you had to get the letter."

It was all right for Maud to carry things off lightly— probably she felt it was her duty—but it didn't help Allis and me so much as she doubtless hoped.

"I think I can promise never to meddle with this sort of thing again," he said gravely. "I'm convinced it was the real thing. Your husband thinks he was responsible. He'll explain to you."

Allis answered the plea that sounded faintly in Fenwick's voice. "Yes, Maud shall have my telepathy theory. I think she'll agree. Maud, do go to the door with Fenwick. There's no fender here, and I don't like to leave ouija."

Maud Allis, as you may have made out, was a good wife who never argued an absurdity if her husband perpetrated it. She preceded Fenwick to the hall.

Allis gripped my hand. "I shall tell Maud exactly what I said. You'll tell nobody anything."

"Of course not. For Mrs. Medford's sake, if nothing else."

Allis relaxed his grip. "Yes—and Fenwick's, too. I've been fond of him for a long time. Perhaps he'll never give himself away again."

"Perhaps not," I agreed. "Asia is a large continent. He may come to believe it was Hilles communicating, you know."

"Well, I rather hope he does. Fenwick's got to live. But you and I don't believe it."

"No, we don't."

"It's queer," Allis mused; "you and I are the only ones of the crowd who know what happened; and the one thing we are most anxious for is that everyone concerned—even Fenwick himself—should be convinced of some explanation we know is wrong. We want Mrs. Medford to believe Mrs. Conway; I want Maud to believe what I said here a while ago; and I even want Fenwick to believe that the dead communicate. We're a scientific lot, aren't we?"

"I'm not sure I wouldn't rather believe any of those things than believe what I do," I said grimly. I remembered Fenwick's face.

"Exactly. Poor science!"

Mrs. Allis returned, and I bade my host and hostess good night. This time I did not go back again.

WINKELBURG[1]

By BEN HECHT

(From *The Smart Set*)

I

THERE was never a man as irritating as Winkelburg. He was an encyclopedia of misfortunes. Everything that can happen to a man had happened to him. He had lost his family, his money and his health. He was, in short, a man completely broken—tall, thin, with a cadaverous face out of which shone two huge lustreless eyes. He walked with an angular crawl that reminded one of the emaciated flies one sees at the beginning of winter. That was Winkelburg to a dot—a creature perversely alive, dragging itself across an illimitable expanse of flypaper.

It was one of Winkelburg's worst habits to appear at unexpected moments. But, perhaps, any appearances he might have made would have had this irritating quality of unexpectedness. One was never looking forward to him, and thus the sight of his wan, uncomfortable smile, his lustreless eyes, his tenacious crawl was invariably an irritating surprise.

I will be frank. It was Winkelburg's misfortune which first attracted me. I listened to his story avidly. He talked in slow words and there was intelligence in the man. He was able to perceive himself, not only as a pain-racked, starving human, but he glimpsed with his large, tired eyes his relation to things outside himself.

It appeared that the man had been lying in a hall bedroom for two weeks dying. An embittered landlady to whom he owed three months rent had tended him. I fancy she was torn between a hope that the miserable fool would

die and give her a chance to rent the room to a more profit-
able customer and a more optimistic greed. He might
recover, get a job and pay her the three months rent he
owed.

Winkelburg wrote to me about it. It was my first
knowledge of the man. He offered his experiences as material for one of the daily stories I was writing for the *News*.
His letter was a document. In it he recounted in good
English and in a few lines the history of his life.

"I have had hard luck all my life," he wrote. "I have
no friends or relatives. My health is broken and I am
without money. I once was somebody, but that doesn't
matter now. I am dying. Lying up here in my room and
hearing the noises in the street all day and all night I got
to thinking about things. I don't mind dying, but to die
all alone in a cheap bedroom with nobody around is too
much. So I got dressed. It took me almost all day to
dress on account of the pain. I had twenty cents left. I
finally managed to walk out of the house and get on a
street car. It was a torture. But I figured if I could reach
the County Hospital they would put me in a bed and
give me treatment, and, anyway, it would not be so bad to
die in a hospital."

Then he went on to relate his experience. He had arrived
at the hospital and been ushered into a receiving room.
Here a group of internes stood around cracking jokes. One
of them finally advised him to take his clothes off. He
retired into one of the booths and stripped. When he
came out the room was empty. So Winkelburg crawled up
on a dirty table and lay there waiting. He waited for an
hour. After an hour an interne popped into the room and
looked at him with some surprise and inquired what the
devil he was doing lying naked on the table. Winkelburg,
more dead than alive, moaned something in reply. Where-
upon the interne examined him. Winkelburg wrote:

"He moved my legs up and down and felt over me for
a minute and then said, 'You're all right. I'll give you a
prescription to fix you up.' And he wrote out a prescription. I put my clothes on slowly and asked him what I
should do. 'Go home,' he said. I told him I couldn't.

Then he asked, 'Well, how did you come here?' I told him it was a torture. So he grinned and said, 'Torture back, then.' I am back in my room now, in bed. I feel worse. I've been thinking about all this. It doesn't make me angry. The world is like that. It has no time for its unfortunates. There are too many healthy ones to take care of. This interne was possibly not a bad fellow. When he talked to me I realized how it was. I was just one of a thousand poor fools, and he was busy with his career and his plans. He didn't mean to be cruel, but that's just human nature, don't you think?"

I wrote the story, adding a few lugubrious details for good measure. I drew a picture of Winkelburg lying on his back, staring at the ceiling and thinking of the busy city whose noises floated in through his window. The next day brought a flood of letters. Philanthropists offered to care for Winkelburg. The hospital authorities denied the incident described by Winkelburg, but offered to make amends and to give him treatment and a bed.

A week later I received a letter of thanks from him. He was in the hospital. Three weeks later another letter came. He had been given a home by an elderly couple. Luck had turned. He had all he wanted. Two more weeks brought another letter. He was living somewhere else now and he would like to hear from me. And then he appeared in person. It was the first time I had ever seen him.

He sat down beside my desk and I looked at him. Death stared out of the man. And I noticed at once the curious kindliness of him. He talked slowly and told me of his experiences. He was courteously brief, and even better than that, he spoke without emotion.

"There is nobody to blame," he said. "Not even myself. It is just the way things go. And if I can't blame myself, how can I blame the world? The city is like that. I'm no good. I'm done. Worn out, useless. People try to take care of the useless ones. There are institutions. Well, I had two good homes and was in two institutions, thanks to the thing you wrote. But they kicked me out. They said I was a faker. Somehow I don't appeal to charitably inclined people."

Later I understood why. It was because of the man's
smile—a feeble, tenacious grimace that seemed to be offer-
ing a sardonic reproof. It could never have been mistaken
for a courageous smile. Philanthropy had taken Winkelburg up and then dropped him. Quickly and definitely.
Because of his smile. The secret of its aggravating quality
was this: in it Winkelburg accused himself of his useless-
ness, his feebleness, his poverty. It was as if he were regarding himself continually through the annoyed eyes of
others and addressing himself with the words of others—
"You, Winkelburg, get out of here. You're a nuisance.
You make me uncomfortable, because you're poor and dis-
eased and full of gloom. Get out. I don't want you
around. Why the devil don't you die?"

And the aggravating thing was that people looked at
Winkelburg's smile as into a mirror. They saw in it a
shrewd reflection of their own attitude toward the man.
They felt that Winkelburg understood what they thought
of him. And they didn't like that. They didn't like to
feel that Winkelburg was aware that deep inside their
minds they were always asking, "Why doesn't this Winkelburg die and have it over with?" Because that made them
out as cruel, heartless people, not much different in their
attitude toward their fellow-man from predatory animals
in their attitude toward fellow predatory animals. And
somehow, although they really felt that way toward Winkelburg, they preferred not to believe it. At least, they
disliked accusation where there should have been only gratitude.

Not that Winkelburg was ungrateful. He was thankful,
obliging and properly humble. But his smile persisted.
And his smile was a mirror that would not let his benefac-
tors escape the truth. And eventually Winkelburg's smile
became for them one of those curious mirrors that exagger-
ate images grotesquely.

Charitably inclined people as well as all other kinds of
inclined people prefer their Winkelburgs more egotistic.
They prefer that unfortunate ones be engrossed in their
misfortunes and not go around wearing sardonic, philosophical smiles.

II

Winkelburg dragged along for six months. He was past fifty-five. Each time I saw him I was certain I would never see him again. I was certain he would die—drop dead while crawling across his flypaper. But he would appear. I would pretend to be vastly busy. He would sit and wait. His consideration was an affront. It said, "Oh, yes, I know you are a very busy man. You are part of the world. But Winkelburg has nothing to do. Nothing but wait. Wait until he dies. So don't hurry. I have plenty of time."

He would never ask alms. I would have been relieved if he had. Instead he would sit and smile, and his smile would say:

"Ah, my friend, you are afraid I am going to ask you for money. Don't worry, please. I would rather die of hunger than ask you. Because it would interfere with our friendship. And I value your friendship more than a bite of food. I won't ask you for money. I won't bother you at all. Yes, yes, I agree with you. I ought to be dead. It would be better for everybody."

We would talk little. He would throw out a hint now and then that perhaps I could use some of his misfortunes for material. For instance, the time his two children had been burned to death. Or the time he had fallen off a street car while in a sick daze and injured his spine for life, and how he settled with the street-car company for five hundred dollars, and how he had been robbed on the way to the bank with the money a month later.

I refused consistently and somewhat curtly his offer of material. This offended Winkelburg. He would pick up the day's paper and sit reading my story through with a show of critical deliberation. Then he would put it down and look at me as if to say:

"This thing you've written about is all right in its way. But it must be obvious to you that, from a purely literary point of view, the material I have to offer is vastly superior."

I saw that his vanity was piqued. I would not have minded this. In fact it was a bit droll. But there was

his smile. Winkelburg's smile rose above his vanity. When
I had returned to the typewriter, feigning industry in the
hope that the man would pick himself up and crawl away,
I would catch a glimpse of the inevitable wan grimace
that came to his lips and the smile would say:

"Yes, yes, I understand. You refuse my material because you don't want to get involved with me. Because
you don't want me to have any more claims on you than
I have. Not that you're afraid I'll ask you for money.
But if I gave you something you're afraid that it would
establish a closer relationship between us. I'm sorry, but
you shouldn't feel that way."

Toward the end Winkelburg's visits grew more frequent.
I gave instructions that he shouldn't be admitted, and that
whenever he called, "I was out." Futile. There were three
things that the rich man couldn't keep out with his high
fence, says the poet—rain, death and tomorrow. And
Winkelburg was gifted with an almost similar aloof tenac-
ity. He crawled past barriers. He melted through walls.
And regardless of subterfuges and instructions, I would
hear his dragging step in the corridor leading to my desk.

He wished to discuss things. He had become suddenly
garrulous. He wished to talk about the city. About its
institutions. About politics. About people. About art.
This phase of Winkelburg was the most unbearable. He
was willing to admit himself an outcast, a thing on a scrap
heap. He was reconciled to the fact that he would starve
to death, and that everybody who had ever seen him would
feel it was a good thing he had finally died.

But he made one plea. He wanted nothing except to
talk and to hear words in order to relieve the loneliness
of his day. He would like abstract discussions that had
nothing to do with Winkelburg and the Winkelburg misfortunes. His smile now said, "I am useless. Worn out
and better off dead. But never mind me. Never mind
Winkelburg and his troubles. My mind is still alive. It
still thinks and works. I wish that it didn't. I wish it
was crippled like Winkelburg is, and that it crawled around
like my body. But it doesn't. So talk to me as if it
were a mind belonging to somebody else, as if it were an

impersonal machine able to pronounce ideas and to argue and to appreciate what you say. Talk to me as if I weren't this insufferable Winkelburg, but somebody of whom you have never heard."

I grew suspicious finally. I began to think there was something vitally spurious about this whole Winkelburg business. And I said to myself, "The man's a downright fake. If anybody were as pathetic and impossible and useless as this Winkelburg is he would shoot himself. Winkelburg doesn't shoot himself. So he becomes illogical . . . unreal."

III

A woman I know belongs to the type that becomes charitable around Christmas time. She makes a glowing pretense of aiding the poor. As a matter of fact she probably does aid them, what with the baskets of food, clothing and necessities she showers upon their hovels. But the point is that she regards the poor as a sort of social and spiritual asset. They afford her the opportunity of appearing in the eyes of her neighbors as a magnanimous soul, of doing something which reflects great credit upon her character. It is certain that she would be unhappy if there were no poor, that Christmas wouldn't be Christmas without the glow of spiritual righteousness and the lift of economic superiority the giving of gifts to deserving inferiors inspires in her. But anyway, she "does good," and if she panders to her own egoism as much as she improves the physical comfort of her charges—that is a complication it will hurt nobody to ignore.

I told this woman about Winkelburg. I became poignant and moving on the subject of Winkelburg's misfortunes, his trials, sufferings, and, above all, his Spartan stoicism. It pleased me to do this. I felt that I was making amends and that the thing reflected great credit upon my character —in her eyes.

So she went to the room on the South Side where Winkelburg lived. And they told her there that Winkelburg was dead. He had died a week ago. She was upset when

she came back and told me about it. She had come too
late. She might have saved him. She accused herself
sorrowfully and I listened with politeness. Her accusation
was a charmingly involved boast. Her sorrow over the
matter was merely her way of telling me all the wonderful things she would have done for Winkelburg. Her regret
that he was dead was obviously enough the disappointment
she felt at not being able to pander to her egoism by
showering poor Winkelburg with largesse.

It was a curious thing—but when she told me that
Winkelburg was dead I felt combatively that it was untrue.
And now since I know certainly that Winkelburg is dead
and buried, I have developed a curious state of mind. I
look up from my desk every once in a while expecting to
see him. In the streets I sometimes find myself actually
thinking:

"I'll bump into him when I turn this corner."

I have managed to discover the secret of this feeling. It
is Winkelburg's smile. Winkelburg's smile was the interpretation of the world's attitude toward him, including my
own, I tell myself. And thus whenever his name comes to
my mind or a thought of him occupies me his smile
appears as if it were the thought in my head. I have only
to think, "He is better off dead," and at once the image of
Winkelburg comes into my eye, repeating the words to me.
This may sound involved, but it is really very simple.
Instead of thinking of Winkelburg I find that I take the
easier way of remembering Winkelburg's smile, and his
smile somehow says for me everything I would have
thought.

And this, in a way, is Winkelburg's revenge, that I am
unable to forget him and that I am unable to say "poor
Winkelburg" without Winkelburg smiling back at me and
saying with a taunting, irritating calm, "Yes, yes, he is
better off dead."

THE TOKEN[1]

By JOSEPH HERGESHEIMER

(From *The Saturday Evening Post*)

WHAT Epes Calef principally thought, walking sharply away from his discharged responsibility at the Custom House, through the thin icy lignt of late afternoon, was that he was glad that was finally done with. It was, he assured himself again, with articulating lips. The next time he went to sea, to the East, to Patagonia and Canton and the Falklands, or lay in the Macao Roads with the Brahminy kites perched high on the rigging, he would be first mate, perhaps even master, of the *Triton,* and no longer a mere supercargo. No words could adequately express how much he hated that position of barterer. Very privately—in view of his father's special characteristic— he hadn't considered it at all a necessary part of his training for the commanding of Calef ships; others of his acquaintance, making like him toward such a superlative destiny, had worked their way progressively aft with no pause over kegs of Spanish dollars and the ridiculous merchants of Co-Hongs and countinghouses. They had always, from the first, been seamen, while he— But he need bother no longer, his seemingly endless wearisome apprenticeship, the tiresome dickering, was over; and in the coming spring, before the lilacs had bloomed in Salem, he would personally, individually, order the last fast holding the *Triton* to earth cast off.

He swore a little, in a manner at once of the sea and of vainglorious youth. Epes Calef was not yet twenty, and his breath congealed in a sparkling mist. He was, he reminded himself with a lifting pleasure, home; the *Triton* had docked at noon, but he had been so busy with the infernal accounts and manifest, the wharfinger and harbor master, that he had hardly dwelt upon his safe and happy return. Neither, he suddenly realized, had he yet seen any member of his family; even Snelling Pingre, their head clerk, had been able only to wave briefly from a distance. His, Epes', father was more often than not at Derby Wharf on the return of one of his ships; either Ira Calef, or Bartlett, the elder son. Now Bartlett, his thoughts ran on, had always been splendidly suited to his appointed activity— an application to the purely financial side of the Calefs' wide trading voyages.

With Bartlett in Salem gradually taking the place of their father, and Epes a master on the sea, the fortunes and prestige of the family would increase in the next generation and the next. But this reflection, or rather its implication, suddenly changed the substance of his thoughts. They settled on Annice Balavan—with an un-accountable, an unreasonable sensation of amazement. Epes recognized that he was about to marry her. He had made this a possibility, no, inevitable, just before he had left on this last voyage. He was in for it, he told himself, in a phrase not wholly gracious, since he had given her the Calef token.

It was remarkable about that—it was an obang, really; a thin gold coin of the East, almost as broad as his palm and stamped with angular signs—because there could be no doubt that when a Calef gave it to a woman, no matter who she was or what the circumstances, he married her. It had come to Salem in the reticule of a ridiculous Dutch girl to whom the obang had been given in the hotel of the Dutch East India Company at Batavia by the first ad-venturous Calef. And after that its tradition, its power, had fast animated it. Epes' attitude toward this, and to Annice Balavan, was consequently fatalistic. Now, after nearly two years on the islands and continents and wide waters of the world, he didn't see how he had come to give the token to Annice. He had, all at once, no great desire for marriage, except to the *Triton;* but with a youthfully philosophical sigh he accepted the impending consequences of his gift as inevitable to life.

There was some consolation in the reflection that Annice

was, it was practically admitted, the prettiest girl in Salem, and there was a permissible question if there were any better looking in Boston. Her considerable part of the Balavan money, too, would be a material assistance to the not inconsiderable Calef funds and ambitions. It was, after all, Epes decided, a very sensible and advantageous arrangement; the more so because he knew beforehand that Annice would not insist on going to sea with him; everyone, in fact, connected with a ship hated a woman, the master's wife, on board. She didn't like the sea, and made no secret of her feeling; the air from it, drawing in through Salem Harbor, took the crispness out of her muslins and made her hair, she declared, look like strings. But that was nonsense; her ashen-gold hair, even in its net, had the softest and most delicate beauty imaginable. Very different it was from Sumatra's; but then, everything about Sumatra, the younger sister, was unlike Annice; particularly the former's exaggerated—Epes called it that—passion for ships and the sea. She carried this to a most unbecoming extent; positively her questions were a nuisance.

He passed the Essex House on the right, and then the Marine Store. The light faded rapidly and it was growing noticeably colder, frigid and still; the sky was a clear pale yellow that flickered in the patches of metallic ice along the gutters, and footfalls, voices, carried surprisingly. Unaccustomed, for a comparatively long period, to winter, he was at once aware of its sting and yet found a gratification, without specially heavy clothes, in disregarding it. He had been hardened to both danger and exposure, and he accepted them with a sense of challenge and victory. How little Salem, the land, compared with the shifting sea, changed; here there was no making or taking in of sail; it didn't matter what happened in the way of weather, the houses, the stone-laid streets, even commonly the trees, were always placidly, monotonously the same. The life in them, as well, went always over the old charted and recharted courses, every morning resembled every other morning, each night all the others. Why, take this latter voyage, twenty-five days from Bombay to Liverpool——

He had reached Summer Street, and turned again, past Mechanics Hall; soon he would be on Chestnut, and then wholly home. Where, he wondered, after he was married to Annice, would he live? Maybe on Bath Street, overlooking Washington Square, or close to the Ammidons. Annice, he thought, would rather prefer that; there was at last a movement away from Chestnut Street toward the square. It made no difference to him; his home primarily —yes, his heart—would be on the quarter-deck of his ship. His wife might arrange all the details on shore. She would do it very well, too; Annice, in addition to her beauty, was capable; she had a direct, positive mind.

He would get the preliminaries of that business over with as soon as possible, and then, late in April, or in May— Where, he speculated already, would he set sail for? There were so many alternatives, so many diverse cargoes to load and progressively discharge. Abruptly he was swinging in between the hand-wrought iron fencing across the Calef dwelling. It was an imposing square house of brick with a square-looking classic portico, a tall elaborate Palladian window above, and four great chimneys at the corners of the white-railed captain's walk that crowned the flattened roof. Epes found the front door unsecured, and entered, calling in a voice that echoed in the bare, dignified hall.

Instantly, from the floor above, his mother replied, but in a voice strangely, almost unrecognizably emotional, and he heard her equally disturbed and hurried approach. The darkly paneled and carved stairway, bending above his head at the tall window over the portico, hid her until she had almost reached him; and then with an involuntary painful contraction of his heart he saw that she was in deep mourning, and that her face was heavy, sodden with tears. Before he could question her, her arms were about his shoulders and she was sobbing again.

"Epes, Epes, I was afraid you weren't coming back either."

"What is it?" he stammered. "Is father——"

She drew slightly away from him, gazing with streaming eyes into his questioning face. "Why, haven't you— But

that is incredible!" She was close to him again. "Bartlett is dead. It—it happened in New York, from a torn
finger and blood poisoning. In two days, Epes; we hardly
got there, saw him. Your father had to go to Boston,
and is just back; but he'll see you almost at once, in the
music room, he said."

How like his father that insistent formality was, Epes
thought; nothing, it seemed, was to shake the dignity, the
aloofness of Ira Calef. His manner positively carried with
it a chill as palpable as that now in the streets. He was,
of course, both to the world at large and to his family, the
perfect shape of integrity; but that, with his rigidly correct
deportment, appeared to be his only conception of what
was owing, through him, to exterior circumstance and
people. All people—Clia, his wife, his two sons—had been
exterior to Ira Calef; it was always evident that he viewed,
weighed every possible development of living solely in the
light of his own unalterable convictions and wishes. They
were, it was true, always carefully studied, logical; nor
were his decisions quickly formed, in any heat, generous
or bitter; it was the inflexible manner, the finality and
detachment of their announcement which made them appear
so unbearably arbitrary.

The music room, like the stair well, was entirely paneled,
walls and ceiling in dark wood, and the mahogany in it,
the waxed floor, even the windows with their multiplicity
of small panes, held in replica the withdrawn, almost
morose effect given by Ira Calef himself. He came presently, in a gait neither slow nor fast, into the music room,
where, without his mother, Epes was waiting. The other's
show of welcome was, for him, unusual; he held Epes'
hand for more than the strictly necessary moment, and at
once indicated a chair and the fact that Epes might sit.
He was a big man, past sixty, handsomely proportioned,
with a handsome face evenly pallid except for the discol-
orations hanging under eyes themselves almost without a
perceptible shading. They were, of course, gray, yet they
were so pale that but for their domineering focus they
rather resembled clear water slightly crystallized with ice.
He made an adequate but brief reference to Bartlett's

death, dwelling for a little on the collapse of the boy's mother; and then leaning back and deliberately, for the time, shifting the conversation, asked Epes Calef for a detailed account of what on his voyage as supercargo he had accomplished.

This Epes, to his considerable relief of mind, was able to explain satisfactorily. The master of the *Triton*, Whalen Dove, had come on board the ship at Gravesend, twenty miles down river from London, and after they had been wind-bound for two weeks at Ramsgate they had proceeded to Madeira for wine, put into Colombo after twenty days, and had gone on almost immediately to the Coromandel Coast, Pondicherry and Madras, where the cargo had been disposed of through Lyss, Saturi & Demonte. Yes, the ship had come home by way of Rotterdam. Lost Teneriffe above the clouds five degrees west. They had made seventeen knots with the main skysail set, when a British ship was under double-reefed topsails. But in a three-quarters gale, west southwest, they carried away a mizzen topsail and the foresail burst.

Ira Calef listened to this in an admirable silence that at the same time conveyed the impression that he was exercising an unnecessary amount of patience in the waiting for details of more importance. Epes quickly recalled himself from his enthusiasm in the mere fact of seamanship. There were close to two hundred cases of indigo in the *Triton's* hold—186, to be precise; about a million pounds of Madras sugar; 460 pieces of redwood; 709 bags of ginger; 830 bags of pepper; 22 chests of tea— The duty, the elder decided, would be over twenty thousand dollars.

"You didn't like this," he said unexpectedly to his son. Epes met his cold gaze fairly. "No, sir," he replied. "Always the taste for mere ships."

To this there was no permissible answer.

"I am sorry for that," the other proceeded, "for, now that Bartlett is dead, it will be needful for you to give up the sea as a career; I shall require you to stay in Salem. There are plenty of good, even faithful masters of ships; but after me you are the only remaining Calef; and it won't do for you to be knocking around the windy reaches of the globe." He stopped, entirely inattentive of Epes' strained lips, his half-lifted hand.

A choking emotion, partly made up of incredulity and in part a burning resentment, fast-rising rebellion, filled Epes Calef. This—this wasn't right, it wasn't fair, it wasn't possible. They couldn't take and, for all his past life, fix his every ambition and hope and standard on the sea, and then in a sentence or two destroy him, ruin everything he was and might be; for what his father had just said amounted to no less. It was inhuman. It couldn't be! Evidently Ira Calef expected him to speak, to acquiesce, for his regular eyebrows mounted ever so slightly. But the thing, the only safety, for Epes now was to remain silent.

"I am not even, completely, certain of Salem," the elder went on in his level voice, after what had almost become an unbearable pause. "I personally shall never live anywhere else; but it may be necessary for you to move into Boston—for a number of years anyhow. I am getting more and more absorbed in marine insurance; and the opportunities for the study of that are moving away from us here. I have spoken to Annice about all this, and since she is a sensible girl with no fancy for a husband eternally below the horizon she is delighted."

"I see," Epes said uncertainly.

Annice Balavan would be delighted with all that his father had just said, especially with the Boston part, the larger society there. She was a natural part of this new, incredibly horrible plan; instantly he identified her with it, saw her moving radiant and content over its monotonous bricks and floors and earth. Something within him, automatic, brought him to his feet. The other glanced up, once.

"You are, of course, upset by the suddenness of the news of your brother's death," he conceded. "If you like you may go to your room with no further discussion at present. There isn't a great deal left to be said—more movements than words. The most advantageous arrangements will be made for Annice and you; her mother has already promised to furnish a Boston house for her in the new style. I am pleased with the manner in which you appear to have accomplished your duties on the *Triton.*"

In his room a fire of coals was burning in the grate, with a faintly audible splitting and small rushes of gaseous flame. It cast a perceptible ruddiness on the immediate oak flooring, while the rest of the room was rapidly dimming; the windows, beyond which the familiar limbs of the elms on the street were sharp and black, showed only rectangles of cold gray; the yellow light had faded from the sky. Epes stood irresolutely, with his gaze lowered, his brow drawn with lines. He could just see his blue sea chest, sent up from the ship earlier in the afternoon; and the brass disks of a nocturnal, his chiefest treasure, hung, he knew, above the chest on the wall. That old instrument of navigation, for finding at night, through the North Star, the hour, seemed to challenge and mock his wretchedness and impotence. That latter word most perfectly held the essence of his tragic situation.

He could do nothing!

Epes slipped into a chair and attempted to combat this. A daring resolution hovered about him, reckless, and yet, he told himself fiercely, entirely justified; he might run away to sea; the sea, the service, he loved. He could ship any day, from any port, as third, probably second mate, and after a single voyage become first officer. That was the reasonable thing to do. He understood that an appeal to his father was worse than useless; the opening of any protest, a difference of opinion, determination, would close Ira Calef to both sympathy and attention. He would be simply, remotely unbending—the eyebrows would climb, his mouth harden, a cutting phrase end the conversation. His father, Epes had realized, was different from the other pleasant fathers he knew; he had always been, well—inhuman. That term in such a connection was new, presumptuous, but Epes in his present mood defiantly allowed it. However, not until now had he acutely suffered from the elder Calef's disposition. Outside he had heard the words "an India liver" applied to his father; yet even Salem was cautious, deferential in its attitude there; Epes could never remember an occasion when his father had been balked in a decision, or even seriously contradicted.

He felt actually as though he hated that frozen parental figure; and he almost blamed Bartlett for dying. That recalled the fact that his brother was dead, that his emotion was neither appropriate nor decent; but the threatened, overpowering wrong to him persisted in dominating every other response. Yes, Epes repeated, he would run away; that—very successfully—had been done before. He'd leave everything, go with only the clothes in which he stood, leaving, out of the sum due him from the *Triton,* payment for them. That act, he recognized, must take him forever from his family, from, as long as Ira Calef lived, his home, Salem. The other would never relent. He thought for a moment of his mother's helpless position; never had he heard her raise her voice, oppose in any particular her husband. He was not, it was true, unkind or discourteous to her, he merely ignored the possibility of her having a single independent desire, a fraction of personality or will. And during Epes' life she had shown no indication that he was wrong. What, Epes now wondered, was the actuality beneath her calm demeanor; maybe she hated, detested Ira Calef. This amazing speculation redirected his thoughts to Annice Balavan.

Or rather, it drew his mind back to the token, the gage of the Calef men. Its reputed, its proved force exerted a species of numbing magic on him; his superstitious regard for it held his imagination as though in chains. Epes had given the obang to Annice, and therefore he was going to marry her; there was no escape from the girl who possessed it. This instinct was so strong that it struck at all his vague planning—Annice, if he knew her, would never consent to marry a runaway sailor, third mate or first or master. No matter what he might project, an unforeseen circumstance, accident, would betray him and marry him to Annice Balavan.

He tried to throw this conviction off, to laugh it away for nonsense; he derided himself unsparingly; rising, he told himself that he would tramp down through the house and out at once; but instead he sank back into his chair. Yet it might be that he could get away, come back successful, rich, in a very few years—one good voyage would secure that—and find Annice waiting for him. This seemed to him an inspiration, and a hard, active spirit welled up within him. After no more than one voyage to China. But again a disability, as gray as the dusk without, flooded him; he couldn't, when the moment came, walk away in that manner from responsibility. No matter what his father was like, he was incontrovertibly his father; already Epes Calef saw his world as the deck of a ship, and the high order, the discipline of that plane was the base of his being. There was, of course, injustice on the sea; tyrannical captains; but the injustice and tyranny could not be met with mutiny. For example, if as a subordinate he were directed to take his ship onto rocks that he could clearly see, what was there for him to do but that? How could he question or penetrate the superior, the totally responsible position?

There had been cases when a master, obviously insane or incapacitated, had been restrained, held in his cabin against the next port inquiry, by his principal officers; but even at the height of his desire Epes couldn't call his father insane. Still seeing his fate as a part of the obsessing sea he told himself that figuratively he had been set ashore on a sterile and deserted beach while his ship, having swung about with her sails filling gloriously, left him for the rush of free water. Accustomed to the open, to hour after hour, day after day, month on month, on deck, he felt all at once that he couldn't breathe in his closed room the confined heat of the coals. Epes, for a little, suffered acutely, in a constriction of nerves. His whole life was to be like this!

A knock sounded at the door, and a servant entered with fresh candles, which he proceeded to fix on the dressing stand, the overmantel, and light. The illumination, at first uncertain, wan, gained in steady brightness. It was time to dress for dinner. There had been no opportunity for him to procure mourning, but he put on his darkest, most formal clothes, and tied a severe black neckcloth.

The candelabra on the dining table showed his mother's place to be empty—she was not yet able to manage the casual—and the chair that had been Bartlett's was pushed against the wall. Ira Calef, seen to extreme advantage at the ceremony of dinner, hardly spoke; he was intent upon his codfish, with a green sauce; and he tasted critically the brown sherry before him in a large goblet of fragile glass flecked with gold. With this, it developed, he was dissatisfied; the wine had, he said curtly, withered; sherry, upon opening, could not withstand delay. He sent out the entire decanter with the order to replace it with another bottling—the Tio Pepe of the *Saragon*. He listed his cellar by the names of the vessels in which the various importations had been made. During this process he maintained an inflexible silence colored with his familiar suggestion of a restraint that no immoderate cause could break. To Epes the sherry, when it arrived, had no more warmth or flavor than was probable in the celebrated muddiness of the Hugli River.

Selecting a cheroot blindly from the box held at his elbow, and lighting it at the tendered spill, he retired mentally in the thin veil of smoke that rose across his face.

"You will, of course, stop in at the Balavans' this evening," his father said presently. Everything he uttered, Epes thought, took subconsciously the form of a direction. Still he must, he supposed, see Annice, if only for the announcement of his return.

The Balavans lived on the north edge of town, their terraced lawn descended to navigable water—to the anchorage, in fact, of the now vanished Balavan merchant fleet, and a deserted warehouse. And, shown through the hall to a drawing-room against the dark, bare garden, Epes found not Annice, as he had expected, but Sumatra. She was glad to see him. She was an indifferent girl, and this was specially noticeable; but he returned, inwardly and visibly, little if any of her pleasure.

"Tell me every shift of the wheel," she demanded, facing him from the long stool of the spinet. "Be a human log."

"I thought Annice was here," he replied.

"She will be soon enough. Did the *Triton* do anything really stirring, outsail seven ships or part both chains in

Table Bay? I hope you came into Derby Wharf with
the sheer poles coach-whipped and cross-pointed Turks'-
heads with double-rose props."

"I assure you, Sumatra," he told her stiffly, "that I
haven't any idea of what you are talking about. And,
what is more, I don't think you have." With this he half
turned from her.

He could still see her, though, a thickly set girl—was
she sixteen yet?—with a rosy, impertinent face and hair
loosely confined in a ribbon. Her name had been given
her from the fact that a Balavan, a master of ships, had
in the eighteenth century discovered pepper growing wild
on the coast of Sumatra. But there was now, Epes told
himself, a far better reason—heaven knew she was peppery.
Rather a detestable child.

Far from being disconcerted by the brevity of his retort
she replied that she had heard it didn't matter what he
understood or didn't understand about the sea—"Now that
you are to be a clerk."

After the stress, the difficulty of his homecoming, and
from Sumatra, this was positively too much; and all the
bitterness banked up by his father's unassailable situation
fell upon her.

"All your life," he asserted, "you have been a joke, with
your language like a crazy ship chandler. You have never
been in the least feminine or attractive, and you never can
be, not by the width of a finger nail. Part of it—being
built like a sampan—you can't help; but that won't help
you, will it? But you might, at least, get a vocabulary
that ought to suit you better. All I say is, you'll notice,
that it ought to. What suits you I shouldn't try to guess.
That's mostly what I think about you; but on this other
subject, where my private affairs, perhaps sorrows, are
concerned, shut up."

This ill-tempered, rasped conclusion came so abruptly
that it surprised even him. He glanced at her a shade
regretfully, and saw with a feeling of satisfaction that
once, anyhow, he had impressed, silenced her. Her head
was bent, her face obscured by her forward-swung hair;
her slippers were very rigidly together.

"I suppose you are right," she admitted after a long breath. "Probably you won't believe it, but I have never thought much about myself or how I affected people. Yes, a lot of them—and you, too—must think I am a joke. So few care for anything as I do for the sea. It used to seem to me that perhaps you did; I was wrong though."

"Didn't I tell you to let me alone?" he cried, again furious. "How do you know what I care for? What do you mean by daring to judge me, you—you——"

"Aren't you leaving the sea for your father's counting-house?" Sumatra calmly demanded of him.

"If I am it's because my duty is there," he replied miserably.

"You are the hell of a sailor," she commented.

Ever since she could walk Sumatra had, on occasion, sworn; at times it had amused Epes Calef, but now it only added to his dislike, his condemnation of her. She should not, he told her severely, have been encouraged to continue it. Her answer was the expressed reflection that he might do better on shore; his delicacy was much too great for salt water.

"Do you honestly hate me?" she asked unaccountably. "I mean, when you are not in a rage."

"No, I don't hate you, in a rage or out of it," he said coldly. "Often you go beyond your years, and you presume a good deal; but after a while you'll make a good wife for the captain of a West India lugger or some fellow trading with Bermuda Hundred."

This was an adroit insult, and pleasurably he watched her flush. She became so unhappy that he was magnanimously touched with remorse, and said with a kindly condescension that it was too bad she hadn't been born a boy.

At that he had it swiftly proven to him that attitudes, interests, vocabularies were misleading, for logical and wholly feminine tears actually streamed over her healthy cheeks. It grew worse, for she rose and came close to him, with clasped desperate hands.

"Don't listen to him!" she begged. "He's a horrid man of snow, even if he is your father; and if you let him he'll spoil your life. Tell him that you have made up your mind to go to sea, and that nothing can change it. You won't be struck dead. He isn't God with a stick of lightning."

"You don't understand," he stammered, backing away from her, intolerably embarrassed. "I am not, as you seem to think, afraid of my father. I have been over and over it all in my head. No, it's something different. You couldn't understand," he repeated. "No girl could."

"You are wrong," she replied slowly. "I see all that you mean, and—yes—I suppose I admire you for it. You can't mutiny"—she echoed his own phrase—"others could, but not a Calef. Yet you make me furious, you are so helpless, so stupid. You will marry Annice and grow fat and nearsighted, that's what'll happen to you."

Annice, in the doorway, asked: "Well, why not?"

Disregarding Sumatra, Epes went forward to meet the girl who possessed the Calef token. He had, in spite of his assertions, forgotten how lovely she was, slender and palely gold; her gray-gold hair was like a cloud in sifted sunlight, her skin had an even, warm pallor that remotely suggested oranges, and her eyes were a cool autumnal brown.

"Epes," she continued, "how burned and well you look."

She took his vigorous hands in hers, held them lightly for a second, and then relinquished him.

"There is an ocean of things for us to talk about and arrange," she proceeded, from a divan; and her glance at Sumatra was a dismissal.

The younger girl made a profound curtsy to them both, surprisingly graceful for her solidity of waist, and disappeared. Epes realized that he ought to kiss Annice, but he felt awkward in the extreme. She held her face delicately to him; it was like a tea rose. He was, he supposed, fortunate; but no sensation of gladness accompanied that supposition. It was so sad about Bartlett, she went on; and how enormously his death had affected them. Wasn't it unexpectedly sweet of her mother to furnish their house —"in miraculous brocades and hangings, with a French boudoir"?

Walking slowly home, the stars, very high above him,

were like a powdering of dry, luminous snow on the polished night. The cold was so intense that his exposed face ached. What an odorous heat there would be over the mooring at the Prince's Ghat in Calcutta! He remembered the firm, light pressure of the northeast trades, the perpetual fleecy trades clouds about the horizon, the bonitos and albacore in the deeply blue, sunny water. Lovely sailing.

Was it true that all that, for him, was already a thing of the past? Epes couldn't believe it, and yet—what other conclusion was possible? Turning his thoughts to the past hour with Annice he tried, in her, to find a recompense for what he was losing, but without success. He was proud of her; in her way she was fine and beautiful. Perhaps what he understood love to be came later; it might be unreasonable to expect the whole measure of joy at once. Annice was cool enough; indeed they had acted as though they had been married for a year or more, as though they had been continuously together instead of having been so lately separated by the diameter of the world.

There was a light in the small room at the rear of the hall, used by his father as an office; and as he laid aside his wraps the elder appeared in the doorway, obviously desiring speech.

"I have seen Mr. Dove," Ira Calef told his son; "and he corroborates your report, with some added praise. I am very well pleased, Epes. Your conduct this evening, too, was admirable. I did not quite expect, at once, such a full comprehension of my intentions. The fact is," he proceeded in a general discursive manner, "that the country is changing very rapidly. A great many men are blind to this, and as a result they will have to suffer. It is not so with me. The days of the colony are at last definitely at an end; from now on not adventure but finance will be the ruling spirit. That is one of the reasons why I am withdrawing you from the sea. Let other paid men—good men, but essentially subordinate—undertake the gales and half gales; it is important for you, a Calef, to be at the center of affairs and safe."

Epes' expression was dull, unrevealing; everything that was being said contradicted and outraged his every fiber.

Safe! Good men, but subordinate! He longed to shout
—for all sailors, before and aft the mast—a contradiction
of his father's cold patronizing periods. He loathed the
money sharks who on land, in houses, traded on the courage and endurance and fidelity of ships' masters and crews.
If Ira Calef was right, and they had grown unimportant,
if their greatness was doomed to vanish—why, then he
wanted to go too.

All this filled his brain and throat, clamored for expression; but not a word, not a protesting sound came from
him. Suddenly he was tired; Epes felt as though the leaden
weight of his future already rested on him. The other
made an approving reference to Annice Balavan; and perversely, for no discoverable reason, in place of the golden
vision of Annice he saw Sumatra, square, like a sampan—
and defiant.

When, for the time, Ira Calef had quite finished the expression of his balanced judgments Epes rose with the
shadow of an instinctive bow.

"Very good, sir." The sea phrase was spoken in a voice
without animation.

Above, close by his room, he was mildly surprised to
find his mother. It was evident that she had been waiting
for him, and followed, carefully closing the door behind
them.

"How did you find Annice?" she asked.

But to his reply that Annice had seemed well enough
she paid no attention. With a quick, nervous gesture she
pressed her handkerchief against her eyes.

"And your father——"

Epes said nothing.

"Epes," she cried, in a sudden realization of all that, it
was now clear, she wanted to say to him, "no matter how
hard and unreasonable he may seem, you mustn't contra-
dict him. It isn't as though he were going to do you harm.
What he plans is right; he can see so much farther than
we can. And you will be very happy, I am sure, with Annice. You'll forget the sea?" her voice rose in inquiry.

"Never," Epes answered.

Clia Calef shivered momentarily. "I was afraid of something like that," she admitted. "And that is why it is necessary for me to speak to you. You must do what your father wants."

This was, he thought, in view of his restraint, all unnecessary. He regarded his mother, seated with her head blurred against the candlelight, with a mature, unsympathetic attention. Women — the characteristic feminine world—were very far outside the scope of his interests and being. Even to his mother he could not explain, seek to justify himself; his inner being had grown obdurate, solitary; life, which had once, in the form of blue water, everywhere surrounded and touched him, had retreated, flowed away, leaving him on that sandy, meaningless beach. Why did she talk and talk?

"You have been wonderfully quiet," she still went emotionally on; "I could tell that from Ira's manner. But I wasn't sure. I'm not yet; and for that reason, to save hideous trouble, I made up my mind to tell you. There is a little strangeness about your father, and it comes out when he is contradicted. Except for that he is splendid. I don't just know what it is, but contradiction makes him wretched; he—he loses control of himself." She was speaking faster, with an obvious increasing difficulty. "I did it, once. We hadn't been married long, and it was in the garden. He had just come back from the counting-house, and he was carrying a light cane, a wanghee. And, Epes, he struck me with it. Oh, not very hard; not, really, too hard. I didn't say a word. I stood for a second, quite frozen, and then I turned to walk out of the garden, to leave him, forever. I intended to go, but it did hurt. I was confused, and instead of finding the gate I walked into the geraniums and fainted. So, you see, I stayed."

Epes Calef drew in an audible harsh breath.

"You mustn't judge him!" she exclaimed eagerly. "I am sure it spoiled a large part of his life. He carried me into the house, and neither of us have referred to it since. Yes, it hurt him beyond speech; for weeks he slept hardly at all. Epes, Epes, I can't have it happen to him again. He is your father and you must help. You love him, too, I am certain; and what he arranges is always, always best."

She was so tremulous, so self-effacing, that he felt he couldn't bear to hear another word. It was terrible, and as wrong as possible.

"He ought to be denied," Epes said in a strong voice. "Now that you have told me this I think it might be what he, what we all need; perhaps I shall have to."

"That is not for you to judge," Clia Calef told him with a resumption of dignity. "You would be very wicked indeed; and not only, perhaps, harm Ira permanently, but me as well. I have to live with him, and not you. Epes, you have the ignorance of youth; but if I can help it I won't have you upsetting our life."

He was, he saw, literally nothing before her love for the man who had struck her with his wanghee.

"It would spoil everything," she half whispered to herself. "I have tried hard, so long."

Epes rose sharply. "You must go to bed," he directed. "If you are not careful you will be sick." He was deathly sick. She clung to him.

"Promise me, promise you will do as he says."

"I have already decided that," he answered in his weary, dead voice.

Epes, with his hand under her arm, conducted her to her room. A wave of warmth flowed into the hall as the door opened and shut, like the soiled enervating breath of a hidden corruption.

It was a physical impossibility, in the temporarily empty days following immediately Epes' arrival home, for his spiritual darkness to stay at its intensest; at least his state of mourning made it unnecessary for him to go to the meaningless parties being then crowded into the heart of the winter season. It was uncomfortable for him at home, and he fell into the habit of lounging through the afternoons in the more informal of the Balavans' drawing-rooms. There, in his special position and license, he was permitted to smoke his cheroots and listen to the light easy run of Annice's voice, so much like the easy light tripping of her fingers over the keyboard of the spinet. He was engaged in exactly this manner an hour or so before Annice's departure for one of the principal cotillons of the year, at

Hamilton Hall; and Annice, who had dressed early so that she could be with him, was sitting erectly by an opposite wall. Sumatra was present, too; a fact to which her elder sister repeatedly called attention by urging the necessity of Sumatra's changing for the ball. Sumatra, Epes had learned, had been half permitted and half coerced into going.

"I can get ready in twelve minutes," she announced.

"I don't doubt that," Annice retorted; "but what will you look like when it is done? In the first place your hair is like wire and takes the longest while to be really possible——"

"It won't matter," said Sumatra; "Epes told me I couldn't make myself attractive, no matter how much we all tried."

"Did you say that, Epes?" Annice asked. "It was rather tactless of you, because, though you'd never guess it, Sumatra is crazy about you. It might even be more than I am."

Epes Calef gazed at Sumatra with a brutal indifference. She met his eyes courageously, and in an even voice replied to her sister.

"I was once," she corrected the other, "when I thought that Epes belonged to the sea. But now he's on land——" She made a gesture of dismissal. "Epes, while I suspect he's very good, is my great disappointment. I don't like good people."

"What experience have you had with bad?" he asked cuttingly. "As usual, you are just talking words. You are a regular sea lawyer."

"Do get dressed, Sumatra," Annice said.

"Something light and feminine," Epes added; "with wreaths of flowers for you to put your feet through."

He couldn't understand why, whenever he talked to Sumatra, he became so vindictive. He had no particular desire to be nasty; it came up in spite of him.

"Perhaps no one will ask me to dance."

"If they do," he advised her, "and it is near supper, don't let go or you'll get no oysters."

"Sumatra, get dressed," Annice commanded.

"Maybe I won't at all."

"Do you mean you'll go like you are?"

"It wouldn't kill anyone, would it? I shouldn't come home and cry if I didn't get an armful of favors; I can get along, for a few minutes anyhow, by myself."

This, Epes thought, promised to be amusing. Peppery Sumatra! Annice glanced at him hastily.

"Please, Sumatra," she entreated; "we simply can't be late. I'll give you my white-ribbed Spanish stockings."

The other serenely answered, "The feet would be too big."

He had never noticed her feet, and to his considerable surprise they were smaller, narrower than Annice's.

"You are a lumpish, impossible child," the elder said acrimoniously. "Why I begged mother to let you start the cotillons I can't imagine. And when we get there you are not to hang about me."

"I won't; you're not seaworthy. You are cut away too much through the middle; you would go over in a good blow."

Epes incautiously laughed.

"Be still," Annice directed him; "she must not be encouraged in such conduct."

"Well," he said pacifically, "you wouldn't, Trinidad." He often substituted the West India island for that from which she was named, reminding her of his matrimonial prediction.

"Yes, sampan," Annice echoed him. "Will you or will you not get dressed?"

"I will, when I have twelve minutes. It doesn't, you know, take me three hours." Nevertheless, she rose. "You haven't been specially nice to me, have you?" she said slowly, carefully avoiding Epes Calef. "You made pretty clear all you thought. I don't believe I could be like that."

Suddenly she gazed full at Epes. "It might be your father in you," she concluded; "if I were you I shouldn't encourage that—for Annice's sake. It would be so hard on her."

"Thank you, but I can take care of myself," Annice assured her brightly; "and it would be nicer to omit the personal history."

"All I say is wrong!" Sumatra declared.

"All," Epes echoed her.

"I must be a sampan."

"Must."

"Square bowed, and only fit for rivers."

"For rivers."

"But even that is better than a desk," she reminded him. She was beside the door, and paused with a hand upon the frame, looking over her shoulder. "What Annice told you was true," she reiterated. "I had a little picture hidden in a drawer, which I am now going up to tear into bits."

When she had gone Annice turned to him in a concili-atory manner.

"There is something I meant to tell you at once, this afternoon, but it slipped from my mind. I hope you won't be angry and I can't imagine how it happened. But the whole thing, of course, is exaggerated; it must be all non-sense at bottom. Still I am sorrier than words can say. Epes, somehow I've lost the token."

He gazed, startled at her, with a stirring of the old Calef superstition within him. However, he concealed it.

"That is too bad. We think it's rather valuable, you know. Perhaps it will turn up; there are so many places you might have left it."

No, she replied; she knew how they felt about it, and she had left it, she was certain, in the lacquer box on her dressing-case. It was very mysterious and uncertain.

"Now," she said with a smile, "you won't have to marry me. The spell, the charm is broken."

This he repudiated in a form correct and stiff. The in-fluence that absurd East Indian coin exerted upon his thoughts was amazing. He repeated, silently, her words—"Now you won't have to marry me." But certainly they had no force, no reality. He was bound to her not by an obang, but by honor. At the same time his feeling was undeniably different; he regarded her from a more de-tached position. What was that Sumatra had hinted—about crying over a scarcity of favors, and taking three hours to dress? It didn't matter to him, nothing did; it

only added to the general weariness, waste of existence.
Epes recalled the promised French boudoir in the threatened Boston house. That was it—his life hereafter was to
be passed in a little scented room choked with brocade and
hangings.

A maid appeared, enveloped Annice in a long cloak lux-
uriously lined with sables, twisted a silvery veiling over her
netted hair, over her lovely regular features, her face with
its indefinite suggestion of golden oranges.

"I thought Sumatra would be late," she declared in an
abstracted exasperation. Then through the veiling she gave
him a metallic and masked kiss. From the hall her voice
sounded, fretful about her carriage boots.

The carriage with Annice and Sumatra departed; he
must go, too; where, he didn't know, it no longer mattered;
home, he supposed. There was a second stamping of hoofs
before the Balavan dwelling, and Mrs. Balavan, in street
wraps, passed the drawing-room door. Epes remembered
that he had heard his mother speak of going to a ballad
soirée with her. Still he remained seated, after the hour
of dinner, and it was nearly nine before he left.

The light in his father's office was, as usual, turned up,
a thin haze of tobacco smoke perceptible. Without the
desire to go up to his room Epes sat in a lower chamber.
Snatches of the conversation—the quarrel, really—between
Sumatra and Annice returned to him. How essentially
different they were. Annice was far, far the lovelier. She
made a business of being beautiful. But at least that, in
a wife, was something; the majority of wives had far less.
What a curious double life it would be—two separate
people with one name, in one house. She could never, he
was sure, mean more to him than she did now. And it
was clear that for her part her demand was no greater.

Sumatra would be the opposite—there was no end to
what she expected, fought for, insisted upon. Strangely
enough, he couldn't see her as a wife—even for that coastwise figure he had so often pictured—at all. He was unable to discover what sort of man would suit her, but
certainly one armed with a belaying pin. He became conscious of a clamor faintly heard from another part of

Salem; it grew more distinct, and he recognized that it was the confused alarms and uproar of a fire. The fire evidently lay in the direction of Marlboro Street; the noise increased rather than subsided; but even this didn't stir him until his father appeared.

"I shall have to neglect my duty this evening," he explained; "there are some questions of foreign exchange. But perhaps you will take my place."

Epes went silently out to the hall, where two leather buckets, painted with the name Active Fire Club, were hanging. He secured them, and a wool scarf, and went unexcitedly in search of the fire. It was, as he had thought, in the vicinity of Marlboro Street, the Baptist Church. The Fire Engine Exchange, he saw, to which generally the men of the Calef family belonged, had secured the place of honor, directly at the conflagration. Its reservoir was connected by hose to another engine, and that latter to a third, which drew from the source of their water. A pandemonium rose about Epes—the hoarse, jeering shouts of the competing companies, authoritative voices magnified by trumpets, the clatter of the hand pump, and the dull roar of the unconquerable flames. A curtain of black smoke, ruddy at its base and, above, poured with live cinders, rolled up across the immaculate green sky and frosty stars.

The members of the Active Fire Club had formed their line for the rapid orderly passing of buckets, and Epes had taken his place at the end, when he saw a short, familiar feminine shape standing alone. It was Sumatra, and it was extremely wrong of her to be there, like that, so late.

He left his position hurriedly and laid a hand on her arm. How, he demanded, had she got there, and why was she by herself?

"Oh, Epes!" she exclaimed with pleasure. "The cotillon nearly killed me, it was so stupid; and then I heard the alarms, and James Saltonstall wanted to come; and so, you see, here we—here I am."

"Where is he? Why did he leave you?"

Before she could answer there was a louder opposed shouting of voices:

"Suck him dry, Exchange!"

"Overwash them, Adams. Drown the damned silk stockings!"

Sumatra clutched his hand excitedly. "Don't you see—they are trying to burst the Exchange engine; we haven't enough men to pump, because some didn't leave Hamilton Hall, and James is at the sweep. You must go, too, Epes. Quick, quick, or it will be too late!"

His negative attitude settled into an active perversity; Epes Calef made up his mind that he wouldn't pump; they could knock the silly engines into painted fragments for all him. Sumatra gave him a strong impatient shove forward, but he resisted her.

"The fire will be over in a few more minutes," he observed.

She damned the fire excitedly; it was the engine she cared about. "I'll pump, myself!" Sumatra cried.

He turned to her with a smile, but that was immediately lost as he saw that she had every intention of fulfilling her threat. Sumatra had started toward the profane companies of men when he caught her by the shoulder.

He said coldly, "You're crazy. Nobody ever heard of such a thing—a girl pumping at a fire! You'd be talked about, insulted in songs all over the country. Come home at once."

She wrenched herself from his hold, and Epes was obliged to stand in front of her with his arms outspread. Sumatra's face grew crimson with rage.

"Get out of my way!" she commanded him. "Do you think everyone is a coward and a ninny like you? I'll pump if I want to, and it doesn't matter who sings about it. I don't care what the other fools of women do."

"No, you won't," he told her grimly.

She gave him a shove, and she was so strong that, unprepared, he staggered. She nearly succeeded in evading him, but he caught her with an arm around her vigorous waist. In an instant they were fighting. Braced, with her hand crushing into his face, she tried to break his hold; then Sumatra struck him in the eye. Infuriated, he wanted to knock her head off, but he had to restrain himself to a negative attack.

"I'll throw you down and sit on you," he gasped; "here, on the street."

By way of reply she kicked his shins until, through the hurt, he could feel the blood sliding into his shoes. Shouts, which now, in his rage, he heard but dimly, derisive and encouraging calls, surrounded him. The girl, the little Amazon, was implored to crack his coco; there were protesting cries of shame, but these were lost in the larger approval and entertainment. By Jupiter, but she was finishing him! This, Epes desperately told himself, was horrible beyond words.

"Stop it!" he said savagely, again and again.

But through set teeth Sumatra replied that she'd pump if she chose, and no—no l-l-land shark could stop her. At this there was a hurrah. Her strength was amazing, and entirely wrong; she was like a maniac. Then with a free arm he punched her directly and rudely in the stomach. Sumatra settled against him limply; and holding her up, dragging her with him past threatening faces wavering in the dark, he succeeded in getting her around a corner to a deserted street.

She was still limp, struggling for breath; her face was pale and her hair in torn disorder. Sumatra slowly recovered, and—amazingly—she smiled. Epes' anger, too, fled; he gazed at her, examining in dismay her clothes with a feeling which might almost have been called admiration. Yet he spoke severely.

"You ought to be in a cage," he told her; "you're just wild."

However was she to fix her clothes, she replied; where could she go? "I ought to go back to Hamilton Hall."

To this he agreed, the Balavan house was far, inconveniently situated; and they decided, since the Calefs and Balavans were now practically one family, to stop at his dwelling for the repairing of her clothes and spirit. He secured his buckets and they hurried back, through a serene air like liquid ice, over Summer Street to Chestnut. The light was still burning in Ira Calef's office, and noiselessly they turned into an opposite room.

Epes went on into the dining room, opening darkly beyond, leaving Sumatra with candles on the floor before a tall mirror. There, bearing a high silver candlestick and a following indeterminate illumination, he discovered a bottle of champagne, tagged the ship *Nautilus* and the year, and gathered two high glasses and some ice. He was tingling with excitement, a disturbance deeper than physical. He felt oddly detached from his late life, the commonplace and irresponsible; his mind was without images, thought—it was like a whirling of crackling colored lights. He found his situation—the uncorked champagne, the two glasses, the unsuspecting near presence of his father, Sumatra, rearranged, entering the dining room—extraordinary and invigorating. The wine foamed whitely through the ice, turning into a silky clear amber that stung his lips. Sumatra observed, sitting down, that she ought to go on to the cotillon at once.

"What," she demanded, "will James Saltonstall think?"

That, Epes replied, was of singularly small importance.

The rose flush had returned to her cheeks, her eyes were shining; she was decidedly more attractive than he had admitted. But that, he made up his mind, he'd never tell her. She sipped and sipped from her glass; that in itself was unusual, startling. No, he corrected his impression, it would have been in any other girl of Sumatra's age, but not in her. The most unexpected, inappropriate things seemed to become her perfectly.

"I don't want to go," she added, so long after her other phrase that he almost lost the connection. "We are so different," Sumatra pointed out; "I hardly ever do what I don't want to. It's a good thing for your father I'm not you."

"It wouldn't make any difference," he said, listlessness again falling over him; "in the end it would be the same; you'd stay or go as he said."

"I would not."

"Oh, yes, but you would."

"He couldn't make me," she insisted; "not about that. It's too terribly important."

Epes became annoyed. "Can't you understand that, to

my father, nothing is important except what he wants?"

"Why argue?" she decided. "After all, I am not you. And yet, even as it is, I believe if I were concerned, which I'm not, I could do what I decided with him."

He laughed. "Try, and if you are successful, why— why, I'd marry you instead of Annice."

The flush deepened painfully in her countenance; she regarded him with startled eyes. For a moment there was a ridiculously tense silence; and then, relaxing, she shook her head negatively.

"It wouldn't be any good; you'd have no regard for me."

"Regard for you!" he exclaimed. "If you did that I'd think more of you than anything else on earth; more than I did of—of the *Triton.*" His voice, his manner darkened. "But you mustn't; there's a lot you don't understand— my father, first of all. He can be very nasty."

"I've told you before, he's only a man," she reminded him. "I shouldn't be afraid." Her direct gaze again challenged him, but Epes shook his head dejectedly. Suddenly she laid a hand over his. "I didn't tear that picture up," she whispered. Then with a sweep of her arm she finished what had been in her glass, and rose. "Come on, he's still in the office."

Epes Calef urged her in careful tones not to be a donkey; he tried, here discreetly, to restrain her; but she went resolutely on, through the front room into the hall. There would be a frightful row, but he couldn't desert Sumatra. However, in the passage she paused, with her lips against his ear.

"Remember, better than the *Triton,* or it would kill me."

Ira Calef looked up from his table, frowning slightly as she entered the office, followed by Epes. The elder's face was as white as marble under the artificial light.

"Why, Sumatra," he greeted her easily.

Epes tried to step between her and his father—disaster —but she held him back, speaking immediately in a voice as level as, but a little faster than, Ira Calef's.

"I suppose you think it's strange to see me here, so late, with Epes; but it is stranger even than you imagine." She put a hand over Epes Calef's mouth. "No," she protested, "you promised to let me speak. Mr. Calef," said the incredible Sumatra, "perhaps I ought to apologize to Mrs. Calef and you—Epes and I are married."

Epes' amazement, which he barely restrained, was no greater than his father's, but the latter's was given, for him, full expression.

"Married!" he repeated in a voice slightly and significantly louder than usual. "Why, that is outrageous! Nothing, nothing at all was said to me. My plan was wholly different."

He rose, beyond the table, with one hand resting beside a paper weight of greenish glass. Epes' eyes fastened upon this.

"It was, as you might guess, in a hurry," Sumatra went on; "we decided only today. You must remember that I am as much a Balavan as Annice, and I suit Epes far better; I understand and agree with his ambition."

The man's manner was colder than the night.

"What ambition?" he demanded.

"To go to sea, of course."

"Epes isn't going to sea," he instructed her.

"He wasn't, as your son," she corrected him; "but married to me, yes."

"No," Ira Calef answered in a restrained, bitter temper that yet had the effect of a shout.

"But he is," Sumatra Balavan retorted. "He is, and now you can't stop him. It doesn't matter what you want, I won't have a husband fastened like a sponge to the earth, and as soft as a sponge." Her anger, equal with Ira Calef's, rose.

The room grew quiet. Epes' attention was still concentrated on the heavy rectangle of glass close by his father's hand. With a sensation like an enveloping breath of winter air he saw the other's fingers reach out and close about the paper weight. He hadn't a second to spare; but Sumatra, too, had seen the instinctive movement on the table.

"I wish you would," she told the man facing her with a set, icy glare. "I'd have you dropped off the end of Derby

Wharf. I'm not your wife or son; there would be no reason for my protecting you, hiding your beastliness from the world. Nothing could be better than having you throw a paper weight at me."

The shadows under Ira Calef's eyes, on the deathly pallor of his face, were like black smudges; a shiver passed over his rigidity. His hand drooped; both hands held the edge of the table before him. Epes, in a swift insight brushed with compassion, saw what was in his father's mind — the huddled light figure crushing the geranium border.

"Get out of here," the elder said to Sumatra in strained, dry tones. "Go, and take him with you."

"To sea?" she insisted.

"If there is any salt water in hell."

But, once more in the hall, she was pitiably shaken.

"What can we do?" she implored Epes, against him.

He reassured her that that was easy enough; a far different, apparently trivial and ill-timed question occupied him.

"Sumatra," he proceeded, "tonight Annice told me that she had lost the obang, the Calef token. Did you find it?"

"No, Epes," she replied, "I didn't find it." Her voice sank, died. "I didn't find it, Epes," she repeated with difficulty. "I couldn't, very well, could I, when I had stolen it?"

THE RESURRECTION AND THE LIFE[1]

By WILLIAM C. G. JITRO

(From *The Little Review*)

THE low country of the lakes with its flowing blue waters, its sunken gray and yellow earth and low skies, is beautiful; yet there have been thrown down in it cities so mean, so cold, so dingy, and so ugly that in them any beautiful thing is marvelous. The eyes strain away out of the cities over the waters and the still, sandy marshes, or turn up into the fathomless heights of the sky; and again and again in springtime, when small clusters of fruit trees and rose vines bloom here and there in the smoke with robins singing in the new sticky foliage, one seeks such spectacles out to walk near them. As for the cities' polyglot people, they are so harsh, so cold and silent, and so monotonous both in appearance and in their fierce activity, that among them any one only beautiful or charming becomes precious; a thrilling deed, a noble character, a great love, a deathless faith, or even a passionate hatred, or profound despair is something to set apart, to cherish in the mind, to hoard and love.

For they dream, the people of those gray and far-off cities by the azure floods, as all must do or die; but their dreams are not good or sweet or high or noble.

Once it was evening in winter in a city and the great blue darkness had fallen upon the low plains, the waters, and the frozen marshes; the darkness had grown gray and misty; and after that, as usual within the city, it had become dead, cold, and dingy black. The long misty streets with their feeble pale-blue lamps were dingy; and though many hurrying people, rattling black gasoline motor vehicles, and broken dirty tram-cars passed in them, yet they remained dreary. One of the half dozen very long streets, which lie across the others and meet in the lower center of the city like the spokes of a half-wheel, was dark when I walked into it. It had large furniture shops full of colored lamps; tobacco and shoe shops well lighted up; and Jews' shops with every sort of cheap glittering merchandise to catch the eyes of the crowd of stupid whites and negroes who occupied this quarter; yet it seemed bleak and dark. The people hurried along silently in the shadows; old snow lay frozen in the dim dirty corners; and the dust was thick. Over the roofs the sky seemed particularly black, foggy and cold.

It was night.

For a time there was no sound except those of the vehicles flying over the rough pavement, the pounding tram-cars that passed, and the shoes of the hurrying people; but at last, at intervals above the other sounds there became audible what seemed to be a voice raised in shouting or speaking; and on coming to a place where two mean dark side streets met I found on the pavement of one of them a short, plump, gentle but very earnest and prepossessing negro of forty who was urging upon passers the principles of Jesus' teaching. He used the inflection and diction of most negroes in this part of the world, but he was neatly dressed and wore a greatcoat, though his head was bare, for he had placed his round black hat against an iron hydrant for the reception of coins. Four or five men who had turned aside from the main street were listening to him; more, however, were going into the half-screened drinking places all about. Besides, the farther side of the street in which he stood contained a row of little dark wooden buildings that held negro brothels.

It was a dusty winter night.

"You men, naow," the negro was crying in a ringing, pleasing voice, "you got to be good! You got to do as God says! It ain't gwine do you no good to pray to God if you don't do as He says! Don't you go to fightin' and killin' and gamblin' and then pray to God. It ain't gwine do you no good! First you got to quit yo' fightin', quit yo' killin', quit yo' drinkin', quit yo' gamblin', quit yo' swarin', quit yo' whore-mongerin: God does not wish you to do these things! Then you go to Him and pray! And he's gwine hear what you say!"

The utterance of these words with such singular force in that stirring melodious voice, and the face and form of this sturdy little man made lovely by joy, faith, an' good will, shone in that bleak cold street, it seemed to me, like a work of glittering gold and jewels amid gutter dust.

I drew nearer and listened to him say that he had come there because he had been bidden by God to go among men and preach the Word, not as preached in worldy churches but as the prophets of Israel and the Apostles preached it long ago. Men must be truthful, kindly, abstemious; then all would be well with them. They must understand one another, sympathize with one another, love one another. That was the Word. When all did so, then God's kingdom would have come on earth. Meantime the few who knew the truth and strove to live by it would, even though they were lonely and cast out, become happy, strong and courageous. Theirs would be a life unattainable by the gross and careless, a life inconceivable by such, yet the life that all men really desired, the life that was man's heritage.

Aside, as it were, for the assurance of timid children, he illustrated some of the workings of God's plan. Once a man received God into his heart and was trying earnestly to live according to His will, God would not desert or neglect him either in this world or any other. He himself was but a humble servant bidden to teach and expound the Word. And since he strove to do this, even though he never succeeded as he wished to, yet God had blessed him forty years with health and strength and the means to live. "The servant am worthy of his hire," God had said, yet so merciful and kind was God that, "Jes' so long as you try the best you can, He'll stand by you. Money an' things is the least, but He'll see to them too. Ah don't have to worry. When Ah get out of money He send me means to get some. Ah don't owe nobody a cent tonight 'cept seventy-five cents fo' coal, and the man said the' wasn't no hurry fo' that; but Ah'm goin' to pay him tomorrow night.

And this week Ah was down to the Boahd of Public Works and they said they'd put me to work next Wednesday mornin' shovelin' up ashes in the alleys. Ah'm gwine be there. So I get on. Kase Ah'm tryin' to do as God said. He'll do jes' the same by you. If you wonder who I am to stand out here and tell you this, Ah'm Brothah Frank Burns, Servant of the Lord, come to preach the Word like ole Isaiah and Jeremiah and ole Jonah—an' like ole Peter an' Paul an' Silas. They said what Ah'm tellin' you naow! Kase that's God's Word that'll make you happy an' strong an' glad!"

Bright earnestness! Steadfast belief! But two grim city policemen, coming through the dark street where the brothels are, making their way swiftly in the gloom, hear the preacher's voice and raise their heads. They are not patrolling and have not their bludgeons, but one immediately gives the other a package he has been carrying and hurries across the street behind the speaker: a short, burly man, pink-faced and contemptuous, active and strong, with the bold insolence and cruelty of the police. The buttons and silver shield glitter on the breast of his clean blue greatcoat; the forepiece and shield shine on his heavy cap. Without a word he takes the speaker from behind by arm and neck, jerks him violently backward, choking him, and all but throws him to the pavement. *"Here! Here! Here!"* he cries. "What are *you* doing?"

Startled, the negro tries to keep his feet and twist his head so as to see his assailant. He strives manfully to explain.

"Where's your *per*mit?" asks the policeman.

"Judge tole me Ah didn't need to have no *per*mit—"

"Git to hell out of here!"

The negro is thrown forward almost to his knees and flung about. Very firmly he declares: "Ah've come here to speak the Word of the Lord like the old prophets in de Bahble. Folks must know this. Judge he tole me—"

At that the policeman fiercely tightens his hold, strikes him on the head with his fist, and hurls him to his knees. The second officer, a taller man, runs in. And the eager crowd that has gathered in the dark during these few minutes of parley closes about to see. Again and again the negro is thrown down, struck, and dragged in the dust. He continues to gasp out his purpose. The dark cold street resounds with the noise of the blows, the scuffle, the negro's voice, and the feet of newcomers running up to see. At length, tossing along in the dark amid the crowd, the preacher is swept round a corner and pushed roughly past a dark little medical school, a cross street, and a long hospital with a dimly lighted colored statue of the Virgin in a front gable. Over the way are a dark cold little park with bare trees and a waterless basin, and beyond this some old public buildings. The negro's once neat clothes are twisted, half pulled from him, and covered with dust and mud, the hand of the policeman chokes him, but he continues to declare his purpose. The policeman, gripping him behind, rushes him along; the other follows carrying the round black hat and half entreating, half commanding the curious crowd to keep off and go away. The captive is taken round another corner and in through the dark basement door of a public building. The second policeman follows and closes the door. Then all go away except me.

I wait for a time, and the tallest policeman comes out and goes off. Soon after the burly attacker comes with his parcel and hurries up the street as if to make up lost time. After an interval the little preacher comes himself, alone and somewhat put to rights; goes quietly back around the corner, past the hospital and medical school and the park and on toward the corner where he was taken. But he seems to consider his work for the night done, and does not stop. He picks his way across the street of business and starts off northward as if beginning a long journey. I follow him curiously for two kilometers or more, but at last, concluding from the way in which he looks about when he passes under the street lights that he suspects that he is being followed, I turn off and go my way.

Next night, however, he is at his corner again, with a large crowd about him this time, for it is the gay free night before the Sabbath when the people have their wages for the week. Crowds are entering and leaving the brothels; loud cheery talk sounds everywhere, in the dark and in the cold blue light of the street lamps; and coins fall steadily into the hat by the hydrant. A tall spectacled friend, well dressed in fur cap and greatcoat with fur collar, accompanies the preacher tonight and treats him disdainfully; but just as before, with the same bright earnestness, the little man tells simply of his "mission," of God's laws and God's promises, and urges obedience to God. Without dismay, even with some zest, he speaks of last night: "Let 'em come an' git me again;" he says, "Ah'll be right back. They'll have to carry me though," he adds quickly. "I ain't gwine to fight 'em. That's what makes all the trouble, men, folks always a-fightin'. You boys," he cries earnestly, "don't you ever go to fightin'; don't you ever go off to no war and kill folks. If they try to make you, don't you care. Let 'em do what they can, but don't you care. The Lord said, 'Don't do it!' He does not wish you to do it! An' God'll look after you. Jes' you obey Him an' don't you worry!"

Introducing his companion, he assures his audience that this is "a splendid speaker," and listens eagerly to the other's halting, practiced: "Ah didn't expect to be called on to speak yeah this evenin'"; and interpolates quick, bright "Amen"s, "Yes, He will"s, and "Bless his Name"s into the exhortation that follows.

That night they were not attacked or molested.

But at a gathering of negroes on a later night I see the same bright strange little man standing unnoticed by himself at one side of the hall, and I go to him and assure him of my sympathy and tell him that I was present the night he was attacked. He passes over that hastily; it was nothing; he has had many such experiences; but when I ask him about himself he answers my questions obligingly, though with some diffidence. He knows nothing of his parents except that before the emancipation one or both were slaves; he has been taught scarcely anything; and has done hard work all his life. In his youth he joined a church and began to preach, but having come soon afterward to see the quality of churches and to be aware of his "mission," he traveled "north" and began to go about working and preaching. He belongs to no church and disapproves of all alike. He has no property, permitting himself nothing but poverty and labor. Already he is looked down upon as improvident by those who know him. His wife has left him, not relishing her lot with him, for they were forced always to lodge in the poorest parts of the towns they visited. The intolerance and hate of white Americans for negro people made their lives harder than they would otherwise have been. Single rooms near small independent "mission houses," when there was one that suited, were their temporary homes; and from one such the wife went at last to visit at the town of Nashville in the distant State of Tennessee, and she has not come back. Her intention to do so was vague at her departure. Her husband has suffered a great deal through her desertion and has humbly and pitifully begged her by letter to return, but he has borne her failure to do so and goes on with his work. He is not loved, nor even much liked by anyone, I find later; he and his preaching, his high standards, his belief, his self-reliance and fearlessness, even his good temper, seem disquieting to others, irritating, a bore, something to escape.

During that year he remained in the city by the floods preaching and working at hard manual labor.

But the next winter, well toward the end, there was an epidemic of pneumonia and my little apostle was stricken suddenly and removed to a cheerless public hospital. There, gasping and choking so horribly that it was almost impossible to watch him, he died the night of his arrival. Nothing but a rickety screen of wood and cloth separated him from a score of other sick men when he died. Next night, washed and dressed in his usual neat clothes, with white linen and a gay colored cravat, the beautiful plump little figure lay in a hideous black coffin with tawdry white lining in the little gloomy mission house that he had found somewhere off on the northern edge of the town. Two or three people watched perfunctorily by the body; but though it was almost spring and the day had been wet, the place grew cold as the night waned, and became almost intolerably dismal and horrible.

The next day, when he was buried, was just such another old winter day, really a wet spring day. The low dirty white sky was heavy with the breath of the lakes; the air was thick with rain; and the filthy snow melted in corners and mingled its muddy dirty water with that which dripped in showers from the soaked and swollen black roofs. The motor vehicles, tramcars and the thousands of feet splashed the water onto the morose people, the buildings, and the shop windows. The negro's wife, not much affected, arrived from Nashville in time to attend the service at the mission house and to go in the cortege to the cemetery.

I left the service early, and riding on various trams and walking part of the time, crossed the low flat scattered city to the great out-of-the-way cemetery off on the western edge where he was to be buried. This tract lay beyond a vast expanse of the dirty little wooden houses of the city, which stand wall to wall along endless monotonous streets; but it lies on the bank of a little winding stream that is tributary to the great one by which the city stands. High stone supports and black iron palings fence the burial place, which stretches away out of sight among poor streets, low flat fields, and woods. Large parts of its surface have been covered with turf or diversified by small artificial mounds and slopes; but it is flat still, and the turf is now gray and dead. The yellow sand of the lake country shows through in places; and the square stones, urns, painted iron benches, and unsubstantial looking tombs that stand in clusters, are tiny. In making the mounds the trunks of many of the trees were buried almost to the branches, and these trees look fat, stubby, and short-legged in the gray mist. A heavy odor of warm, salty grease hangs in the lower air, a suggestive stench from a factory for reducing fats somewhere in the neighborhood. There are winding macadam roads through the cemetery.

When I have waited a little while at a place which has recently been added for the graves of poor people, the great black motor coach, splashed with mud, appears suddenly out of the city and enters one of the small stone gateways at the southeastern corner. There is a stone lodge there, and a bell over the gates tolls briefly as the coach comes in. Then the vehicle follows a road parallel to a lonely bare wet red-paved street outside, in which long dingy trolley cars pass at intervals; and comes quickly to where I am. The sand here is entirely bare; the few old forest trees are neglected; and the graves lie in long close rows. They have no stones, but there are dead rotten flowers on some of the newest, fluttering forlornly from cardboard frames wound with lead foil and adorned with letters of crinkly purple paper. Some graves have been covered with white cotton cloth fastened to the ground by pegs; but that is all. Ragged rotten brown leaves lie in the hollows of the sand, where brown weeds stand; and wet newspapers are blown about by the cold wind.

In this shabby somber place on the dun earth of the boundless lake country, beside the harsh ugly city in which he has been an unwelcome stranger, but under the great white sky, too, the body of the servant of God is to be laid.

The coach stops in the muddy road, and the escort, all negroes except the undertaker and his agile assistant, descend in the mist. Those who are to carry the coffin gather uncertainly, and with the assistance of the undertaker and his man take it down. Then an irregular procession is formed, the bearers take off their hats, and slowly and stumblingly all move off up the slope on a mat of tan jute with two red stripes, that has been laid on the mud, and make their way among the graves. Shabby, ordinary people in their greatcoats and hats of different dull colors, with their umbrellas and rubber storm shoes, no one of them is much moved as they creep with their dead man like tiny worms on the yellow sand beneath the sky. When the poor black coffin has been put down on the canvas bands of the wooden frame around the grave, all stand back quietly while something that I cannot hear at my distance is read or said. Some of the women sob out then. The coffin descends slowly from sight into the damp yellow sand.

Out at a distance over the swampy fields beyond the stream, large black crows flap noisily around a lone tree; from a tiny locomotive on railway trackage far away white steam rises with a faint roar. The mist in the air is rapidly turning to falling rain.

After a short pause the party straggles back to the coach, some who have started first pausing to look at the other graves and the dead flowers. A few remain for a moment by the open grave looking down. But very soon all are again in their places and the coach is rolling away among the slopes. It passes out at the stone gate and back into the city. And then old German laborers, who have been waiting not far off, approach the grave rheumatically and set aside the few flowers that have been left on the pile of fresh sand, which is partly covered by a green waxed cloth and evergreen branches. They put on and screw down the lid of the new wooden overbox; earth is thrown in; and before the early gloomy rainy nightfall the grave of Brother Frank Burns, Servant of the Lord, is almost filled.

But I go from the place almost unmindful of the irony of what has happened, almost unmindful of the night and the mist and the vastness of the wet sky; so touching and agitating have been this fair bright vain dream which I have glimpsed, and this pure and simple heart which, dreaming, has been able to meet its destiny so calmly and so bravely, has been able so undeniably and so thoroughly to conquer life and to conquer death.

THE GOLDEN HONEYMOON[1]

By RING W. LARDNER

(From *The Cosmopolitan*)

MOTHER says that when I start talking I never know when to stop. But I tell her the only time I get a chance is when she ain't around, so I have to make the most of it. I guess the fact is neither one of us would be welcome in a Quaker meeting, but as I tell Mother, what did God give us tongues for if He didn't want we should use them? Only she says He didn't give them to us to say the same thing over and over again, like I do, and repeat myself. But I say:

"Well, Mother," I say, "when people is like you and I and been married fifty years, do you expect everything I say will be something you ain't heard me say before? But it may be new to others, as they ain't nobody else lived with me as long as you have."

So she says:

"You can bet they ain't, as they couldn't nobody else stand you that long."

"Well," I tell her, "you look pretty healthy."

"Maybe I do," she will say, "but I looked even healthier before I married you."

You can't get ahead of Mother.

Yes, sir, we was married just fifty years ago the seventeenth day of last December and my daughter and son-in-law was over from Trenton to help us celebrate the Golden Wedding. My son-in-law is John H. Kramer, the real estate man. He made $12,000 one year and is pretty well thought of around Trenton; a good, steady, hard worker. The Rotarians was after him a long time to join, but he kept telling them his home was his club. But Edie finally made him join. That's my daughter.

Well, anyway, they come over to help us celebrate the Golden Wedding and it was pretty crimpy weather and the furnace don't seem to heat up no more like it used to and Mother made the remark that she hoped this winter wouldn't be as cold as the last, referring to the winter previous. So Edie said if she was us, and nothing to keep us home, she certainly wouldn't spend no more winters up here and why didn't we just shut off the water and close up the house and go down to Tampa, Florida? You know we was there four winters ago and staid five weeks, but it cost us over three hundred and fifty dollars for hotel bill alone. So Mother said we wasn't going no place to be robbed. So my son-in-law spoke up and said that Tampa wasn't the only place in the South, and besides we didn't have to stop at no high price hotel but could rent us a couple rooms and board out somewheres, and he had heard that St. Petersburg, Florida, was *the* spot and if we said the word he would write down there and make inquiries.

Well, to make a long story short, we decided to do it and Edie said it would be our Golden Honeymoon and for a present my son-in-law paid the difference between a section and a compartment so as we could have a compartment and have more privatecy. In a compartment you have an upper and lower berth just like the regular sleeper, but it is a shut in room by itself and got a wash bowl. The car we went in was all compartments and no regular berths at all. It was all compartments.

We went to Trenton the night before and staid at my daughter and son-in-law and we left Trenton the next afternoon at 3.23 P. M.

This was the twelfth day of January. Mother set facing the front of the train, as it makes her giddy to ride backwards. I set facing her, which does not affect me. We reached North Philadelphia at 4.03 P. M. and we reached West Philadelphia at 4.14, but did not go into Broad Street. We reached Baltimore at 6.30 and Washington, D.C., at 7.25. Our train laid over in Washington two hours till another train come along to pick us up and I got out and strolled up the platform and into the Union Station. When I come back, our car had been switched on to another track, but I remembered the name of it, the La Belle, as I had once visited my aunt out in Oconomowoc, Wisconsin, where there was a lake of that name, so I had no difficulty in getting located. But Mother had nearly fretted herself sick for fear I would be left.

"Well," I said, "I would of followed you on the next train."

"You couldn't of," said Mother, and she pointed out that she had the money.

"Well," I said, "we are in Washington and I could of borrowed from the United States Treasury. I would of pretended I was an Englishman."

Mother caught the point and laughed heartily.

Our train pulled out of Washington at 9.40 P. M. and Mother and I turned in early, I taking the upper. During the night we passed through the green fields of old Virginia, though it was too dark to tell if they was green or what color. When we got up in the morning, we was at Fayetteville, North Carolina. We had breakfast in the dining car and after breakfast I got in conversation with the man in the next compartment to ours. He was from Lebanon, New Hampshire, and a man about eighty years of age. His wife was with him and two unmarried daughters and I made the remark that I should think the four of them would be crowded in one compartment, but he said they had made the trip every winter for fifteen years and knowed how to keep out of each other's way. He said they was bound for Tarpon Springs.

We reached Charleston, South Carolina, at 12.50 P. M. and arrived at Savannah, Georgia, at 4.20. We reached Jacksonville, Florida, at 8.45 P. M. and had an hour and a quarter to lay over there, but Mother made a fuss about me getting off the train, so we had the darkey make up our berths and retired before we left Jacksonville. I didn't sleep good as the train done a lot of hemming and hawing, and Mother never sleeps good on a train as she says she is always worrying that I will fall out. She says she would rather have the upper herself, as then she would not have to worry about me, but I tell her I can't take the risk of having it get out that I allowed my wife to sleep in an upper berth. It would make talk.

We was up in the morning in time to see our friends from New Hampshire get off at Tarpon Springs, which we reached at 6.53 A. M.

Several of our fellow passengers got off at Clearwater and some at Belleair, where the train backs right up to the door of the mammoth hotel. Belleair is the winter headquarters for the golf dudes and everybody that got off there had their bag of sticks, as many as ten and twelve in a bag. Women and all. When I was a young man we called it shinny and only needed one club to play with and about one game of it would of been a-plenty for some of these dudes, the way we played it.

The train pulled into St. Petersburg at 8.20 and when we got off the train you would think they was a riot, what with all the darkeys barking for the different hotels.

I said to Mother, I said:

"It is a good thing we have got a place picked out to go to and don't have to choose a hotel, as it would be hard to choose amongst them if every one of them is the best."

She laughed.

We found a jitney and I give him the address of the room my son-in-law had got for us and soon we was there and introduced ourselves to the lady that owns the house, a young widow about forty-eight years of age. She showed us our room, which was light and airy with a comfortable bed and bureau and washstand. It was twelve dollars a week, but the location was good, only three blocks from Williams Park.

St. Pete is what folks calls the town, though they also call it the Sunshine City, as they claim they's no other place in the country where they's fewer days when Old Sol don't smile down on Mother Earth, and one of the newspapers gives away all their copies free every day when the sun don't shine. They claim to of only give them away some sixty-odd times in the last eleven years. Another nickname they have got for the town is "the Poor Man's Palm Beach," but I guess they's men that comes

there that could borrow as much from the bank as some of
the Willie boys over to the other Palm Beach.

During our stay we paid a visit to the Lewis Tent City,
which is the headquarters for the Tin Can Tourists. But
maybe you ain't heard about them. Well, they are an
organization that takes their vacation trips by auto and
carries everything with them. That is, they bring along
their tents to sleep in and cook in and they don't patronize
no hotels or cafeterias, but they have got to be bona fide
auto campers or they can't belong to the organization.

They tell me they's over 200,000 members to it and they
call themselves the Tin Canners on account of most of
their food being put up in tin cans. One couple we seen
in the Tent City was a couple from Brady, Texas, named
Mr. and Mrs. Pence, which the old man is over eighty
years of age and they had came in their auto all the way
from home, a distance of 1,641 miles. They took five
weeks for the trip, Mr. Pence driving the entire distance.

The Tin Canners hails from every State in the Union and
in the summer time they visit places like New England
and the Great Lakes region, but in the winter the most of
them comes to Florida and scatters all over the State.
While we was down there, they was a national convention
of them at Gainesville, Florida, and they elected a Fre-
donia, New York man as their president. His title is
Royal Tin Can Opener of the World. They have got a
song wrote up which everybody has got to learn it before
they are a member:

> The tin can forever! Hurrah, boys! Hurrah!
>   Up with the tin can! Down with the foe!
> We will rally round the campfire, we'll rally once again,
>   Shouting, "We auto camp forever!"

That is something like it. And the members has also
got to have a tin can fastened on to the front of their
machine.

I asked Mother how she would like to travel around that
way and she said:

"Fine, but not with an old rattle brain like you driving."

"Well," I said, "I am eight years younger than this Mr. Pence who drove here from Texas."

"Yes," she said, "but he is old enough to not be skittish."

You can't get ahead of Mother.

Well, one of the first things we done in St. Petersburg was to go to the Chamber of Commerce and register our names and where we was from as they's great rivalry amongst the different States in regards to the number of their citizens visiting in town and of course our little State don't stand much of a show, but still every little bit helps, as the fella says. All and all, the man told us, they was eleven thousand names registered, Ohio leading with some fifteen hundred-odd and New York State next with twelve hundred. Then come Michigan, Pennsylvania and so on down, with one man each from Cuba and Nevada.

The first night we was there, they was a meeting of the New York-New Jersey Society at the Congregational Church and a man from Ogdensburg, New York State, made the talk. His subject was Rainbow Chasing. He is a Rotarian and a very convicting speaker, though I forget his name.

Our first business, of course, was to find a place to eat and after trying several places we run on to a cafeteria on Central Avenue that suited us up and down. We eat pretty near all our meals there and it averaged about two dollars per day for the two of us, but the food was well cooked and everything nice and clean. A man don't mind paying the price if things is clean and well cooked.

On the third day of February, which is Mother's birthday, we spread ourselves and eat supper at the Poinsettia Hotel and they charged us seventy-five cents for a sirloin steak that wasn't hardly big enough for one.

I said to Mother: "Well," I said, "I guess it's a good thing every day ain't your birthday or we would be in the poorhouse."

"No," says Mother, "because if every day was my birthday, I would be old enough by this time to of been in my grave long ago."

You can't get ahead of Mother.

In the hotel they had a cardroom where they was several men and ladies playing five hundred and this new fangled whist bridge. We also seen a place where they was dancing, so I asked Mother would she like to trip the light fantastic toe and she said no, she was too old to squirm like you have got to do now days. We watched some of the young folks at it awhile till Mother got disgusted and said we would have to see a good movie to take the taste out of our mouth. Mother is a great movie heroyne and we go twice a week here at home.

But I want to tell you about the Park. The second day we was there we visited the Park, which is a good deal like the one in Tampa, only bigger, and they's more fun goes on here every day than you could shake a stick at. In the middle they's a big bandstand and chairs for the folks to set and listen to the concerts, which they give you music for all tastes, from Dixie up to classical pieces like Hearts and Flowers.

Then all around they's places marked off for different sports and games—chess and checkers and dominoes for folks that enjoys those kind of games, and roque and horseshoes for the nimbler ones. I used to pitch a pretty fair shoe myself, but ain't done much of it in the last twenty years.

Well, anyway, we bought a membership ticket in the club which costs one dollar for the season, and they tell me that up to a couple years ago it was fifty cents, but they had to raise it to keep out the riffraff.

Well, Mother and I put in a great day watching the pitchers and she wanted I should get in the game, but I told her I was all out of practice and would make a fool of myself, though I seen several men pitching who I guess I could take their measure without no practice. However, they was some good pitchers, too, and one boy from Akron, Ohio, who could certainly throw a pretty shoe. They told me it looked like he would win the championship of the United States in the February tournament. We come away a few days before they held that and I never did hear if he win. I forget his name, but he was a clean cut young fella and he has got a brother in Cleveland that's a Rotarian.

Well, we just stood around and watched the different games for two or three days and finally I set down in a checker game with a man named Weaver from Danville, Illinois. He was a pretty fair checker player, but he wasn't no match for me, and I hope that don't sound like bragging. But I always could hold my own on a checkerboard and the folks around here will tell you the same thing. I played with this Weaver pretty near all morning for two or three mornings and he beat me one game and the only other time it looked like he had a chance, the noon whistle blowed and we had to quit and go to dinner.

While I was playing checkers, Mother would set and listen to the band, as she loves music, classical or no matter what kind, but anyway she was setting there one day and between selections the woman next to her opened up a conversation. She was a woman about Mother's own age, seventy or seventy-one, and finally she asked Mother's name and Mother told her her name and where she was from and Mother asked her the same question, and who do you think the woman was?

Well, sir, it was the wife of Frank M. Hartsell, the man who was engaged to Mother till I stepped in and cut him out, fifty-two years ago!

Yes, sir!

You can imagine Mother's surprise! And Mrs. Hartsell was surprised, too, when Mother told her she had once been friends with her husband, though Mother didn't say how close friends they had been, or that Mother and I was the cause of Hartsell going out West. But that's what we was. Hartsell left his town a month after the engagement was broke off and ain't never been back since. He had went out to Michigan and become a veterinary, and that is where he had settled down, in Hillsdale, Michigan, and finally married his wife.

Well, Mother screwed up her courage to ask if Frank was still living and Mrs. Hartsell took her over to where they was pitching horseshoes and there was old Frank, waiting his turn. And he knowed Mother as soon as he seen her, though it was over fifty years. He said he knowed her by her eyes.

"Why, it's Lucy Frost!" he says, and he throwed down his shoes and quit the game.

Then they come over and hunted me up and I will confess I wouldn't of knowed him. Him and I is the same age to the month, but he seems to show it more, some way. He is balder for one thing. And his beard is all white, where mine has still got a streak of brown in it. The very first thing I said to him, I said:

"Well, Frank, that beard of yours makes me feel like I was back north. It looks like a regular blizzard."

"Well," he said, "I guess yourn would be just as white if you had it dry cleaned."

But Mother wouldn't stand that.

"Is that so!" she said to Frank. "Well, Charley ain't had no tobacco in his mouth for over ten years!"

And I ain't!

Well, I excused myself from the checker game and it was pretty close to noon, so we decided to all have dinner together and they was nothing for it only we must try their cafeteria on Third Avenue. It was a little more expensive than ours and not near as good, I thought. I and Mother had about the same dinner we had been having every day and our bill was $1.10. Frank's check was $1.20 for he and his wife. The same meal wouldn't of cost them more than a dollar at our place.

After dinner we made them come up to our house and we all set in the parlor, which the young woman had give us the use of to entertain company. We begun talking over old times and Mother said she was a-scared Mrs. Hartsell would find it tiresome listening to we three talk over old times, but as it turned out they wasn't much chance for nobody else to talk with Mrs. Hartsell in the company. I have heard lots of women that could go it, but Hartsell's wife takes the cake of all the women I ever seen. She told us the family history of everybody in the State of Michigan and bragged for a half hour about her son, who she said is in the drug business in Grand Rapids, and a Rotarian.

When I and Hartsell could get a word in edgeways we joked one another back and forth and I chafed him about being a horse doctor.

"Well, Frank," I said, "you look pretty prosperous, so I suppose they's been plenty of glanders around Hillsdale."

"Well," he said, "I've managed to make more than a fair living. But I've worked pretty hard."

"Yes," I said, "and I suppose you get called out all hours of the night to attend births and so on."

Mother made me shut up.

Well, I thought they wouldn't never go home and I and Mother was in misery trying to keep awake, as the both of us generally always takes a nap after dinner. Finally they went, after we had made an engagement to meet them in the Park the next morning, and Mrs. Hartsell also invited us to come to their place the next night and play five hundred. But she had forgot that they was a meeting of the Michigan Society that evening, so it was not till two evenings later that we had our first card game.

Hartsell and his wife lived in a house on Third Avenue North and had a private setting room besides their bedroom. Mrs. Hartsell couldn't quit talking about their private setting room like it was something wonderful. We played cards with them, with Mother and Hartsell partners against his wife and I. Mrs. Hartsell is a miserable card player and we certainly got the worst of it.

After the game she brought out a dish of oranges and we had to pretend it was just what we wanted, though oranges down there is like a young man's whiskers; you enjoy them at first, but they get to be a pesky nuisance.

We played cards again the next night at our place with the same partners and I and Mrs. Hartsell was beat again. Mother and Hartsell was full of compliments for each other on what a good team they made, but the both of them knowed well enough where the secret of their success laid. I guess all and all we must of played ten different evenings and they was only one night when Mrs. Hartsell and I come out ahead. And that one night wasn't no fault of hern.

When we had been down there about two weeks, we spent one evening as their guest in the Congregational Church, at a social give by the Michigan Society. A talk was made by a man named Bitting of Detroit, Michigan, on How I was Cured of Story Telling. He is a big man in the Rotarians and give a witty talk.

A woman named Mrs. Oxford rendered some selections which Mrs. Hartsell said was grand opera music, but whatever they was my daughter Edie could of give her cards and spades and not made such a hullaballoo about it neither.

Then they was a ventriloquist from Grand Rapids and a young woman about forty-five years of age that mimicked different kinds of birds. I whispered to Mother that they all sounded like a chicken, but she nudged me to shut up.

After the show we stopped in a drug store and I set up the refreshments and it was pretty close to ten o'clock before we finally turned in. Mother and I would of preferred tending the movies, but Mother said we mustn't offend Mrs. Hartsell, though I asked her had we came to Florida to enjoy ourselves or to just not offend an old chatterbox from Michigan.

I felt sorry for Hartsell one morning. The women folks both had an engagement down to the chiropodist's and I run across Hartsell in the Park and he foolishly offered to play me checkers.

It was him that suggested it, not me, and I guess he repented himself before we had played one game. But he was too stubborn to give up and set there while I beat him game after game and the worst part of it was that a crowd of folks had got in the habit of watching me play and there they all was, looking on, and finally they seen what a fool Frank was making of himself, and they began to chafe him and pass remarks. Like one of them said:

"Who ever told you you was a checker player!"

And:

"You might maybe be good for tiddle-de-winks, but not checkers!"

I almost felt like letting him beat me a couple games. But the crowd would of knowed it was a put up job.

Well, the women folks joined us in the Park and I wasn't going to mention our little game, but Hartsell told about it himself and admitted he wasn't no match for me.

"Well," said Mrs. Hartsell, "checkers ain't much of a game anyway, is it?" She said: "It's more of a children's game, ain't it? At least, I know my boy's children used to play it a good deal."

"Yes, ma'am," I said. "It's a children's game the way your husband plays it, too."

Mother wanted to smooth things over, so she said:

"Maybe they's other games where Frank can beat you."

"Yes," said Mrs. Hartsell, "and I bet he could beat you pitching horse-shoes."

"Well," I said, "I would give him a chance to try, only I ain't pitched a shoe in over sixteen years."

"Well," said Hartsell, "I ain't played checkers in twenty years."

"You ain't never played it," I said.

"Anyway," says Frank, "Lucy and I is your master at five hundred."

Well, I could of told him why that was, but had decency enough to hold my tongue.

It had got so now that he wanted to play cards every night and when I or Mother wanted to go to a movie, why one of us would have to pretend we had a headache and then trust to goodness that they wouldn't see us sneak into the theater. I don't mind playing cards when my partner keeps their mind on the game, but you take a woman like Hartsell's wife and how can they play cards when they have got to stop every couple seconds and brag about their son in Grand Rapids?

Well, the New York-New Jersey Society announced that they was going to give a social evening too and I said to Mother, I said:

"Well, that is one evening when we will have an excuse not to play five hundred."

"Yes," she said, " but we will have to ask Frank and his wife to go to the social with us as they asked us to go to the Michigan social."

"Well," I said, "I had rather stay home than drag that chatterbox everywheres we go."

So Mother said:

"You are getting too cranky. Maybe she does talk a

little too much but she is good hearted. And Frank is always good company."

So I said:

"I suppose if he is such good company you wished you had of married him."

Mother laughed and said I sounded like I was jealous. Jealous of a cow doctor!

Anyway we had to drag them along to the social and I will say that we give them a much better entertainment than they had given us.

Judge Lane of Paterson made a fine talk on business conditions and a Mrs. Newell of Westfield imitated birds, only you could really tell what they was the way she done it. Two young women from Red Bank sung a choral selection and we clapped them back and they gave us Home to Our Mountains and Mother and Mrs. Hartsell both had tears in their eyes. And Hartsell, too.

Well, some way or another the chairman got wind that I was there and asked me to make a talk and I wasn't even going to get up, but Mother made me, so I got up and said:

"Ladies and gentlemen," I said. "I didn't expect to be called on for a speech on an occasion like this or no other occasion as I do not set myself up as a speech maker, so will have to do the best I can, which I often say is the best anybody can do."

Then I told them the story about Pat and the motorcycle, using the brogue, and it seemed to tickle them and I told them one or two other stories, but altogether I wasn't on my feet more than twenty or twenty-five minutes and you ought to of heard the clapping and hollering when I set down. Even Mrs. Hartsell admitted that I am quite a speechifier and said if I ever went to Grand Rapids, Michigan, her son would make me talk to the Rotarians.

When it was over, Hartsell wanted we should go to their and play cards, but his wife reminded him that it was after 9.30 P. M., rather a late hour to start a card game, but he had went crazy on the subject of cards, probably because he didn't have to play partners with his wife. Anyway, we got rid of them and went home to bed.

It was the next morning, when we met over to the Park, that Mrs. Hartsell made the remark that she wasn't getting no exercise so I suggested that why didn't she take part in the roque game.

She said she had not played a game of roque in twenty years, but if Mother would play she would play. Well, at first Mother wouldn't hear of it, but finally consented, more to please Mrs. Hartsell than anything else.

Well, they had a game with a Mrs. Ryan from Eagle, Nebraska, and a young Mrs. Morse from Rutland, Vermont, who Mother had met down to the chiropodist's. Well, Mother couldn't hit a flea and they all laughed at her and I couldn't help from laughing at her myself and finally she quit and said her back was too lame to stoop over. So they got another lady and kept on playing and soon Mrs. Hartsell was the one everybody was laughing at, as she had a long shot to hit the black ball, and as she made the effort her teeth fell out on to the court. I never seen a woman so flustered in my life. And I never heard so much laughing, only Mrs. Hartsell didn't join in and she was madder than a hornet and wouldn't play no more, so the game broke up.

Mrs. Hartsell went home without speaking to nobody, but Hartsell staid around and finally he said to me, he said:

"Well, I played you checkers the other day and you beat me bad and now what do you say if you and me play a game of horseshoes?"

I told him I hadn't pitched a shoe in sixteen years, but Mother said:

"Go ahead and play. You used to be good at it and maybe it will come back to you."

Well, to make a long story short, I give in. I oughtn't to of never tried it, as I hadn't pitched a shoe in sixteen years, and I only done it to humor Hartsell.

Before we started, Mother patted me on the back and told me to do my best, so we started in and I seen right off that I was in for it, as I hadn't pitched a shoe in sixteen years and didn't have my distance. And besides, the plating had wore off the shoes so that they was points right where they stuck into my thumb and I hadn't throwed more than two or three times when my thumb was raw and it pretty near killed me to hang on to the shoe, let alone pitch it.

Well, Hartsell throws the awkwardest shoe I ever seen pitched and to see him pitch you wouldn't think he would ever come nowheres near, but he is also the luckiest pitcher I ever seen and he made some pitches where the shoe lit five and six feet short and then schoonered up and was a ringer. They's no use trying to beat that kind of luck.

They was a pretty fair size crowd watching us and four or five other ladies besides Mother, and it seems like, when Hartsell pitches, he has got to chew and it kept the ladies on the anxious seat as he don't seem to care which way he is facing when he leaves go.

You would think a man as old as him would of learnt more manners.

Well, to make a long story short, I was just beginning to get my distance when I had to give up on account of my thumb, which I showed it to Hartsell and he seen I couldn't go on, as it was raw and bleeding. Even if I could of stood it to go on myself, Mother wouldn't of allowed it after she seen my thumb. So anyway I quit and Hartsell said the score was nineteen to six, but I don't know what it was. Or don't care, neither.

Well, Mother and I went home and I said I hoped we was through with the Hartsells as I was sick and tired of them, but it seemed like she had promised we would go over to their house that evening for another game of their everlasting cards.

Well, my thumb was giving me considerable pain and I felt kind of out of sorts and I guess maybe I forgot myself, but anyway, when we was about through playing Hartsell made the remark that he wouldn't never lose a game of cards if he could always have Mother for a partner.

So I said:

"Well, you had a chance fifty years ago to always have her for a partner, but you wasn't man enough to keep her."

I was sorry the minute I had said it and Hartsell didn't

know what to say and for once his wife couldn't say nothing. Mother tried to smooth things over by making the remark that I must of had something stronger than tea or I wouldn't talk so silly. But Mrs. Hartsell had froze up like an iceberg and hardly said good night to us and I bet her and Frank put in a pleasant hour after we was gone.

As we was leaving, Mother said to him: "Never mind Charley's nonsense, Frank. He is just mad because you beat him all hollow pitching horseshoes and playing cards."

She said that to make up for my slip, but at the same time she certainly riled me. I tried to keep ahold of myself, but as soon as we was out of the house she had to open up the subject and begun to scold me for the break I had made.

Well, I wasn't in no mood to be scolded. So I said:

"I guess he is such a wonderful pitcher and card player that you wished you had married him."

"Well," she said, "at least he ain't a baby to give up pitching because his thumb has got a few scratches."

"And how about you," I said, "making a fool of yourself on the roque court and then pretending your back is lame and you can't play no more!"

"Yes," she said, "but when you hurt your thumb I didn't laugh at you, and why did you laugh at me when I sprained my back?"

"Who could help from laughing!" I said.

"Well," she said, "Frank Hartsell didn't laugh."

"Well," I said, "why didn't you marry him?"

"Well," said Mother, "I almost wished I had!"

"And I wished so, too!" I said.

"I'll remember that!" said Mother, and that's the last word she said to me for two days.

We seen the Hartsells the next day in the Park and I was willing to apologize, but they just nodded to us. And a couple days later we heard they had left for Orlando, where they have got relatives.

I wished they had went there in the first place.

Mother and I made it up setting on a bench.

"Listen, Charley," she said. "This is our Golden Honeymoon and we don't want the whole thing spoilt with a silly old quarrel."

"Well," I said, "did you mean that about wishing you had married Hartsell?"

"Of course not," she said, "that is, if you didn't mean that you wished I had, too."

So I said:

"I was just tired and all wrought up. I thank God you chose me instead of him as they's no other woman in the world who I could of lived with all these years."

"How about Mrs. Hartsell?" says Mother.

"Good gracious!" I said. "Imagine being married to a woman that plays five hundred like she does and drops her teeth on the roque court!"

"Well," said Mother, "it wouldn't be no worse than being married to a man that expectorates towards ladies and is such a fool in a checker game."

So I put my arm around her shoulder and she stroked my hand and I guess we got kind of spooney.

They was two days left of our stay in St. Petersburg and the next to the last day Mother introduced me to a Mrs. Kendall from Kingston, Rhode Island, who she had met at the chiropodist's.

Mrs. Kendall made us acquainted with her husband, who is in the grocery business. They have got two sons and five grandchildren and one great-grandchild. One of their sons lives in Providence and is way up in the Elks as well as a Rotarian.

We found them very congenial people and we played cards with them the last two nights we was there. They was both experts and I only wished we had met them sooner instead of running into the Hartsells. But the Kendalls will be there again next winter and we will see more of them, that is, if we decide to make the trip again.

We left the Sunshine City on the eleventh day of February, at 11 A. M. This give us a day trip through Florida and we seen all the country we had passed through at night on the way down.

We reached Jacksonville at 7 P. M. and pulled out of there at 8.10 P. M. We reached Fayetteville, North Carolina, at nine o'clock the following morning, and reached Washington, D. C., at 6.30 P. M., laying over there half an hour.

We reached Trenton at 11.01 P. M. and had wired ahead to my daughter and son-in-law and they met us at the train and we went to their house and they put us up for the night. John would of made us stay up all night, telling about our trip, but Edie said we must be tired and made us go to bed. That's my daughter.

The next day we took our train for home and arrived safe and sound, having been gone just one month and a day.

Here comes Mother, so I guess I better shut up.

HE LAUGHED AT THE GODS[1]

By JAMES OPPENHEIM

(From *Broom*)

DURING the course of some psychological investigations I was making, I found it necessary to visit an insane asylum near New York. The building was no more than an ill-smelling barracks, very desolate; but the young interne, who guided me through the place, finally took me to a series of private rooms, which were homelike and pleasant and had windows facing the fields and the hills. He told me by the way that I must above all things see Dr. Farraday. Dr. Farraday, he explained, knew a great deal about the human soul; so much so that the young doctors often consulted him about puzzling and unusual cases.

"He is the most interesting man here," he told me.

"And what is he suffering from?" I asked.

He smiled. "You'll have to get his own diagnosis," he said. "Between you and me, I think he has a high regard for our free board and lodging. He has the sort of insanity of the hobo, of the I-Won't-Works. But he came to it too late in life to make freight cars and hay-lofts at all attractive. He was too settled down to wander the world, and too—well, insane to work."

"Well!" I laughed, "I daresay there are many like him —only they are quartered on relatives, or wives, or friends. . . . In ancient days that form of insanity was highly honorable. It is, isn't it, the insanity of the artist?"

His answer was to knock at a door, and a deep and rather pleasing voice cried, "Come in." So we went in.

The light flooded brightly through the tall wide window, so that at first I only saw a dark bulk coming toward us.

[1] Copyright, 1921, by *Broom*.
Copyright, 1923, by James Oppenheim.

But I noticed the walls hung with many strange and brilliant drawings, all of a symbolical nature, mythic animals and gods, stars and moons, and landscapes that never were. When I was through blinking, and had my man on the darker side of me, I saw him quite plainly. He was rather bulky and large, swarthy and something about his face resembling the face of a turtle.

His manner was very courteous, but a little absent. The young interne excused himself, with a private wink at me, as much as to say: "I won't interfere"; and so we were left alone.

I offered him a cigar, which pleased him, and we sat in comfortable armchairs by the window, and were soon plunged in scientific discussion. . . . But I saw he was restless. I noticed, too, now, that his clothes were ill-fitting, worn out, patched and rather dirty; that his nails and fingers were sooted up with crayon and stained with ink; that his cheeks and chin needed a shave and his hair was rather longer than we wear it.

His restlessness increased. He rubbed his chin, gazed about abstractedly, swung his leg back and forth in a too obvious rhythm. And at last he spoke in a voice which did not seem his at all—a voice which appeared to me to belong to some other person. The voice he had used was quiet and cool, although sympathetic. This new voice was personal, hot, and almost bitter.

"What is the use of all this talk?" he cried out. "It gets us nowhere. Intellect! science! theory! brain-spinning! Young man, that is our modern Devil. Kill him . . . strangle him out of your soul. He is the Devil of the ice, of the cold polar regions. Better a hundred times the old Devil of the burning hell, for in fire there is also God!"

For a moment I thought I was coming to psychic fisticuffs with him; but I reflected, and at once swallowed my pride.

"I see," I said, looking him in the eyes, "you knew this modern Devil very well; perhaps intimately."

He glanced at me.

"You sit there," he cried, "a bit of ice yourself. I feel no warmth from you; I am not a human being to you, but just another case. Everywhere I look for Christ and find a Devil. But you scientists will never save the world without love—yea, and hate, too. Fire cleanses and resurrects, but the ice freezes and slays. You would embalm me too in your waste places; and there is no healing in it. Feel this asylum—chilly and cold and full of living death—and the blasted crowd waiting for a great lover to cast out their demons. He is late in coming; He is late in coming."

The something that was strange in his voice, his manner and in his words troubled me deeply.

"You are quite right," I said simply. "Forgive me for my attitude."

He looked at me attentively and spoke more softly.

"There is some hope for you, then," he murmured. "Look," and he reached and brought a sheet of drawing paper from the little table beside him.

He had drawn a picture in crayon, and done it very well. There was a powerful man, with arms crossed on his chest, standing like a Napoleon on an ice-sheathed rock, and out of the sky a lightning in the form of a great serpent had leaped down and was about to fasten his fangs into the man's eyes.

"Wonderful!" I cried. "And it means?"

"You tell me what it means," he commanded.

It flashed intuitively across my mind that it meant: "He who sees too much must be struck blind." I told him and he was highly pleased: he regarded me affectionately.

"This is the first human contact I have had in a long time," he said. "Except, of course, some of the lunatics. . . ."

"But how," I asked, "can a man see too much, and why is such a man like Napoleon?"

"Ah," he said, "when Christ was shown the kingdoms of the world from a high mountain, he chose then between Cæsar and the Galilean. Seeing, man—to see, to know—knowledge, they say, is power. . . . But when one is blind then one sees truly . . . sees inwardly. 'They have eyes, but they see not'. . . ."

I felt his meaning, though, to use the word in his sense, I did not see it.

"And what is the serpent?" I asked.

"The gods."

"Then you believe in the gods?"

"I have always believed in them," he said in his strange voice again, "but I laughed at them. The great Dr. Farraday laughed at the gods. Believed? Of course. The fool says in his heart, There is no God. And the intellectual says in his heart, There are gods, and I laugh at them."

We sat in silence, smoking, and now and then I felt him trying to pierce me with a look. At last he said:

"You are troubled, my friend."

"Yes, I am troubled," I admitted. "We are all troubled in these days."

"The days of the great ice," he murmured. "The second Glacial Period." He paused, then spoke abruptly. "I have a strange feeling for you, very unusual. I am going to tell you something. You may forget it as soon as you have heard it. You may say to yourself: 'It is the phantasy of an insane man.' Or you may find it material for analysis and so enrich your science. Or perhaps if I am not wholly demented, you may take it into your being and find it a gift of the gods. . . . It is a story—one of the few that have meaning for me. And it is about a man I knew—oh, knew very well. Most intimately. . . . Perhaps it is the story of our age. Who knows?"

I looked at him. Our eyes met.

"Tell me," I said.

And he told me. . . .

"His name was Trudo. That name after all is as good as another. . . . I must tell you a little about his childhood . . . not much . . . it is not very important. Trudo was a sensitive child; he couldn't compete with the boys; he was a coward and a stay-at-home. He felt everything so intensely that he suffered incessantly. He could not fight, he could not play ball. And his father, whom he worshipped, died. And his mother was practical and embittered by her struggles and her poverty. Trudo felt he was a worm. Yes, he was vermin. Until he made a discovery. . . . If you couldn't beat others with your fists or your skill or your leadership, you could beat them with your mind. And that was the beginning of the end for Trudo. . . .

"He resolutely killed all his feelings. It can be done, you know. You become like the snail. His body is soft and fragile; but he draws it into his shell when there is danger of attack. This is what Trudo did. And for the rest, he studied. He became a physician and a man of research. He developed his intellect in a truly marvelous way. And he rose, and was well on the path toward greatness.

"I won't bore you with the details. They are the same for everyone who succeeds. Think of your own successes. Merely imagine Trudo at the top of his profession, living in a very fine house near Central Park on a chaste side street. Respectability, luxury, the waiting room with old masters on the wall, the tiled and shining laboratory, the cushioned library, and so on, and so on. . . . It is not important, is it?

"I pause a moment to speak of his wife. She was a very fine woman, doubtless. Of one of the old New York families. If I mentioned the name, you'd know all about it, I'm sure. And she was religious, in a way, though her god was rather a crude one, a sort of hybrid, not of the sphinx variety exactly, but a good respectable American god. I am not cynical about it either. That god has given us much of America. . . . Let me describe him in a word, a line: He was a puritan who believed in hard work, righteousness and business. And he believed in kindness and purity. You see my wife, don't you? She wanted me to be honest and upright, respectable and wealthy, and at the same time lowly and obedient—down on my knees to her deity. . . . She found me then an anomaly: I was honest, I was wealthy, I was upright; but I was proud and vain and consumed in myself. I had no love in my heart. You know there was John Brown to prove that a puritan can love like a blast of fire. But also, as you know, a puritan can be a peak of ice.

"Now I must tell you a great joke. My patients thought me a second Jesus. Actually. And why? Because I was remarkably intuitive. I could pierce direct into their souls, and so I knew just what to say and to do to make them feel I was in full sympathy with them. Is there anything more devilish than that? I ask you. Think. To use the art of love to serve merely one's ambition and one's egotism. To wear the mask of Christ in order to be a great doctor. Good old American bluff, isn't it?"

He paused, and took a puff on his cigar. It was as if he had forgotten my presence. Indeed he did not seem to realize that he had dropped speaking of "Trudo" and was speaking directly of himself, in the first person.

Then he went on, his voice growing warm and poignant.

"My wife warned me, often. She said I had slain my soul, and was headed for a great crash. She pointed out how many of our great business-men make forced marches on success and are killed or driven insane or into a sanitarium before they are fifty. I agreed with her. But what could I do? The greatest tragedy of my life was the fact that it was a comedy. I knew all the facts, but I didn't care a snap of my fingers. I could not feel the tragedy. I was perfectly happy on the ice—that is, if you can call it happy. Perhaps, to put it more honestly, I was neither glad nor sad, but busy, alert and keen.

"Then the symptoms came. I will not enter into the details. Palpitation of the heart, for instance—a very bad symptom, as you know. You see, I had no heart; so it was just there that the gods began to make mischief. Ah, yes, I knew then that the gods I had laughed at were preparing a little doomsday for me. Man does not live by intellect alone. If thou hast two loaves of bread, sell one, and buy hyacinths for thy soul. Lord! I said those very words to myself at the time. But of what avail?

"Obviously there was nothing I could do—except one thing. I could put away Mammon—I could give up my practice, my fine house, my scientific researches. But what modern successful man can do it? It was exactly like the rich young man who went to Jesus. And Jesus asked him if he could give up his wealth; leave all, and follow. And the young man could not. That was I.

"No. My pride and revolt increase, if anything. And I even became cold toward my wife. And this killed her. I looked on her dead face, and not even then could I break through the ice, and drop one poor tear of pity or self-pity.

"You see, I was utterly lost. And now with my wife dead, and no children, and no true friends, you might have thought that it would be easy to let go of the power of the world. But not so. Not so. The decks were cleared for action, that was all. I was going to do a great bit of scientific writing. . . .

"Then the lightning struck me. Oh, it was so simple, so simple. I was walking one night on a side-street on the lower west side. And a prostitute accosted me. I had a sudden burning curiosity. I was curious about the psychology of prostitution. I would go with this woman, and study her. I had no desire. I was a puritan. I did not want to touch her. Ugh! as a physician I knew too much about the diseases of vice. . . .

"She took me then to her dingy hall bedroom in a cheap lodging house. I sat on the cot; she sat on a soap-box. And in the gaslight I saw her; a very thin woman, a little tall, and perhaps tubercular. Shining eyes and glowing cheeks. And she was very poor."

He groaned, and stopped. Then he whispered:

"Now the story begins. . . . I began questioning her, when suddenly she burst out on me:

" 'But you are not a human being. You are terrible. I feel as if the Devil himself were in this room.'

"I was startled. I asked her:

" 'Who are you? Where do you come from?'

" 'I am a Russian,' she said, 'and a Jewess. My name is Losha.'

" 'But are not you in league with the Devil also?'

" 'No,' she cried defiantly, rising before me and clenching her fists. 'I am driven by need and loneliness; but you are only vain and learned. You are a lost soul.'

" 'Yes,' I admitted in my honest way, 'I *am* lost. What's to be done about it?'

" 'You know you are lost,' she cried, 'and yet ask me that? Oh, this is terrible. This is the eternal damnation they talk about. . . .'

" 'That doesn't help me,' I said. 'Talk has never helped me. I can talk myself.'

She stared at me, and leaned toward me.

" 'You are right. Only an infinite love could help you.'

"That was the way we talked. And suddenly I forgot that I was the questioner and had a great desire to tell her about myself. I told everything, just as I have told you. It was amazing enough; an ignorant sick woman of the gutter, one whose body was common merchandise, and who had no life of her own, and I, the learned scientist, the respectable and wealthy doctor.

"Three times I went to see her. And at the third the lightning passed through me. She was weeping when I entered and would not rise from the bed. Her face was buried in her hands.

" 'Why are you crying Losha?' I asked.

" 'I weep,' she said, 'because you are to be pitied more than I am. We are both prostitutes. But the Devil in me is a god, and you have no god.'

"I stood, silent, but quite calm. Then she rose slowly and flung her arms about my neck. I had not expected it. She whispered passionately:

" 'I love you. I love you. I love you.'

" 'Why do you love?' I asked.

" 'Because I am your lost soul.'

"And I saw the truth. I saw that what lay buried in me was not only divine love, but also the great beast, and that this woman was both. And first I felt a burning steal through my body, a hot and primal fire, the smoky breath of hell itself, and for the first time I could remember, I had the horrible cannibal lust to tear a human body limb from limb. But while I was convulsed with this, something strangely other came up and mingled with the lust. It was as if I saw the Christ. It was holy and ecstatic and divine. . . . Yes, yes, yes, it was love. . . .

"You can imagine an earthquake that raises some monstrous buried formation to the surface and buries what it finds there. That happened to me. . . . It was like a conversion. But in my conversion both Christ and the beast came up and tore asunder the great Dr. Farraday— the fine intellect, the high-minded ego. . . .

"In short, I went suddenly mad, and gave a great shriek,

tearing off my clothes and foaming at the mouth. I called Losha 'the goddess' and prostrated myself before her. Then I shrieked aloud for the torture and agony and had something very like a fit of epilepsy.

"She was terrified. She finally put me to bed, and soothed me. She nursed me tenderly. I would lie quiescent for hours, in a fever. Then the spell was on me. I saw great beasts, kings and gods. I was ground by terrible passion and ecstasy. It was a death. . . ."

He paused; then smiled sadly. . . .

"You can imagine the sequel. I could not return to my house. It was all ended. All my interest in my work, my position, my power and place in the world, had vanished. Everything, but the emotions that swept me, was quite unreal. And so I ruined myself.

"I married Losha. It seemed a simple matter. And we opened a little stationery shop and kept it together. . . . And then I began to draw: I became an artist. I was alive from head to foot, and yet quite tormented—tormented by these terrible passions and ecstacies, these perverted and glorious impulses which for years had festered in my darkness, and which, when they came upon me, came more like monsters than divinities. . . .

"What can I say of Losha? She was the one woman whom I never knew. My intuition failed me. I never understood. Was she ugly or beautiful? stupid or wise? base or noble? I cannot tell. I only could know her simple and undivided love, which never forsook me. It was those fires in which I became as ashes.

"As ashes, ashes. . . . One cold morning she coughed a great big racking spasm. . . . Then she whispered to me:

" 'Trudo, I love you.'

"And she died. . . . I closed the shop. . . . I did not need the shop. I needed only my own soul, which began to dawn in me like the sun in spring. . . . And being quite insane, I came here. . . ."

We were silent. He fussed about among his papers and murmured: "I suppose it isn't much of a story."

I smiled at him, but said nothing. Then he showed me a portrait he had made of Losha.

She was dark and thin, even gaunt, and a look almost of
madness in the eyes. . . . The tears rolled down the Doctor's cheeks. . . .

A little later I said goodby to him. We stood, facing each
other and he held my hand.

"I am insane," he said, "do not forget that. And out
there—" he waved his other hand in the direction of New
York, "live the sane ones. Losha is dead, and Dr. Farraday is dead. You know the ancients," he smiled quaintly,
"thought the insane were close to the gods. But that's a
fable, isn't it?"

I closed the door on him very softly, troubled in spirit.

IN THE METROPOLIS[1]

By BENJAMIN ROSENBLATT

(From *Brief Stories*)

SHE sat in a show window of a large department store. "A prize to those who make her laugh," read a conspicuous sign over her head. An American flag was wrapped around her slim figure; a sword which she clutched with both hands rested on her lap with its point towards a placard announcing a bargain sale.

She sat motionless, her eyes wide open, her face hardly betraying a trace of life.

All day long she sat there, while multitudes passing on the sidewalk turned their heads towards her and wondered: "Is it a living woman or a wax figure?" It was this puzzle which held the pedestrian, and caused the manager of the store to chuckle at his own cleverness. When he saw in the morning this bashful country girl shuffling into the store and asking inaudibly for a job, he caught at the chance for novelty in the advertising of his sale. Her features were so immobile; she appeared, on the whole, so lifeless that his agile mind had promptly pictured her in her present setting.

Unceasingly the crowd surged before the window. Newsboys with bundles under their arms, messengers in uniform, girls with lunch boxes in their hands, even trim-looking business men—all forgot their errands for a few minutes, and directed their mingled breath towards that window. Some of the boys stood for hours, sticking out their tongues, puffing up their cheeks, grinning and grimacing in a vain effort to get a smile from that grim apparition.

Though she was alone inside the window, still it seemed to her as if she were thrown into that seething mass before her, as if jostled and mercilessly kicked about. How strange everything! How confusing to her!

In the morning, when she learned there was work for her at the store, she was so happy that she thought of writing home at once about her good luck. But in the evening, after her first day's work, she was so exhausted that the girls of the establishment who took her to their boarding-house, had to lead her under her arms. She walked and wondered: the manager had said there was absolutely no work attached to her job.

At the supper-table, the girls, good naturedly, poked fun at her; and she grew livelier. Later, some of them had a romp, and decided that the feet of the uncouth lass were surely more used to follow the cows to pasture, than to dance.

The next morning the girls hurried feverishly. They paid little attention to the "rustic clown." Some had slept too late; they looked anxious and careworn. Last evening's warmth had all evaporated, and the "wax figure" felt a strange chill and a sinking at the heart.

Again she took her seat in the show window. She was faint, not having been in the mood for breakfast, and before long dizziness overtook her. She felt as if she looked into some deep water from which a wave suddenly emerged—a huge wave that roared, groaned, moved towards her, striving to engulf her, to carry her away.

Still, she appeared on that second day conscious of things she had not observed at first. The cars that thundered back and forth seemed new, and she noted the elevated overhead. The crowds were again as large and again as busy making "faces" which frightened her into immobility, so that it became harder for the people to get her attention, and most of them wondered: "Will she ever smile?"

In the afternoon it rained. The electric lights began to twinkle early, and a sea of umbrellas moved, moved endlessly before the motionless figure in the window.

She stared at the rumbling taxis that splashed hither and thither; at the zig-zag drizzle, the steady downpour, and her eyes suddenly filled. Thoughts of home were awakened within her by the rain. Her brain and heart.

hitherto as if congealed by the terror of the strange world before her, now thawed and filled her with a gnawing sadness and self-pity. How is it at home now? her thoughts ran. How is it at home? It rains. There is the muddy road, the ruts and the pools. Father is indoors now, back from the field. The gray dusk falls. Mother sits with folded arms by the window and gazes longingly out into the dark.

"Are you looking for me?" the figure in the window, forgetting herself, suddenly wailed. "Mother, mother dear, take me to you. I ain't used to this; I'm so lonely and afraid."

Her lips trembled visibly. A spasm shot across her face and contracted it—and many of the crowd outside who made "mouths" at her, burst into a triumphant hurrah. "She laughed!" roared a colored man so loud that it reached the manager, who forthwith decided to discharge the "figure." "I get the prize," yelled others. "I made her laugh! I made her laugh!"

FROM THE OTHER SIDE OF THE SOUTH[1]

By WILBUR DANIEL STEELE

(From *The Pictorial Review*)

THE day had been dead hot. Under the weight of the afternoon one would have thought it could never be cool again in the Mzab. But immediately the sun had dipped behind the cliff that guards the western rim of the oasis the thin air emptied itself, and the night-chill, penetrating and treacherous, flowed over the dry bottom of the *oued*.

The town stirred. Under my gallery there came and went a word-fight between Berber muleteers from the north. After that I heard the evening call of the muezzin dropping down from the mosque-tower on the crowded hill, arid, sinuous, like the note of another wooden well-wheel shrilling above the desert floor. Then somewhere under a house arose the hollow voice of a tambour struck with a thumb, and a man sang. In a rift of silence a wandering breeze threshed all the date-fronds in the *oued*-bottom with a phantom of distant applause. Nearer at hand a foot-scuffle in the dusk. A choked laugh. And all around in the heavy shadows of that quarter the subdued giggling, the rustling, and jewel-clanking of the women of dark delight.

"What's wrong with the Ouled Naïl girls to-night?" I asked along the gallery. Abd, son of Abdallah the Mozabite, rose to his feet on the tiles near the stair, a white wraith.

"*Kain kairouan ja, sidi.*" (There is a caravan come.)

Drums banged; women scurried. The momentous night was established and stars sprinkled the sky, large and restless stars, always flickering a little to the eye in that air without body.

273

I sat at an island crossroads of the western Sahara, where the pale, blurred sand-courses, like the wakes of ships, come up the bald skin of the globe from the green mysteries that lie months away on the other side of the south.

"Abd!" I called, "where does the caravan come from, east or west?"

Abd was gone. On the tiles I heard the fall of a Christian boot. Borak, the Englishman, came toward me in the shadows.

"I wonder you're not out," he said. "The caravan comes from the south."

"Not——!"

"Rather! This is a real one—like the old days again. Right away up from under. You'd better have a look at the beggars; you're romantic, you know. Might not have another chance in a year."

I put on my coat and went with him. Borak has been too long in Africa, one part and another. He has forgotten that it is the Dark Continent. As we walked he went on in his habitual vein of banter.

"It's a tidy lot of heroes for you. You may imagine. Seven 'moonlights' on the trek, and I lay a pound sterling not a man in the crowd has washed in the thirty weeks."

"Thirty weeks!" I couldn't help echoing it. "Lord!"

"There ought to be a story there, eh? As a matter of fact there isn't. I insist again that there's more story, more poetry and romance in the life of a Whitechapel coster than you'll hear in a year listening to these people. They lack imagination. They want the mental whip of civilization; that's it in a nutshell."

I felt like saying "Bosh!" Borak is too dogmatic.

We were passing into the thick of the "low town," and on our right loomed the ugly oblong of the douane, the French custom-house that stands at the converging of the deep-Sahara routes. Borak looked at it and chuckled.

"Old Arnauld" (the customs official) "is in a fair pother. There's a frightful mixture in the trek, blacks and browns from a dozen different basins down below, and you may imagine there's a lack of passports. So tha s Arnauld's job; to divine. Or rather it's Bou Dik's job, for the orderly has all the work. When I passed the market coming to you Bou Dik was tackling an old chap who claims to be Senegal but looks away east of that, a pot-bellied old swine, black as a chimney-pot, solemn as an archbishop, and blind as a bat. I gather all he wants is to be let pass quietly on his way to Holy Mekka, where he hopes to die. Bou Dik, though, is full of wild and horrid notions. He has crossed the trail lately of a dervish man who has the word that Mouley Saa* is now booked to descend in the guise of a blackamoor, and naturally, having a fat berth with the Infidel, Bou Dik isn't going to let the Deliverer into *his* department—not if he can help it. So just now Bou Dik is death and leprosy on niggers. I wish you could have heard the row."

I was to hear it presently. We had arrived at a chain swung across the black street and, ducking under it, we came into the open market square. I had seen the place a hundred times, by sun and moon and stars, and still familiarity had not quite worn off my first sense of it as a haven between the winds, the anchorage of a remote white port of call lost in the ocean of stone. To-night that illusion was deepened a dozenfold. There is no other metaphor in speech so true as "ships of the desert." They were here. To-night I knew that I had known before only the small fry of that dry sea world, only the shore-huggers, the humble brotherhood of the coastwise trade. Here to-night was the creature of the main, the deep-sea squadron, the tall fleet.

From where we stood, clear to the further shore of dim arcades, the ground was hidden under the mass of kneeling beasts and heaped bales, a tumbled thing, monstrous in sleep. We picked our way through the ruck, lighting matches from time to time when we found ourselves trapped in blind alleys between bales and humps, or felt our way barred by the hairy neck of a camel curving waist-high across the night. Mountains whisked fat tails at us; sleeping legs sprawled from beneath hills of cargo like dead men pinned under wreckage. Borak took hold of my elbow.

*The Napoleonic Messiah of Mohammedan prophecy.

"This way," he said. "I hear the voice of Bou Dik."

I heard it too, impassive, obstinate. There was a small fire of brush-roots throwing a glow around a ring of specters in the center of the field of ruin. The burnooses, all the same color of desert dust, might indeed have been winding-sheets; the hooded faces, gaunt, bone-built, played upon by the weak and tricky illumination from beneath, might have been skulls. And in the midst of the communing dead Bou Dik, enveloped in his red robe of authority, was the devil himself presiding.

His voice had ceased. As we settled behind him a man got to his feet on the side beyond the fire. With a gesture which had in it something of the trained orator he put back the hood of his burnoose, baring his strong neck and his round, blue-black, kinky-polled negroid head.

"Thou hast demanded, sidi, who is this man who is the father of my father. Thou hast demanded whence he comes, whither he goes, what he desires. Now I will tell thee all these things, I, Belkano, who am not without power in the country which is under Kalgou."

He spoke a quaint Arabic in which all the throat-sounds were brought forward and softened—such a tongue, Borak told me, as black boys pick up in the Mohammedan *zaouias* at Sikasso and Timbuktu—quaint, and yet more easily understood in the Mzab than dialects not so far away, in Tunis, say, or the Moroccan uplands.

"The father of my father," he said, "is a very great and holy man."

In the pause that followed all the eyes turned upon the object deposited at the speaker's feet. It was discerned to be human.

"Black as a chimney-pot, solemn as an archbishop, blind as a bat." Like many of Borak's observations, that one had everything in it but the essential. The essential thing was the man's enormous separation. Whether it was the infirmity of his great age or whether it was his "holiness" (which may account for many things), he was removed to a distance which could not be measured. He lived on another planet. He lived within another sky, the sky of his own skin.

There was something majestic in the completeness of
his immobility. Save for a faint, slow, rhythmical pulse of
his swollen lower lip there was nothing visibly alive in him.
Not once did the dead eyeballs, sustained in little cups of
rheum, shift from the line of dead ahead. From the first
to the last of that audience he remained in the attitude in
which I imagine he must have been deposited, a sphinx
thing in ebony, content with memories. Memories gorgeous
or infernal. His lip fascinated me. I could not get my
eyes away from that pendulous and extraordinary tissue,
throbbing with faint, ordered convulsions in the orange
light. It was as if the creature's heart, appalled by something under the black sky of skin, had broken prison and
escaped so far, only to be caught on the threshold and hang
there eternally, beating.

I had to shake myself. In a whisper, to Borak: "What's
that he was saying? The tall one."

"He says that his grandfather is bound on the pilgrimage to Mekka because he is tremendously holy, and he is
tremendously holy because he has a huge sin on his soul.
Not bad, eh? It has happened before."

Bou Dik's voice was heard. "What then is that sin?"

The dark orator looked around the circle beneath him.

"It is known in Andiorou and Adar. It is known in
Damagarin country and even in Manga country in the
east." He looked at Bou Dik. "Now I will recount thee
that history, sidi."

His gaze returned to the fire. I shall not soon forget
him as he stood there against the stars of the desert night,
tall, glossy, vibrant, speaking out in a strong voice the
story of the moribund flesh beside him.

"Know thou then that it was in the years before the
missionaries of God (to whom be the prayer) and of his
Prophet (be his bliss eternal by the streams that never
cease!) had brought to my tribe the Word and the Flame
of Islam. Glory to the One God!"

"Glory to the One God!" the echo rustled around the
ring.

"In those days then the men of my people lived in darkness. They performed no ablutions. Their prayers were

to images made with their hands. The strongest and
bravest of the young men of that tribe was Djeba, who
was later called Djim, as I will recount to thee, sidi, and
who was to become the father of my father, and who is
this man. The young man who was next to Djeba in
strength and courage was Moa. These two were brothers
of the milk. Of these two, each was the other's breath.
When these two went into the bush to hunt, the animals
said to one another, 'Strike if thou wilt amongst seven
men, but avoid the Brothers of the Milk!' So lived Djeba
and Moa in those days. Djeba was the spear of Moa;
Moa was Djeba's shield.

"In those days then came a war-party from the south,
from the country of Gando under Sokoto, the country of
braggarts and thieves. They came out of the bush in the
morning and moved toward the village, casting their spears
aloft and beating on drums. The warriors of my people
did not fail to answer them. They advanced out of the
stockade. Nikato, the Headman, was in the forefront, and
at his two shoulders went Djeba and Moa. That sunrise
Djeba slew five of the sons of Gandoland. Moa slew five.
Neither cut nor bruise was on their bodies. *Sing the Valor
of the Brothers of the Milk!*"

The apostrophe rang out, absorbed, deep-throated, across
the sleeping caravan. My eyes went to the flesh on the
ground. Into that dark house had those words been able
to penetrate? Had their ringing set some hidden echo
ringing? How could one say? The lip that was like the
man's drawn heart pulsed in the same laggard, imperturb-
able count; the dead eyeballs did not shift. But perhaps
they were dead only that they might see the better the
sunlight of that vanished and heroic myth.

"*Sing the Valor and the Victory of the Brothers of the
Milk!*

"That war-party was beaten; its dead soiled the ground;
its living fled into the bush. That day the drums were
beaten in the village and muttons were killed; that night a
feast was made. The young men danced and the old men
made sacrifice to their images.

"But the images of those days were idolatrous and had

no power over good and ill. *La illah il allah!** Accordingly then it was written that the survivors of that war-party, gathering again in the bush and being drunk with the desire of revenge, fell once more upon the village in the hour when the young men were full-fed and their weapons away. So in that night many of my tribe were slain. The stockades were thrown down; the houses were given to the flame. In the light of that flame many virgins were desecrated, many old men disemboweled, many children spun on spears. But those of good growth and being were taken away. Djeba and Moa were taken away.

"How can I recount to thee, sidi, the days of that march? Am I then another Errendi, that the words of my lamentation should fall like burning oil on a new wound? But the history is well known in all the country above the River, for my father's brother, Ahmed ben Djeba, he who had it out of the mouth of Djeba, has made it a chant at a hundred feasts and sung it under a hundred council-trees. He has sung the days of that going, the weeks, each week after the other through the hotness of that bush-trail. He has told the tale of the moons. In the roof of his mouth he has recalled the song of the lash that fell on those men's shoulders and made of their flesh the flesh of goats that is hung on the stockade to cure. He has stirred the dung-heaps to bring in memory the meat that was given them at evening before they fell down to sleep. With his tongue he has made the clank of the chain that bound them together, the heavy chain of iron that bound together even those two who were bound by the strong bond of the breast that gave them suck!

"Many among them died. When they died their bodies were cut from the chain with swords. Djeba and Moa grew thin. When Djeba looked at Moa he saw a skeleton that he did not know. When Moa looked at Djeba he saw a thing which filled him with terror. At night each bade the other farewell, saying, 'In the morning I shall be dead.' But they were strong and they did not die. Only their minds became empty.

"Then they came at last to the banks of a great lake.

* There is no god but God.

This lake was so great that when they had been sold to a white boatman and when they had come out in the boat so far that they could no longer see the bank behind them, then they could yet see no bank before, and the water was all about them to the sky like the sand in the desert of Djouf. To my father's brother Djeba has recounted that they were more than the length of a moon in that going, but it must be recalled that his mind was empty, since no lake to be compared with that is in our knowledge. A wind arose on that lake and water came into the boat. They were athirst, but when they drank of that water it was sour and their thirst consumed them tenfold after. What man is there master of words sufficiently bitter to recount that going upon the lake of those men who were captive?

"Then they came at last to the other bank of that lake, and they were taken up swiftly into the bush of the country beyond, for there were war-boats of other white men on the water. And on another day they came to a great *ksar* of a hundred shelters, and in the market-place of that *ksar* they were exposed for sale. They were nine. Nine men left out of sevenscore strong men! What battle in the memory of the tribes so disastrous as that going! What ambush so bloody as that march of the companions of the Brothers of the Milk!"

For a moment after the outcry the orator's lips closed over the firelit sheen of his white teeth. I suppose that he (like his paternal uncle) had recited this tropic saga a hundred times in the villages of the black south. I doubt not that at this point he had been accustomed to pause, to receive for a moment the sweet applause of a groan.

"And so," he resumed, "they were sold that day into labor. And of the Brothers of the Milk, those whose eyes saw a single thing and whose lips spoke the same, Moa was taken one way and Djeba another, and their hearts died. Djeba, the blood-child of chieftains, was driven like a bullock up into the bush by a white driver, and when his weakness grew on him and he stumbled that driver struck him with a thong.

"That country beyond the great lake is a fat country, full of plantings of maize and cotton in the uplands where the bush is cleared. It is known by the name of Djoja, and in extent it lies from the banks of the lake into the interior many marches away. Djeba was taken to a certain planting and thrown into a *dar* in a stockade as great as a small *ksar*. There he had the company of other captives from the River, from the Camaroun, and from the River Greater than the River in the south. Some there were who had been there so great a time that they had forgotten their own tongues and knew only the Djoja speech, and some had been born in that stockade.

"Then they were driven into the fields to labor. In his weakness the sun beat upon the head of Djeba and made him forget. Then he was driven back to the stockade, and the rain came through the thatch of the *dar* and wet his body and fever consumed his heart. But already his heart was dead; only when he slept and saw Moa in a dream did he live.

"And that driver said to him, 'How art thou called?' And he said, 'Djeba.' And the driver laughed and cried, 'That is no name for a black boy; I christen thee Djim; and Djim thou art!'" And he went away, still laughing as if he had turned a word of wit. So a hate of him came into Djeba, and Djeba would have killed him, only that he was a tall, great-bodied man, and Djeba, who had been worth five warriors in his strength, was like a child in weakness now.

"That fever burned his heart and his bowels. He was given to eat of a cous-cous made of sour maize and swineflesh. Then his stomach turned over. He vomited. He said, 'Now at last I am to die.'

"But then a woman came into that *dar*. She laid a hand on his head and called him Djim, but the hand was cool, and the anger went from his heart. She gave him milk to drink, and his pain ceased. His sickness passed. In the darkness of that shelter that woman was like the healing benignity of the moon when it has come an hour high in the east. She spoke in tones of compassion, and he was made whole.

" 'Who then is that woman?' he asked of the men, 'and how is she called?'

" 'She is Mis'us, and she lives in the *dar kebir*' (the Big House).

" 'Is she then the woman of that driver?' he asked.

"His companions laughed. 'Nay, she is the woman of Maas Djo.'

" 'Who then is Maas Djo?'

" 'Maas Djo is the Maasa, the Headman. It is his silver with which thou wert got.'

" 'Why then have I not seen this Headman?'

" 'For the reason that since thou hast come he has been gone with a war-party to fight the Yankis to the north.'

" 'He has gone then to take other captives?'

" 'Nay he has gone to save those he has got.' And then they recounted to Djeba: 'The war-parties of the Yankis who come from behind the rivers of the north choke the trails. The bush never sleeps for the sound of their drums. Their torches are amongst the settlements. The long peace of the white men is broken; new confederations are formed; terror is loosed abroad. The lust of booty and of blood is aflame in the Yankis. It is said that they devour babes; it is known that when they make prayer in their holy places their ablutions are performed in the blood of a lamb. Such are they!'

"Then they recounted to Djeba how Maas Djo and the other Headmen, the holders of plantings, all the young men, how they had gathered to the war-drums in the trails, how they had chosen chiefs and gone away into the bush, and how the sky above them was that day the color of gore.

"And Djeba asked them, 'Which is then the stronger?' And they answered, 'The party of Maas Djo is the stronger. Mayhap even now it has driven the Yankis back across their rivers. Mayhap to-morrow he will return home!'

"But one amongst them who had been born into labor in that stockade in Djoja and who was now an old man said, 'Mayhap not.' That same man, who was called by the name of Moz, came into the *dar* at night and said in a low voice to Djeba, 'The Yankis are like the leaves of the pepper-tree; they are small, but their number is beyond count. Hark thou well when the bush is sleeping and thou wilt hear their powder-guns in the north.'

"Then Djeba harkened, but he heard no guns. Nevertheless he sharpened his reaping-tool. But he was not yet strong from his sickness.

"From time to time that woman from the *dar kebir* came to bring him sweet milk and speak in tones of compassion. And it was written that the heart of Djeba, the son of chieftains, should grow soft and meek. But when that driver perceived Mis'us ministering to the captive's weakness he jeered with mocking laughter, and the woman cowered before it as though she had been afraid and fled away to the Big House. And Djeba's hatred of that man grew like a pain.

" 'When I am stronger I will kill him,' he said.

"So he grew stronger.

"On another night that man called Moz came in secret and said to Djeba, 'Hark thou well in the night, and before another moon has gone thou wilt hear the drums of the tribesmen of the north.' And when he saw Djeba take up his reaping-tool he said, 'Rather shouldst thou sing for joy. For these men here who are ignorant *niggahs* have told thee things apart from the truth. Thou hast spoken to me of they milk-brother who is called Moa, who was sold into the planting of Maas Djoj Blaak. It has come to my knowledge that Moa has fled from that planting, and with others from other plantings has gone to fight in the war-parties of the Yankis, where they are received with honors. Is it probable that such men eat babes? No, Djim, I repeat to thee, these here are child-headed *niggahs,* who know not that the Yankis come to set them free out of labor in the plantings. No, Djim, rather shouldst thou sing for joy, for when thou see'st the Yankis thou wilt see thy milk-brother in their train.'

"Then Djeba's heart sang for joy.

" 'Again, again I shall see my brother!' he cried. 'Again our eyes shall behold one thing and our breaths shall be one!' And he said to Moz, 'Now I too will run away from the stockade and I will go to meet Moa.'

"And Moz said, 'But the driver will prevent thee.'

"And Djeba said, 'No, for I will kill the driver before I go.'

"And Djeba waited, feeding his heart on the thought of Moa and on the promise of the death of that white man who had laughed.

"There came an evening when he watched and saw the driver going out of the stockade into the edge of the bush. So Djeba took up his sharp reaping-tool and followed, creeping near the ground. He came near to the driver. He saw him very clearly. The driver was dressed in finery, with a hat like a deep drum fashioned of fur, and a tunic of blue cloth with buttons of silver. Djeba saw him against the light of dusk in the sky. But the driver was not alone. Mis'us was there, where she had stolen for solitude. It was she that the driver had followed, as the desert hyena slinks slavering after the lone gazelle. The fear was in Djeba that if he struck the man, then the woman would give the alarm and he would be taken again. He might have struck both. But his heart was softened by the compassion of the woman, and what was written in the book of the future he was not given yet to read. Had he known! Had he but known to strike—the driver afterward, perhaps —but the woman first.

"But while he hesitated, already it was too late. He saw the driver step forward and grasp the woman's arm, uttering words he could not understand. He saw the woman, standing quietly, turn her head and spit once and spit twice in the driver's face.

"She continued to stand quietly, like stone. But the driver flung off toward the stockade, laughing terribly in his deep chest.

"Then Djeba would have returned and waited another chance at the man. But the thought of Moa was strong on him, and the bush was at his back. So he said to himself, 'I will return with Moa,' and he crept away.

"All that night he walked swiftly. He hid himself and slept in the day and advanced by night again. He did not know where he went, but the image and affection of his milk-brother were so powerful in Djeba that it seemed he would come truly to Moa. Because of that he remained strong. His stomach was empty but his heart was fed, and he penetrated the bush with the swiftness of a panther.

He would have wished to speak with others and know his way, but if he saw slaves in the fields then he saw with them a white driver, and he was afraid.

"There came a time when he saw a Senegal man working at the edge of a maize-planting, and no driver was in sight. So he showed himself, and he asked, 'Where then are the Yankis?' And the man answered him, 'Go thou to Tlaanta. I know nothing, but at Tlaanta all things are known.'

" 'Where then is Tlaanta?' Djeba demanded. And the man said, 'If thou knowest not Tlaanta then indeed thou art an ignorant *niggah*. Turn thy face to the north, and at nightfall thou wilt behold a great *ksar* which is Tlaanta, which is the chief place of Djoja, where all things are known—"

("Tlaanta." Something queer was happening down in the subconscious regions of my brain. "Tlaanta, the chief place of Djoja." The reader may laugh, but so firmly was my attention fixed in the picture of some fabulous tropical mid-African scene that the familiar syllables, blurred in the Arab utterance, touched still too lightly to make a breach. "Tlaanta Djoja—" I glanced uneasily at Borak, as though he could help. He returned my stare with a supercilious grin, as much as to say, "My word! you're not letting yourself be taken in by this fantastic claptrap!" *"Tlaanta,* the chief place of *Djoja"* — *"Maas Djo"* — *"Yankis"* — *"Moz"* — *"Djim"* — The equatorial forest-walls were trying their hardest to topple over in my dull brain. But there was no time. I had to get back to the saga unfolding in the strong voice of the orator in that ember-lit Sahara night.)

"—And when the night fell Djeba saw before him in the sky a pillar of light. And he came on a hill and saw a great settlement in flames. And then all about him came people fleeing in confusion through the dark bush, carrying on their heads their mills and cooking-pots and crying, 'The Yankis! The Yankis are come!'

"Then Djeba was glad. He went down toward burning Tlaanta. The flame was in his face and his heart was hot, and he stood and called aloud the name of his brother of the milk. But he saw no man. A lad ran out of a shelter that took fire. Djeba caught that lad by the arm and cried, 'Where are the Yankis?' And the lad screamed, 'Gone! Gone!' and he fell down with his eyes wide open, and Djeba saw that he was dead.

"And Djeba said to himself, 'If the Yankis are gone and Moa with them, then it will be his thought to lead them to that planting where I was a slave, to kill that driver and set me free.' So he turned his back on the burning *ksar*. He ran all through that night. Others ran with him; other slaves freed by the war-party's passage. They turned this way and that in the darkness, chanting the war-chants of the Yankis, and their paths through the bush were ruin. In the night they pillaged and burned stockades, in the morning they marched in bands, in the afternoon they slept along the trails. But by day and by night their minds were turned with freedom, and when Djeba ran amongst them demanding word of Moa their answers were without sense.

"There was a night when Djeba came upon a clearing. He saw a stockade in flames. The light of those flames showed him the fields, and then he recognized that planting and his spirit leaped with joy. He said, 'Now Moa has come here seeking me, and his revenge is before my eyes!'

"And Djeba ran bounding across the fields and came into the flame of the stockade, and he called Moa's name. He shouted the war-call of their tribe. He shouted the hunting-call that had been fixed between the milk-brothers in the old days in the bush.

"Then it seemed to Djeba that he heard the answer to the hunting-call, but in the crackling of the flames he could not say whence it came. Then he bounded on in the stockade. In that circle of fire he saw a man standing. It was a white man he had never seen. His breast was black with blood, his head hung down, and he wept. Djeba went toward him boldly.

" 'Tell me, then, where is Moa?'

"The man looked at him with dull, heavy eyes from which the tears ran down, and for answer he said, 'Where is my wife, boy? Where are my servants? I am Maas Djo. I have come home.'

"Then Djeba perceived that the man was possessed, so he did not harm him, but ran on. He leaped like a panther through all the stockade. He bounded through the wall and stood in the lighted field, and there was nothing there but his shadow. Then he ran toward the bush, and there he saw a figure. He pursued, and the figure ran into the bush, but Djeba was too swift, and overtook it, and he saw it was that woman, who crouched like a terrified gazelle and watched his coming with large eyes.

"And he said, 'It is I.'

"When the woman heard that she trembled with relief and took hold of his arm and whispered, 'It is thou, Djim! I thought it was *he*. I thought thou wert that drunken monster pursuing me still!'

"When he heard that, there came into Djeba's mind the memory and the hate of that driver. And he said, 'Where is he now?' And the woman, grasping his arm more tightly at that instant, whispered, 'Hush, thou, and hark! He comes!'

"Then near them Djeba heard the fall of feet and he saw the man advancing through the bush. He saw his shape plain and black against the glow beyond the leaves; the shape of that fur hat he remembered, in the form of a deep drum, tilted wildly; the shoulders thrust out with that tunic of silver buttons, the elbows swaggering. And he saw that the figure was drunk and lustful and that he came in cunning silence amongst the leaves, and he knew that the time of his revenge was at hand.

"So Djeba sprang through the leaves and caught the man's neck in his fingers. They fell down in the dark on the ground, and there they fought. But Djeba's powerful hands were about the man's throat, and the man lay quiet and breathed no more. Then Djeba went back, but the terrified woman was gone.

"Then Djeba returned across the field toward the stockade, calling Moa's name again, and in the field near the stockade he saw lying the body of a man. The man was despoiled of his clothes and naked, and his head cut three-quarters from his trunk. And Djeba looked and saw that it was that driver.

"Then Djeba said to himself, 'The night is full of infernal creatures, witches and *djinoun*. I have slain the driver in his finery in the bush, and here he lies an hour dead and naked in the field. The night is red with devilwork.' A fear came on him and his teeth knocked together. Nevertheless he went back to the bush, laid hold of that other man's feet, and pulled him through the bush to the field, and there he looked at the face of the man he had slain.

"He looked at the face of the man he had slain!"

The syllables of the loud repetition went away across the sleeping floor of the square and played among the invisible arcades, echoes deep-toned, momentous, tragic. And in the glow of the embers I saw the lip of that oblivious clay pulsing, pulsing, with the same laggard and monotonous beat. I continued to stare at it. You may be certain now that I stared. The short hairs at the back of my skull stood up and pricked the skin. For the wonder of it. Even to that Senegal orator himself the saga he repeated remained fabulous, an epic of equatorial rivers. Chanted first by son and then by grandson at a hundred feasts and under a hundred village council-trees and grown into the body of mid-African legendry, not till this night had it come to ears that heard; to eyes that saw with the eyes of that ancient, moribund, blind, black wanderer. For now I knew that I had heard the tale of that incendiary night on a "Djoja planting" before, not once, but many, many times; not in the glow of a Sahara camp-fire, but in the ember light of a Hancock County chimney-nook, where my own grandmother Peyton used to sit before bedtime thirty years agone, reciting a saga of her own.

The narrator's voice was heard again, rushing, staccato.

"Then Djeba ran through the bush to find that woman, his one thought that he might now slay her too. For he perceived now that she must be a witch-doctress, thus by compassion to have blinded his eyes. He ran with all his power. How long he ran, what man can say? Sometimes he seemed to see that woman as a shadow in the bush before him and sometimes as a bird flying before him through the trees. In him there was no hunger save the hunger for her killing, no thirst save the thirst for her blood, no weariness save the weariness of the damned soul.

"And then there was a time when it seemed to Djeba that he was in the midst of many men. He saw that they were white men and that they moved in a thousand ranks. Ruin lay behind them and thunder ran around. And he remembered the words of Moz: 'The Yankis are like the leaves of the pepper-tree; they are small, but their number is beyond count.' And when the nights came Djeba saw their camp-fires, and even their fires were beyond count.

"A forgetfulness came on Djeba. He ran from fire to fire, crying, 'Where is Moa?' And those men mocked him, saying, 'Moa what?' But Djeba screamed at them and ran on. Or sometimes they named him *Samboh,* saying, 'Hold, *Samboh.* Sit down with us now and sing!' Then Djeba thanked them, and sat down with them and sang, and the war-chant of the Yankis filled the sky.

"And after many days Djeba came with the war-party to the banks of that lake, and there he beheld a bearded chieftain sitting on a horse, and he fell down on his face and wept. And he implored, 'That I come again to my own country beyond this water, where Moa, my brother, has returned, and where he awaits me in the village of my tribe!' And that chieftain heard.

"In after-days then was Djeba placed in a boat, together with many of the River and the Cameroun, and he returned across that lake where the waters lay to the sky like the sands in the desert of Djouf. Then they made a village on the shore. But Djeba left them. He penetrated the bush through which he had marched many years before, bound to that chain. He penetrated the country of enemies and he passed through. Then Djeba came to his own village again. There were old men there who knew him when he spoke his name. They rejoiced and made a feast. All night they feasted. And one of the old men said to Djeba, 'Moa, thy brother of the milk was taken with thee. Where then is Moa?'

"And Djeba said, 'I do not know.' And he took none of the feast.

"And in the years afterward, when Djeba had taken

wives and got sons, there came into our country the missionaries of God (to whom be the prayer) and of his Prophet (may his bliss never decrease)——

"*La illah il allah!*

"And they spoke the word of the Koran to Djeba, and Djeba's heart turned in his breast. And he said then, 'My heart can no longer contain a lie. Hark all to the truth. Moa, my brother of the milk—which bond is sacred—Moa, my brother, him I slew with my own hands in that land which is beyond the great water. I slew him, being tricked by a witch-woman. And that witch-woman I was not able to slay! That then is my sin!'

"That then is the sin of Djeba. I have spoken, I, Belkano, who am the son of his son!"

In the hush that followed that deep-toned verbal signature my breath whistled small in my throat.

"Lord! Lord! Oh, my Lord!"

Borak eyed me with a smirk and a grunt. The black fellow showed his shining teeth again. He took another breath into his lungs.

"For the length of thirty Ramadans the father of my father has not opened his mouth to any man in speech. Because of that sin, because he would not look at any man, his eyes have become blind. He would not hear, and his ears are deaf. Thus men know that he is holy. So they come for many marches to touch his hand. Sometimes then his lips are opened, and for their ears he will sing again that war-chant of the Yankis. And then those men will give him offerings against his pilgrimage, that he may see Holy Mekka and ease him of that sin and die——"

The voice was rising.

"They give him offerings of broad copper! They throw down pieces of silver before him! *They throw down gold!*"

I heard the wind going out of Borak's chest at that; an obscure thoracic collapse. A snort.

"At last! At last the plot unfolds. Now the old bird will render that popular ditty entitled, 'The Unwritten War-song of the Wild Yankis of Yankisland,' and the company will contribute. And strangely enough the ringmaster's eye is fastened unerringly on *you*."

"For God's sake, man——"

"Yes, but you'lll see," he persisted. "You'll note that his toe even now is prodding the old one in the ribs."

It was true. I saw the nudging and peremptory toe. I stared at that lip hanging in the ember-light. I beheld a disorder and quickening of that fleshy pulse. I heard an obedient sound issuing forth. It was a very small, shallow, creaking sound. It emerged from that emotionless mask of senility; it rose and fell in mechanical lengths of tone like a bent wire and went away and was lost in the night of the packed Sahara square. It was a queer chant.

"Cock and bull!" grunted Borak.

"For God's sake, man, hush!"

I stared and I listened. Yes, it was a very queer chant indeed. The short hairs were beginning to stand up again at the back of my skull.

On the ground, red with the firelight, a copper sou was tossed. I saw another fall, and another. I took out my wallet and found a hundred-franc note, and I let it flutter into the circle over the shoulder of Bou Dik.

Borak got hold of me.

"*Lord!* I say, now! What's *that* for?"

"To help and ease him of that 'sin.'"

"But my dear simple chap—all that rigmarole——"

"Of the greatest of all African wars——"

He tilted his head at me with the absurdest suspicion about my wits.

"Come away!" he said.

I got up and went with him out into the black ruck of the camels. He was groaning audibly over that squandered bank-note. "Man, man, and you were really taken in by that beggar's claptrap. Why — look you — in that old chap's day there weren't enough white men in Central Africa all put together——"

"Borak!" I said. "*Will* you listen to that song!"

In the hollow of the market, above the grunt and snore of the caravan, the thin war-chant of the "Yankis" wound on, repeating, repeating,

John B'own's body lahs amoldin' in the g'ave,
John B'own's body lahs amoldin' in the g'ave,
John B'own's body lahs amoldin' in the g'ave,
But his soul goes mahchin' on——

In that Sahara darkness where the pale courses come from beyond the South I saw Atlanta burning. Sherman was on the march.

THE COFFIN[1]

By CLEMENT WOOD

(From *The Pagan*)

IT stood in the middle of the sitting-room. It was all black, except for the silver shine of the handles. There were flowers on the floor beside it, vague blotches of dulled white and yellow. The burdened odor of honeysuckle, a ground-clinging, unhealthy sweetness, came to the man's nostrils; there was a stiff, pungent scent, too, that he could not place. On the mantel, more flowers; the glimmer of the bracket lamp washed these feebly—its wick was so low that the flame seemed next door to dying at any moment. Flowers filled the stiff-backed chair beneath the lamp. There were two other chairs in the room, both empty.

Thomas Rice loitered at the open doorway, taking in the sparse furnishings. He had stood for ten minutes within the dining room, while Aunt Teby Riggs, Charley's own aunt on his mother's side, whispered harshly all he needed to know, and much that he did not.

"Won't yer have just a bite, Mr. Rice?" she insisted stridently, unable to keep her eyes off the twisted half of his face.

"I et my supper already, thank yer."

"Just a mite of this chicken? Or a cup of somethin' warm, to stay by yer?"

"No 'm, Miss Riggs." He fumbled uneasily with his sweaty felt hat, drooping from his right hand; his coat hung limp over his arm. It was a hot, stirless night; serving writs up the county tired feet and spirit; and the final walk from Belle Ellen to Dolomite was a good eight miles.

She indicated the crowded hat-rack. "Yer can find

room. . . . Louella's eatin' her supper now." The shrill syllables rasped his ear.

Her disquieting footfall followed him to the sitting-room. Her arm gestured past him. "They got it from undertaker Norton, in Bessemer," she volunteered chattily under her breath.

"Yes."

The dining-room door creaked to at last. He stood, rubbing the ball of his right thumb with his forefinger, as if to cleanse each of invisible irritating dust from the felt hat. The hat was gone; its absence was a momentary annoyance, a perceptible gap in things.

There were two chairs. Both were against the same wall, toward the front of the house. The mantel, the chair with flowers, the two empty chairs, and . . . it. . . . His restless mind took an unconscious inventory. Instinctively he put off thinking about what lay within it.

He took the farther chair. They were almost a room's length apart, and this one was slightly nearer what had been the man he had loved. She—the woman that he despised—could hardly think that his mere sitting there could poison the air for her.

His mind wandered on. Honeysuckles were great flowers for funerals. That sharp, stiff odor—it was like the look of dahlias, stiff, waxy. There were some in old man Lunsford's side yard. Maybe these came from there. He could afford to give away, especially if it cost him nothing: flowers . . . advice. . . . Butting into people's business, with his skinny little face and weedy little beard, like his own weedy front yard.

The dining-room door creaked open. A firmer step thudded on the carpet. She came into the room, a thin hand shading her eyes, to make him out. Then she sat in the empty chair.

"Evenin', Louella." It was her house, now; decency demanded that much.

"Evenin'." The word was spat out.

She sat stiff on the chair-edge, white hands folded upon black skirt. Her eyes pointed straight down the room. She said no more; he kept still. The odor of the kerosene-lamp swayed with that of the honey-suckles, mingled with a soiled scent he at last imagined must come from the middle of the room.

She had not meant to speak beyond this. But she should have made it civil. Maybe she had been a bit short. "Aunt Teby tol' me yer were here."

His answer was framed after a pause. "Yes. I saw her."

There was nothing more to be said about it. Each nursed sullen dislike.

The stolid minutes passed. Occasional remote noises entered, looked about, left swiftly. A pan banged from the rear of the house; a horse neighed listlessly; doors creaked open and shut with exaggerated quietness. These subsided. The stillness of death spread from the middle of the room to the house and the farm without.

He could watch her profile, in the lamp's withdrawn glimmer. She stared stonily down the room, away from him; there was no harm in observing her unbeknown. Her hair was knotted in the back, a skimpy knot; it lay flat and black above her forehead . . . black, like her dress. Her cheeks were thinner than he remembered seeing her have. Her teeth stuck out, as always. They seemed the whitest thing in the room; their stony inactivity held his imagination. He licked his lips unconsciously.

There had not been a sound from the house for half an hour. He stirred uncomfortably; the chair squeaked. "It doesn't set comfortable, to some," she said, shortly.

"Not very."

"Some folks think they've a right to be partic'lar." Her tone was sour, complaining.

He did not answer. Time drawled along; the tired minutes plodded unendingly. Funny of Charley to want him and—her, who'd never teamed a bit. Think of being married to such as her! Who wouldn't die? . . . Well, talk would make the night pass quicker.

He broke the icy silence. "Crowded tonight?" His right hand gestured a vague circle.

"Yes. Two to a bed upstairs. Aunt Teby and Mary— cot in the kitchen. Two of the boys in the dining room.

Lucky yer don't have to be fixed for. Nowhere left." She laughed without mirth.

His curious eyes travelled around. "Nothing to sleep on here." They returned to the middle of the room in fascination, as if he had waited this excuse to revisit what was there. Afraid that she had caught the morbid fancy, that there was a gruesome, yet possible, couch, he hastened on. "Not that I can't sleep in a chair, though. But I reckon we won't do much sleeping tonight."

"No." The spiteful warning that she would not trust herself asleep, with him around, spoke in the sneering monosyllable.

In the hush that followed, his mind returned to the cold body lying near. He fought against thinking of Charley Hawkins as a corpse; it was of the young Charley, the chum of the years before the marriage, that thoughts came. Memory after memory woke to life out of him, with dizzying rapidity: memories remote from this musty, close room; memories stained with vivid sunlight on fields of black-eyed Susans, with shadow-dapple on the creek's windings, with starry stretches of windy night. A lively, vigorous Charley Hawkins had featured these . . . a good looker, not like himself, his face spoiled from birth. . . .

Yes, Charley had been a lively kid. . . . Baseball, a scrap, a hay-ride to the river, especially whenever a girl was mixed up in it—Charley was chain-lightning. There was that kid widow, Mamie Fagin. Just one trick she had: when you kissed her—God! Her teeth against your neck! The teeth were like Louella's, he reflected, looking over at Charley's widow. Maybe Charley liked 'em with teeth that way; they were always livelier to love.

His mind fondled Louella and the live Charley together for a moment, then returned to earlier time. After Mamie, there had been her unmarried sister, Gussie; Charley switched quick. . . . That scare, when he confided that they were afraid he'd gotten the girl into trouble! False alarm, of course. . . . And the three Bennet girls—not that they were anything. . . . His mind lengthened the roll.

Muscles cramped with sitting in the one position, he rose

awkwardly. To cover the act, he walked over to the mantel, and smelled the flowers. "Pretty," he grudged.

The woman followed slowly, doing over her duty as guide of the occasion. "Those were from Judge O'Rear's; these, Miss Lunsford." She named the others, eager to talk, yet letting tone and look lash her forced listener. Her manner was agitated; the hushed watching must be getting on her nerves, he judged.

Silently she stood beside him, before that black thing in the middle of the room. She must say something. Her hand reached out and touched it. "Plush," she said.

He nodded.

"The best undertaker Norton had."

"It came from him?"

"Yes. He won't have any shiftless funeral," she concluded with bitterness.

They went back to the chairs. The impulse to talk dominated her, and Rice hitched his chair a few steps closer, so that their remarks might be sufficiently low-voiced not to disturb—well, not to disturb what lay in the plush-covered thing. Shivering slightly, she drew hers a bit nearer.

"Shiftless," she had said. He recalled that this was her favorite adjective for him—and he Charley's side-partner, even best man at the wedding! Never a jaunt or a spree that they had not gone on together, until Charley took a fancy to Louella. That was Charley's luck again; Tom had known Louella longer, fancied her first . . . been mad for her, finally. She was too quiet for Charley then; and sometimes . . . sometimes she hadn't frowned at Tom, when he sat near her, itching and miserable. Of course, if he had spoken, she would have laughed . . . with that twisted face of his!

So she and Charley had hitched up. At first, Charley had made him come around . . . insisted. She let him know soon enough and plain enough, that this was no place for him. "Shiftless," she'd called him; she said he was too shiftless to marry. . . . No, she never could have meant that, that he should have spoken. She would have laughed. . . . Not that!

It got worse. She'd scold Charley sharply when he was around. Her hints got too pointed; he'd had the good sense to stay away. Everybody said she had a mean tongue—mean as garbroth.

The woman half faced him now; and her thoughts dwelt on the same period as his. He had done his best to spoil Charley for her, this dirty Tom "Grits." He'd egged him on to drink, and fight, and gamble . . . and chase women. Used to come up to their house and sit around in the way; then tease Charley off into some devilment, when he wanted to stay home. Too lazy, too backward, to open his lips to a girl; he'd kept her fooling around, until she had really wanted—well, not him . . . something. . . . She'd shown him his place at last; out of the door. A squint-faced loafer, a hanger-on around the sheriff's office. . . . Fine friend for her husband! Charley at least would work regular. And now "Grits" sat there like a whipped dog, as he always did when he saw her. Slinking cur of a man!

Something urged him to pretend sympathy for her; she had lost her husband. "He didn't suffer?"

"No. He was well and up Sunday; and now—and now —" She pressed her forehead and cheeks fiercely against her cupped hands; her shoulders trembled rhythmically.

"There, there." He tried awkwardly to feign tenderness. Like as not her tongue had whipped the man to death.

To death. . . . His thoughts opened unwillingly to Charley now—to Charley dead. Queer thing, lying so close— couldn't say a thing, do a thing! . . . It wasn't the Charley he had known; not the same at all. Preachers must be right; the man he had known had gone—somewhere. That thing—cold, uncanny, staring through closed eyelids, with hair and finger-nails still alive, growing horribly—this foul thing was all that was left. Served Louella right! This was what she had made of Charley.

His fancy began to weave thoughts of the dead thing and the woman. She was wrapped in introspection now; his eye measured her from hair to barked black oxfords. One by one his mind stripped off the garments of mourning, and what lay beneath the black shell: a restless fancy cast her in intimate scenes with the man who was gone.

Morbidly the thoughts persisted, were embroidered. What if the chill, dead, bristle-faced thing should hold her as husband holds wife! A fit punishment. . . . Something deep within him lingered on the details.

The after-midnight coolness slunk between them. She shivered, wondering if he had felt it. He was her guest, after all. "I'll get your coat," she whispered, leaning close. She got it, and a wrap to throw around her own shoulders.

It seemed somehow warmer when their chairs were close, she thought. Of course, Tom Rice couldn't help being what he was born to be. And she had thought a lot of him before she knew Charley. If he'd only spoken! . . . And —to come here tonight, when he hadn't been around for five years . . . of course, just because her dead man had wished it. . . .

The friend watched her bent body, as sobs overcame her. The sneer dissolved from his face. Poor thing! She wasn't such a plain-looking woman, even now; she had been decent-looking, as a girl. Even those teeth; they might —they might at least thrill a man.

Rising silently, she flung herself on her knees beside what had been her husband. Her weight ground the flowers into the carpet; the smell of bruised honey-suckle eddied dizzyingly. With terrible quietness she sobbed and sobbed. The unearthly vigil, on top of the shut-mouthed hours when she had to preserve some calmness, and arrange for the funeral, had been too much; the bars were down, the hysteric flood burst through.

At last her agony shook Tom Rice. The woman would cry herself sick. He walked to her side in the dimness; the lamp seemed weaker than before. He stood, uncertain what to do or say. The sobbing pulsed on.

He knelt beside her, stroking her shoulders with nervous hand. A twitch of repugnance bothered him at touching her. The stroking had no effect at first; low words of endearment, caressing modulations, came, and his touch became more soothing. The disgust wore off. "There, there! I know it hurts. Don't take on so. It won't help. There—"

She became sensible of his presence. Her overburdened

heart overflowed toward him; few men would have done
what he was doing. She turned to him, mouth open word-
lessly, pale teeth showing. She clung desperately to his
shoulders, while the sobs twisted and wracked her. His
arms closed upon her; her head burned against his neck.
He smelt the odor of kerosene upon her, where she must
have been fixing the lamps; then the acrid newness of the
mourning cloth. His body felt unnaturally warm where
she lay awkwardly bunched against him.

She tried to speak. "He was all I had." Unnerved
again, she threw herself across the plush top, forcing her
face into it. He looked back longingly at his deserted
chair. No, he had helped calm her; it wasn't such an unpleasant sensation, despite the smell of kerosene and new
goods . . . and an unpleasant, dirtier odor that he had
feared at first came from the corpse, but now localized as
coming from her or her clothes. He knelt beside her
again.

His touch quieted her; it made him restless. His mind
throbbed now with her; under any other circumstances,
with a woman so close, he could not hold her so unmovedly.
The very vision of her under other circumstances made him
more restless; his touch upon her was spasmodic, provocative.

Gradually he rose from his knees to a place beside her,
sprawled over the plush. His arm rounded her shoulders,
and unconsciously drew her toward him. Still sobbing,
she threw herself against his bosom. He began to kiss
away the tears. The tang of the moist salt in her eyes
quickened him. Their lips met. He felt the pressure of
those insidious, insistent teeth—their touch tortured him.

As they clung, the lamp flared up once, then sputtered
out. There was the stinging odor of burnt kerosene and
charred wick. They did not notice it, nor the clinging
sweetness of the bruised honeysuckle.

Tom Rice had one clear thought. The house was
crowded; every other room was filled. Out of the moist
fervor of the moment the woman realized that her head
was against the flowers on the floor—the back of her head,
and not her face. She was too weakened from hysteric

sobbing to protest when she found herself lying along the
soft fragrant surface; nor did she longer wish to. He felt
on the tense skin of his neck the touch of those madden-
ing teeth. Their lips met again in the breathing darkness.

She stirred out of his arms, when the bony fingers of
gray-bodied dawn reached through the closed shutters and
touched the crushed flowers on which they still were.

"Come, dear," she whispered softly, the gray pallor
twisting her plain face into a grotesque tenderness. She
kissed his twisted cheek with shy eagerness. He took it
passively; the taut thrill of the past hours had gone.

He watched her, as her fingers set the flowers to rights.
Meditatively he replaced the two chairs at the two ends
of the front wall, where they had first been. They should
be found so.

The two watchers took up their almost ended vigil.
Morning, and Aunt Teby's black coffee, should find them
so—the morning of the funeral.

THE YEARBOOK OF THE AMERICAN
SHORT STORY
OCTOBER, 1921, TO SEPTEMBER, 1922

ADDRESSES OF MAGAZINES
PUBLISHING SHORT STORIES

NOTE. *This address list does not aim to be complete, but is based simply on the magazines which I have consulted for this volume, and which have not ceased publication.*

Ace-High Magazine, 799 Broadway, New York City.
Adventure, Spring and Macdougal Streets, New York City.
Ainslee's Magazine, 79 Seventh Avenue, New York City.
All's Well, Gayeta Lodge, Fayetteville, Ark.
American Boy, 142 Lafayette Boulevard, Detroit, Mich.
American Magazine, 381 Fourth Avenue, New York City.
American Scandinavian Review, 25 West 45th Street, New York City.
Arch, 32 Waverley Place, New York City.
Argosy All-Story Weekly, 280 Broadway, New York City.
Asia, 627 Lexington Avenue, New York City.
Atlantic Monthly, 8 Arlington Street, Boston, Mass.
Ave Maria, Notre Dame, Indiana.
Black Cat, Book Hill, Highland Falls, New York.
Black Mask, 25 West 45th Street, New York City.
Blue Book Magazine, 36 South State Street, Chicago, Ill.
Bookman, 244 Madison Avenue, New York City.
Breezy Stories, 112 East 19th Street, New York City.
Brief Stories, 714 Drexel Building, Philadelphia, Pa.
Broom, 3 East 9th Street, New York City.
Catholic World, 120 West 60th Street, New York City.
Century, 353 Fourth Avenue, New York City.
Chicago Tribune, Chicago, Illinois.
Christian Herald, Bible House, New York City.
Clay, 3325 Farragut Road, Brooklyn, N. Y.
Collier's Weekly, 416 West 13th Street, New York City.
Cosmopolitan Magazine, 119 West 40th Street, New York City.
Delineator, Spring and Macdougal Streets, New York City.
Designer, 12 Vandam Street, New York City.
Detective Story Magazine, 79 Seventh Avenue, New York City.
Dial, 152 West 13th Street, New York City.
Double Dealer, 819 Baronne Street, New Orleans, La.
Everybody's Magazine, Spring and Macdougal Streets, New York City.
Extension Magazine, 223 West Jackson Boulevard, Chicago, Ill.
Follies, 25 West 45th Street, New York City.
Freeman, 32 West 58th Street, New York City.
Gargoyle, 7, rue Campagne, Paris 1, France.
Good Housekeeping, 119 West 40th Street, New York City.
Harper's Bazar, 119 West 40th Street, New York City.

Harper's Magazine, Franklin Square, New York City.
Hearst's International Magazine, 119 West 40th Street, New York City.
Holland's Magazine, Dallas, Texas.
Ladies' Home Journal, Independence Square, Philadelphia, Pa.
Liberator, 34 Union Square, East, New York City.
Little Review, 24 West 16th Street, New York City.
Live Stories, 35 West 39th Street, New York City.
McCall's Magazine, 236 West 37th Street, New York City.
McClure's Magazine, 80 Lafayette Street, New York City.
MacLean's Magazine, 143 University Avenue, Toronto, Canada.
Magnificat, Manchester, N. H.
Menorah Journal, 167 West 13th Street, New York City.
Metropolitan, 432 Fourth Avenue, New York City.
Midland, 3415 Iowa Street, Pittsburgh, Pa.
Modern Priscilla, 85 Broad Street, Boston, Mass.
Munsey's Magazine, 280 Broadway, New York City.
Open Road, 248 Boylston Street, Boston, Mass.
Outlook, 381 Fourth Avenue, New York City.
Pagan, 23 West 8th Street, New York City.
Pearson's, 34 Union Square, New York City.
People's Home Journal, 76 Lafayette Street, New York City.
People's Popular Monthly, 801 Second Street, Des Moines, Iowa.
Pictorial Review, 216 West 39th Street, New York City.
Popular Magazine, 79 Seventh Avenue, New York City.
Queen's Work, 626 North Vandeventer Avenue, St. Louis, Mo.
Red Book Magazine, North American Building, Chicago, Ill.
Reviewer, 809½ Floyd Avenue, Richmond, Va.
Saturday Evening Post, Independence Square, Philadelphia, Pa.
Saucy Stories, 25 West 45th Street, New York City.
Scribner's Magazine, 597 Fifth Avenue, New York City.
Short Stories, Garden City, Long Island, N. Y.
Smart Set, 25 West 45th Street, New York City.
Snappy Stories, 35 West 39th Street, New York City.
Sunset, 460 Fourth Street, San Francisco, Cal.
Telling Tales, 799 Broadway, New York City.
10-Story Book, 538 South Dearborn Street, Chicago, Ill.
Today's Housewife, Cooperstown, N. Y.
Top-Notch Magazine, 79 Seventh Avenue, New York City.
Town Topics, 2 West 45th Street, New York City.
True Story Magazine, 119 West 40th Street, New York City.
Wave, 5513 West Iowa Street, Chicago, Ill.
Western Story Magazine, 79 Seventh Avenue, New York City.
Woman's Home Companion, 381 Fourth Avenue, New York City.
Woman's World, 107 South Clinton Street, Chicago, Ill.
World Fiction, Houston Publishing Company, New York City.
Young's Magazine, 112 East 19th Street, New York City.
Youth, 66 East Elm Street, Chicago, Ill.

THE BIOGRAPHICAL ROLL OF HONOR
OF AMERICAN SHORT STORIES

OCTOBER, 1921, TO SEPTEMBER, 1922

NOTE. *Only stories by American authors are listed. The index figures 1, 2, 3, 4, 5, 6, 7, and 8 prefixed to the name of the author indicate that his work has been included in the Rolls of Honor for 1914, 1915, 1916, 1917, 1918, 1919, 1920, and 1921 respectively. The list excludes reprints.*

ADAMS, BILL (BERTRAM M. ADAMS). Born at Sevenoaks, England, February 24, 1879, of Anglo-Irish parentage. Educated at elementary schools and Weymouth College. On father's death went to sea in sail. Ill health brought him ashore. First story " The Bos'un of the Goldenhorn's Yarn," Adventure, January 20, 1922. Lives at Lindsay, California.
  Sailor's Way.
  Twinkle-Bright.

AIKEN, CONRAD (POTTER). Born at Savannah, Georgia, August 5, 1889. Harvard graduate. Married. Contributing editor to the *Dial*, 1917. Author of " Earth Triumphant," 1914; " Turns and Movies," 1916; " The Jig of Fo slin," 1916; " Nocturne of Remembered Spring," 1917; " Charnel Rose," 1918; " Scepticisms," 1919; " House of Rust," 1920; " Punch: the Immortal Liar," 1921; " Priapus and the Pool," 1921. Editor of " Modern American Poets," 1922. Lives in England.
  Dark City.

(8) ALLEN, JAMES LANE (*for biography, see* 1921).
  Miss Locke.

(345678) ANDERSON, SHERWOOD (*for biography, see* 1917).
  Contract.
  I'm a Fool.

(34567) BABCOCK, EDWINA STANTON (*for biography, see* 1917).
  Strange Flower.

(45) BEER, THOMAS (*for biography, see* 1917).
  Casual.
  Rope.

BELLAMY, FRANCIS RUFUS. Born at New Rochelle, New York, December 24, 1886. Educated at Williams College and Cornell University. Has been farmer, book salesman and special corre-

spondent. Author of "Balance," 1917; "Flash of Gold," 1922.
Lives at Holliston, Mass.
>   Talk.

(78) BERCOVICI, KONRAD (*for biography, see* 1920).
>   Death of Murdo.
>   Father and Son.
>   Ghitza.
>   Hazi, Wife of Sender Surtuck.
>   Mincu.
>   Murdo:
>   Tanasi.
>   When a Man Rules.

BIGGS, JR., JOHN. Born at Wilmington, Delaware, October 6, 1895.
Educated at Princeton and Harvard. Lawyer. First short story
"Corkran of the Clamstretch," Scribner's Magazine, December,
1921. Lives at Wilmington, Delaware.
>   Wind Witch.

BODENHEIM, MAXWELL.
>   Insanity.

BOOGHER, SUSAN M.
>   Unknown Warrior.

(3) BOOTH, FREDERICK. Born in Hamilton County, Indiana,
October 16, 1882. Lived on the farm and was a farmer until
1906. Educated in Indiana public schools and Earlham College,
Richmond, Indiana. Has been engaged In book selling, carpentry,
concrete and steel construction, newspaper and advertising work
coincident with unceasing but slow creative effort, under material
and psychic difficulties. Has a novel in preparation. Lives in
New York City.
>   Helpless Ones.

BROWN, BERNICE. Born at Webster City, Iowa, 1890. Graduate
of Wells College. Has been Associate Editor of Every Week and
Fiction Editor of Collier's Weekly. Lives in New York City.
>   Miracle.

(7) BRYNER, EDNA CLARE (*for biography, see* 1920).
>   Forest Cover.

BUCK, OSCAR MACMILLAN. Born at Cawnpore, India, February 9,
1885. Educated in India and at Ohio Wesleyan University and
Drew Theological Seminary. Has taught in Bareilly Theological
Seminary in India. Now professor at Drew Theological Seminary,
Madison, New Jersey. First short story, 1917. Joint author of
"India Beloved of Heaven," 1918. Especially interested in
history of Asiatic peoples. Lives in Madison, New Jersey.
>   "Kismet" — a Tale of Rohilkind.

(5678) CABELL, JAMES BRANCH (*for biography, see* 1918).
   Candid Footprint.

(5) CARVER, GEORGE. Born at Cincinnati, Ohio, December 19,
   1888. Educated at University of Alabama, University of Chicago,
   and Miami University. College instructor at present, but has
   been mill worker, student, reporter and soldier. Chief interest:
   trying to find expression for ideas better suggested than described
   by the phrase: forlorn minstrels sighing for banished kings. First
   story "In a Moment of Time," Stratford Journal, September,
   1918. Lives at Harvey, Illinois.
   Singer.

CHAPMAN, FRANCES NORVILLE. Born at Chillicothe, Missouri,
   December 31, 1876. Educated at Chillicothe Normal School,
   and has studied music and languages in Chicago, Boston, and
   abroad. Has travelled extensively. First story "The Quality
   of Genius," in the Cavalier, 1908. Lives at Brookline, Massachusetts.
   Prisoners of the Dead.

(23458) COBB, IRVIN S. (*for biography, see* 1917).
   Alas, the Poor Whiffletit!

COHEN, ROSE GOLLUP. Born in a Russian village, April 2, 1880.
   Came to America, 1892. Sweatshop and factory life, working
   fourteen hours a day. Health broke down when seventeen.
   Learned to read English from the Bible in a hospital. Has studied
   short story writing at Hunter College and Columbia University.
   Author of "Out of the Shadow," 1918. First short story "Sifted
   Earth," Touchstone, July, 1920. Lives in New York City.
   Natalka's Portion.

(7) CORLEY, DONALD.
   Book of Debts.

CRAVEN, THOMAS JEWELL. Born at Salina, Kansas, age thirty-three
   Graduate of Kansas Wesleyan University. First short story
   "Love in Smoky Hill," Dial, January, 1922. Author of "Paint,"
   1922. Chief interests literature and painting. Critic of æsthetics.
   Lives at Brookhaven, Long Island, New York.
   Love in Smoky Hill.

(4568) DOBIE, CHARLES CALDWELL (*for biography, see* 1917).
   Vision.

EHLERT, FAY. Born in New York City of Hungarian stock, April 12,
   1886. Married. Educated privately, and at Columbia College
   of Expression and University of Chicago. Chief interests drama,
   psycho-pathology, and the human "driftwood." First story
   "The Undertow," Pearson's Magazine (N. Y.), November, 1921.
   Lives in Chicago. Illinois.
   Vow.

(78) FINGER, CHARLES J. (*for biography, see* 1920).
Jade Piece.
My Friend Julio.
Shame of Gold.

FITZGERALD, F. SCOTT. Born at St. Paul, Minnesota, September 24, 1896. Educated at Princeton. First story "Babes in the Woods," Smart Set, August, 1919. Author of "This Side of Paradise," 1920; "Flappers and Philosophers," 1920; "The Beautiful and Damned," 1922; "Tales of the Jazz Age," 1922. Interested in play-writing. Lives in Minnesota.
Two for a Cent.

(48) FRANK, WALDO (*for biography, see* 1917).
Candy Cigar and Stationery.
John the Baptist.
Murder.

FREDERICK, JOHN TOWNER. Born on a farm near Corning, Iowa, February 1, 1893. Public school education. Graduate of State University of Iowa. Instructor in English there, and later head of the English Department of the State Normal School, Moorhead, Minnesota. Two years of farming in Michigan. Now Assistant Professor of English, University of Pittsburgh. Married. Founder and editor of The Midland. Author of "Druida," 1923. First short story "The Legacy," Smart Set, October, 1921.
Legacy.

FREEDMAN, DAVID. Born in Roumania, April 26, 1898. Brought to America at the age of two. Graduate of the City College of New York. Has been editor of a weekly journal and superintendent of an orphan asylum. Chief interests bowling, mathematics and metaphysics. First short story "Mendel Marantz — Housewife," Pictorial Review, April, 1922. Lives in Brooklyn, N. Y.
Mendel Marantz — Housewife.
Mendel Marantz Moves.
Quest of Sarah.

FURMAN, LUCY. Born in Henderson, Kentucky. Educated privately. Has been settlement worker in Kentucky mountains for over fifteen years. Author of "Stories of a Sanctified Town," 1897; "Mothering on Perilous," 1914; "Quare Women," 1923. Chief interest Hindman Settlement School. Lives at Hindman Kentucky.
Fourth of July.
Quare Women.
Taking the Night.

(12345678) GEROULD, KATHARINE FULLERTON (*for biography, see* 1917).
Belshazzar's Letter.
Nature of an Oath.

GILKYSON, WALTER. Born at Phoenixville, Pennsylvania, December 18, 1880. Educated at Swarthmore College and University of Pennsylvania. Lawyer. First story " The Illumined Moment," Atlantic Monthly, April, 1921. Lives in Philadelphia, Pennsylvania.
  Spoken in Jest.

(56) GOODMAN, HENRY (*for biography, see* 1918).
  Thomas.

(3) GRAEVE, OSCAR. Born in New York City, 1885. Public school education. First story published in McClure's Magazine about 1910. Author of " The Keys of the City," 1914; " Youth Goes Seeking," 1919; " Brown Moth," 1921. Lives in New York City.
  Headlines.

HARRIS, FRANK. Born in Galway, Ireland, 1854. Emigrated to the United States in 1870. Educated at numerous American and European Universities. Married. Practised law in Kansas. Has been editor of London Evening News, Fortnightly Review, and Saturday Review. Author " Elder Conklin," 1892; " The Bomb," 1909; " The Man Shakespeare," 1909; " Montes the Matador," 1910; " The Women of Shakespeare," 1911; " Unpath'd Waters," 1913; " Vales of Isis," 1914; "Contemporary Portraits," (3 series) 1914, 1919, 1921; " Great Days," 1914; " Love in Youth," 1914; " England or Germany," 1915; " The Life and Confessions of Oscar Wilde," 1916. Editor of Pearson's Magazine (N. Y.). Lives in New York City.
  Mad Love.

(8) HART, FRANCES NOYES (*for biography, see* 1921).
  American.

(35) HAWES, CHARLES BOARDMAN. Born at Clifton Springs, New York, January 24, 1889. Educated at Bowdoin College. Editor of " The Open Road." Author of " The Mutineer," 1920; " The Great Quest," 1921. Lives at Gloucester, Massachusetts.
  Out of the Storm.
  Peter Ronco.

(2568) HECHT, BEN (*for biography, see* 1918).
  Winkelburg.

(567) HERGESHEIMER, JOSEPH (*for biography, see* 1918).
  Token.

(123) HOPPER, JAMES MARIE. Born in Paris, July 23, 1876. Came to America in 1887. Educated at University of California. Has practised law, been newspaper reporter, college instructor, editor and war correspondent. Author of " Caybigan," 1906; " Goosie," 1910; " Freshman," 1912; " What Happened in the Night," 1913. Lives at Carmel, California.
  Ship in the Bottle.

HULL, ALEXANDER. Born at Columbus, Ohio, September 15, 1887. Educated at Muskingum College and University of Pennsylvania. Head of Music Department, Pacific College. Married. Musical composer. First story " The Lilac Scented Envelope," All-Story Weekly, November 6, 1915. Lives at Newberg, Oregon.
Bain's Hole.

HUNT, LIAN. Born at Glen Gardner, New Jersey. Spent childhood in Roanoke, Virginia. High school education. Special student at Columbia University. Lives at Port Washington, Long Island, New York.
King of the Reef.

JITRO, WILLIAM C. G. Born near Lansing, Michigan, December 29, 1890. Education by private study. Has been publishing stories under several signatures since 1910. Lives in Detroit, Michigan.
Resurrection and the Life.

KILMAN, JULIAN. Born at Drummondsville, Canada, March 26, 1878. Studied law at University of Michigan. Practised law at Buffalo. Now engaged in Bureau of Naturalization at Buffalo. First story " Dan Alders' Revenge," Short Stories, September, 1914. Lives at Buffalo, New York.
Laugh.

(78) KOMROFF, MANUEL (for biography, see 1921).
Burning Beard.

LANE, ROSE WILDER. Born at De Smet, Dakota Territory, December 5, 1877. Public school education. Author of " Henry Ford's Own Story," 1917; " Diverging Roads," 1919; (with Frederick O'Brien) " White Shadows In the South Seas," 1919; " The Making of Herbert Hoover," 1920. Lives at Mansfield, Missouri.
Innocence.

LARDNER, RING W. Born at Niles, Michigan, March 6, 1885. Educated in public schools and at Armour Institute of Technology. Married. Sporting writer and editor for American newspapers since 1907. Author of " Bib Ballads," 1915; " You Know Me, Al," 1915; " Gullibles Travels," 1917; " Own Your Own Home," 1917; " Treat 'Em Rough," 1918; " The Real Dope," 1918; " My Four Weeks in France," 1918; " The Young Immigrants," 1919; " Symptoms of Being 35," 1921; " The Big Town," 1921. Lives at Great Neck, New York.
Golden Honeymoon.

(4) LEE, JENNETTE (for biography, see 1917).
Man Who Made Poetry Hum.

MCPEAK, IVAL. Born near Fulton, Iowa, May 10, 1889. Educated at State University of Iowa. Engaged in public health publicity and education. First story " Long — Short — and a Long," Midland, October, 1915. Lives in Minneapolis, Minnesota.
Prairie Symphony.

MAHONEY, JAMES. Born at Greeneville, Tennessee, September 7, 1893. Educated at Emory and Henry College, Virginia, and Columbia University. Teacher in Choir School, Cathedral of St. John the Divine, New York City. In French Ambulance Service during the war. Received the Croix de Guerre. Studied art in Paris. First story " The Showing Up of Henry Widdemer," McCall's Magazine, August, 1920. Fond of swimming. Has studied play writing with George Pierce Baker at Harvard. Lives at Bristol, Virginia.

Taxis of Fate.

MERWIN, SAMUEL. Born at Evanston, Illinois, October 6, 1874. Educated at Northwestern University. Married. Author (with H. K. Webster) " The Short Line War," 1899; (with H. K. Webster) " Calumet K.", 1901; " The Road to Frontenac," 1901; " The Whip Hand," 1903; " His Little Hour," 1903; " The Merry Anne," 1904; " The Road Builders," 1905; " Comrade John," 1907; " Drugging a Nation," 1908; " The Citadel," 1912; " The Charmed Life of Miss Austin," 1914; " Anthony the Absolute," 1914; " The Honey Bee," 1915; " The Trufflers," 1916; " Temperamental Henry," 1917; " Henry Is Twenty," 1918; " The Passionate Pilgrim," 1919; " Hills of Han," 1920; " In Red and Gold," 1921; " Goldie Green," 1922. Editor of Success, 1909–11. Lives at Concord, Massachusetts.

Axiom of Peter Bell Ivor.

MONTROSS, LYNN. Born in Nebraska, October 17, 1895. Educated at University of Nebraska. Journalist. Member of American Expeditionary Force in France. First story " In the Dark," Adventure, 1920. Author of " Town and Gown," (with Lois Seyster Montross), 1923. Lives in Chicago, Illinois.

Pagan.

(235) MYERS, WALTER L. (for biography, see 1918).
Summoned.

NORDHOFF, CHARLES B. Born of American parents in London, February 1, 1887. Graduate of Harvard. Free lance. First story " Savagery," Harper's Magazine, April, 1922. Author of " The Fledgling," 1919; (with James Norman Hall) " The Lafayette Flying Corps," 1920; (with James Norman Hall) " Faery Lands of the South Seas," 1921. Now in Tahiti.

Savagery.

(57) OPPENHEIM, JAMES (for biography, see 1918).
He That Laughed at the Gods.

(27) PICKTHALL, M. L. C.
Black Hand.
Luck.
Man They Pitied.
Men Who Climbed.

(12378) POST, MELVILLE DAVISSON (*for biography, see* 1920).
Mountain School Teacher.

(6) RABENEL, BEATRICE (*for biography, see* 1919).
Great-Granduncle Sebastian.

ROSEBORO, VIOLA. Born in Pulaski, Tennessee, 1857. Education
by desultory reading. Writer, editor, critic and guide. Author
of " Old Ways and New," 1898; " The Joyous Heart," 1903;
" Players and Vagabonds," 1904; " The Storms of Youth," 1920.
Fiction editor of McClure's Magazine. Lives in New York City.
Aaron Westcott's Funeral.

(2347) ROSENBLATT, BENJAMIN (*for biography, see* 1917).
In the Metropolis.

(57) RUSSELL, JOHN (*for biography, see* 1918).
Adversary.

SAMUEL, MAURICE. Born in Roumania, February 8, 1895. Went
to Manchester, England, in 1901. Educated at Manchester
University. Emigrated to America, 1914. In the American army
in France, during the war. Attached to the Morgenthau Com-
mission to Poland 1919. Public stenographer in Paris, Berlin
and Vienna. Returned to America in 1920. Author of " The
Outsider," 1920; " The Masquerader," 1922. Lives in New York
City.
Masquerader.

SEIFERT, SHIRLEY L. Born in St. Peter's, Missouri. Graduate of
Washington University. Did secretarial work for the Red Cross
and War Loan Organizations during the war. First story " The
Girl Who Was Too Good Looking," American Magazine, July,
1919. Lives in St. Louis, Missouri.
Lady of Sorrows.

(1234567) SINGMASTER, ELSIE (*for biography, see* 1917).
Magic Mirror.

SPEARS, RAYMOND S. Born at Bellevue, Ohio, August 2, 1876.
Public school education. Married. Has been reporter, special
article writer and forester. On staff of Adventure. Author,
" Camping on the Great River," 1912; " Camping on the Great
Lakes," 1913; " The Cabin Boat Primer," 1913; " Trip on the
Great Lakes," 1913; " The River Prophet," 1920; " Diamond
Tolls," 1920; " Driftwood," 1921. Lives at Little Falls, New York.
Ripe Peach.

(34578)SPRINGER, FLETA CAMPBELL (*for biography, see* 1917).
Realities.

(2345678) STEELE, WILBUR DANIEL *(for biography, see 1917).*
Anglo-Saxon.
From the Other Side of the South.
" He That Hideth His Secret."
Mad.
Man Who Sat.
Marriage in Kairwan.

(345678) VENABLE, EDWARD CARRINGTON *(for biography, see 1921).*
Reverend James E. Markison.

(345678) VORSE, MARY HEATON *(for biography, see 1917).*
Halfway House.

WALDO, SIDNEY. Born in Boston, December 14, 1883. Graduate
of Harvard. Engaged in the building material business. First
story " Footprints in Water," Detective Story Magazine, March
30, 1920. Lives at Brookline, Massachusetts.
Sons and Brothers.

WARREN, MAUDE (LAVINIA) RADFORD. Born at Wolfe Island,
Canada. Educated at University of Chicago. Author " King
Arthur and His Knights," 1907; " The Land of the Living," 1908;
" Peter Peter," 1909; " The Main Road," 1913; " Barbara's
Marriages," 1915; " Robin Hood," 1915; " Little Pioneers,"
1916; " The White Flame of France," 1918. Lives at Ithaca,
New York.
On the Run.

WATTS, MARY STANBERY. Born in Delaware County, Ohio, Novem-
ber 6, 1868. Convent education. Married. Author of " The
Tenants," 1908; " Nathan Burke," 1910; " The Legacy," 1911;
" Van Cleve," 1913; " The Rise of Jennie Cushing," 1914; " The
Rudder," 1916; " The Boardman Family," 1918; " From Father
to Son," 1919. Has also written plays. Lives in Cincinnati, Ohio
Reward of Virtue.

(5678) WILLIAMS, BEN AMES *(for bio raphy, see 1918).*
Likeness of a Form.

WOOD, CLEMENT. Born at Tuscaloosa, Alabama, September 1,
1888. Educated at University of Alabama and Yale. Married.
Practised law, has been assistant city attorney and recorder of
Birmingham, Alabama, and taught at several private schools.
Vice-Principal Dwight School, New York, 1920–22. Author
" Glad of Earth," 1917; " The Earth Turns South," 1919;
" Jehovah," 1920 ;" Mountain," 1920; " Nigger," 1922. Lives
at Hastings-on-Hudson, New York.
Coffin.

THE ROLL OF HONOR OF FOREIGN SHORT STORIES IN AMERICAN MAGAZINES

OCTOBER, 1921, TO SEPTEMBER, 1922

NOTE. *The index figures* 1, 2, 3, 4, 5, 6, 7, *and* 8 *prefixed to the name of the author indicate that his work has been included in the Rolls of Honor for* 1914, 1915, 1916, 1917, 1918, 1919, 1920, *and* 1921 *respectively. The list excludes reprints.*

I. ENGLISH AND IRISH AUTHORS

(12345678) AUMONIER, STACY.
> Accident of Crime.
> Miss Bracegirdle Does Her Duty.

BARRINGTON, E.
> Mystery of Stella.

(348) BERESFORD, J. D.
> Looking Glass.
> Soul of an Artist.

(1235678) BLACKWOOD, ALGERNON.
> Dance of Death.
> Woman's Ghost Story.

BUTTS, MARY.
> Change.
> Speed the Plough.

CHESTERTON, G. K.
> Temple of Silence.
> Vengeance of the Statue.

(8) COPPARD, A. E.
> Black Dog.
> Broadsheet Ballad.

CORKERY, DANIEL.
> By-Product.
> Colonel MacGillicuddy Goes Home.
> Ember.
> Price.
> Unfinished Symphony.

(6) DE LA MARE, WALTER.
> Tree.

(6) EDGINTON, MAY.
   Mary Gets Married.

(1234568) GALSWORTHY, JOHN.
   Feud.
   Man Who Kept His Form.
   Santa Lucia.

(28) GIBBON, PERCEVAL.
   By Consent.
   Saint Flossie.

KAYE-SMITH, SHEILA.
   Mrs. Adis.
   Mockbeggar.
   Old Gadgett.

KINROSS, ALBERT.
   Traitors.

(47) LAWRENCE, D. H.
   Episode.
   Dick Collier.

" MALET, LUCAS."
   Conversion.

MANSFIELD, KATHERINE.
   Fly.

MAXWELL, W. B.
   Romance of It.

MOORE, GEORGE.
   Peronnik the Fool.

(456) MORDAUNT, ELINOR.
   Fighting Cocks.
   " Genius."
   Heart of a Ship.
   Kelly O'Keefe.
   Parrots.

(4) PERTWEE, ROLAND.
   Chap Upstairs.
   Empty Arms.
   Summer Time.

(78) SINCLAIR, MAY.
   " Heaven."

(578) STEPHENS, JAMES.
   Hunger.

(278) WALPOLE, HUGH.
   Conscience Money.
   Major Wilbraham.

II. Translations

(47) ANDREYEV, LEONID.
Luckiest Man in the World.

ARTZYBASHEFF, MIKHAIL.
Old Story.

(5) BERTHEROY, JEAN.
Reign of the Spirit.

(67) BLASCO, IBANEZ VICENTE.
Sunset.

BOJER, JOHAN.
Skobelef.

BUNIN, IVAN.
Gentleman from San Francisco.
Kasimir Stanislavovitch.

(5) MAUPASSANT, GUY DE.
Story of a Wise Man.

MORAND, PAUL.
Roman Night.

SADOVEANU, MICHAIL.
Spring.

SIWERTZ, SIGFRID.
Leonard and the Fisherman.

TIMMERMANS, FELIX.
Beguine Symforosa.

VALLE-INCLAN, RAMON DEL.
My Sister Antonia.

THE BEST BOOKS OF SHORT STORIES
OF 1922

AMERICAN AUTHORS

1. CABELL. Chivalry. McBride.
2. CABELL. Gallantry. McBride.
3. CLEMENS. Mysterious Stranger. Harper.
4. COBB. Sundry Accounts. Doran.
5. COLCORD. Instrument of the Gods. Macmillan.
6. CRANE. Men, Women, and Boats. Boni & Liveright.
7. FRANK. City Block. The author: Darien, Conn.
8. GEROULD. Valiant Dust. Scribner.
9. HURST. Vertical City. Harper.
10. MELVILLE. Apple-Tree Table. Princeton.
11. O'HIGGINS. Some Distinguished Americans. Harper.

ENGLISH AND IRISH AUTHORS

12. BERESFORD. Signs and Wonders. Putnam.
13. BLACKWOOD AND WILSON. Wolves of God. Dutton.
14. CORKERY. Hounds of Banba. Huebsch.
15. DAVEY. Pilgrim of a Smile. Doran.
16. ELLIS. Kanga Creek. Brentano.
17. HUXLEY. Mortal Coils. Doran.
18. LAWRENCE. England, My England. Seltzer.
19. MACHEN. House of Souls. Knopf.
20. MANSFIELD. Garden Party. Knopf.
21. MOORE. In Single Strictness. Boni & Liveright.
22. MORRISON. Tales of Mean Streets. Boni & Liveright.
23. TOMLINSON. London River. Knopf.
24. WOOLF. Monday or Tuesday. Harcourt.

TRANSLATIONS

25. ALEICHEM. Jewish Children. Knopf.
26. CHEKHOV. Cook's Wedding. Macmillan.
27. GOLDBERG, *translator*. Brazilian Tales. Four Seas.
28. GORKY. Through Russia. Dutton.
29. HEIDENSTAMM. Charles Men. American-Scandinavian Foundation.
30. MAUPASSANT. Boule de Suif. Knopf.
31. MAUPASSANT. Mademoiselle Fifi. Knopf.
32. NERVAL. Daughters of Fire. Brown.
33. POPOVIC, *translator*. Jugo-Slav Stories. Duffield.
34. SCHNITZLER. Shepherd's Pipe. Brown.
35. UNDERWOOD, *translator*. Famous Stories from Foreign Countries. Four Seas.

VOLUMES OF SHORT STORIES
PUBLISHED IN THE UNITED STATES

OCTOBER, 1921, TO SEPTEMBER, 1922

NOTE. *An asterisk before a title indicates distinction. This list includes single short stories, collections of short stories, and a few continuous narratives based on short stories previously published in periodicals. Volumes announced for publication in the autumn of 1922 are listed here, though in some cases they had not yet appeared at the time this book went to press.*

I. AMERICAN AUTHORS

ABDULLAH, ACHMED. Alien Souls. McCann.

ADAMS, ADELINE (MRS. ADELINE VALENTINE POND). *Amouretta Landscape. Houghton, Mifflin.

ADAMS, SAMUEL HOPKINS. From a Bench in Our Square. Houghton, Mifflin.

ANDREWS, MARY RAYMOND SHIPMAN. *His Soul Goes Marching On. Scribner.

Yellow Butterflies. Scribner.

BABBITT, ELLEN C. More Jataka Tales. Century.

BEAUMONT, GERALD. Riders Up! Appleton.

BESKOW, ELIZABETH MARIA. Christmas Homecoming. Augustana Book Concern.

BRENNING, MARGARET. You Know Charles. Holt.

CABELL, JAMES BRANCH. *Chivalry. McBride.

*Gallantry. McBride.

CLEMENS, SAMUEL LANGHORNE (MARK TWAIN). *Mysterious Stranger. Harper.

COBB, IRVIN S. *Sundry Accounts. Doran.

COHEN, OCTAVUS ROY. Assorted Chocolates. Dodd, Mead.

Highly Colored. Dodd, Mead.

COLCORD, LINCOLN. *Instrument of the Gods. Macmillan.

" CONNELL, RICHARD." Sin of Monsieur Pettipon. Doran.

CORBIN, LILYAN STRATTON. Reno. Colyer.

CORTHELL, ROLAND. On the Sidewalk. Cornhill.

CRANE, HILLIS. Dawn. Augustana Book Concern.

CRANE, STEPHEN. *Men, Women and Boats. Boni and Liveright.

DERIEUX, SAMUEL A. Frank of Freedom Hill. Doubleday, Page.

DICKSON, HARRIS. Old Reliable in Africa. Stokes.

EDWARDS, HARRY STILLWELL. *Mam'selle Delphine. Holly Bluff Pub. Co.

FERBER, EDNA. *Gigolo. Doubleday, Page.

FISHER, LENA LEONARD. River Dragon's Bride. Abingdon Press.

FITZGERALD, F. SCOTT. *Tales of the Jazz Age. Scribner.

FORD, SEWELL. Torchy as a Pa. Clode.
> Trilby May Crashes In. Harper.

FRANK, WALDO. *City Block. The author (Darien, Conn.).

FRENCH, JOSEPH LEWIS, editor. Great Pirate Stories. Brentano's.

GEROULD, KATHARINE FULLERTON. *Valiant Dust. Scribner.

HARRISON, ELIZABETH. Misunderstood Children. Macmillan.
> Offero, the Giant. Macmillan.

"HENRY, O." (WILLIAM SIDNEY PORTER.) *Selected Stories. Doubleday, Page.

HUNTINGTON, MRS. FLORA CLARKE. Handkerchief and the Sword. Authors and Publishers Corp.

HURST, FANNIE. *Vertical City. Harper.

KNAPP, SHEPHERD. Old Joe. Abingdon Press.

KYNE, PETER BERNARD. Cappy Ricks Retires. Cosmopolitan Book Corp.

LAW, FREDERICK HOUK, editor. Modern Essays and Stories. Century.

LENK, MARGARETE KLEE. Patrick's First Christmas. Augustana Book Concern.

McSPADDEN, JOSEPH WALKER, editor. Famous Mystery Stories. Crowell.

MARQUIS, DON. Revolt of the Oyster. Doubleday, Page.

MARSHALL, EDISON. Heart of Little Shikara. Little, Brown.

MATTHEWS, BRANDER. Vignettes of Manhattan; Outlines in Local Color. Scribner.

MAYO, KATHERINE. Mounted Justice. Houghton, Mifflin.

MAYO, MARGERY. Russians Abroad. Stratford Co.

MELVILLE, HERMAN. *Apple-Tree Table; and Other Sketches. Princeton.

MORLEY, CHRISTOPHER. Plum Pudding of Divers Ingredients. Doubleday, Page.

MUSSER, HOWARD ANDERSON. Jungle Tales. Doran.

NICHOLSON, MEREDITH. Best Laid Schemes. Scribner.

O'BRIEN, EDWARD J., editor. Best Short Stories of 1921. Small, Maynard.

O'HIGGINS, HARVEY. *Some Distinguished Americans. Harper.

PARKER, DUDREA. Pig Iron. Norman, Remington.

PEARSON, ADELAIDE. Laughing Lion. Dutton.

PENCE, RAYMOND WOODBURY, editor. Short Stories by Present Day Authors. Macmillan.

RAMSAY, ROBERT L., editor. *Short Stories of America. Houghton, Mifflin.

RINEHART, MARY ROBERTS. More Tish. Doran.

RUSSELL, CHARLES M., editor. Rawhide Rawlins Stories. Montana Newspaper Assn.

SOCIETY OF ARTS AND SCIENCES. O. Henry Memorial Award Prize Stories of 1921. Doubleday, Page.

SQUIER, EMMA LINDSAY. Wild Heart. Cosmopolitan Book Corp.

STOCK, RALPH. South of the Line. Doubleday, Page.

STOVALL, DENNIS H. Spell of the Shang Kambu. Standard Pub. Co.

STRINGER, ARTHUR. Twin Tales. Bobbs-Merrill.
TARBELL, IDA M. He Knew Lincoln. Macmillan.
TASSIN, ALGERNON. Rainbow String. Macmillan.
TERHUNE, ALBERT PAYSON. Further Adventures of Lad. Doran.
TILDEN, WILLIAM TATEM, 2d. It's All in the Game. Doubleday, Page.
WALKER, GUY MORRISON. Skeletons. Stratford.
WILEY, HUGH. Lily. Knopf.

II. ENGLISH AND IRISH AUTHORS

ATKEY, BERTRAM. Winnie O'Wynn and the Wolves. Little, Brown
BARRINGTON, E. *"The Ladies!" Atlantic Monthly Press.
BECK, L. ADAMS. *Ninth Vibration. Dodd, Mead.
BERESFORD, JOHN DAVYS. *Signs and Wonders. Putnam.
BIBESCO, PRINCESS ELIZABETH. Balloons. Doran.
"BIRMINGHAM, GEORGE A." (JAMES OWEN HANNAY). Lady Bountiful. Doran.
BLACKWOOD, ALGERNON *and* WILSON, WILFRED. *Wolves of God. Dutton.
BONE, DAVID W. *"Broken Stowage." Dutton.
CHESTERTON, GILBERT KEITH. *Man Who Knew Too Much. Harper.
CORKERY, DANIEL. *Hounds of Banba. Huebsch.
DAVEY, NORMAN. *Pilgrim of a Smile. Doran.
DELL, ETHEL MAY. Odds, and Other Stories. Putnam.
DRINKWATER, JOHN. Cotswold Characters. Yale.
ELLIS, HAVELOCK. *Kanga Creek. Brentano's.
*English Short Stories from Fifteenth to Twentieth Century. (Everyman's Library.) Dutton.
EYTON, JOHN. Dancing Fakir. Longmans.
HOWARD, F. MORTON. *Happy Rascals. Dutton.
HUXLEY, ALDOUS. *Mortal Coils. Doran.
JAMES, MONTAGU RHODES. *Five Jars. Longmans.
KINROSS, ALBERT. *Truth About Vignolles. Century.
KIPLING, RUDYARD. Selected Stories. Doubleday, Page.
LAWRENCE, D. H. *England, My England. Seltzer.
LYONS, A. NEIL. *Market Bundle. Dodd, Mead.
MACHEN, ARTHUR. *House of Souls. Knopf.
"MALET, LUCAS." *Da Silva's Widow. Dodd, Mead.
MANSFIELD, KATHERINE. *Garden Party. Knopf.
MERRICK, LEONARD. *To Tell You the Truth. Dutton.
MONTMORENCY, JAMES EDWARD GEOFFREY DE. Never-Ending Road. Oxford University Press.
MOORE, GEORGE. *In Single Strictness. Boni and Liveright.
MORRISON, ARTHUR. *Tales of Mean Streets. Boni and Liveright.
O'BRIEN, EDWARD J. *and* COURNOS, JOHN, *editors.* Best British Short Stories of 1922. Small, Maynard.
OSBOURNE, LLOYD. Wild Justice. Appleton.
OWEN, H. COLLINSON. Adventures of Antoine. McCann.
"ROHMER, SAX." Tales of Chinatown. Doubleday, Page.
"SAKI." Reginald. McBride.

TOMLINSON, H. M. *London River. Knopf.
WOOLF, VIRGINIA. *Monday or Tuesday. Harcourt, Brace.

III. TRANSLATIONS

" ALEICHEM, SHALOM." (*Yiddish.*) *Jewish Children. Knopf.
CHEKHOV, ANTON. (*Russian.*) *Cook's Wedding. Macmillan.
" FRANCE, ANATOLE." (JACQUES-ANATOLE THIBAULT.) (*French.*)
    *Count Morin, Deputy. Dodd, Mead.
    *Marguerite. Dodd, Mead.
GOLDBERG, ISAAC, *translator.* (*Portuguese.*) *Brazilian Tales.
    Four Seas.
GORKY, MAXIM. (*Russian.*) *Through Russia. Dutton.
HEIDENSTAMM, VERNER VON. (*Swedish.*) *Charles Men. 2 vols.
    American-Scandinavian Foundation.
LEBLANC, MAURICE. (*French.*) Eight Strokes of the Clock.
    Macaulay.
MACKLIN, ALYS EYRE, *translator.* (*French.*) Twenty-Nine Tales
    from the French. Harcourt, Brace.
MAUPASSANT, GUY DE. (*French.*) *Boule de Suif. Knopf.
    *Mademoiselle Fifi. Knopf.
NERVAL, GERARD DE. (*French.*) *Daughters of Fire. N. L. Brown.
POPOVIC, PAVLE, *editor.* (*Jugo-Slav.*) *Jugo-Slav Stories.
    Duffield.
SCHNITZLER, ARTHUR. (*German.*) *Shepherd's Pipe. N. L. Brown.
UNDERWOOD, EDNA WORTHLEY, *translator.* *Famous Stories from
    Foreign Countries. Four Seas.

ARTICLES ON THE SHORT STORY

OCTOBER, 1921, TO SEPTEMBER, 1922

Authors of articles are printed in capital letters.

The following abbreviations are used in this index:

Book. (N. Y.)..........Bookman (New York)
Cath. W...............Catholic World
Cen...................Century
Corn..................Cornhill Magazine
Dial..................Dial
D. D..................Double Dealer
Eng. R...............English Review
Free..................Freeman
John..................John o'London's Weekly
L. H. J..............Ladies' Home Journal
Lib...................Liberator
L. Merc..............London Mercury
Nat. (N. Y.)..........Nation (New York)
Nat. (London)........Nation (London)
New A................New Age
New S................New Statesman
N. Rep...............New Republic
N. Y. Times..........New York Times Review of Books
Post.................New York Evening Post Literary Review
Queen................Queen
Scr..................Scribner's Magazine
Wave.................Wave

Adams, Adeline.
    By J. W. Krutch. Nat. (N. Y.) July 26. (115 : 99.)
Ade, George.
    By Thomas L. Masson. Book. (N. Y.) Oct., '21. (54 : 116.)
AIKEN, CONRAD.
    Fyodor Dostoevsky. Free. Dec. 28, '21. (4 : 378.)
    Katherine Mansfield. Free. June 21. (5 : 357.)
ALDEN, RAYMOND M.
    Oscar Wilde. Post. Dec. 3, '21. (2 : 228.)
ALDINGTON, RICHARD.
    James Joyce. Post. March 11. (2 : 491.)
American Short Story.
    By Brander Matthews. N. Y. Times. Sept. 17. (27 : 2.)
    By Gilbert Seldes. Dial. April. (72 : 427.)
    By Johan J. Smertenko. Nat. (N. Y.) (114 : 779.)

ANDERSON, JOHN D.
  Thomas Hardy. N. Y. Times. May 28. (10.)
Anderson, Sherwood.
  Anonymous. Nat. (N. Y.) Nov. 23, '21. (113 : 602.)
  Anonymous. Nat. (London.) Feb. 4. (30 : 695.)
  Anonymous. Times Lit. Suppl. July 13. (21 : 457.)
  By C. E. Bechhofer. Times Lit. Suppl. Jan. 19. (21 : 44.)
  By William Rose Benét. Post. Nov. 26, '21. (2 : 200.)
  By Mary M. Colum. Free. Nov. 30, '21. (4 : 281.)
  By J. W. Krutch. Nat. (N. Y.) Nov. 23, '21. (113 : 602.)
  By Robert Morss Lovett. N. Rep. Nov. 23, '21. (28 : 383.)
  By Robert Morss Lovett. Dial. Jan. (72 : 79.)
  By Edwin Muir. Free. June 14. (4 : 321.)
  By Albert Jay Nock. Free. Feb. 8. (4 : 513.)
  By Forrest Reid. Nat. (London.) July 8. (31 : 510.)
  By Paul Rosenfeld. Dial. Jan. (72 : 29.)
  By Gilbert Seldes. N. Y. Times. Dec. 4, '21. (10.)
  By Carl Van Doren. Nat. (N. Y.) Oct. 12, '21. (113 : 407.)
  By Rebecca West. New S. Feb. 18. (18 : 565.)
  By Rebecca West. New S. July 22. (19 : 443.)
  By T. K. Whipple. Post. March 11. (2 : 481.)
  By Walter Yust. D. D. March. (3 : 161.)
Andreyev, Leonid.
  By Alexander Kaun. N. Rep. June 28. (31 : 133.)
ARNOLD, WILLIAM HARRIS.
  Robert Louis Stevenson. Scr. Jan. (71 : 53.)
Balzac, Honoré de.
  Anonymous. Times Lit. Suppl. Jan. 5. (21 : 9.)
  By Desmond MacCarthy. New S. Dec. 10, '21. (18 : 288.)
BARNES, DJUNA.
  James Joyce. D. D. May. (3 : 249.)
Baroja, Pio.
  By J. B. Trend. Nat. (London.) April 1. (31 : 26.)
Barrios, Eduardo.
  By Ernesto Montenegro. Post. Dec. 10, '21. (2 : 259.)
BATEMAN, MAY.
  John Galsworthy. Cath. W. March. (114 : 732.)
BEACH, JOSEPH WARREN.
  Thomas Hardy. N. Rep. Aug. 23. (31 : 366.)
BECHHOFER, C. E.
  Sherwood Anderson. Times Lit. Suppl. Jan. 19. (21 : 44.)
Beerbohm, Max.
  By Max Eastman. Lib. June. (5 : 5.)
  By J. W. Krutch. Nat. (N. Y.) Oct. 12, '21. (113 : 413.) Post.
    Nov. 19, '21. (2 : 186.)
  By Philip Littell. N. Rep. May 17. (30 : 347.)
  By George Q. Moore. D. D. Jan. (3 : 55.)
BELGION, MONTGOMERY.
  Paul Jean Toulet. Free. Jan. 18. (4 : 453.)
BENET, WILLIAM ROSE.
  Sherwood Anderson. Post. Nov. 26, '21. (2 : 200.)

Bercovici, Konrad.
    Anonymous. Nat. (N. Y.) Nov. 30, '21. (113 : 625.)
    By Padraic Colum. Dial. Dec., '21. (71 : 711.)
    By Johan J. Smertenko. Post. Nov. 19, '21. (2 : 183.)
Bibesco, Elizabeth.
    By Clarence Day, Jr. N. Rep. March 22. (30 : 115.)
    By Ludwig Lewisohn. Nat. (N. Y.) March 1. (114 : 261.)
    By Rebecca West. New S. March 4. (18 : 621.)
Blackwood, Algernon.
    Anonymous. Post. March 25. (2 : 523.)
    By Alma Newton. N. Y. Times. April 2. (16.)
    By Kathleen Shackleton. John. Sept. 3, '21. (612.)
Blasco Ibáñez, Vicente.
    Anonymous. Times Lit. Suppl. Nov. 10, '21. (20 : 733.)
Bone, David W.
    By Felix Riesenberg. Post. July 8. (2 : 787.)
BOYD, ERNEST.
    Gustave Flaubert. Post. Dec. 17, '21. (2 : 280.)
BOYNTON, H. W.
    W. H. Hudson. Post. Feb. 4. (2 : 398.)
BRENNECKE, HENRY.
    E. T. A. Hoffmann. N. Y. Times. June 25. (15.)
BROCK, A. CLUTTON.
    W. H. Hudson. Times Lit. Suppl. Aug. 24. (21 : 542.)
BROWN, HEYWOOD.
    Harvey O'Higgins. Book. (N. Y.) Oct., '21. (54 : 156.)
BUELL, LLEWELLYN M.
    Robert Louis Stevenson. Scr. Feb. (71 : 184.)
Bunin, Ivan.
    Anonymous. Times Lit. Suppl. April 20. (21 : 256.)
    By J. W. Krutch. Nat. (N. Y.) July 26. (115 : 99.)
    By J. Middleton Murry. Nat. (London.) June 24. (31 : 444.)
BURKE, KENNETH.
    Gustave Flaubert. Dial. Feb. (72 : 147.)
Cabell, James Branch.
    Anonymous. Times Lit. Suppl. Jan. 26. (21 : 57.)
    By Carl Van Doren. Nat. (N. Y.) Dec. 7, '21. (113 : 664.)
    By Ben Ray Redman. Post. Dec. 17, '21. (2 : 276.)
    By Vincent Starrett. D. D. Nov., '21. (2 : 203.)
    By Rebecca West. New S. May 13. (19 : 156.)
    By Cuthbert Wright. Free. Sept. 6. (5 : 621.)
CANBY, HENRY SEIDEL.
    Joseph Conrad. Post. Feb. 4. (2 : 393.)
    John Russell. Post. Dec. 10, '21. (2 : 251.)
CANE, MELVILLE H.
    Brander Matthews. Free. May 24. (5 : 260.)
Chambers, Robert W.
    Anonymous. Post. Dec. 3, '21. (2 : 227.)
Chekhov, Anton.
    By Francis Hackett. N. Rep. March 1. (30 : 23.)
    By Martha Harris. N. Y. Times. July 23. (27 : 8.)

By Alexander Kaun. Free. March 1. (4 : 592.)
By J. Middleton Murry. Nat. (London.) April 8. (31 : 57.)
By J. Middleton Murry. N. Rep. March 22. (30 : 114.)
By Allan Nevins. Post. Nov. 26, '21. (2 : 200.)
By L. A. Sulveritsky. N. Rep. May 10. (30 : 312.)
By M. P. Willcocks. Eng. R. March. (34 : 207.)
By Jacob Zeitlin. Nat. (N. Y.) April 5. (114 : 400.)

Cobb, Irvin S.
    By Hildegarde Hawthorne. N. Y. Times. May 14. (14.)
COLTON, ARTHUR.
    Short Story. Post. Oct. 1, '21. (2 : 49.)
COLUM, MARY M.
    Sherwood Anderson. Free. Nov. 30, '21. (4 : 281.)
    Daniel Corkery. Free. Aug. 2. (5 : 498.)
COLUM, PADRAIC.
    Konrad Bercovici. Dial. Dec., '21. (71 : 711.)
    James Joyce. N. Y. Times. June 11. (10.)
    James Stephens. Dial. Nov., '21. (71 : 601.)
Conrad, Joseph.
    By Henry Seidel Canby. Post. Feb. 4. (2 : 393.)
Coppard, A. E.
    By Ludwig Lewisohn. Nat. (N. Y.) March 1. (114 : 261.)
Corkery, Daniel.
    By Mary M. Colum. Free. Aug. 2. (5 : 498.)
COWLEY, MALCOLM.
    Katherine Mansfield. Dial. Aug. (73 : 231.)
CRANE, CLARKSON.
    Gérard de Nerval. Free. Aug. 23. (5 : 572.)
Crane, Stephen.
    Anonymous. Free. Jan. 18. (4 : 455.)
CROCE, BENEDETTO.
    G. Flaubert. L. Merc. March. (5 : 487.)
    Guy de Maupassant. L. Merc. May. (6 : 61.)
Davis, Richard Harding.
    Anonymous. Post. July 29. (2 : 839.)
DAWSON, N. P.
    Fannie Hurst. Post. April 15. (2 : 579.)
DAY, JR., CLARENCE.
    Elizabeth Bibesco. N. Rep. March 22. (30 : 115.)
Diaz-Garces, Joaquin.
    By Ernesto Montenegro. Post. Dec. 10, '21. (2 : 259.)
Dostoevsky, Fyodor.
    By Conrad Aiken. Free. Dec. 28, '21. (4 : 378.)
    Anonymous. Times Lit. Suppl. Jan. 12. (21 : 25.)
    By N. Bryllion Fagin. D. D. Dec., '21. (2 : 267.)
    By Edwin Muir. Free. Sept. 13. (6 : 17.)
    By J. Middleton Murry. Nat. (London.) Dec. 24, '21. (30 : 505.)
    By William Lyon Phelps. N. Y. Times. Jan. 15. (8.)
    By Manya Gordon Strunsky. Post. March 18. (2 : 505.)
    By Avrahm Yarmolinsky. N. Rep. Nov. 30, '21. (29 : 15.)
    By Avrahm Yarmolinsky. N. Rep. Sept. 27. (32 : 115.)

EASTMAN, MAX.
Max Beerbohm. Lib. June. (5 : 5.)
EATON, WALTER PRICHARD.
Brander Matthews. N. Y. Times. Jan. 8. (11.)
English Short Story.
Anonymous. Times Lit. Suppl. July 6. (21 : 440.)
FAGIN, N. BRYLLION.
Fyodor Dostoevsky. D. D. Dec., '21. (2 : 267.)
Ferber, Edna.
Anonymous. Book. (N. Y.) Jan. (54 : 434.)
FIELD, LOUISE MAUNSELL.
Ellen Glasgow. N. Y. Times. July 30. (21.)
Lucas Malet. N. Y. Times. July 9. (27 : 21.)
Flaubert, Gustave.
Anonymous. Times Lit. Suppl. Jan. 5. (21 : 12.)
Anonymous. Times Lit. Suppl. Dec. 15, '21. (20 : 833.)
By Ernest Boyd. Post. Dec. 17, '21. (2 : 280.)
By Kenneth Burke. Dial. Feb. (72 : 147.)
By Benedetto Croce. L. Merc. March. (5 : 487.)
By Austin Hay. N. Y. Times. Jan. 15. (6.)
By Charles Leonard Moore. Post. Jan. 28. (2 : 382.)
By T. Sturge Moore. Times Lit. Suppl. Dec. 29, '21. (20 : 876.)
By J. Middleton Murry. Dial. Dec., '21. (71 : 625.)
FOOTNER, HULBERT.
Arthur Machen. Post. June 17. (2 : 736.)
FORMAN, HENRY JAMES.
D. H. Lawrence. Nat. (N. Y.) (27 : 12.)
FREEMAN, JOHN.
Robert Louis Stevenson. L. Merc. April. (5 : 617.)
Freeman, Mary E. Wilkins.
Anonymous. Post. July 22. (2 : 823.)
Fuller, Henry Blake.
By Carl Van Doren. Nat. (N. Y.) Dec. 21, '21. (113 : 729.)
By Carl Van Vechten. D. D. June. (3 : 289.)
FULLER, HENRY B.
Hamlin Garland. Free. Nov. 9, '21. (4 : 210.)
Galantière, Lewis.
Marcel Schwob. Free. June 14. (330.)
Galsworthy, John.
By May Bateman. Cath. W. March. (114 : 732.)
Gana, Federico.
By Ernesto Montenegro. Post. Dec. 10, '21. (2 : 259.)
Garland, Hamlin.
Anonymous. Times Lit. Suppl. Aug. 31. (21 : 554.)
By Henry B. Fuller. Free. Nov. 9, '21. (4 : 210.)
By Hildegarde Hawthorne. N. Y. Times. July 30. (27 : 10.)
By Robert Morss Lovett. N. Rep. Sept. 27. (15.)
By Constance Lindsay Skinner. Post. Dec. 3, '21. (2 : 218.)
By Carl Van Doren. Nat. (N. Y.) Nov. 23, '21. (113 : 596.)
GEROULD, GORDON HALL.
Joseph Hergesheimer. Post. June 17. (2 : 735.)

Glasgow, Ellen.
  By Louise Maunsell Field. N. Y. Times. July 30. (21.)
Gordon, Vera.
  Short Story. Free. Dec. 14, '21. (4 : 332.)
Hackett, Francis.
  Anton Chekhov. N. Rep. March 1. (30 : 23.)
Hardy, Thomas.
  By John D. Anderson. N. Y. Times. May 28. (10.)
  By Joseph Warren Beach. N. Rep. Aug. 23. (31 : 366.)
  By Llewelyn Powys. Dial. March. (72 : 286.)
Harris, Frank.
  By J. W. Krutch. Nat. (N. Y.) July 5. (115 : 19.)
Harris, Martha.
  Anton Chekhov. N. Y. Times. July 23. (27 : 8.)
Harte, Bret.
  Anonymous. Times Lit. Suppl. March 16. (21 : 169.)
  By H. M. Tomlinson. Nat. (London.) March 11. (30 :
    861.)
Hawthorne, Hildegarde.
  Irvin S. Cobb. N. Y. Times. May 14. (14.)
  Hamlin Garland. N. Y. Times. July 30. (10.)
  Albert Kinross. N. Y. Times. May 7. (2.)
Hawthorne, Nathaniel.
  Anonymous. Times Lit. Suppl. April 6. (21 : 225.)
  By Robert Lynd. New S. April 22. (19 : 68.)
Hay, Austin.
  Gustave Flaubert. N. Y. Times. Jan. 15. (6.)
Hearn, Lafcadio.
  By John S. Kendall. D. D. June. (3 : 313.)
  By Lucile Rutland. D. D. Feb. (3 : 96.)
Henderson, Archibald.
  Jack London. N. Y. Times. April 16. (10.)
Henry, O.
  Anonymous. Free. Jan. 11. (4 : 431.)
  By George MacAdam. N. Y. Times. Aug. 6. (27 : 5.)
  By Hyder E. Rollins. Post. March 18. (2 : 505.)
  By Hyder E. Rollins. Post. Jan. 7. (2 : 332.)
  By Hyder E. Rollins. Post. June 17. (2 : 736.)
  By Carl Van Doren. Nat. (N. Y.) March 1. (114 : 260.)
Herford, Oliver.
  "Say It with Asterisks!" L. H. J. June. (28.)
Hergesheimer, Joseph.
  Anonymous. Book. (N. Y.) May. (55 : 247.)
  By Gordon Hall Gerould. Post. June 17. (2 : 735.)
  By Carl Van Doren. Nat. (N. Y.) Dec. 7, '21. (113 : 664.)
Herrick, Robert.
  Hugh Walpole. Post. Oct. 8, '21. (2 : 65.)
Hoffmann, E. T. A.
  By Henry Brennecke. N. Y. Times. June 25. (15.)
Houghton, Elizabeth.
  Katherine Mansfield. Post. June 17. (2 : 737.)

Hudson, W. H.
>   Anonymous. N. Rep. Sept. 27. (32 : 113.)
>   By H. W. Boynton. Post. Feb. 4. (2 : 398.)
>   By A. Clutton Brock. Times Lit. Suppl. Aug. 24. (21 : 542.)

Hurst, Fannie.
>   By N. P. Dawson. Post. April 15. (2 : 579.)

Huxley, Aldous.
>   By Edward Shanks. L. Merc. June. (6 : 212.)
>   By George Stevens. Post. July 1. (2 : 771.)
>   By Rebecca West. New S. May 13. (19 : 156.)

Jacob, Max.
>   By Pierre Robert. New A. May 18. (31 : 32.)

Jacobsen, Jens Peter.
>   By Ben Ray Redman. Nat. (N. Y.) (115 : 311.)

James, Henry.
>   Anonymous. Free. Feb. 8. (4 : 526.)
>   Anonymous. Times Lit. Suppl. Dec. 22, '21. (20 : 849.)
>   By Joseph Pennell. Cen. Feb. (103 : 543.)
>   By Gilbert Seldes. Dial. Oct., '21. (71 : 472.)

Jammes, Francis.
>   By Ben Ray Redman. Nat. (N. Y.) Sept. 27. (115 : 311.)

Joyce, James.
>   By Richard Aldington. Post. March 11. (2 : 491.)
>   By Djuna Barnes. D. D. May. (3 : 249.)
>   By Padraic Colum. N. Y. Times. June 11. (10.)

KAUN, ALEXANDER.
>   Leonid Andreyev. N. Rep. June 28. (31 : 133.)
>   Anton Chekhov. Free. March 1. (4 : 592.)
>   Vladimir G. Korolenko. Post. March 4. (2 : 470.)

KENDALL, JOHN S.
>   Lafcadio Hearn. D. D. June. (3 : 313.)

Kinross, Albert.
>   By Hildegarde Hawthorne. N. Y. Times. May 7. (2.)

Korolenko, Vladimir G.
>   By Alexander Kaun. Post. March 4. (2 : 470.)
>   By Avrahm Yarmolinsky. Nat. (N. Y.) March 1. (114 : 254.)

KRUTCH, J. W.
>   Adeline Adams. Nat. (N. Y.) July 26. (115 : 99.)
>   Sherwood Anderson. Nat. (N. Y.) Nov. 23, '21. (113 : 602.)
>   Max Beerbohm. Nat. (N. Y.) Oct. 12, '21. (113 : 413.) Post.
>   Nov. 19, '21. (2 : 186.)
>   I. A. Bunin. Nat. (N. Y.) July 26. (115 : 99.)
>   Frank Harris. Nat. (N. Y.) July 5. (115 : 19.)
>   Katherine Mansfield. Nat. (N. Y.) July 26. (115 : 99.)

Larrain, Ines Echeverria de.
>   By Ernesto Montenegro. Post. Dec. 10, '21. (2 : 259.)

Latorre, Mariano.
>   By Ernesto Montenegro. Post. Dec. 10, '21. (2 : 259.)

Lawrence, D. H.
>   By Henry James Forman. Nat. (N. Y.) (27 : 12.)
>   By Paul Rosenfeld. N. Rep. Sept. 27. (32 : 125.)
>   By Rebecca West. New S. June 24. (19 : 326.)

LE GALLIENNE, RICHARD.
    Oscar Wilde. Book. (N. Y.) Oct., '21. (54 : 162.)
LEWISOHN, LUDWIG.
    Elizabeth Bibesco. Nat. (N. Y.) March 1. (114 : 261.)
    A. E. Coppard. Nat. (N. Y.) March 1. (114 : 261.)
    Virginia Woolf. Nat. (N. Y.) March 1. (114 : 261.)
Lillo, Baldomero.
    By Ernesto Montenegro. Post. Dec. 10, '21. (2 : 259.)
LISLE, GEORGE.
    Robert Louis Stevenson. Corn. Dec., '21. (706.)
LITTELL, PHILIP.
    Max Beerbohm. N. Rep. May 17. (30 : 347.)
LITTELL, ROBERT.
    Katherine Mansfield. N. Rep. July 5. (31 : 166.)
London, Jack.
    Anonymous. Times Lit. Suppl. Nov. 3, '21. (20 : 709.)
    By Archibald Henderson. N. Y. Times. April 16. (10.)
    By Lewis Mumford. N. Rep. March 29. (30 : 145.)
    By Carl Van Doren. Nat. (N. Y.) March 1. (114 : 260.)
LOVETT, ROBERT MORSS.
    Sherwood Anderson. Dial. Jan. (72 : 79.)
    Sherwood Anderson. N. Rep. Nov. 23, '21. (28 : 383.)
    Hamlin Garland. N. Rep. Sept. 27. (15.)
LYND, ROBERT.
    Nathaniel Hawthorne. New S. April 22. (19 : 68.)
MACADAM, GEORGE.
    O. Henry. N. Y. Times. Aug. 6. (27 : 5.)
MACCARTHY, DESMOND.
    Honoré de Balzac. New S. Dec. 10, '21. (18 : 288.)
    Leo Nikolaevich Tolstoi. New S. July 15. (19 : 417.)
Machen, Arthur.
    By Hulbert Footner. N. Y. Post. June 17. (2 : 736.)
    By Albert Jay Nock. Free. Aug. 2. (5 : 502.)
    By Paul Jordan Smith. Wave. June. (35.)
Malet, Lucas.
    By Louise Maunsell Field. N. Y. Times. July 9. (27 : 21.)
    By Charles Leonard Moore. Post. July 8. (2 : 794.)
Mansfield Katherine.
    By Conrad Aiken. Free. June 21. (5 : 357.)
    Anonymous. Nat. (London.) March 25. (30 : 949.)
    Anonymous. Times Lit. Suppl. March 2. (21 : 137.)
    Anonymous. Times. (London.) July 27.
    By Malcolm Cowley. Dial. Aug. (73 : 230.)
    By Elizabeth Houghton. Post. June 17. (2 : 737.)
    By J. W. Krutch. Nat. (N. Y.) July 26. (115 : 99.)
    By Robert Littell. N. Rep. July 5. (31 : 166.)
    By Edward Shanks. Queen. March 25. (360.)
    By Rebecca West. New S. March 18. (18 : 678.)
MASSON, THOMAS L.
    George Ade. Book. (N. Y.) Oct., '21. (54 : 116.)

MATTHEWS, BRANDER.
    American Short Story. N. Y. Times. Sept. 17. (27 : 2.)
Matthews, Brander.
    By Melville H. Cane. Free. May 24. (5 : 260.)
    By Walter Prichard Eaton. N. Y. Times. Jan. 8. (11.)
Maugham, W. Somerset.
    Anonymous. Nat. (London.) Jan. 14. (30 : 593.)
    Rebecca West. New S. Nov. 5, '21. (18 : 140.)
Maupassant, Guy de.
    By Benedetto Croce. L. Merc. May. (6 : 61.)
    By T. R. Ybarra. N. Y. Times. Jan. 22. (1.)
Mauriac, Francois.
    Anonymous. Times Lit. Suppl. March 9. (21 : 152.)
Melville, Herman.
    By Carl Van Vechten. D. D. Jan. (3 : 9.)
Middleton, Richard.
    Anonymous. Times Lit. Suppl. July 20. (21 : 472.)
Milanesi, Guido.
    Anonymous. Times Lit. Suppl. Aug. 17. (21 : 532.)
MONAHAN, MICHAEL.
    Oscar Wilde. D. D. Nov., '21. (2 : 229.)
MONTENEGRO, ERNESTO.
    Eduardo Barrios. Post. Dec. 10, '21. (2 : 259.)
    Joaquin Diaz-Garces. Post. Dec. 10, '21. (2 : 259.)
    Federico Gana. Post. Dec. 10, '21. (2 : 259.)
    Ines Echeverria de Larrain. Post. Dec. 10, '21. (2 : 259.)
    Mariano Latorre. Post. Dec. 10, '21. (2 : 259.)
    Baldomero Lillo. Post. Dec. 10, '21. (2 : 259.)
    Pedro Prado. Post. Dec. 10, '21. (2 : 259.)
    Fernando Santivan. Post. Dec. 10, '21. (2 : 259.)
    Augusto Thomson. Post. Dec. 10, '21. (2 : 259.)
MOORE, CHARLES LEONARD.
    Gustave Flaubert. Post. Jan. 28. (2 : 382.)
    Lucas Malet. Post. July 8. (2 : 794.)
MOORE, GEORGE Q.
    Max Beerbohm. D. D. Jan. (3 : 55.)
MOORE, T. STURGE.
    Gustave Flaubert. Times Lit. Suppl. Dec. 29, '21. (20 : 876.)
Morand, Paul
    By J. Middleton Murry. Nat. (London.) April 29. (31 : 161.)
MUIR, EDWIN.
    Sherwood Anderson. Free. June 14. (321.)
    Fyodor Dostoevsky. Free. Sept. 13. (6 : 17.)
MUMFORD, LEWIS.
    Jack London. N. Rep. March 29. (30 : 145.)
MURRY, J. MIDDLETON.
    Ivan Bunin. Nat. (London.) June 24. (31 : 444.)
    Anton Chekhov. N. Rep. March 22. (30 : 114.)
    Anton Chekhov. Nat. (London.) April 8. (31 : 57.)
    Fyodor Dostoevsky. Nat. (London.) Dec. 24, '21. (80 : 505.)

Gustave Flaubert. Dial. Dec., '21. (71 : 625.)
Paul Morand. Nat. (London.) April 29. (31 : 161.)

Nerval, Gérard de.
By Clarkson Crane. Free. Aug. 23. (5 : 572.)
By Ben Ray Redman. Nat. (N. Y.) Sept. 27. (115 : 311.)

NEVINS, ALLAN.
Anton Chekhov. Post. Nov. 26, '21. (2 : 200.)

NEWTON, ALMA.
Algernon Blackwood. N. Y. Times. April 2. (16.)

NOCK, ALBERT JAY.
Sherwood Anderson. Free. Feb. 8. (4 : 513.)
Arthur Machen. Free. Aug. 2. (5 : 502.)

O'Higgins, Harvey.
By Heywood Brown. Book. (N. Y.) Oct., '21. (54 : 156.)

OSBOURNE, LLOYD.
Robert Louis Stevenson. Post. Dec. 24, '21. (2 : 297.)

PENNELL, JOSEPH.
Henry James. Cen. Feb. (103 : 543.)

PHELPS, WILLIAM LYON.
Fyodor Dostoevsky. N. Y. Times. Jan. 15. (8.)

Pirandello, Luigi.
Anonymous. Times Lit. Suppl. April 13. (21 : 243.)

Poe, Edgar Allan.
By Raymond A. Preston. Post. July 22. (2 : 830.)
By Theodore Stanton. Post. July 22. (2 : 830.)

POWYS, LLEWELYN.
Thomas Hardy. Dial. March. (72 : 286.)

Prado, Pedro.
By Ernesto Montenegro. Post. Dec. 10, '21. (2 : 259.)

PRESTON, RAYMOND A.
Edgar Allan Poe. Post. July 22. (2 : 830.)

REDMAN, BEN RAY.
James Branch Cabell. Post. Dec. 17, '21. (2 : 276.)
Jens Peter Jacobsen. Nat. (N. Y.) Sept. 27. (115 : 311.)
Francis Jammes. Nat. (N. Y.) Sept. 27. (115 : 311.)
Gérard de Nerval. Nat. (N. Y.) Sept. 27. (115 : 311.)
Arthur Schnitzler. Nat. (N. Y.) Sept. 27. (115 : 311.)

REID, FORREST.
Sherwood Anderson. Nat. (London.) July 8. (31 : 510.)

Riesenberg, David W.
David W. Bone. Post. July 8. (2 : 787.)

ROBERT, PIERRE.
Max Jacob. New A. May 18. (31 : 32.)

ROLLINS, HYDER E.
O. Henry. Post. March 18. (2 : 505.)
O. Henry. Post. Jan. 7. (2 : 332.)
O. Henry. Post. June 17. (2 : 736.)

ROSENFELD, PAUL.
Sherwood Anderson. Dial. Jan. (72 : 29.)
D. H. Lawrence. N. Rep. Sept. 27. (32 : 125.)

Russell, John.
  By Henry Seidel Canby. Post. Dec. 10, '21. (2 : 251.)
RUTLAND, LUCILE.
  Lafcadio Hearn. D. D. Feb. (3 : 96.)
Santivan, Fernando.
  By Ernesto Montenegro. Post. Dec. 10, '21. (2 : 259.)
Schnitzler, Arthur.
  By Ben Ray Redman. Nat. (N. Y.) Sept. 27. (115 : 311.)
Schwob, Marcel.
  Anonymous. Times Lit. Suppl. Jan. 19. (21 : 37.)
  By Lewis Galantière. Free. June 14. (330.)
SELDES, GILBERT.
  American Short Story. Dial. April. (72 : 427.)
  Sherwood Anderson. N. Y. Times. Dec. 4, '21. (10.)
  Henry James. Dial, Oct., '21. (71 : 472.)
SHACKLETON, KATHLEEN.
  Algernon Blackwood. John. Sept. 3, '21. (612.)
SHANKS, EDWARD.
  Aldous Huxley. L. Merc. June. (6 : 212.)
  Katherine Mansfield. Queen. March 25. (360.)
  H. G. Wells. L. Merc. March. (5 : 506.)
Short Story.
  By Vera Gordon. Free. Dec. 14, '21. (4 : 332.)
  By Orlo Williams. Times. (London.) May 3.
SKINNER, CONSTANCE LINDSAY.
  Hamlin Garland. Post. Dec. 3, '21. (2 : 218.)
SMERTENKO, JOHAN J.
  American Short Story. Nat. June 28. (114 : 779.)
  Konrad Bercovici. Post. Nov. 19, '21. (2 : 183.)
SMITH, PAUL JORDAN.
  Arthur Machen. Wave. June. (35.)
Somaré, Enrico.
  Anonymous. Times Lit. Suppl. Aug. 24. (21 : 544.)
STANTON, THEODORE.
  Edgar Allan Poe. Post. July 22. (2 : 830.)
STARRETT, VINCENT.
  James Branch Cabell. D. D. Nov., '21. (2 : 203.)
Stephens, James.
  By Padraic Colum. Dial. Nov., '21. (71 : 601.)
Sternheim, Carl.
  Anonymous. Nat. (London.) Dec. 17, '21. (30 : 478.)
STEVENS, GEORGE.
  Aldous Huxley. Post. July 1. (2 : 771.)
Stevenson, Robert Louis.
  By William Harris Arnold. Scr. Jan. (71 : 53.)
  By Llewellyn M. Buell. Scr. Feb. (71 : 184.)
  By John Freeman. L. Merc. April. (5 : 617.)
  By George Lisle. Corn. Dec., '21. (706.)
  By Lloyd Osbourne. Post. Dec. 24, '21. (2 : 297.)
  By Henry Van Dyke. Scr. Aug. (72 : 161.)

ARTICLES ON THE SHORT STORY 335

STRUNSKY, MANYA GORDON.
Fyodor Dostoevsky. Post. March 18. (2 : 505.)
SULVERITSKY, L. A.
Anton Chekhov. N. Rep. May 10. (30 : 312.)
Tarkington, Booth.
Anonymous. Book. (N. Y.) Nov., '21. (54 : 218.)
Anonymous. N. Y. Times. June 25. (22.)
Thomson, Augusto.
By Ernesto Montenegro. Post. Dec. 10, '21. (2 : 259.)
TOLSTOI, COUNTESS SOPHIE.
Leo Nikolaevich Tolstoi. Free. May 17, 31; June 14, 28; July
12, 26. (5 : 229, 277, 325, 372, 421, 467.)
Tolstoi, Leo Nikolaevich.
Anonymous. Times Lit. Suppl. July 13. (21 : 456.)
By Desmond MacCarthy. New S. July 15. (19 : 417.)
By Countess Sophie Tolstoi. Free. May 17, 31; June 14, 28;
July 12, 26. (5 : 229, 277, 325, 372, 421, 467.)
By T. R. Ybarra. N. Y. Times. June 4. (5.)
TOMLINSON, H. M.
Bret Harte. Nat. (London.) March 11. (30 : 861.)
Toulet, Paul Jean.
By Montgomery Belgion. Free. Jan. 18. (4 : 453.)
TREND, J. B.
Pio Baroja. Nat. (London.) April 1. (31 : 26.)
Miguel de Unamuno. Nat. (London.) Nov. 19, '21. (30 :
316.
Turgenev, Ivan.
Anonymous. Times Lit. Suppl. Dec. 8, '21. (20 : 813.)
TYNAN, JOSEPH L.
Oscar Wilde. Free. July 5. (5 : 395.)
Unamuno, Miguel de.
By J. B. Trend. Nat. (London.) Nov. 19, '21. (30 : 316.)
VAN DOREN, CARL.
Sherwood Anderson. Nat. (N. Y.) Oct. 12, '21. (113 : 407.)
James Branch Cabell. Nat. (N. Y.) Dec. 7, '21. (113 : 664.)
Hamlin Garland. Nat. (N. Y.) Nov. 23, '21. (113 : 596.)
O. Henry. Nat. (N. Y.) March 1. (114 : 260.)
Joseph Hergesheimer. Nat. (N. Y.) Dec. 7, '21. (113 : 664.)
Jack London. Nat. (N. Y.) March 1. (114 : 260.)
VAN DYKE, HENRY.
Robert Louis Stevenson. Scr. Aug. (72 : 161.)
VAN VECHTEN, CARL.
Henry Blake Fuller. D. D. June. (3 : 289.)
Herman Melville. D. D. Jan. (3 : 9.)
Von Heidenstam, Verner.
Anonymous. Times Lit. Suppl. April 20. (21 : 257.)
Walpole, Hugh.
Anonymous. Nat. (N. Y.) Nov. 30, '21. (113 : 625.)
By Robert Herrick. Post. Oct. 8, '21. (2 : 65.)
Wells, H. G.
By Edward Shanks. L. Merc. March. (5 : 506.)

WEST, REBECCA.
　　Sherwood Anderson. New S. Feb. 18. (18 : 564.)
　　Sherwood Anderson. New S. July 22. (19 : 443.)
　　Elizabeth Bibesco. New S. March 4. (18 : 621.)
　　James Branch Cabell. New S. May 13. (19 : 156.)
　　Aldous Huxley. New S. May 13. (19 : 156.)
　　D. H. Lawrence. New S. June 24. (19 : 326.)
　　Katherine Mansfield. New S. March 18. (18 : 678.)
　　W. Somerset Maugham. New S. Nov. 5, '21. (18 : 140.)
WHIPPLE, T. K.
　　Sherwood Anderson. Post. March 11. (2 : 481.)
Wilde, Oscar.
　　By Raymond M. Alden. Post. Dec. 3, '21. (2 : 228.)
　　By Richard Le Gallienne. Book. (N. Y.) Oct., '21. (54 : 162.)
　　By Michael Monahan. D. D. Nov., '21. (2 : 229.)
　　By Joseph L. Tynan. Free. July 5. (5 : 395.)
Willcocks, M. P.
　　Anton Chekhov. Eng. R. March. (34 : 207.)
WILLIAMS, ORLO.
　　Short Stories. Times. (London.) May 3.
Woolf, Virginia.
　　By Ludwig Lewisohn. Nat. (N. Y.) March 1. (114 : 261.)
WRIGHT, CUTHBERT.
　　James Branch Cabell. Free. Sept. 6. (5 : 621.)
YARMOLINSKY, AVRAHM.
　　Fyodor Dostoevsky. N. Rep. Nov. 30, '21. (29 : 15.)
　　Fyodor Dostoevsky. N. Rep. Sept. 27. (32 : 115.)
　　Vladimir Korolenko. Nat. (N. Y.) March 1. (114 : 254.)
YBARRA, T. R.
　　Guy de Maupassant. N. Y. Times. Jan. 22. (1.)
　　Leo Tolstoy. N. Y. Times. June 4. (1.)
YUST, WALTER.
　　Sherwood Anderson. D. D. March. (3 : 161.)
ZEITLIN, JACOB.
　　Anton Chekhov. Nat. (N. Y.) April 5. (114 : 400.)

INDEX OF SHORT STORIES IN BOOKS

OCTOBER, 1921, TO SEPTEMBER, 1922

The following abbreviations are used in the index:

Prize C. .... Prize. O. Henry Memorial Prize Stories of 1921.
Ramsay .... Ramsay. Short Stories of America.
Tarbell .... Tarbell. He Knew Lincoln.
Twain .... Twain. Mysterious Stranger.
Underwood B. ... Underwood. Famous Stories from Foreign
               Countries.
Woolf .... Woolf. Monday or Tuesday.

I. AMERICAN AUTHORS

ADAMS, ADELINE.
  Amouretta Landscape. Adams. 1.
  Artist's Birthday. Adams. 228.
  Bits of Clay. Adams. 45.
  " C'est Une Taupe." Adams 96.
  Face Called Forgiveness. Adams.
    198.
  Marquis Goes Donkey-Riding.
    Adams. 168.
  Speaking of Angels. Adams. 141.
  Their Appointed Rounds. Adams.
    105.
  Young Lady In Blue. Adams. 57.
ALLEN, MARYLAND. (MRS. EDWARD
    TYSON ALLEN.)
  Urge. Prize C. 45.
AMES, JOSEPH B.
  Lion and the Mouse. Law B. 253.
ANDERSON, SHERWOOD. (1876– .)
    (*See 1920 and 1921.*)
  Brothers. Anderson B. 102;
    O'Brien E. 3.
  Door of the Trap. Anderson B.
    116.
  Dumb Man. Anderson B. 3.
  Egg. Anderson B. 46.
  I Want to Know Why. Anderson
    B. 5.
  Man In the Brown Coat. Anderson
    B. 97.
  Man With the Trumpet. Anderson
    B. 268.
  Motherhood. Anderson B. 168.
  New Englander. Anderson B.
    134.
  Other Woman. Anderson B. 33.
  Out of Nowhere Into Nothing.
    Anderson B. 171.
  Seeds. Anderson B. 21.
  Senility. Anderson B. 93.
  Unlighted Lamps. Anderson B.
    64.
  War. Anderson B. 161.
ANDREWS, MARY RAYMOND SHIPMAN.
    (*See 1918 and 1920.*)
  His Soul Goes Marching On.
    Andrews C.
ANONYMOUS.
  The Pipe. McSpadden D. 110.
ATHERTON, GERTRUDE. (1857– .)
  Pearls of Loreto. Ramsay. 161
BEER, THOMAS. (1889– .) (*See
    1920.*)
  Mummery. Prize C. 66.
BENET, WILLIAM ROSE. (1886– .)
  Chinaman's Head. Law B. 230.

BERCOVICI, KONRAD. (1882– .)
    (*See 1921.*)
  Fanutza. O'Brien, E. 13.
BURT, MAXWELL STRUTHERS. (1882–
    .) (*See 1921.*) (*See 1918,
    1920, 1921.*)
  Experiment. O'Brien E. 28.
CABELL, JAMES BRANCH. (1879– .)
    (*See 1920 and 1921.*)
  Actors All. Cabell D. 111.
  Adhelmar at Puysange. Cabell
    B. 35.
  April's Message. Cabell D. 139.
  Castle of Content. Cabell B. 173.
  Casual Honeymoon. Cabell D. 63.
  Conspiracy of Armaye. Cabell B.
    145.
  Ducal Audience. Cabell D. 303.
  Heart of Gold. Cabell D. 247.
  In Necessity's Mortar. Cabell B.
    113.
  In the Second of April. Cabell D.
    171.
  In Ursula's Garden. Cabell B.
    203.
  Love at Martinmas. Cabell D.
    39.
  Love-Letters of Falstaff. Cabell B.
    63.
  Porcelain Cups. Cabell B. 229.
  Rhyme to Porringer. Cabell D. 91.
  Scapegoats. Cabell D. 275.
  Semper-Idem. Cabell B. 257.
  Simon's Hour. Cabell D. 3
  Story of the Choices. Cabell C. 99.
  Story of the Fox-Brush. Cabell C.
    247.
  Story of the Heritage. Cabell C.
    185.
  Story of the Housewife. Cabell C.
    127.
  Story of the Navarrese. Cabell C.
    221.
  Story of the Rat-Trap. Cabell C.
    73.
  Story of the Satraps. Cabell C.
    159.
  Story of the Scabbard. Cabell C.
    195.
  Story of the Sestina. Cabell C.
    15.
  Story of the Tenson. Cabell C. 45.
  "Sweet Adelais." Cabell B. 87.
  Wedding Jest. Cabell B. 9.
CATHERWOOD, MARY HARTWELL.
  Windigo. Ramsay. 191.

II. ENGLISH AND IRISH AUTHORS

III. TRANSLATIONS

MAGAZINE AVERAGES

OCTOBER, 1921, TO SEPTEMBER, 1922

The following table includes the averages of distinctive stories in certain American periodicals published from October, 1921, to September, 1922, inclusive. One, two and three asterisks are employed to indicate relative distinction. " Three-asterisk stories " are of somewhat permanent literary value. The list excludes reprints.

PERIODICALS (OCT.–SEPT.)	NO. OF STORIES PUBLISHED	NO. OF DISTINCTIVE STORIES PUBLISHED			PERCENTAGE OF DISTINCTIVE STORIES PUBLISHED		
		*	**	***	*	**	***
Asia	10	9	6	1	90	60	10
Atlantic Monthly	26	23	16	7	88	62	27
Broom	23	20	16	10	87	69	43
Century	42	39	32	17	93	76	40
Collier's Weekly	109	18	3	1	17	3	1
Delineator	40	11	4	3	28	10	8
Dial	22	22	21	14	100	95	64
Double Dealer	21	12	8	2	57	38	10
Everybody's Magazine	66	9	2	1	14	3	2
Good Housekeeping	44	6	3	1	14	7	2
Harper's Magazine	44	39	23	14	89	52	32
Hearst's International	63	18	4	1	29	6	2
Ladies' Home Journal	42	8	3	2	19	7	5
McClure's Magazine (March–September)	46	13	2	1	28	4	2
Metropolitan	87	17	9	6	19	10	7
Pictorial Review	65	44	31	22	66	48	33
Red Book Magazine	115	27	4	2	24	4	2
Saturday Evening Post	245	34	14	7	14	6	3
Scribner's Magazine	52	37	19	7	71	37	14
Smart Set	127	44	9	5	35	7	4
World Fiction (August–September)	22	21	11	5	95	50	23

*The following tables indicate the rank, during the period between
October, 1921, and September, 1922, inclusive, by number and per-
centage of distinctive short stories published, of eighteen periodicals
coming within the scope of my examination which have published an
average of 15 per cent or more of distinctive stories. The lists exclude
reprints, but not translations.*

By Percentage

1. Dial 100%
2. World Fiction (August–September) 95%
3. Century 93%
4. Asia 90%
5. Harper's Magazine 89%
6. Atlantic Monthly 88%
7. Broom 87%
8. Scribner's Magazine 71%
9. Pictorial Review 66%
10. Double Dealer 57%
11. Smart Set 35%
12. Hearst's International 29%
13. McClure's Magazine (March–September) 28%
14. Delineator 28%
15. Red Book Magazine 24%
16. Metropolitan 19%
17. Ladies' Home Journal 19%
18. Collier's Weekly 17%

By Number

1. Pictorial Review 44
2. Smart Set 44
3. Century 39
4. Harper's Magazine 39
5. Scribner's Magazine 37
6. Red Book Magazine 27
7. Atlantic Monthly 23
8. Dial 22
9. World Fiction (August–September) 21
10. Broom 20
11. Hearst's International 18
12. Collier's Weekly 18
13. Metropolitan 17
14. McClure's Magazine (March–September) 13
15. Double Dealer 12
16. Delineator 11
17. Asia 9
18. Ladies' Home Journal 8

*The following periodicals have published during the same period
ten or more " two-asterisk stories." The list excludes reprints, but not
translations. Periodicals represented in this list during 1915, 1916,*

1917, 1918, 1919, 1920, and 1921 are represented by the prefixed letters a, b, c, d, e, f, *and* g, *respectively.*

1.	abcdefg	Century	32
2.	bcdefg	Pictorial Review	31
3.	abcdefg	Harper's Magazine	23
4.	fg	Dial	21
5.	abcdef	Scribner's Magazine	19
6.		Broom	16
7.	cdef	Atlantic Monthly	16
8.	abcde	Saturday Evening Post	14
9.		World Fiction (August–September)	11

The following periodicals have published during the same period five or more " three-asterisk stories." The list excludes reprints, but not translations. The same signs are used as prefixes as in the previous list.

1.	bcdefg	Pictorial Review	22
2.	abcdefg	Century	17
3.	fg	Dial	14
4.	abcdefg	Harper's Magazine	14
5.		Broom	10
6.	cdef	Atlantic Monthly	7
7.	abcdef	Scribner's Magazine	7
8.	abc e	Saturday Evening Post	7
9.	a c ef	Metropolitan	6
10.		World Fiction (August–September)	5
11.	def	Smart Set	5

Ties in the above list have been decided by taking relative rank in other lists into account.

INDEX OF SHORT STORIES PUBLISHED
IN AMERICAN MAGAZINES

OCTOBER, 1921, TO SEPTEMBER, 1922

All short stories published in the following magazines, and news-papers, October, 1921, to September, 1922, inclusive, are indexed:

Short stories of distinction only, published in the following maga-zines during the same period, are indexed:

Live Stories
MacLean's Magazine
Magnificat
Munsey's Magazine
Open Road
People's Home Journal
People's Popular Monthly
Popular Magazine
Queen's Work
Reviewer
Saucy Stories
Short Stories

Snappy Stories
Telling Tales
10-Story Book
Today's Housewife
Top-Notch Magazine
Town Topics
True Story Magazine
Wayside Tales
Western Story Magazine
Woman's World
Young's Magazine

Certain stories of distinction published in the following magazines during this period are indexed, because they have been specially called to my attention:

Jewish Daily News
Junior League Bulletin

New York Nation
Photoplay

I have considered several other magazines without finding any stories of distinction. One, two, or three asterisks are prefixed to the titles of stories to indicate distinction. Three asterisks prefixed to a title indicate the more or less permanent literary value of the story, and entitle it to a place on the annual " Rolls of Honor." Cross references after an author's name refer to previous volumes of this series. (H.) after the name of an author indicates that other stories by this author, published in American magazines between 1900 and 1914, are to be found indexed in " The Standard Index of Short Stories," by Francis J. Hannigan, published by Small, Maynard and Company, 1918. The figures in parentheses after the title of a story refer to the volume and page number of the magazine. In cases where successive numbers of a magazine are not paged consecutively, the page number only is given in this index.

The following abbreviations are used in the index:

Adv.	Adventure
Ain.	Ainslee's Magazine
Am.	American Magazine
Am. B.	American Boy
Asia	Asia
Atl.	Atlantic Monthly
A. W.	All's Well
B. C.	Black Cat
Blue	Blue Book Magazine
Book	Bookman (N. Y.)
Br. St.	Brief Stories
Broom	Broom
Cath. W.	Catholic World
Cen.	Century
Chic. Trib.	Chicago Tribune (Syndicate Service)

I. American Authors

A

ABBOTT, ELEANOR HALLOWELL. (MRS. FORDYCE COBURN.) (1872– .) (See 1915, 1918, 1920, 1921.) (H.)
　Gift of the Probable Places. L. H. J. Jan. (5.)
　Ye Greate Astonishments. L. H. J. Dec. '21. (3.)
ABDULLAH, ACHMED. (ACHMED ABDULLAH NADIR KHAN EL-DURANI EL-IDRISSYEH.) ("A. A. NADIR.") (1881– .) (See 1915, 1916, 1917, 1918, 1919, 1920, 1921.) (H.)
　*Affair of the Chinese Vase. Col. Oct. 22, '21. (7.)
　*Affair of the Nauratama Amulet. Col. Dec. 10, '21. (7.)
　*Affair of the Shiva Natarajah. Col. Dec. 24, '21. (7.)
　**Black Poppies. T. T. Nov., '21. (10 : 12.)
　**Matter of Face. McCall. June (8.)
　*Most Just Among Moslems. Cos. July. (97.)
　*Tale the Drum Told. Cos. Aug. (95.)
　*Vase of Ancient Precepts. T. T. Oct., '21. (9 : 204.)
ADAMS, ADELINE.
　**Marquis Goes Donkey-Riding. Atl. April. (129 : 474.)
" ADAMS, BILL." (BERTRAM M. ADAMS.) (1879– .)
　*Amos Tregenna. Adv. Aug. 10. (157.)
　*Bosun of the Goldenhorn's Yarn. Adv. Jan. 20. (86.)
　*Debt at Sea. Adv. March 10. (55.)
　***Sailors' Way. Des. March. (20.)

　*Time Comes. Adv. May 20. (35.)
　***Twinkle-Bright. Adv. Sept. 30. (98.)
ADAMS, FRANK R. (1883– .) (See 1915, 1916, 1921.)
　Gentlemen Once. Cos. July. (81.)
　Jongleur of Hollywood. Cos. Sept. (39.)
　Mrs. You. Cos. Oct. '21. (26.)
　Two of Them. Cos. Aug. (83.)
ADAMS, SAMUEL HOPKINS. (1871– .) (See 1915, 1916, 1917, 1918, 1919, 1920, 1921.) (H.)
　Isle O'Dreams. Red Bk. Aug. (46.)
　*Plooie of Our Square. Col. Oct. 29, '21. (7.)
　Town That Wasn't. Red Bk. Dec., '21. (81.)
ADDINGTON, SARAH.
　Jill Fools the Jack of Hearts. L. H. J. June. (14.)
　Mrs. Dumpty's Dilemma. L. H. J. Sept. (20.)
AIDLINE-TROMMER, ELBERT.
　**Ten Percent. Nat. (N. Y.) June 28. (114 : 774.)
AIKEN, CONRAD POTTER. (1889– .)
　***Dark City. Dial. April. (72: 345.)
　**Soliloquy on a Park Bench. Dial. June. (72 : 601.)
AIKEN, RALPH.
　Their Wedding Anniversary. Les. W. March 25. (134 : 406.)
ALBERT, ROSE.
　Alley Rat. Pag. (Dec.- Jan.) (29.)
ALDIS, MARY REYNOLDS. (MRS. ARTHUR T. ALDIS.) (1872– .) (See 1916.)
　*Mosque of the Empress. Dial. March. (72 : 273.)

BANNING, MARGARET CULKIN.
  Sauce for the Gander. Met. March. (26.)
  With Luxury Tax. Met. Feb. (12.)
BARNARD, LESLIE GORDON. (See 1920.)
  *Twilight. Mod. P. Dec., '21. (14.)
BARRETT, RICHMOND BROOKS. (See 1920, 1921.)
  Art for Art's Sake. S.S. April. (103.)
  Sins of the Father. S.S. May. (39.)
BARRIE, CASWELL.
  Out of the Night. Met. Oct., '21. (34.)
BARROWS, FRANKLYN.
  Jimmy and the Ultimatum. Am. Jan. (28.)
  Ryan's Decision. Ev. Jan. (156.)
BARTLETT, FREDERICK ORIN. (1876– .) (See 1915, 1916, 1917, 1918, 1919, 1920, 1921.) (H.)
  Cliff Dwellers. S. E. P. June 24. (20.)
  Cubs. Del. Nov., '21. (16.)
  His Mother's Son. Red Bk. Nov., '21. (37.)
  Without End. Del. April. (10.)
BARTLEY, NALBRO. (1888– .) (See 1917, 1918, 1919, 1921.)
  Dizzy. McCall. April. (5.)
BARTON, BRUCE. (1886– .) (See 1921.)
  Secret Society of Wives. W. H. C. April. (15.)
  Spring of Eternal Youth. W. H. C. Oct., '21. (12.)
BATCHELOR, HAZEL DEYO.
  Romance. S. S. May. (83.)
BEACH, REX. (ELLINGWOOD) (1877– .) (See 1919, 1921.)
  White Brant. Cos. Sept. (85.)
BEARD, WOLCOTT LE CLEAR. (1867– .) (See 1915, 1919, 1920, 1921.) (H.)
  *Wedding Gift. McC. Sept. (66.)
BEAUMONT, GERALD. (See 1921.)
  Bull Baiters. Red Bk. June. (54.)
  Christmas Handicap. Red Bk. Jan. (48.)
  Elephant. Red Bk. Oct., '21. (62.)
  Gambling Chaplain. Red Bk. Dec., '21. (32.)
  Golden Moment. Red Bk. Nov., '21. (62.)
  Miracle. Red Bk. May. (38.)
  Mud and 95. Red Bk. Sept. (60.)
  Oh, Susanna! Red Bk. March. (48.)
  Ol' Joe Slump. Red Bk. July. (87.)
  Star. Red Bk. April. (38.)
  Thoroughbreds. Red Bk. Feb. (41.)
  When Johnny Comes Marching Home. Red Bk. Aug. (71.)
BEER, THOMAS. (1889– .) (See

1917, 1918, 1919, 1920, 1921.)
  *Addio. S. E. P. Oct. 29, '21. (16.)
  *Balliol. S. E. P. May 13. (12.)
  *By Parables. S. E. P. Aug. 26. (16.)
  ***Casual. Pop. July 20. (106.)
  *Citizens of Hidj. S. E. P. March 18. (14.)
  Don Carlos Vittori. S. E. P. Jan. 21. (10.)
  **Enemy. Cen. May. (104 : 30.)
  *Fifty and Fifty. Harp. M. Sept. (145 : 467.)
  *Lips. S. E. P. Sept. 9. (12.)
  ***Rope. S. E. P. March 25. (12.)
  *Tact. S. E. P. July. 1. (8.)
BEHRMAN, S. N. (See 1917, 1918, 1919, 1920, 1921) and NICHOLSON, J. K.
  *Holiday. S. S. June. (89.)
  Rupert Goes on the Loose. S. S. March. (53.)
BELGION, MONTGOMERY.
  La Dame de Carreaux. Pearson. March. (29.)
BELLAMANN, HENRY.
  Man Who Was Lonely. D. D. Dec., '21. (2 : 239.)
BELLAMY, FRANCIS RUFUS. (1886– .)
  ***"Talk." Harp. M. Dec., '21. (144 : 35.)
BENET, STEPHEN VINCENT. (1898– .) (See 1916, 1920.)
  *Goobers-à la Française. Del. Aug. (5.)
  Mad Americans. Met. Jan. (12.)
BENTINCK, RICHARD. (See 1919.)
  Goldfish Bowl. Sun. Nov., '21. (20.)
BENTON, MARGARET. (See 1921.)
  God Gives Husbands. Am. April. (25.)
  World that Judith Found. W. H. C. Aug. '21. (17.)
BERRANGER, CLARA.
  Spun Gold. Met. April. (40.)
BERCOVICI, KONRAD. (1882– .) (See 1920, 1921.)
  ***Death of Murdo. Pict. R. July. (12.)
  ***Father and Son. Cen. March. (103 : 668.)
  ***Ghitza. (R.) Pearson. July. (30.)
  ***Hazi, Wife of Sender Surtuck. Broom. Dec., '21. (1 : 162.)
  ***Mincu. Pict. R. March. (12.)
  ***Murdo. Pict. R. Dec. '21. (16.)
  ***Tanasi. Cen. June. (104 : 163.)
  ***When a Man Rules. Pict. R. May. (12.)
  *Yahde, the Proud One. (R.) Pearson. May. (18.)
BIGGERS, EARL DERR. (1884– .) (See 1916, 1917, 1921.)
  Heart of the Loaf. S. E. P. Aug. 5. (5.)

BRUBAKER, HOWARD. (1892– .)
(*See 1915, 1916, 1917, 1918, 1919, 1920, 1921.*) (*H.*)
Two Birds. Col. Oct. 1, '21. (7.)

BRUNO, GUIDO. (1884– .) (*See 1915, 1920.*)
Alma. Pearson. Oct., '21. (47 : 165.)

BRYNER, EDNA CLARE. (*See 1920.*)
***Forest Cover. Book. Jan. (54 : 454.)

BUCK, OSCAR MACMILLAN. (1885– .) (*See 1920.*)
***" Kismet " — a Tale of Rohilkund. Asia. Aug. (22 : 595.)

BUCKLEY, F. R.
Gold-Mounted Guns. Red Bk. March. (91.)

BULGER, BOZEMAN. (*See 1915, 1916, 1917, 1919, 1920, 1921.*)
Flight of Sadie. Ev. April. (99.)
BULGER, BOZEMAN, *see* RUNYON, DAMON, *and* BULGER, BOZEMAN.

BURKE, KENNETH. (*See 1920.*)
David Wassermann. Lit. R. Autumn, '21. (24.)

BURNET, DANA. (1888– .) (*See 1915, 1916, 1917, 1918, 1919, 1920.*)
Minnow. Book. April. (55 : 152.)
Pity. Pict. R. April. (10.)
Reggie. S. E. P. April 29. (6.)
Spider's Web. Hear. Dec., '21. (9.)
Wandering Daughters. Hear. July. (26.)

BURT, MAXWELL STRUTHERS. (1882– .) (*See 1915, 1917, 1918, 1919, 1920, 1921.*)
**Inheritors. Pict. R. Nov., '21. (14.)
Inhibiting Wattles. Red Bk. May. (58.)

BURT, WILL.
*Things That Live Under the Floor. McC. May. (97.)

BUTLER, ELLIS PARKER. (1869– .) (*See 1915, 1916, 1917, 1918, 1919, 1920, 1921.*) (*H.*)
Liar. Sun. March. (12.)
*Martin Forgot. Del. July. (18.)
Sane Hearts. Pict. R. Jan. (24.)
Sheer Silk. Pict. R. Dec., '21. (18.)
Short Skirts. Pict. R. Feb. (26.)
Sic Semper Susans! Pict. R. March. (23.)
*Use Common Sense. Mun. July. (210.)

" BYRNE, DONN." (BRYAN OSWALD DONN-BYRNE.) (1888– .) (*See 1915, 1916, 1917, 1918, 1919, 1920, 1921.*) (*H.*)
By Ordeal of Justice. Hear. Oct., '21. (10.)
*Dramatis Personæ. Scr. Aug. (72 : 147.)

Happy Ending. Hear. April. (11.)
Thing Called Gratitude. Hear. Jan. (41.)
Triangle. Ev. Sept. (85.)
*Wisdom Buildeth Her House. Cen. Dec., '21. (103 : 161.)

C

CABELL, JAMES BRANCH. (1879– .) (*See 1915, 1918, 1919, 1920, 1921.*) (*H.*)
***Candid Footprint. Cen. May. (104 : 3.)

CAMP, (CHARLES) WADSWORTH. (1879– .) (*See 1915, 1916, 1917, 1918, 1920, 1921.*) (*H.*)
Defiance. Col. Dec. 24, '21. (3.)

CAMPBELL, EVELYN.
Happiness. Ev. May. (164.)

CANFIELD, DOROTHY. (DOROTHEA FRANCES CANFIELD FISHER.) (1879– .) (*See 1915, 1916, 1918, 1919, 1921.*) (*H.*)
*Colonel Sharp. Outl. April 12. (130 : 595.)
*Great Love. Outl. Feb. 8. (130 : 219.)
*" Old Man Warner." Outl. Jan. 11. (130 : 56.)
*Uncle Giles. Outl. Feb. 22. (130 : 306.)
*Yankee Mother In Israel. Outl. May 3. (131 : 22.)

CARNE, MARY A.
Fetters of Gold. Cath. W. Sept. (115 : 756.)

CARROLL, GRACE IRENE.
Katrinka's Belated Childhood. Cath. W. May. (115 : 230.)

CARVER, GEORGE. (1888– .) (*See 1918, 1920.*)
***Singer. Mid. March. (8 : 95.)

CARY, LUCIAN. (1886– .) (*See 1918, 1919, 1921.*)
Dashing Stranger. McCall. Sept. (10.)
Don't Go Near the Water. Red Bk. Aug. (62.)
Glass Husbands. Harp. B. Nov., '21. (44.)
Once a Flirt. McCall. Oct., '21. (14.)
Way These Things Happen. McCall. Aug. (7.)
What Galatea Said. Ev. July. (98.)

CASTLE, EVERETT RHODES. (*See 1917, 1918, 1919, 1920.*)
Tip. S. E. P. April 29. (14.)

CAVENDISH, JOHN C. (*See 1919, 1920, 1921.*)
Convert. S. S. Dec., '21. (119.)
Reformed Man. S. S. June. (119.)

CHAMBERLAIN, LUCIA. (*See 1917, 1920, 1921.*) (*H.*)
Passion in the Park. Met. Nov., '21. (11.)

CRAVEN, THOMAS JEWELL. (1889- .)
***Love In Smoky Hill. Dial. Jan.
(72 : 1.)
CURTIS, EDITH R.
Something Ere the End. S. S.
Aug. (117.)
CURTIS, MARGUERITE.
Joseph's Coat. S. E. P. April 29.
(10.)
Shining Column. S. E. P. Sept. 9.
(34.)
CURTISS, PHILIP (EVERETT). (1885 —
.) (See 1915, 1916, 1917,
1918, 1919, 1920, 1921.) (H.)
Sumac and Goldenrod. L. H. J.
Feb. (8.)
CURWOOD, JAMES OLIVER. (1878- .)
(See 1917, 1918, 1919, 1921.)
(H.)
Message to His Master. Cos. Oct.,
'21. (70.)

D

DALLETT, MORRIS. (See 1920, 1921.)
Pursuit. S. S. Jan. (53.)
DANE, YARDLEY.
*Requiscat. S. S. Aug. (70.)
DAVIS, CHARLES BELMONT. (1866- .)
(See 1915, 1916, 1919, 1920,
1921.) (H.)
*Ethics of Nelson Cole. Scr. Jan.
(71 : 23.)
DAVIS, J. FRANK. (See 1917, 1918,
1919.)
Bill Titus Comes Back. Red Bk.
March. (73.)
Cranked In Gear. Red Bk. April.
(85.)
Fallen Arches. Red Bk. May.
(77.)
No Dramatis Personæ. Chic.
Trib. April 9.
DAY, JR., CLARENCE. (See 1915, 1916,
1921.)
Quick Ripplers. Met. Feb. (33.)
DAY, CURTISS LA Q. (See 1919.)
Son of a Sidewalk. Sun. Jan.
(46.)
DAY, HOLMAN FRANCIS. (1865- .)
(See 1915, 1918, 1919, 1920,
1921.) (H.)
Jode's People. Col. June 24. (7.)
DEAN, WILLIAM HARPER. (See 1921.)
Horseshoe for Luck. L. H. J.
Jan. (8.)
Pompadour Days. L. H. J. Oct.,
'21. (16.)
DE JAGERS, DOROTHY. (See 1916,
1920.)
Average Woman. S. E. P. April
8. (10.)
Special Case. S. E. P. July 29.
(9.)
Tears, Idle Tears. S. E. P. Sept.
23. (6.)
DELANO, EDITH BARNARD. (See 1915,
1917, 1918, 1920, 1921.) (See
" H " under BARNARD, EDITH

and DELANO, EDITH BARNARD.
*Nor Iron Bars. L. H. J. Sept.
(10.)
Provided For. Chic. Trib. Jan. 8.
**Rosellen. L. H. J. May. (10.)
Somebody's Sweetie. Pict. R.
Oct., '21. (25.)
*Sycamore Tree. W. W. Jan. (7.)
DE LEON, WALTER. (See 1921.)
Blessed Meek. Ev. Sept. (113.)
Broken-Hearted Success. Ev.
Oct., '21. (49.)
Dicky's Continuity. Ev. Feb.
(33.)
Her Majesty Molly. S. E. P.
Sept. 23. (10.)
Lovely Bounder. Ev. Jan. (76.)
Short Vamps. Ev. March. (37.)
Sweet and Sour. Ev. June.
(171.)
Turtle Doves. Ev. Nov., '21.
(129.)
DERIEUX, SAMUEL A. (1881–1922.)
(See 1916, 1917, 1918, 1919,
1920, 1921.)
An Act of God. Am. March.
(29.)
Billy Thompson's Plan for
Revenge. Am. July. (46.)
Comet. Am. Dec., '21. (38.)
Invisible Huntsman. Am. June.
(28.)
Joe Goes After the Doctor. Am.
Nov., '21. (51.)
Old Shad's Chippendale. Del.
July. (14.)
Sixth Shot. Red Bk. July. (78.)
DERRY, SELMA.
White Playground. Wave. Jan.
(9.)
DEUTSCH, HERMANN BACHER. (See
1916.)
Apogee. D. D. Jan. (3 : 45.)
DICKENSON, EDWIN C. (See 1918,
1921.)
Border Stuff. W. H. C. Nov., '21.
(23.)
DICKEY, BASIL.
Bad News. Ev. May. (115.)
DICKSON, HARRIS. (1868- .) (See
1915, 1916, 1917, 1918, 1919,
1920, 1921.) (H.)
Cannie the Uncanny. Col. May 6.
(11.)
Moccasin Slough. Col. Aug. 12.
(3.)
Trapping of Judge Pinkham.
S. E. P. Sept. 9. (24.)
DINGLE, CAPTAIN.
Ocean Magic. S. E. P. Sept. 30.
(10.)
DIVINE, CHARLES. (See 1917, 1921.)
Snake-charmer of Kairwan. Ev.
June. (82.)
Street of Sapphire Doors. Sun.
April. (32.)
Symbolic Shoes of Mr. Bullis.
S. S. June. (112.)

DOBIE, CHARLES CALDWELL. (1881–
.) (See 1916, 1917, 1918
1919, 1920, 1921.)
***Vision. Cen. Jan. (103 : 415.)
DODD, LEE WILSON. (1879–   .)
(See " H.")
Little Rufo. Red Bk. Nov., '21.
(86.)
DONNELL, ANNIE HAMILTON. (1862–
.) (See 1915, 1920.) (H.)
Last Straw. McCall. Oct., '21. (13.)
DOUGLAS, FORD. (See 1920, 1921.)
(H.)
Fraternal Spirit. S. S. April.
(29.)
Majesty of the Law. S. S. July.
(31.)
Mr. Worthington's Black Eye.
S. S. Nov., '21. (63.)
DOUNCE, HARRY ESTY. (See 1917,
1919, 1920.)
Cobblestone Flies Up. Col. Aug.
26. (7.)
Trapped. Ev. May. (58.)
DRAGO, HARRY SINCLAIR.
Rain. Met. April. (53.)
DREHER, CARL.
Fifth Decade. S. S. Feb. (115.)
DUGANNE, PHYLLIS. (See 1919, 1920.)
Amateur Rebel. L. H. J. Feb. (6.)
Fulla — Pep! L. H. J. April. (8.)
Vanishing Girl. L. H. J. Jan. (6.)
DUNBAR, OLIVIA HOWARD. (OLIVIA
HOWARD DUNBAR TORRENCE.)
(1873–   .) (See 1915, 1919.)
(H.)
*Classic Pattern. Scr. Feb. (71 :
218.)
*Home of Her Own. Scr. Jan.
(71 : 89.)
DUNN, JOSEPH ALLAN. (1872–   .)
(See 1915, 1921.) (H.)
*Crimson Corpuscle. McC. Aug.(17.)
DUTTON, LOUISE ELIZABETH. (See
1915, 1916, 1917, 1918, 1919,
1920, 1921.) (H.)
Magic Music. S. E. P. Feb. 18.
(28.)
One Night in June. Met. April.
(9.)
Spooning. S. E. P. Feb. 11. (24.)
DWYER, JAMES FRANCIS. (1874–   .)
(See 1915, 1916, 1917, 1918,
1919, 1920, 1921.) (H.)
**Camp o' Sunset Glory. Del. May.
(10.)
DYER, WALTER ALDEN. (1878–   .)
(See 1915, 1916, 1917, 1918,
1920, 1921.) (H.)
Dog Doctor. Del. June. (14.)

E

EASTMAN, REBECCA LANE HOOPER.
(MRS. WILLIAM FRANKLIN
EASTMAN.) (1877–   .) (See
1915, 1919, 1920, 1921.) (H.)
Gentleman with Plaid Eyes. Scr.
July. (72 : 60.)

Idyl of Madison Square. McC.
Sept. (49.)
EDGINGTON, HARTLEY.
His Fourth Born. Sun. Feb. (20.)
EDSON, C. L.
Smartest Man In America. S. S.
May. (96.)
EHLERT, FAY. (1886–   .)
*Punishment. Pearson. Jan. (48 :
25.)
Undertow. Pearson. Nov., '21.
(47 : 208.)
***Vow. Pearson. Feb. (29.)
ELDRIDGE, PAUL. (See 1918, 1919,
1920.)
Back to Methusaleh. S. S. Dec.,
'21. (73.)
ELLERBE, ALMA MARTIN ESTABROOK.
(1871–   ) and ELLERBE, PAUL
LEE. (See 1915 under ESTA-
BROOK, ALMA MARTIN; 1917
under ELLERBE, ALMA ESTA-
BROOK; 1919, 1920, 1921 under
ELLERBE, ALMA MARTIN ESTA-
BROOK, and ELLERBE, PAUL
LEE.) (See " H " under ELLERBE,
PAUL LEE.)
Down But Not Out. Col. April
22. (15). April 29. (13.)
**" Some People Say They are
Married." Cen. April. (103 :
846.)
ELLIOTT, FRANCIS PERRY. (1861–   .)
Surgeon's Knife. L. H. J. July.
(12.)
EMBREE, ALICE.
Price of Paint. G. H. Aug. (50.)
ENGLAND, GEORGE ALLAN. (1877–   .)
(See 1916, 1919, 1921.) (H.)
Sauce. Ev. March. (131.)
ESTY, ANNETTE. (See 1921.)
Immune. Cath. W. July. (115 :
527.)
*" Rights." Scr. July. (72 : 87.)
EVANS, IDA MAY. (See 1915, 1916,
1917, 1918, 1919, 1920, 1921.)
(H.)
His Wife's Money. Cos. July.
(69.)
Out of the Golden Pack. Chic.
Trib. Aug. 27.
To Him That Hath. S. E. P.
March 11. (24.)
Voice of Blanche Perkins. S. E. P.
June 17. (18.)
Way a Girl Treats Her Father.
S. E. P. Sept. 23. (14.)
Yellows. G. H. Nov., '21. (52.)
EVERMAN, PAUL.
Oh, Ballyhoo! Ev. March. (171.)

F

FAGIN, N. BRYLLION.
**Dream. Am. H. Nov. 11, '21.
(42 : 695.)
FARAGOH, FRANCIS EDWARDS.
*Chop Suey. Lib. Nov., '21.
(15.)

FARNHAM, MABEL.
Virginia, Aged Ten Years. Cath.
W. Jan. (114 : 520.)
FARRAR, JOHN. (CHIPMAN.) (1896–
.)
*Edge of Cobbler's Wood. Book.
Dec., '21. (54 : 342.)
FERBER, EDNA. (1887–   .) (See
1915, 1916, 1917, 1918, 1919,
1920, 1921.) (H.)
*Afternoon of a Faun. Col. Nov.
12, '21. (3.)
FINCH, ANITA.
*Tennessee Baby. McC. April.
(90.)
FINGER, CHARLES J. (1871–   .)
(See 1919, 1920, 1921.)
**Hyenas. A. W. Feb. (2 : 43.)
*Incongruity. A. W. Nov., '21.
(R.) (1 : 255.)
***Jade Piece. D. D. April. (3 : 176.)
***My Friend Julio. Cen. July.
(104 : 323.)
**Romero Hotel. Youth. Jan.
(1 : 3.)
***Shame of Gold. Cen. March.
(103 : 749.)
FITZGERALD, FRANCIS SCOTT KEY.
(1896–   .) (See 1920, 1921.)
**Curious Case of Benjamin Button.
Col. May 27. (5.)
Popular Girl. S. E. P. Feb. 11.
(3.)
***Two For a Cent. Met. April.
(23.)
FITZ-HUGH, MILDRED.
King's Son. Ev. March. (84.)
FLEMING, BOYD.
When Romance Flirted. Am.
Sept. (53.)
FOHN, M. POWELL.
Wishes That Were Granted. S. S.
May. (107.)
FOLSOM, ELIZABETH IRONS. (1876–   .)
(See 1916, 1917, 1918, 1919,
1920, 1921.)
**In the Audience. Met. Feb. (23.)
FOOTE, JOHN TAINTOR. (See 1915,
1916, 1918, 1919, 1920, 1921.)
(H.)
Economic Independence. S. E. P.
Dec. 10, '21. (3.)
Shame On You. S. E. P. Oct.
8, '21. (5.)
Song of the Dragon. S. E. P. Nov.
12, '21. (3.)
White Grouse. S. E. P. Sept. 9.
(6.)
FORRESTER, IZOLA L. (See 1918 under
FORRESTER, IZOLA L. and PAGE,
MANN; see 1921 under FORRES-
TER, IZOLA L., see " H," under
FORRESTER, IZOLA L.)
" Beloved Son of ———— " Del.
June. (11.)
FOSTER, CHARLES C.
*" My Son, My Son Absalom! "
McC. Aug. (104.)

On Stony Lonesome. McC. Sept.
(87.)
Tie that Binds. McC. Aug. (106.)
FOSTER, JULIA B. (See " H.")
Wild-Feather Pillow. Sun. Sept.
(5.)
FOSTER, MAXIMILIAN. (1872–   .)
(See 1915, 1917, 1918, 1920.)
(H.)
Between Friends. S. E. P. Sept.
23. (18.)
Bubbles. S. E. P. Jan. 7. (8.)
Bucket Boob. S. E. P. June 17.
(14.)
Knock-Out. S. E. P. Feb. 4. (8.)
My Wife's Money. S. E. P. March
25. (5.)
Tape. S. E. P. April 15. (12.)
FOXHALL, GEORGE.
Blood Will Tell. Col. July 22.
(7.)
FRAENKEL, H. E.
*Yellow Quilt. Lib. Dec., '21.
(11.)
FRANK, WALDO. (1890–   .) (See
1916, 1917, 1921.)
***Candy Cigar and Stationary.
Broom. Jan. (252.)
***John the Baptist. Dial. Sept.
(72 : 312.)
***Murder. Broom. June. (2 :
220.)
FRAZER, ELIZABETH. (See 1915, 1916,
1920.) (H.)
Two-Job Girl. S. E. P. June 10.
(32.)
FREDERICK, JOHN TOWNER. (1893–   .)
Associate Professor Quinby of the
English Department. S. S. Jan.
(108.)
***Legacy. S. S. Oct., '21. (119.)
*Mirage. S. S. July. (119.)
FREEDMAN, DAVID. (1898–   .)
*Intellectual Lover. Pict. R. July.
(6.)
***Mendel Marantz–Housewife. Pict.
R. April. (12.)
***Mendel Marantz Moves. Pict. R.
June. (10.)
***Quest of Sarah. Pict. R. Aug.
(14.)
FREEMAN, MARY E(LEANOR) WILKINS.
(1862–   .) (See 1915, 1916,
1917, 1918, 1920.) (H.)
*Mother-Wings. Harp. M. Dec.
'21. (144 : 90.)
*Return. W. H. C. Aug., '21.
(21.)
FUESSLE, KENNETH.
Wife of a Man of God. S. S. Oct.,
'21. (31.)
FURMAN, LUCY. (See " H.")
***Fourth of July. Atl. July. (130 :
68.)
***Quare Women. Atl. May. (129 :
594.)
***Taking the Night. Atl. June.
(129 : 756.)

G

GALE, ZONA. (1874– .) (See 1915, 1916, 1917, 1918, 1919, 1920, 1921.) (H.)
*For Show. Del. July. (5.)
**Simon and the Thief. Cen. Jan. (103 : 337.)

GARRETT, GARET. (1878– .) (See 1917, 1920, 1921.)
*Goose-Man. Cen. Sept. (104 : 669.)
House a Wop Built. McC. June. (65.)

GATLIN, DANA. (See 1915, 1916, 1917, 1918, 1919, 1921.) (H.)
Girl In the Scandal. Cos. Oct., '21. (83.)
Its Triteness Recommends It. Chic. Trib. Nov. 6, '21.

GAUL (HARRIET) AVERY. (See " H.")
Billboard. McC. May. (104.)

GAUSS, MARIANNE. (See 1915, 1920.) (H.)
Sweet Violet. McC. May. (52.)

GEER, GERTRUDE MARSHALL.
Boston Calling. Atl. Aug. (130 : 207.)

GELZER, JAY. (See 1920, 1921.)
In Time of Storm. G. H. July. (31.)
New York Gets Margy Frances. G. H. Aug. (36.)
Something to Remember. G. H. May. (81.)
Sunday Wives. Hear. April. (25.)

GEROULD, KATHERINE FULLERTON. (1879– .) (See 1915, 1916, 1917, 1918, 1919, 1920, 1921.) (H.)
***Belshazzar's Letter. Met. June. (15.)
***Nature of an Oath. Scr. Aug. (72 : 208.)

GERRY, MARGARITA SPALDING. (1870– .) (See 1915, 1916, 1917, 1920, 1921.) (H.)
Indirect Lighting. Harp. M. Oct., '21. (143 : 602.)

GIBBS, GEORGE. (1870– .) (See 1919.) (H.)
Face In the Fog. Mod. P. Feb. (14.)
False Pretenses. Mod. P. Sept. (10.)

GILBERT, GEORGE. (1874– .) (See 1916, 1918, 1919, 1920, 1921.)
Son Who Looked Down On His Father. Am. Sept. (20.)

GILBERT, KENNETH.
Burden of Procyon. Sun. April. (10.)
Debt of the Wilderness. Sun. Jan. (32.)
Great Feud of Talking River. Am. Nov., '21. (38.)
Outlaw. Met. Oct., '21. (17.)
Patriarch of the Peak. Sun. Aug. (21.)

GILKYSON, WALTER. (1880– .) (See 1921.)
**Empty Bottles. Scr. Feb. (71 : 234.)
***Spoken in Jest. Atl. April. (129 : 506.)

GINGER, BONNIE R. (See 1915, 1919.) (H.)
Decoy. Cen. Oct., '21. (102 : 899.)
One-Piece Pattern. McCall. May. (14.)
Working With a Will. Ev. April. (87.)

GIZYCKA, ELEANOR.
Polonaise. Harp. B. Dec., '21. (23.)

GLENN, MENDEL G.
*His Last Sermon. J. For. Nov. '21. (4 : 1051.)

GODFREY, WINONA. (1877– .) (See 1919, 1920, 1921.) (H.)
Dauntless Lysander. Chic. Trib. Jan. 15.

GOLD, MICHAEL.
*Password to Thought — to Culture. Lib. Feb. (14.)

GOLDMAN, RAYMOND LESLIE. (See 1917, 1918.)
*House of the Crying Child. Met. April. (48.)

GOLDRICK, HATTIE B.
Perennials. Pict. R. Feb. (12.)

GOODHUE, STODDARD.
Accusing Voice. Ev. April. (145.)
First Stone. Ev. March. (72.)
Magic Wheel. Ev. Feb. (43.)
Test-tube Necromancy. Ev. Jan. (145.)

GOODLOE, ABBIE CARTER. (1867– .) (See 1915, 1916, 1918, 1919, 1920, 1921.) (H.)
*Her Story. Hol. May. (16.)
**Palmore. Scr. May. (71 : 576.)

GOODMAN, HENRY. (See 1921.)
**Berth. Clay. Spring. (1 : 3.)
*In His Cups. Clay. Summer No. (36.)
***Thomas. Mid. May. (8 : 145.)

GRAEVE, OSCAR. (1885– .) (See 1915, 1916, 1917, 1918, 1919, 1920, 1921.) (H.)
***Headlines. S. S. April. (55.)

GRANGER, HENRY FRANCIS.
" Gee! Let's Go! " Ev. Sept. (23.)

GRANT, BRUCE.
Sob Stuff. Youth. Jan. (1 : 49.)

GREENE, OLIVE WARD. (See 1919.)
Lantern. Met. April. (27.)

GREGORY, FRANCIS and KILMAN, JULIAN. **Pull-Up. D. D. April. (3 : 197.)

H

HAAREM, PAUL J.
Man Who Sought Experience. Sun. Feb. (65.)

6

HARRIS, KENNETH. (contd.)
  Concerning Joe and Jemima.
    S. E. P. Aug. 5. (9.)
  Father Was Right. S. E. P. Feb.
    25. (5.)
  Sensitive Soul. Red Bk. Sept.
    (42.)
  To One Thing Constant Never.
    S. E. P. Dec. 17, '21. (8.)
HART, FRANCES NOYES. (1890–   .)
    (See 1921.)
  ***American. Pict. R. Nov., '21.
    (12.)
  Aunt Rita. L. H. J. May. (8.)
  Concerning Dearly Beloved —.
    L. H. J. June. (18.)
  *Delilah. Pict. R. Dec., '21. (26.)
  Light Magic. McCall. Aug. (8.)
    Sept. (15.)
  O Young Lochinvar! L. H. J.
    Sept. (14.)
  Penelope and the Poet. L. H. J.
    Aug. (12.)
  *Philip the Gay. L. H. J. Feb. (3.)
  *Prince Rides By. L. H. J. April.
    (3.)
  *There Was a Lady. S. E. P. Feb.
    18. (10.)
HARTMAN, LEE FOSTER. (1879–   .)
    (See 1915, 1917, 1918, 1920.)
    (H.)
  Honest Luella. Hear. May. (39.)
  **Out of the Air. Harp. M. Sept.
    (145 : 490.)
  *Parrot. Red Bk. Jan. (53.)
  **Poppies of Wu Fong. Harp. M.
    Nov., '21. (143 : 739.)
HATCH, LEONARD. (See 1915, 1920,
    1921.) (H.)
  " My Heart Leaps Up —." Outl.
    Nov. 23, '21. (129 : 477.)
HAWES, CHARLES BOARDMAN. (1889–
    .) (See 1916, 1917, 1918,
    1919.)
  **Man on the Raft. O. R. Feb. (9.)
  ***Out of the Storm. O. R. Dec., '21.
    (5.)
  ***Peter Ronco. O. R. Oct., '21. (29.)
  **Zenk. O. R. Nov., '21. (4.)
HEARN, LAFCADIO. (1850–1904.) (See
    " H.")
  **Chemise of Margarita Pareja.
    D. D. Oct., '21. (2 : 128.)
HECHT, BEN. (1896–   .) (See 1915,
    1917, 1918, 1919, 1921.)
  *Adventure of the Broken Mirror.
    Harp. B. Sept. (64.)
  At the Feet of the Goddess. S. S.
    Nov., '21. (99.)
  ***Winkelburg. S. S. March. (77.)
HEFFERNAN, DEAN L.
  He Was Serving Two Masters —
    One of Them Golf. Am. Oct.
    '21. (11.)
HELLMAN, SAM.
  Outguesser. S. E. P. June 3. (10.)
  Shoshone Catapult. S. E. P.
    July 29. (12.)

Tiny Skims the Cream. S. E. P.
    Sept. 9. (14.)
  Twosome at Tuara. S. E. P. Aug.
    26. (6.)
HENRIKSON, CARL I. (See 1915, 1916.)
  **Keeping House in Boytime. P. P.
    M. June. (6.)
  **Music in Boytime. P. P. M.
    April. (7.)
HEPBURN, ELIZABETH NEWPORT.
  Doctor's Wife. G. H. July. (36.)
HERGESHEIMER, JOSEPH. (1880–   .)
    (See 1915, 1916, 1917, 1918,
    1919, 1920, 1921.) (H.)
  *Tea Houses. S. E. P. March 4.
    (8.)
  *Tide Runner. S. E. P. Dec. 3, '21.
    (5.)
  ***Token. S. E. P. Oct. 22, '21. (12.)
  **Traveler's Repose. S. E. P. April
    8. (8.)
  *Wasps. S. E. P. May 13. (5.)
HERRICK, ELIZABETH. (See 1915, 1917,
    1919.) (H.)
  Matter With Peter. Scr. April.
    (71 : 465.)
  Wall Dog. Scr. Sept. (72 : 315.)
HERRICK, ROBERT. (1868–   .) (See
    1916.) (H.)
  *Weakest Link. Mun. March.
    (215.)
HEWES, ROBERT E. (See 1919, 1920.)
  Maria San Ramon. Met. July.
    (55.)
HEWES, WILLIAM G.
  Two Gentlemen of Venice. D. D.
    Sept. (4 : 111.)
HICKS, JANE. (See 1921.)
  *Justice on Rattlesnake. McC.
    Aug. (39.)
  Pi-Anna Gentleman. Del. Feb. (5.)
HOPPER, ELSIE VAN DE WATER.
  *Flight of the White Herons. Scr.
    Nov., '21. (70 : 593.)
HOPPER, JAMES. (MARIE.) (1876–   .)
    (See 1915, 1916, 1917, 1918,
    1919, 1920, 1921.) (H.)
  Bond. G. H. Sept. (69.)
  From the Dregs. Les. W. Dec.
    3, '21. (133 : 766.)
  Glass Cage. G. H. May. (34.)
  *In the Fog. Les. W. Jan. 14.
    (134 : 46.)
  **Jerrup. Cen. Aug. (104 : 580.)
  *Nonpareil. S. S. May. (5.)
  Quick Readjustment. Les. W.
    Feb. 18. (134 : 222.)
  Santa O'Toole. Les. W. Dec.
    17, '21. (838.)
  ***Ship in the Bottle. G. H. Jan.
    (10.)
  Soldadera. Les. W. Oct. 8, '21.
    (133 : 481.)
HORN, R. DE S. (See 1920.)
  Flying Norseman. Col. Sept. 2.
    (10.)
  Jinx of the Shandon Belle. Col.
    Sept. 30. (9.)

LEA, FANNY HEASLIP. (contd.)
It Gives a Lovely Light. G. H. March. (10.)
Love-in-a-Mist. Chic. Trib. Feb. 19.
Mothers. G. H. Aug. (22.)

LEACH, PAUL R. (See 1920, 1921.)
From the High Places. Col. Oct. 15, '21. (3.)
Still in the Service. Col. July 1. (13.)
Way to a Man's Heart. Col. June 3. (9.)

LE BOUTILLIER, CORNELIA GEER. (1894–   .) (See 1917, 1918, 1919 under GEER, CORNELIA THROOP; 1920 under LE BOUTILLIER, CORNELIA GEER.)
Banter. W. H. C. Feb. (22.)

LEE, JENNETTE. (BARBOUR PERRY.) (1860–   .) (See 1915, 1916, 1917, 1918, 1919, 1921.) (H.)
*Island Window. Harp. M. Aug. (145 : 295.)
***Man Who Made Poetry Hum. Scr. July. (72 : 109.)

LEE, MUNA. (See 1915, 1920, 1921.)
Embarkation to Cytherea. S. S. Aug. (127.)
Small-Town Episode. S. S. May. (111.)

LENGEL, WILLIAM C. (See 1921.)
Song He Was Ashamed Of. Met. May. (40.)

LEONARD, ORVILLE H. (See 1921.)
*Bad Ike. W. St. Dec. 17, '21. (108.)
*Green Gold. W. St. Oct. 15, '21. (72.)
*Last of the Vigilantes. W. St. Dec. 10, '21. (47.)
*Same Breed. W. St. Aug. 12. (48.)
Seein' It's Christmas. W. St. Dec. 24, '21. (51.)
*Strain of Two Deserts. W. St. July 1. (51.)
*Well Matched Pair. W. St. March 11. (87.)
*Young and Spry. W. St. Nov. 19, '21. (44.)

"LESSING, BRUNO." (RUDOLPH BLOCK.) (1870–   .) (See 1916, 1919, 1920, 1921.) (H.)
All In a Night. Hear. June. (70.)
Business Before Matrimony. Hear. March. (37.)
Christmas Episode. Hear. Dec., '21. (49.)
Envy—A Parable. Hear. Jan. (48.)
Humorous Story of Natzi. Hear. Oct., '21. (50.)
Lapidowitz Dines Out. Hear. July. (77.)
Love and Crime. Hear. April. (37.)
Wedding Present. Hear. May. (24.)

What Nicolo Never Knew. Hear. Nov., '21. (46.)

LETHBRIDGE, OLIVE.
Sheik's Wife. McCall. April. (10.)

LEVICK, MILNES. (See 1919, 1920, 1921.)
**Echo from Another Century. S. S. Dec., '21. (81.)

LEWIS, ADDISON. (1889–   .) (See 1917, 1918, 1919, 1920.)
People First — Blouses Second. Col. Feb. 11. (7.)

LEWIS, CHARLOTTE E.
Intelligibles. G. H. July. (49.)

LEWIS, LLOYD D. (See MACARTHUR, CHARLES G. and LEWIS LLOYD D.)

LEWIS, ORLANDO FAULKLAND. (1873–   .) (See 1918, 1919, 1920, 1921.)
Alibi. Red Bk. March. (64.)
Back Draft. Red Bk. July. (59.)
Crime Is Crime. Red Bk. June. (98.)
Day of Judgment. Red Bk. Oct. '21. (86.)
Man Smith. Red Bk. May. (55.)
Return of Ainsworth. Col. Jan. 28. (7.)
Twenty Minutes. Red Bk. April. (43.)

LEWIS, OSCAR.
*Essie Compton Letters. S. S. July. (104.)

LIEBE, HAPSBURG. (See 1915, 1918, 1919, 1921.) (H.)
Beyond the River. Col. March 25. (9.)

LINDSAY, DONALD. (See 1920.)
*Bondage. Pag. Dec.–Jan. (18.)

LISTER, WALTER B. (See 1921.)
Helpmeet. S. S. Sept. (48.)

LIVINGSTON, ARMSTRONG. (See 1918.)
Beyond the Horizon. Met. Jan. (31.)
God's Machinery. Met. Feb. (24.)

LIVINGSTON, DOROTHY.
Love-Vine. Scr. Feb. (71 : 209.)

LOCKWOOD, SCAMMON. (See 1916, 1920, 1921.)
Done by Statistics. Les. W. May 20. (134 : 664.)
Revenge. Les. W. April 8. (134 : 472.)

LOFTING, HILARY.
Blanco Loop. Met. March. (25.)

LONG, E. WALDO. (See 1921.)
Four Words to the Wise. Am. Feb. (40.)

LONG, HANIEL.
**Abdication of Young Rome. Wave. June. (3.)
**Amirace In Rhidago. D. D. April. (3 : 187.)
*Antonia and Dionigi. Wave. Feb. (19.)
*City of the Chameleons. Free. April 26. (5 : 151.)

MARQUAND, J. P. (*See 1921.*)
Different from Other Girls. L. H.
J. July. (8.)
Eight Million Bubbles. S. E. P.
Jan. 28. (8.)
How Willie Came Across. S. E. P.
July 8. (5.)
Land of Bunk. S. E. P. Sept. 16.
(5.)
Only a Few of Us Left. S. E. P.
Jan. 14. (3.)
MARSDEN, GRIFFIS. (*See 1919, 1920,
1921.*)
Out of Nothing. Pag. Oct.–Nov.,
'21. (20.)
MARSH, GEORGE T. (*See 1915, 1916,
1917, 1919, 1921.*) (*H.*)
McCleod's Partner. Red Bk.
Jan. (37.)
MARSHALL, ANDREW.
Felicitas. McC. April. (73.)
MARSHALL, EDISON. (1894–   .)
(*See 1916, 1917, 1918, 1920,
1921.*)
*Furs. Red Bk. April. (75.)
MARSHALL, RACHEL *and* TERRELL,
MAVERICK. (*See 1917.*)
From the Diary of Ninea Sru.
Sun. Oct., '21. (44.)
MARTIN, HUGH S.
Man from Headquarters. Ev.
April. (50.)
Missing Plans. Ev. June. (52.)
Pearls of Novgorod. Ev. Aug.
(123.)
Vengeance. Ev. July. (113.)
MASON, ELMER BROWN. (*See 1915,
1920.*) (*H.*)
Soviet In Ward Eleven. McC.
April. (54.)
MASON, GRACE SARTWELL. (1877–   .)
(*See 1915, 1916, 1917, 1918,
1919, 1920, 1921.*)
Certain Something. Red Bk.
May. (86.)
MASON, LAURA KENT. (*See 1920,
1921.*)
Wife's Side. S. S. Sept. (107.)
MATTER, JOHN.
Team Work. Met. June. (56.)
MAURY, REUBEN H.
*Man Who Could Shovel. Red
Bk. Aug. (76.)
One Minute On the 600. Red Bk.
May. (90.)
Success. Red Bk. Sept. (65.)
MEANS, E(LDRED). K(URTZ). (1878–
.) (*See 1918, 1919, 1920,
1921.*) (*H.*)
*Hoodoo Sermon Text. Mun.
Oct., '21. (129.)
*Trouble-Scooter. Mun. March.
(334.)
MELLETT, BERTHE KSVATVOLD. (*See
1915, 1916, 1917, 1921.*)
Allison Shoots a Line. Col.
Dec. 3, '21. (9.)
Glad Eyes. Del. Oct., '21. (15.)

Kidnapping of Puppy Losher.
Col. April 29. (7.)
Miss Bolivar. Del. Dec., '21.
(15.)
No Bomb in Gilead. Del. Aug.
(12.)
Party Was a Knockout. Col.
Jan. 21. (7.)
Retreat. Col. June 24. (11.)
Sabine Woman. Col. July 15.
(7.)
Weakly Bugle. Col. Feb. 18. (7.)
MEZQUIDA, ANNA BLAKE. (*See 1915,
1920.*)
Dancing Feet. Ev. Nov., '21.
(28.)
Judge Not! Am. May. (21.)
MERWIN, SAMUEL. (1874–   .) (*See
1915, 1920, 1921.*) (*H.*)
"Armagedeon." S. E. P. Feb. 25.
(12.)
***Axiom of Peter Bell Ivor. S. E. P.
April 1. (8.)
Breathing Time. S. E. P. March
4. (13.)
Gold One. Chic. Trib. April 16.
It'll Always Be Something. S. E.
P. Jan. 21. (14.)
Slack Wire. S. E. P. Feb. 11. (13.)
Tone. S. E. P. Oct. 29, '21. (13.)
Washington Avenue. S. E. P.
Oct. 15, '21. (5.)
MESSIER, ARTHUR J.
"It's a Long, Long Road —."
Mod. P. March. (16.)
METTA, V. B.
*Lover of Balkis. Pearson. May.
(36.)
MILLER, ALICE DUER. (1874–   .)
(*See 1915, 1916, 1919, 1920,
1921.*) (*H.*)
Morning After. S. E. P. July 29.
(5.)
Return to Normalcy. S. E. P.
April 22. (3.)
Revolt of the Bookkeeper. S. E.
P. July 8. (8.)
MILLER, HELEN TOPPING. (*See 1915,
1916, 1917, 1919, 1920, 1921.*)
Cakie. S. E. P. Sept. 2. (30.)
Road That Leads Back. McCall.
Feb. (11.)
Velvet Feet. McC. July. (64.)
Yellow Streak. Am. Jan. (20.)
MILLER, THOMAS SAMSON. (*See " H."*)
House of McLeod. McC. April.
(94.)
Ivory Poacher. McC. March. (37.)
MILLER, WARREN H. (1876–   .)
(*See 1919, 1921.*)
Crash Dive. McC. May. (74.)
MILLS, DOROTHY CULVER. (*See 1918,
1919, 1921.*)
John Jordan's Fan. S. E. P. Sept.
2. (16.)
MILN, LOUISE JORDAN.
Sword of Chastity. Met. May.
(31.)

NORDHOFF, CHARLES B. (1887–   .)
***Savagery. Harp. M. April. (144 :
545.)

NORRIS, KATHLEEN. (1880–   .) (See
1915, 1916, 1917, 1919, 1920.)
(H.)
Real Thing. G. H. Dec., '21. (10.)
Rose's Tiny Laddeen. Cos. Sept.
(59.)
Second Choice. G. H. Feb. (29.)
True Believer. McCall. Dec., '21.
(5.)
Unbecoming Conduct of Annie.
Cos. Aug. (36.)

NORTON, ROY. (1869–1917.) (See
1915, 1916, 1917, 1919.) (H.)
*To the Lights. Blue. April. (1.)
*Way of the Waves. Pop. July 7.
(182.)
*Woman On the Beach. Cos. Oct.,
'21. (32.`

O

OEMLER, MARIE CONWAY. (1879–   .)
(See 1915, 1916, 1918.) (H.)
**Fear. Pearson. Feb. (24.)

OLIVER, OWEN. (See 1915, 1920, 1921.)
Sack. Chic. Trib. July 9.

O'MALLEY, ELEANOR. (See 1921.)
Little House. S. S. Nov., 21.
(109.)

O'NEILL, HUGH. (See " H.")
Restless Riata. S. E. P. Oct. 29,
'21. (10.)

OPPENHEIM, JAMES. (1882–   .) (See
1920.)
Bert Beamish and the Sacred Cow.
Col. March 11. (13.)
*Dolly of Logan Square. Ev.
Aug. (23.)
***He Laughed at the Gods. Broom.
Nov., '21. (1 : 46.)
*Shagan. Ev. Dec., '21. (17.)

OSBORNE, WILLIAM HAMILTON. (1873–
.) (See 1915, 1916, 1917,
1918, 1919, 1920, 1921.) (H.)
Double Trouble, Delaware. S. E.
P. Oct. 1, '21. (14.)
Road Closed: Detour. Chic.
Trib. Oct. 16, '21.
Sensational Disclosure. S. E. P.
May 27. (30.)

OSBOURNE, LLOYD. (1868–   .) (See
1915, 1917, 1919, 1920, 1921.)
(H.)
Our Consul at Jampoke. Red Bk.
March. (31.)

O'SHASNAIN, BRIAN P.
*Coming of the Danes. Cath. W.
Feb. (114 : 655.)

ONSLEY, CLARE.
" Of the House of Faith." Pag.
Oct.–Nov., '21. (5.)

P

PAEZ, CATALINA V. (See 1916.)
*Thicker Than Water. Cath. W.
Nov., '21. (114 : 236.)

PAINE, RALPH DELAHAYE. (1871–   )
(See 1915, 1916, 1918, 1920,
1921.) (H.)
Four Stars of Destiny. Red Bk.
Aug. (92.)

PAKE, MARIE.
Pluck of a Little Woman. Am.
March. (48.)

PANGBORN, GEORGIA WOOD. (1872–
.) (See 1915, 1916, 1917,
1920, 1921.) (H.)
*Carnoc. Des. March. (8.)
*Peak. Des. May. (14.)
Purple Lady. Chic. Trib. Aug. 20.
Snow In the Pass. Chic. Trib.
Dec. 25, '21.
*Two of a Kind. Des. June. (14.)

PARK, J. EDGAR. (1879–   )
Our Christmas Criminal. W. H.
C. Dec., '21. (14.)

PARKER, AUSTIN.
On Wings of Vengeance. Col.
Sept. 16. (5.)

PARKER, SIR GILBERT. (1862–   )
(See 1915.) (H.)
**After the Ball. Scr. May. (71 :
565.)

PARKER, LOCKIE.
**After the Murder. Dial. Nov.,
'21. (71 : 556.)
**Minnie. Mid. May. (8 : 169.)

PARSONS, MARION RANDALL.
Red Gods and Mr. Norton S. S.
Oct., '21. (57.)

PATERSON, ISABEL. (See 1921.)
Many Waters. Del. Jan. (15.)
Perfect Wife. McCall. March. (14.)

PATTULLO, GEORGE. (1879–   ) (See
1915, 1916, 1917, 191⁻, 1919,
1920, 1921.) (H.)
Ledger of Life. S. E. P. March 4.
(10.)
Old Granite Face. S. E. P. Feb. 4.
(14.)
'Tain't Right. S. E. P. April 12. (6.)
Tar and Feathers. S. E. P. Sept.
23. (3.)
Thumbs Down. S. E. P. Dec. 10,
'21. (14.)

PAYNE, WILL. (1855–   .) (See 1915,
1916, 1917, 1918, 1919, 1920,
1921.) (H.)
*Musham's Essay. Chic. Trib.
July 16.

PEARCE, THEODOCIA. (See 1920.)
Mother Kind. L. H. J. June. (20.)

PECK, LELAND W.
Yellow. Sun. Jan. (28.)

PELLEY, WILLIAM DUDLEY. (See 1916,
1917, 1918, 1919, 1920, 1921.)
*Birds of Passage. Sun. April. (20.)
*Gamble Terrible. Sun. May. (5.)
Money to Burn. Mod. P. Aug.
(10.)
*Three Fingers of Hooch. Red Bk.
Nov., '21. (48.)
*Woman-Hater. Red Bk. April.
(89.)

Society Seeks Its Own Level. S. E. P. July 8. (12.)

Uprising Generation. S. E. P. April 15. (28.)

R

RABELL, DU VERNET. (*See 1920, 1921.*)
Ex-Champion and the Lady. McC. April. (59.)

RAMOS, ELEANOR.
*Captains. S. S. Nov., '21. (85.)

RAMOS, ELEANOR, *and* ROBERTS, W. ADOLPHE.
Music. S. S. July. (83.)

RANKIN, KATHERINE.
Skyrockets. McCall. May. (15.)

RAPHAELSON, SAMPSON. (*See 1920, 1921.*)
*Day of Atonement. Ev. Jan. (44.)
Duel for Lydia. Hear. March. (21.)
*Happiness of Rebecca. Hear. Feb. (48.)
Lizette. Ev. April. (37.)
White Roses and Red. Met. Sept. (51.)

RAVENEL, BEATRICE WITTE. (1870– .) (*See 1919, 1920, 1921.*)
*Clonmoyle Returns. Ain. May. (61.)

RAVENEL, BEATRICE.
***Great-Granduncle Sebastian. Harp. M. July. (145 : 177.)
*Hate Story. Harp. M. Aug. (145 : 366.)

RAY, MARIE BEYNON. (*See 1920, 1921.*)
Great Simpleton. Harp B. March. (62.)
" Prologue to Adventure." Harp. B. June. (54.)
Their Beautiful Woman. Harp. B. July. (42.)
Very Shiny Girl. Harp. B. Feb. (60.)

RAYMAN, LOUIS A.
Red Sholem's Kaddish. J. D. N. Oct.–Nov., '21.

REDINGTON, HELEN. (*See 1921.*)
Her Family. Ev. Feb. (135.)
New House. Ev. Sept. (16.)

REELY, MARY KATHARINE. (*See 1917, 1918, 1921.*) (*H.*)
**Hands. Mid. April. (8 : 113.)

REESE, LOWELL OTUS. (1866– .) (*See 1916, 1917, 1918, 1919, 1920, 1921.*)
Midnight Sons. Col. Nov. 5, '21. (7.)
Spiders. S. E. P. Oct. 8, '21. (9.)

RHODES, HARRISON (GARFIELD). (1871– .) (*See 1915, 1918, 1919, 1920, 1921.*) (*H.*)
Thomas Robinson and the Servant Problem. S. E. P. Nov. 19, '21. (14.)
Thomas Robinson Sees Life. S. E. P. Jan. 14. (8.)

RHYS, M. THORNTON.
Les Illusions. Pag. Dec.–Jan. (37.)

RICHTER, CONRAD. (*See 1915, 1916, 1917, 1918, 1919, 1920.*) (*H.*)
" Over the Hill to the Rich House." Outl. Sept. 6. (132 : 25.)

RILEY, A. DALE.
*Between. Asia. Nov., '21. (21 : 918.)

RINEHART, MARY ROBERTS. (1876– .) (*See 1915, 1916, 1917, 1918, 1919, 1920.*) (*H.*)
Midsummer Knight's Dream. S. E. P. Dec. 17, '21. (3.) Dec. 24, '21. (18.)
Tish Plays the Game. S. E. P. March 4. (3.)

" RISSAKOFF, ARKADY." (JOHN BERRY.) (*See 1916 under* BERRY, JOHN.)
*Revenge of Sarras. 10-St. Jan. (24.)

ROBBINS, LEONARD H. (1877– .) (*See 1920, 1921.*)
Sightseers. W. H. C. Feb. (17.)

ROBERTS, CHARLES GEORGE DOUGLAS. (1860– .) (*See 1915, 1917, 1918, 1921.*) (*H.*)
Citadel in the Grass. S. E. P. July 8. (20.)
Star-Nose of the Under Ways. Sun. May. (20.)

ROBERTS, ISABEL J.
*Ship o' Dreams. Scr. March. (71 : 363.)

ROBERTS, WALTER ADOLPHE. (1886– .) (*See 1920.*)
Minister of Education and Fine Arts. S. S. March. (125.)

ROBERTS, W. ADOLPHE. (*See* RAMOS, ELEANOR, *and* ROBERTS, W. ADOLPHE.)

ROCHE, MAZO DE LA. (*See 1915, 1916, 1919, 1920.*) (*See " H " under* DE LA ROCHE, MAZO.)
*Adopting Granfa. W. H. C. Feb. (11.)

ROE, VINGIE E. (*See 1915, 1916, 1917, 1918, 1919, 1920, 1921.*) (*H.*)
Bucky. Sun. March. (5.)
Miss Putty Face. Chic. Trib. March 19.
Silvershine. Pict. R. March. (10.)

ROGERS, ELLEN.
Lunch Table Liaison. S. S. Dec., '21. (97.)

ROOF, KATHARINE METCALF. (*See 1915, 1918, 1919, 1920, 1921.*) (*H.*)
*Perfume of the Night. Way. T. April. (104.)

ROSEBORO', VIOLA. (1857– .) (*See 1915.*)
***Aaron Westcott's Funeral. McC. May. (37.)

ROSENBLATT, BENJAMIN. (1880– .) (*See 1915, 1916, 1917, 1919, 1920, 1921.*) (*H.*)
***In the Metropolis. Br. St. Dec., '21. (11.)

VENABLE, EDWARD CARRINGTON.
(1884– .) (See 1915, 1916, 1917, 1918, 1919, 1921.)
Angela. Scr. June. (71 : 714.)
***Reverend James E. Markison. Scr. Jan. (71 : 81.)

VORSE, MARY (MARVIN) HEATON. (MARY HEATON VORSE O'BRIEN MINOR.) (See 1915, 1916, 1917, 1918, 1919, 1920, 1921.) (H.)
***Halfway House. Harp. M. Oct., '21. (143 : 557.)
**Hero. Lib. Aug. (17.)
" Men are Beasts." W. H. C. Sept., '21. (19.)
Poor Old Edna. Del. Dec., '21. (8.)

W

WAAGE, C. M.
*When the Gods Died. Cath. W. Dec., '21. (114 : 333.)

WALDO, SIDNEY. (1883– .) (See 1921.)
*Mrs. Melvin:Judge and Jury. B. C. July. (5.)
***Sons and Brothers. Pict. R. Feb. (14.)

WALLACE, FREDERICK WILLIAM.
**Tea from China. MacL. July 15. (9.)

WARREN, MAUDE (LAVINIA) RADFORD. (1875– .) (See 1915, 1916, 1917, 1918, 1921.) (H.)
*Girl Who Wanted a Fairy Prince. L. H. J. Nov., '21. (10.)
***On the Run. Cen. Jan. (103 : 388.)

WATTS, MARY S(TANBERY). (1868– .) (See 1915.) (H.)
***Reward of Virtue. Harp. M. May. (144 : 707.)

WEAVER, JOHN VAN ALSTYNE. (See 1921.)
Enamel. Met. June. (11.)

WEBSTER, HENRY KITCHELL. (1875– .) (See 1915, 1916, 1917, 1918. (H.)
Flashlight. Chic. Trib. Sept. 17.
Sister Anne. Chic. Trib. April 30.
$10,000 Beauty. Chic. Trib. July 23.

WEIMAN, RITA. (1889– .) (See 1915, 1919, 1920, 1921.)
Law Unto Ourselves. Cos. July. (87.)

WEITZENKORN, LOUIS. (1893– .) (See 1920, 1921.)
Millicent. Chic. Trib. March 26.
Tricks. Chic. Trib. Dec. 11, '21.

WELLES, HARRIET OGDEN DEEN. (See 1917, 1918, 1919, 1920, 1921.)
*Painted Canyon. Scr. July. (72 : 42.)
*Runaway Blimp. Scr. Dec., '21. (70 : 689.)

WERNER, CARL AVERY.
Pockets. Am. May. (60.)

WESTON, GEORGE. (T.) (1880– .) (See 1915, 1916, 1917, 1918, 1919, 1920, 1921.) (H.)
Cold Molasses. S. E. P. Dec. 17, '21. (10.)
Girl with Money. S. E. P. Aug. 26. (10.)
Golden Eggs. S.E.P. April 15. (24.)
Maggot of Misty Mountain. S. E. P. Aug. 19. (5.)
Old Rip. S. E. P. Sept. 30. (16.)
One Clever Idea a Day. S. E. P. Oct. 8, '21. (14.)
Sent On Approval. S. E. P. Jan. 14. (14.)

WHARTON, MABEL H. (See 1918.)
Accommodating? — I'll Say He Is! McC. Aug. (62.)

WHITE, ETHEL.
Extra Half-Ounce. Met. Dec.,'21. (25.)
Third Eye. Met. March. (54.)

WHITE, NELIA GARDNER. (See 1920, 1921.)
Wife Who Was Old at 35. Am. May. (30.)

WHITMAN, STEPHEN FRENCH. (1880– .) (See 1915, 1919, 1920, 1921.) (H.)
*Two Roses. Red Bk. Jan. (27.)

WHITTEMORE, C. W.
*Last Lot. Pearson. May. (28.)
*" Odd Stick." Pearson. Sept. (19.)

WIDDEMER, MARGARET. (MARGARET WIDDEMER SCHAUFFLER.) (See 1915, 1917, 1918, 1920, 1921.) (H.)
Little Queens. Col. March 4. (11.)
Once to Every Married Man. Col. June 10. (11.)

WILBER, W. C. (See 1921.)
Real Womanly Woman. S. S. Oct., '21. (49.)

WILCOXSON, ELIZABETH GAINES. (See 1917, 1918.) (H.)
Five Jacobs. Met. Oct., '21. (25.)

WILEY, HUGH. (1894– .) (See 1917, 1918, 1919, 1920, 1921.)
Black Angel. S. E. P. Jan. 28. (16.)
Manchu Blood. S. E. P. March 25. (14.)
*Mates Adrift. S. E. P. March 4. (24.)
Red Tape Cutter. S. E. P. Sept. 2. (36.)
Single, Double, Trouble. S. E. P. May 27. (24.)
Survival of Sin. S. E. P. Aug. 19. (12.)
Three and Out. Sun. Sept. (12.)
Tide of Fortune. S. E. P. Jan. 7. (12.)
Wildcat Joss. Sun. Aug. (12.)
Wildcat Thirteen. S E. P. Oct. 15, '21. (12.)
Wishbone Luck. Sun. July. (5.)

WOLJESKA, HELEN. (*See 1915, 1920.*) (*H.*)
Freewoman. S. S. Oct., '21. (89.)
WOOD, CLEMENT. (1888– .)
***Coffin. Pag. Dec.-Jan. (5.)
WOOD, JULIA FRANCIS. (*See 1918, 1919.*) (*H.*)
Their Own Lives. W. H. C. Oct., '21. (13.)
WOODROW, MRS. WILSON. (NANCY MANN WADDEL WOODROW.) (*See 1915, 1921.*) (*H*).
Rose Royale. Met. Dec., '21. (16.)
WOOLLEY, EDWARD MOTT. (1867– .) (*See 1921.*) (*H.*)
Keys to Ausable. Red Bk. Nov. '21. (81.)
Pirate Exploration Company. Red Bk. July. (68.)
WORMSER, GWENDOLYN RANGER. (*See 1919, 1920, 1921.*)
**Devil's Leap. Col. March 11. (7.)
WORTS, GEORGE FRANK. (1892– .) (*See 1918, 1919, 1920, 1921.*)
Fresh Water Methods. Col. Dec. 17, '21. (7.)
Furnace for Your Foe. Col. Feb. 4. (7.)
Little Ice Devils. Col. Nov. 19, '21. (11.)
Nothing but the Best. Col. May 20. (12.)

" Oh, Michael, How Could You?" Col. Nov. 26, '21. (7.)
Ship to Catch a Sailor. Col. Dec. 31, '21. (9.)
Soup and Fish. Ev. June. (135.)
WRATH, CALEB. (*See 1921.*)
Keys of the City. McC. July. (81.)
WRIGHT, CUTHBERT.
Midwinter Night's Dream. S. S. March. (121.)
*Photograph of Jesus Christ. Gargoyle. July.
WYNN, ALICE GORTON.
Cajans. D. D. Jan. (3 : 21.)

Y

YATES, DORNFORD. (*See 1921.*)
Tameless Terror. Met. Oct., '21. (36.)
YATES, L. B. (*See 1915, 1916, 1918, 1919, 1920, 1921.*) (*H.*)
Flowers of Fancy. Red Bk. Feb. (66.)
This Man's War. S. E. P. Sept. 23. (16.)
YOUMANS, ELEANOR WILLIAMS.
Man Who Wanted a Dog That Would Kill. Am. Oct., '21. (22.)
YUST, WALTER. (*See 1921.*)
**Belles-Lettres. Youth. Jan. (1 : 41.)

II. ENGLISH AND IRISH AUTHORS

A

ARLEN, MICHAEL. (*See 1921.*)
Tea at the Ritz. S. S. Dec., '21. (127.)
ARMSTRONG, MARTIN.
*Poets and the Housewife. Broom. May. (112.)
ARNOLD, EDWIN L. (*See 1915.*)
Cupidity of Syad. Les. W. Dec. 31, '21. (910.)
ATKEY, BERTRAM. (1880– .) (*See 1919, 1921.*)
Even That Which He Hath. Ev. March. (23.)
Winnie and the Dunoon System. S. E. P. March 11. (5.)
Winnie and the Poison Runner. S. E. P. Dec. 17, '21. (14.)
Winnie and the Rajah. S. E. P. Oct. 22, '21. (15.)
AUMONIER, STACY. (1887– .) (*See 1915, 1916, 1917, 1918, 1919, 1920, 1921.*)
***Accident of Crime. S. E. P. March 11. (20.)
***Miss Bracegirdle Does Her Duty. Pict. R. Sept. (10.)
AUSTIN, FREDERICK BRITTEN. (1885– .) (*See 1915, 1917, 1918, 1919, 1920, 1921.*) (*H.*)
*One Night In Venice. Hear. March. (29.)

**Red Shawl. Hear. Feb. (8.)
S. O. S. Red Bk. Sept. (46.)

B

BAILY, F(RANCIS). E(VANS). (1887– .) (*See 1921.*)
Felicia the Fortunate. Hear. Feb. (37.)
Iris, the Sun-Kissed. Hear. Jan. (12.)
Not Even Eve. Hear. Nov., '21. (14.)
VingieDarling. S.E.P. Sept. 30. (14.)
BARRINGTON, EMILIE ISABEL WILSON. (MRS. RUSSELL BARRINGTON.) (*See 1921.*)
***Mystery of Stella. Atl. March. (129 : 311.)
BECHHOFER, C. E. (*See 1921.*)
*Fifth Bull. S. S. Feb. (39.)
BECK, L. ADAMS. (*See 1920, 1921.*)
**Flute of Krishna. Asia. Jan. (22 : 28.)
**Loveliest Lady of China. Asia. Oct., '21. (21 : 843.)
**Round-Faced Beauty. Atl. Dec., '21. (128 : 750.)
Wisdom Which Is One with Love. Asia. Sept. (22 : 733.)
BELL, J(OHN). J(OY). (1871– .) (*See 1915, 1916, 1917, 1918, 1919, 1921.*) (*H.*)
*Culvert. Chic. Trib. March 5.

384 THE YEARBOOK

F

FARNOL, (JOHN)JEFFERY. (1878– .)
(*See 1917.*) (*H.*)
*Cupboard. Way. T. April. (1.)
FLOWER, (WALTER) NEWMAN. (1879–
.) (*See 1921.*) (*H.*)
*Lady in Lavender. S. E. P.
March 18. (22.)
FRIEDLAENDER, V. H. (*See 1916, 1918,
1919, 1920.*)
*Risk. Scr. Oct., '21. (70 : 464.)
*Top Dog. Harp M. March.
(144 : 442.)
**Wrong Horse. Harp. M. July.
(145 : 242.)

G

GALSWORTHY, JOHN. (1867– .)
(*See 1915, 1916, 1917, 1918,
1919, 1920, 1921.*) (*H.*)
***Feud. Del. Feb. (7); March. (13.)
***Man Who Kept His Form. Del.
Oct., '21. (8.)
***Santa Lucia. Del. April. (5.)
GEORGE, W. L. (1882– .) (*See
1917, 1920, 1921.*)
*Eileen. Chic. Trib. June 25.
GIBBON, PERCEVAL. (1879– .) (*See
1915, 1916, 1917, 1918, 1920,
1921.*) (*H.*)
***By Consent. Red Bk. Aug. (98.)
**Deal in Exchange. S. E. P. July 1.
(23.)
**Gold that Glitters. Pop. Jan. 20.
(63 : 109.)
*Good Uncles. S. E. P. April 1.
(18.)
*Looters. Chic. Trib. Feb. 5.
*Man of Principle. S. E. P. April 8.
(20.)
*Man Who Remembered. Mun.
May. (75 : 598.)
***Saint Flossie. S. E. P. Dec. 3, '21.
(10.)
**When America Goes East. S. E. P.
May 20. (14.)
GRIMSHAW, BEATRICE. (*See 1915, 1916,
1920, 1921.*) (*H.*)
Isles of Peace. Red Bk. Oct., '21.
(72.)
Something Lost. Red Bk. April.
(57.)
Woman in the Cage. Chic. Trib.
Sept. 10.

H

HACKETT, FLORENCE. (1884– .)
*My Surprise. Pearson. Jan.
(48 : 11.)
**Streal. W. F. Sept. (111.)
HARRINGTON, KATHERINE. (MRS.
ROLF BENNETT.) (*See 1920,
1921.*)
Matter of Luck. Les. W. Nov. 5,
'21. (133 : 622.)
" HAY, IAN." (JOHN HAY BEITH.)
(1876– .) (*See 1915, 1917.*)
Cure. Met. May. (13.)
Fowl Play. Met. March. (18.)

HERBERT, A. P. (*See 1919, 1921.*)
*War that Ended War. W. F.
Sept. (30.)
HORN, HOLLOWAY. (1886– .) (*See
1921.*)
Sting. Harp. B. Oct. '21. (69.)
HOWARD, FRANCIS MORTON. (1880–
.) (*See 1921.*)
*Kind Assistance. Sh. St. Oct. 25,
'21. (71.)
" HOWARD, KEBLE." (JOHN KEBLE
BELL.) (1875– .) (*See 1915,
1921.*) (*H.*)
Saint In Pajamas. Hear. March.
(25.)

K

KAYE-SMITH, SHEILA.
**Good Wits Jump. Harp. M.
March. (144 : 483.)
***Mrs. Adis. Cen. Jan. (103 : 321.)
***Mockbeggar. Harp. M. Feb.
(144 : 331.)
Old Gadgett. Harp. M. Aug.
(145 : 342.)
KENNEY, ROWLAND. (*See 1920.*)
**Nailed. Dial. Dec., '21. (71 : 639.)
KINROSS, ALBERT. (1870– .) (*See
1915, 1916, 1921.*) (*H.*)
**Elysian Fields. Atl. Jan. (129 :
33.)
**Profiteer. Cen. Nov., '21. (103 :
28); Dec., '21 (103 : 290).
***Traitors. S. S. April. (93.)

L

LANCASTER, G. B. (*See 1915, 1916,
1918.*) (*H.*)
*Big Punch. Met. March. (40.)
*Lone-Patrol Sangar. Sh. St.
June 25. (119.)
LAWRENCE, DAVID HERBERT. (1885–
.) (*See 1915, 1917, 1919,
1920, 1921.*) (*H.*)
***Episode. Dial. Feb. (72 : 143.)
**Fragment of Stained Glass. (*R.*)
Pearson. March. (7.)
***Sick Collier. (*R.*) Pearson. Feb.
(10.)

M

MACHEN, ARTHUR. (1863– .) (*See
1917, 1919.*)
**Marriage of Panurge. Wave.
Jan. (2.)
**Secret Glory. Wave. Feb. (41.)
" MALET, LUCAS." (MARY ST. LEGER
HARRISON.) (*See 1921.*)
***Conversion. W. F. Aug. (64.)
MANSFIELD, KATHERINE. (MRS. J.
MIDDLETON MURRY.)
***Fly. Cen. Sept. (104 : 743.)
MAUGHAM, W. SOMERSET. (1874– .)
(*See 1921.*)
**Fear. Cen. March. (103 : 712.)
*His Majesty's Representative.
McC. May. (25.)
*Honolulu. Ev. Oct., '21. (4.)
**Philosopher. McC. April. (20.)
*Sullivan. McC. May. (89.)

SINCLAIR, MAY. (*See 1915, 1917, 1920, 1921.*) (*H.*)
***"Heaven." Pict. R. June. (12.)
SINGLETON, A. H.
  *Hairy Mary. Atl. May. (129 : 623.)
  **Jack the Robber. Atl. Feb. (129 : 174.)
  **Larry. Atl. March. (129 : 364.)
SNELL, EDMUND.
  Amber Goddess. Met. Feb. (21.)
SOUTAR, ANDREW. (1879–   .) (*See 1915, 1916, 1917, 1918, 1919.*)
  **Golden Toys. Red Bk. Jan. (86.)
STACPOOLE, HENRY DE VERE. (1865–   .) (*See 1916, 1918, 1920, 1921.*) (*H.*)
  *Deaf Mute. Pop. April 7. (149.)
  *Luck. Pop. Jan. 7. (184.)
  *Story of Gombi. Pop. Feb. 7. (184.)
STEPHENS, JAMES. (1882–   .) (*See 1915, 1918, 1920, 1921.*) (*H.*)
  ***Hunger. Broom. Nov., '21. (1: 3.)
STERN, G. B. (MRS. GEOFFREY LISLE HOLDSWORTH.) (1890–   .)
  *One Year to Live. Fol. July. (55.)

T

TERRILL, G. APPLEBY.
  Bristol Eyes. S. E. P. Nov. 26, '21. (16.)
  Hotel Remember. S. E. P. May 13. (52.)

W

WALLACE, EDGAR. (1875–   .) (*See 1915, 1916, 1917, 1918, 1919, 1920.*) (*H.*)
  Barons of the Nimble. S. E. P. June 3. (12.)
  Cinema Picture. McC. March. (67.)
  Lamp That Never Went Out. McC. April. (100.)
  Limp of the Clan Chen. Ev. Oct., '21. (100.)
  Student of Men. McC. June. (89.)

WALPOLE, HUGH. (1884–   .) (*See 1915, 1920, 1921.*)
  **Come Out of the Kitchen. Pict. R. April. (6.)
  ***Conscience Money. Pict. R. May. (22.)
  **Dance. Pict. R. June. (14.)
  ***Major Wilbraham. Chic. Trib. Nov. 13, '21.
  **Night-Raiders. Pict. R. Sept. (15.)
  *Poodle. Pict. R. Aug. (22.)
  **Saladin and the Black Bishop. Pict. R. July. (24.)
WENNERBERG, FREDERICK.
  *Passing of McCartenay. Cath. W. Aug. (115 : 646.)
WEYMAN, STANLEY JOHN. (1855–   .)
  *Two Pages. Pearson. April. (18.)
WILLIAMS, MARGERY. (MRS. FRANCESCO BIANCI.) (*See 1921.*)
  *Cupboard on the Stairs. Hol. March. (9.)
  *Little Wooden Doll. Harp. B. Aug. (70.)
  *Spring Fire. S. S. July. (63.)
WODEHOUSE, PELHAM GRENVILLE. (1881–   .) (*See 1915, 1916, 1917, 1918, 1919, 1920, 1921.*) (*H.*)
  Bertie Changes His Mind. Cos. Aug. (101.)
  Heel of Achilles. Chic. Trib. June 11.
  Long Hole. McC. March. (59.)
  Metropolitan Touch. Cos. Sept. (99.)
  Purity of the Turf. Cos. July. (103.)
WRAY, ROGER. (*See 1917.*)
  Lascivious Bird. S. S. Jan. (79.)
WYLIE, I(DA). A(LENA). R(OSS). (1885–   .) (*See 1916, 1917, 1918, 1919, 1921.*)
  **Greatness and Jamey Pobjoy. G. H. Nov., '21. (16.)
  *Release. G. H. April. (16.)

III. TRANSLATIONS

A

ALBERT-JEAN. (*French.*)
  Battle of Flowers. Broom. Sept. (3 : 133.)
ALBUJAR, ENRIQUE LOPEZ. (*Spanish.*)
  **Knight of Death. W. F. Aug. (87.)
ANDERSEN, HANS CHRISTIAN. (1805–1875.) (*Danish.*)
  Two Brothers. Scan. July. (10 : 412.)
ANDREYEV, LEONID NIKOLAEVICH. (1871–1919.) (*Russian.*) (*See 1916, 1917, 1920.*) (*See " H " under* ANDREIEFF.)
  ***Luckiest Man in the World. W. F. Aug. (57.)

ARTZYBASHEFF, MIKHAIL. (*Russian.*) (*See 1915.*)
  ***Old Story. W. F. Sept. (39.)
AVERTCHENKO, ARCADIJI. (*Russian.*) (*See 1915, 1916, 1919.*)
  **Silent Man. W. F. Aug. (113.)

B

" BERTHEROY, JEAN." (BERTHE CARIANNE LE BARILLIER.) (1860–   .) (*See 1918, 1919, 1920, 1921.*) (*French.*)
  Armistice Anniversary. N. Y. Trib. Aug. 27.
  Black Dress. N. Y. Trib. March 12.
  Cecilia at Seventeen. N. Y. Trib. April 9.

HIRSCHFELD, GEORG. (1873– .)
(*German.*)
*Changing Places. W. F. Sept.
(70.)

I

IBANEZ, VICENTE BLASCO. (*See* BLASCO
IBANEZ, VICENTE.)

J

JALOUX, EDMUND. (*French.*)
Passionate Angler. N. Y. Trib.
March 19.

L

LARBAUD, VALERY. (*French.*)
**Hour with the Face. Free. April
12. (5 : 103.)
LATZKO, ANDREAS. (*See 1921.*)
(*Austrian.*)
**Double Patriot. Free. July 5.
(5 : 392.)
LEBLANC, MAURICE. (1864– .) (*See
1915.*) (*H.*) (*French.*)
At the Sign of Mercury. Met.
July. (25.)
Case of Jean Louis. Met. Dec.,
'21. (38.)
Footprints In the Snow. Met.
June. (25.)
In the Dining Car. Met. March.
(43.)
Lady With the Hatchet. Met.
May. (45.)
On the Top of the Tower. Met.
Oct., '21. (12.)
Tell-Tale Film. Met. Jan. (36.)
Water Bottle. Met. Nov., '21.
(35.)
LUCATELLI, LUIGI. (*Italian.*)
*Bibi. S. S. Aug. (96.)
*Diogenes. S. S. Sept. (90.)
*History of an Idiot. S. S. Aug.
(99.)
*How Asmodeo Ribelli Did Not
Make His Fortune. S. S. Sept.
(88.)
*Little Victim. S. S. Aug. (95.)
*Man for the Ages. S. S. Aug.
(101.)
**Petitioner. S. S. Aug. (98.)
*Pierino. S. S. Sept. (87.)
*Sentiment. S. S. Sept. (89.)
Signor Saverio's Nose. S. S. June.
(57.)
*Signora Dora's Little Economics.
S. S. Aug. (97.)
Teodoro Nasica. S. S. July. (75.)

M

MARDRUS, LUCIE DELARUE. (*See 1917,
1918, 1919, 1920, 1921.*) (*French.*)
Burglar and the Cat. N. Y. Trib.
Aug. 6.
Lesson of the Eglantine. N. Y.
Trib. March 5.
Lesson of the Fire. N. Y. Trib.
May 21.

*Lottery Ticket. N. Y. Trib. Jan.
15.
Old Maid's Marriage. N. Y. Trib.
Dec. 4, '21.
*On the Other Side of the Mirror.
N. Y. Trib. Oct. 30, '21.
*Sorcerer. N. Y. Trib. April 16.
MAUPASSANT, HENRI RENE ALBERT
GUY DE. (1850–1893.) (*See
1918.*) (*H.*) (*French.*)
***Story of a Wise Man. Hear.
May. (11.)
MILLE, PIERRE. (1864– .) (*See
1917, 1918, 1919, 1920, 1921.*)
(*French.*)
Day's Work Along the Marne.
N. Y. Trib. Dec. 18, '21.
*Heroine of the Wilderness. N. Y.
Trib. Oct. 16, '21.
*Poilu Who Said He Was Deaf.
N. Y. Trib. Nov. 27, '21.
MOLNAR, FRANZ. (1879– .) (*See
1916.*) (*Hungarian.*)
**Coal-Thieves. Free. Oct. 26, '21.
(4 : 151.)
**Snow-Man. Cen. Sept. (104 :
649.)
MORAND, PAUL. (*See 1921.*) (*French.*)
***Roman Night. Broom. Feb.
(291.)
MULLER, ANDRE. (*French.*)
Double Retribution. Pearson.
May. (26.)

O

OHANIAN, ARMEN.
Dancer of Shamakha. Asia. April.
(22 : 251.)

P

PAOLIERI, FERDINANDO. (1878– .)
(*Italian.*)
*Ambush. W. F. Sept. (102.)
PERET, BENJAMIN. (*French.*)
*At 125 Boulevard St. Germain.
Broom. Aug. (3 : 31.)
PICARD, HELENE. (*French.*)
Crimes of King Myrrhus. N. Y.
Trib. April 30.
PILNIAK, BORIS. (*Russian.*)
**At the Doors. Broom. Aug.
(3 : 57.)
PUAUX, RENE. (*French.*)
*Miracle. Del. Jan. (16.)

R

RAMEAU, JEAN. (*See 1919, 1920.*)
(*French.*)
In Quest of the Knife. N. Y. Trib.
July 16.
REGIS, ROGER. (*See 1916, 1920.*) (*H.*)
(*French.*)
Feathered Love Affair. N. Y. Trib.
Aug. 13.
RHAIS, ELISSA. (*French.*)
**Kerkeb. W. F. Aug. (39.)